Love and Other Ruins

BY KAREN X. TULCHINSKY

POLESTAR
An Imprint of Raincoast Books

Polestar Books and Raincoast Books gratefully acknowledge the support of the Government of Canada through the Book Publishing Industry Development Program, the Canada Council and the Department of Canadian Heritage. We also acknowledge the assistance of the Province of British Columbia through the British Columbia Arts Council.

The author gratefully acknowledges the British Columbia Arts Council for a creative writing grant to write the first draft of this manuscript.

Edited by Lynn Henry
Text design by Ingrid Paulson

NATIONAL LIBRARY OF CANADA CATALOGUING IN PUBLICATION DATA

Tulchinsky, Karen X.
Love and other ruins

ISBN 1-55192-554-0

I. Title.
PS8589.U603L67 2002 C813'.54 C2001-911678-0
PR9199.3.T76L67 2002

Library of Congress Control Number: 2002102383

Polestar Book Publishers
An Imprint of Raincoast Books
9050 Shaughnessy Street
Vancouver, British Columbia
Canada, V6P 6E5
www.raincoast.com

In the United States:
Publishers Group West
1700 Fourth Street
Berkeley, California
94710

At Raincoast Books we are committed to protecting the environment and to the responsible use of natural resources. We are acting on this commitment by working with suppliers and printers to phase out our use of paper produced from ancient forest. This book is one step toward that goal. It is printed on 100% ancient-forest-free paper (100% post-consumer recycled), processed chlorine- and acid-free, and supplied by New Leaf Paper. It is printed with vegetable-based inks. For further information, visit our website at www.raincoast.com. We are working with Markets Initiative (www.oldgrowthfree.com) on this project.

1 2 3 4 5 6 7 8 9 10

Printed and bound in Canada by Friesens.

Love and Other Ruins is a sequel to *Love Ruins Everything* (Press Gang, 1998). It picks up where the first book left off, but like *Love Ruins Everything*, can be enjoyed on its own.

CONTENTS

SPRING 1999

Y2K AND OTHER HYSTERICAL DELUSIONS

All anyone talks about these days is the approaching millennium. The year 2000. Y2K. 2000 years After Death. The naysayers were right. Armageddon approaches. Computers all over the world are going to crash, wreaking utter havoc in their electronic wake. Traffic lights will freeze. Streetlights will shut off. Phone service will be disrupted. Hydro will go down. Waterlines will burst. Airplanes will crash. Trains will derail. Automated teller machines will self-destruct. The entire World Wide Web will have a nervous breakdown and implode. Judgement day is here.

People are hoarding bottled water, Kraft Dinner and canned tuna, sparkling wine and beef. They're buying generators in case the power goes down. Tiny battery-powered TVs and CD players. Extra batteries for their cell phones. Candles, flashlights, solar-powered heaters, Coleman cookstoves, sub-zero sleeping bags and Arctic proof, down-filled parkas.

Computer nerds are making a fortune reprogramming. Y2K compliant. Y2K ready. Y2K proof. Y2K efficient. Y2K this and Y2K that. People are afraid to fly on New Year's Eve. They're worried about heat, light, food and water. What if the Russians aren't Y2K ready? Will we all go up in a puff of nuclear smoke at the stroke of midnight? Will long- and short-range missiles be dispatched at exactly twelve a.m. Greenwich Time? Is Thailand

Y2K compliant? Will their short-range missiles speed toward the Kremlin's and crash in the air above New Jersey? Will aliens land in the tiny village of Eston, Saskatchewan, and perform sadistic experiments on card-carrying members of the Reform Party? The year 2000 is almost here. There is so much to worry about. It's a worldwide worry-fest.

Personally, I'm not concerned. The way my health is deteriorating, I doubt I'll be here to see it. Roger doesn't know the whole truth. I've been hiding it from him. He knows about my KS lesion. Only one so far, knock on mahogany, right in the middle of my back. He *has* noticed my lingering cough. I keep telling him I'm still getting over that bad cold from the winter. But it's not that. It's the virus. I've been HIV positive since 1986. Haven't been sick yet. Not really. The KS doesn't hurt. And it hasn't spread. Still, the virus has been growing inside me, eating away at me. Consuming me. I can feel it stalking me, like an escaped convict. Desperate, crazy and scared. A hulking hungry giant.

Everyone wants to know what I'll be doing when the calendar turns over to the year 2000. Personally, I'd be happy to be right here. On the living room couch, in the apartment I share with the one man I've ever truly loved: Roger. That would be enough for me.

My father has permanently moved into our den. He's hiding out. Solly used to be involved with the Mob. Not the mob you're thinking of — not Don Corleone of Sicily. Not someone Al Pacino would play in the movie. More likely Jerry Seinfeld, or Alan Arkin. Maybe even Richard Dreyfuss, if you get the picture. It was a long time ago, when I was a little boy. In the sixties my father got involved in the fringes of Jewish organized crime in Toronto, in an insurance scheme that was supposed to make a lot of people rich. Solly was the patsy. The front man. The proverbial deer in the headlights. He was trapped, caught, tried and convicted. He served six years in Kingston Penitentiary and got out when I was twelve. Managed to stay clean for most of my teen years and my twenties. Then he disappeared again, to Florida, only to resurface on my doorstep, last November, with his

Cuban cigars and ever-present bottle of Jack Daniel's. He's been here ever since and shows no sign of leaving.

A late afternoon sun beats inside the living room through the balcony door of our third-floor apartment on Alexander Street — just off Church, south of Wellesley, in the heart of Toronto's Gay Ghetto. The centre of the universe, as far as I'm concerned. My father has gone out for the evening. A card game at his friend Stan Birmbaum's house. He promised he'd be out late. Thank God. Roger and I have scarcely had a moment alone together since Solly's been here. I'm cooking a beautiful dinner: my famous baked salmon with pepper cream sauce, asparagus tips lightly sautéed in extra virgin olive oil and dry white wine, basmati rice and a Caesar salad with real anchovies and fresh Parmesan. There's a smart bottle of Sauvignon Blanc chilling in the fridge.

I open the kitchen cupboard, grab my apron, slip it over my neck, cross the belt behind my back and tie it in a bow in the front. It's a silly apron. Designed for a woman. A *feminine* woman. All pink and frills, the kind that covers your bosom and flows to just above the knee in a flurry of lace. Roger bought it for me as a joke, for my thirty-eighth birthday, but I just love it. Makes me feel like Natalie Wood in *West Side Story. I feel pretty. Oh so pretty. I feel pretty and witty and gay* ... And now, well ... I just can't seem to cook without it.

I glance at the clock. Roger will be home any minute. I pirouette like our former Prime Minister, Pierre Elliott, I pirouette into the dining room to set the table. I choose the good china. Nothing but the best for my hard-working man. I set out candles, light them, then race back to the kitchen to blend the Grand Marnier chocolate sauce for the fresh strawberries I picked up this morning in Kensington Market.

I hear Roger's key in the lock. Halfway across the living room, I slip the apron over my head and toss it on the couch. I'm wearing an old pair of tight jeans that are ripped in several strategic locations, and a black tank top. Roger loves my street-butch look. A queer contrast to the Doris Day apron. I have plans for after dinner.

"Henry," Roger grins, taking in the scene.

We embrace. He's dressed in his nurse's uniform — loose green cotton pants and matching shirt. Over top he wears his black leather jacket. Roger's a real butch. Tall, dark and handsome, with jet-black hair and a little curl over his forehead like Superman. The stuff of my childhood dreams. He's such a hunk, sometimes I can't believe he wants to be with little ol' me.

He looks around the room. "Your father's out?"

"For the entire evening."

"Great. Let's dance," says Roger, with a glint in his eye.

"Dance?"

"Yeah." He flashes me his widest dimpled smile. "You know? Dance." He crosses the room to the stereo, pops in a CD, tosses his jacket onto the sofa. The room is filled with the familiar opening chords of Marvin Gaye's "Sexual Healing." Roger takes me in his big, strong arms. He's taller and brawnier than I am. His five o'clock shadow scratches against my cheek. We dance our way through the song. By the end, we are kissing. My hands are in Roger's hair and he is tugging at my T-shirt, ripping it over my head.

There is the sound of a key in the lock. The apartment door swings open.

"Aw jeez," Solly says, shielding his eyes from the sight of us.

Roger and I move apart.

Solly steps inside the apartment and slams the door shut abruptly. "Come on. Come on. What is this, Henry? The homo honeymoon suite?"

"It *is* our apartment, Pop," I say indignantly, folding my arms across my naked chest.

"Yeah, yeah. Whatever. But you could have a little whatcha-callit? Propriety." Solly hangs his brown felt fedora on our tasteful, black and chrome hat rack. Frank Sinatra meets Calvin Klein.

"Propriety?"

"Yeah, you know. Manners." He puffs on a stub of a thick cigar, pouring putrid black smoke into our apartment.

"Manners?"

"Yeah, Henry. Some things are better left, you know, behind closed doors." He blows clouds of smoke in our direction.

Roger waves at the smoke with one hand.

"Pop, I told you when you moved in here, Roger and I weren't going to hide our relationship."

"Yeah, yeah. Listen, it's okay by me, fellas. What the fuck I care what kinda disgusting things you two do with each other —"

"Pop —" I warn.

"But when there's company present, you gotta have a little whatchacallit? ... Discretion."

"Company? What company?" I look around the apartment. There's only the three of us here.

Solly puffs on his cigar.

The smoke catches in my throat, makes me cough. "Pop, put out the cigar."

"What?"

"The cigar."

"Oh." It's as if he has forgotten about our no smoking policy. He opens the door a few inches, drops the cigar on the hallway carpet, sticks one foot through the opening and crushes the butt on the floor. There is a shadow on the wall and quiet murmuring. Is there somebody in the hall?

"Pop! You can't just leave it there."

"Why not?"

"Pop —"

"Awright, awright. Don't get your girdle in a knot, Henry." He laughs at his own joke, opens the door wider, bends to pick up the crushed cigar.

"I thought you were playing cards?" My hands drop to my hips. I feel like an angry housewife. "At Stan's." There is a shrill tone to my voice.

My father shrugs. "Well, it didn't work out. His wife came home early. So we're playing over here." He opens the door wider. "Come on, guys," he says toward the hall.

"What?"

"Don't worry, Henry. I can see you're busy out here." The sarcasm drips from Solly's voice. "We're going into my room." Solly removes his wrinkled black trench coat, hangs it on the rack. Stan Birmbaum steps into the apartment, followed by Meyer Katz and Lou Greenberg, longtime friends of my father's — all in their sixties, and in various states of disrepair. Potbellies, receding hairlines, drooping chins, greying hair. Stan carries a collapsed card table, Lou grips a full bottle of whisky by the neck, Meyer holds a grease-stained take-out pizza box. They file past Roger and me.

"Hiya Henry." Lou tips his hat.

"Henry. Long time no see," Stan breathes heavily from the strain of lugging the table.

"Is that Henry?" asks Meyer, squinting behind Coke-bottle glasses.

"All right. Come on, guys. Follow me," orders my father. They parade past us toward Solly's room at the back of the apart-ment. The room that used to be our den.

I am furious. He'd promised to stay out late, to give Roger and me some time alone. I want to kill my father. I stand in the middle of the living room, fists at my sides. I will follow him into the den and strangle him. Wring his neck until he's dead.

"Great." I sulk.

I expect Roger to be upset, but he laughs. "Let's just go out for dinner, Henry."

"But I spent all afternoon making a fabulous dinner."

"Well, then ..." He moves toward me, runs one hand down my bare chest. "Let's take dinner into the bedroom."

When I get up the next morning, Roger has gone to work. I throw on a pair of sweatpants and a T-shirt, stumble through the living room and into the kitchen. Everything is a mess. The dishes and pots and pans from our dinner are strewn on the counter and in the sink. There's also an empty pizza box, glasses and plates. I feel hungover, even though I only had one glass of wine — my limit. I can't deal with this mess yet. I need coffee first. I fill the coffee grinder with beans, dump the grounds into the filter, pour water into the machine. I glance at the stove-top clock. Early. Eight-fifteen. The paper won't arrive for at least another hour. It's part of my morning ritual, to scour the pages of the *Toronto Star*.

Four months ago, local journalist Rick Jackson interviewed members of my ACTOUT group. We've been working with a doctor from New York, Albert Maxwell, who believes that HIV is not a natural occurrence, but was intentionally invented by the U.S. military in the 1970s as a form of biological warfare. The man-made virus was then tested out on an unsuspecting gay community in 1978 in Manhattan and San Francisco, slipped into an experimental vaccine for hepatitis B, says Albert. The article was supposed to run in the *Star* months ago, but it hasn't appeared yet. Every morning I check the papers. I'm too irritated this morning to wait for the paper to be delivered, so I slip on my runners and my black leather motorcycle jacket and step out of the apartment.

Outside the sun is shining. There is a chill in the air, but spring has arrived. I walk down Alexander to Church Street, wave to a couple of boys from the neighbourhood. In the small parkette by The 519 — Toronto's gay and lesbian community centre — there are already a couple of queens lying on blankets on the grass in Speedos, getting a head start on their tans. I used to do the very same thing before Dr. Green discovered the KS lesion on my back. Now I stay out of the sun unless I'm covered in clothing from head to toe and wearing a sunbonnet. In the convenience store, I grab a carton of milk, a bottle of OJ, a package of Smarties — my one true addiction — and a copy of the *Star*.

Inside the apartment the coffee is ready. I pour a cup, add milk, grab the paper and head out to the balcony. We face south and there's no sun on our side of the building yet, but it's just warm enough, even in the shade, to be pleasant. I settle onto a white plastic chair and flip through the first section of the paper. On page fourteen I find it: Rick's article. My heart speeds up. I sit straight in my chair. Finally. We've been waiting since

December, when he wrote and filed the story, for it to be published. His editor, he's told us, keeps putting it on hold, waiting for the right time. Whatever that means.

The headline reads, "ACTOUT Acts Out," and the subtitle says, "AIDS Victims Yell Government Conspiracy." I scan the brief article quickly. Albert is quoted several times. My name is mentioned as a spokesperson for ACTOUT. As I read, my belly twists in anger. We sound like lunatics. Like those people who live in trailer parks in Utah and report flying saucers. It reads like a *National Enquirer* exposé. According to the article, members of ACTOUT claim that the government of the United States purposely infected the gay community with AIDS back in 1978, which is sort of true, but the way it's worded, we sound like nut-cakes. Complete and utter weirdos. Escapees from the local loony bin. I am mortified. I am livid. How could Rick do this to us? After we trusted him? After Albert trusted him. I throw the newspaper down, stomp into the living room and dial Rick's number.

"Hello?"

I recognize the voice. It's Philip, the nurse Rick hired last time he was sick. Which should be my first clue. I lace into him without thinking.

"Where the hell is Rick? I can't believe he had the nerve to publish such utter illiterate trash about ACTOUT and Albert. And to misquote me so entirely. I mean, who does he think he is? I just hope Albert hasn't seen this. Makes Al look like the Nutty Professor, and me like a drug-addled, bra-burning political fanatic. And I thought Rick had a thing for Albert. Well, if that's how he treats his lovers, I'd hate to see what he writes about his exes. Where is the spineless, despicable, sellout of a traitor anyway? Put him on the phone, will you?"

"Can't," says Philip.

"Oh yeah? Why the hell not?"

"Not here."

"Oh yeah? Where the hell is he?"

"Hospital," Philip answers calmly.

"Oh. Shit." I take a deep breath, let it out slowly. Feel like a dumb-ass. "Which hospital?"

"Which do you think?"

"Oh." All AIDS patients go to St. Michael's. It's kind of like Gay Pride Parade in the AIDS ward. Roger works at St. Michael's Hospital. Whenever I go to pick up Roger after work, I see people I know. Ex-tricks, ex-lovers, ex-friends. I've spent some time there myself. Not for a while, mind you, knock on polished parquet, but I've done some time. "What happened?" I ask Philip.

"PCP again. Fifth time."

"Oh shit. Listen, Phil?"

"Uh huh?"

"Sorry."

"Uh huh."

At the nurses' station I ask for Rick's room. The walk down the hall is endless. I hate walking in the first time after someone has been admitted. That's the worst. You never know what state you'll find them in. My runners squeak on the freshly waxed linoleum floor. Fluorescent lights glare down on me. The heavy smells of disinfectant, fear and unwashed bodies mingle in the air. A harried orderly rushes by. I pass a cart filled with half-eaten lunch trays: fish sticks, overcooked carrots and peas, red Jell-O. My belly tightens. Clutching my copy of the paper under one arm, I step slowly into Rick's room. He is awake, sitting up in bed, with several pillows arranged behind him. He is hooked up to an IV and wears an oxygen mask. I wave and enter. Sit on the hard vinyl chair beside his bed. I notice a copy of this morning's paper on his bedside table, opened to the page with his article. He glances at it. Then at me. He moves the oxygen mask to one side to speak. Rick's pale blond hair is thin, his skin translucent, almost blue. He looks terrible, like he's aged twenty years in the four months since I last saw him. I try not to stare.

"You saw it?" he asks.

I nod grimly.

"It wasn't ... my ... fault ... Henry." It is difficult for him to speak. He takes short, shallow breaths between each word. He replaces the oxygen mask and breathes.

I nod. Wait.

He moves the mask. "Editor ... cut it ... to ribbons. Didn't know. Not until ... I saw it ... here." He points feebly with a weak wrist at the paper, replaces the mask. Closes his eyes. Breathes. Quick, short, pained breaths. I gulp as deep a breath as I can in sympathy.

"Your editor? I thought you said he was behind you on this one."

Rick grunts; his eyes are hard.

"Isn't that what you said?"

He sighs, nods and sums up the problem in one word. "Betrayal."

"Uh huh," I say. "It's okay, Rick. I was mad at first. But I understand." And I do. I know enough about the media to know how little power a freelance writer has. In my old life I was a staff photographer at a low-budget gay paper in New York, and later at *Xtra*, a slick gay news and entertainment magazine in Toronto. This was about a million years ago, in my youth. Before I retired to look after my plague-ridden body. I get a disability insurance cheque once a month and Roger takes care of the rest. It's probably true, what Rick says. He probably didn't know what his editor did to his piece before it was printed. And I can't imagine that he would have written the piece the way it appears. Such a condescending tone.

"Have you talked to Albert?" I ask.

Albert Maxwell was the impetus for the project. Over the past seven years, he has gathered and compiled boxes of research supporting his theory. When he approached my ACTOUT group for help last year, we asked Rick to write an article about Albert's findings and submit the piece to the *Toronto Star*. We thought they'd run it as a hard news story on the front page. We imagined international coverage. The president of the United States would be called to question. People would demand the truth.

Obviously the newspaper's editors thought Rick's article was a big joke — a human interest piece about a quack doctor and crazy militant AIDS activists.

"Albert knows," Rick says tersely.

I get the feeling that love isn't exactly blooming between them anymore. "He's mad?"

Rick nods solemnly, eyes fixed, jaw set, as if that is a supreme understatement.

"Does he know you're here?"

Rick shrugs. He looks sad and defeated. I pat his arm again. Then the coughing starts. He leans forward and gasps for breath between short, racking coughs. I rub his back. A nurse runs in, shoves me out of the way, fiddles with the oxygen tank.

"You better go," the nurse says to me, as if I have caused the coughing.

"You hang in there, Rick."

He closes his eyes and smiles weakly. The nurse helps him lay back against the pillows. I leave the room.

In the hospital corridor I have a mini-nervous breakdown. It comes over me all at once. Fear swirls in my belly, rises to my throat. I sob involuntarily. Embarrassed, I turn to face the wall and cry into my hand. Let the tears flow. Let the grief pour out. I hear people walking around me. I ignore them. It's all so fucking sad. It's not Rick I'm crying over. I hardly know Rick. It's the enormity of the thing. I've been here in this ward to visit dying friends more times than I can remember. I can't recall half of the people who have died. They all blur into one big hospital visit. Their faces merge. My first boyfriend, an ex-roommate, my first bf's ex, my first bf's ex's ex, an ex-trick, a gym buddy, a guy I used to work with, a roommate's ex, my ex's ex. It's a war zone, and I am a soldier, watching my buddies blown to bits beside me in the trenches. With no backup. No air cover. Down to our last few rounds. The horror only ends with death.

I cry myself out, then turn around, wipe my face with my sleeve. Breathe. Behind me at the nurses' desk, an orderly has been watching me. He smiles weakly when I catch his eye.

"You okay?" He speaks softly.

I shrug.

In the hall a young man sits in a wheelchair, emaciated and in the final stages. Beside him on a chair sits an older woman, probably his mother. She holds a plastic glass of water in front of him while he sips from a bent paper straw. She tenderly wipes his chin when he dribbles some water. I think about my mother, Belle. I've been trying to tell her about my HIV status for years, but it's been difficult. She's not exactly what you would call a good listener. My mother is in perpetual crisis. She's always breaking up with her boyfriend, Bernie, or depressed or thinking of trying Prozac or threatening to kill herself. Or complaining about my father, whom she divorced twenty-five years ago. I've just never had the heart to tell her about me. But in this moment outside Rick's room, watching a mother wipe her son's chin, I want *my* mother. When I end up here, I want her to visit me and wipe *my* chin. I pull myself together and leave the hospital.

I've decided to head uptown to my mother's place in the suburbs before I lose my nerve. I'm going to break the news. Today is Tuesday, one of her days off work. I know she will be home, probably doing her nails or cleaning her apartment. At Yonge Street I enter the subway station, struggle in my pocket for change. Mid-morning the subway car is not too crowded. I slouch in a seat near the back. The rhythmic rumbling of the train settles my nerves. Most of the trip is underground, inside the dark tunnel. The train only occasionally bursts out into the open air and sunlight. Even in the suburbs, spring is beautiful. Trees in the ravine are heavy with ripe buds, ready to burst into bloom. In my mind, I plan out what I will tell my mother.

Hi Ma, I have bad news ... no, too grim. *Ma, I have good news and bad news.* What's the good news? God, this reminds me of coming out. Except that was easier. I didn't have to break the news at all. My mother arrived home unexpectedly early and walked into my bedroom, to find me down on my knees sucking Morris Silverberg's cock. You know the saying — a picture's worth a thousand words. She pretty well got it right away. What's not to get?

At the Finch Station, my belly is in knots. I'm determined to go through with this, but I'm nervous. I find half a pack of Smarties in my pocket and crunch on a handful. The subway doors open. I step out. Walk upstairs, wait for a bus to take me to Bathurst Street. Maybe I should just act it out for my mother. I should have rented an oxygen tank and an IV stand, wheeled into her apartment in a chair, dressed in a hospital gown, looking thin and tired and drawn, covered in purple lesions, gasping for my every breath.

Get it, Ma?

Outside my mother's building, I take a deep breath and push the intercom buzzer. She lives in a high-rise overlooking Bathurst Street, has lived in the same building for thirty years. When my father went to jail the first time, she moved uptown to the suburbs.

"Yes, who is it?" My mother's voice over the intercom.

"It's your favourite son."

"Henry?! Come on up." She buzzes me in.

Inside her apartment I can see she's been crying.

"Ma? What's the matter?"

"Bernie's left me."

"Again?" My mother's been dating Bernie Warshovsky off and on for the past fifteen years. Several times a year they break up. He's asked her many times to marry him, but she refuses. This way, she gets to live alone, which suits her. And Bernie is obliged to court her. He brings her flowers and chocolates, takes her out on the town. She's convinced this would all stop if she married him. She's probably right.

She fetches a bunched-up Kleenex from her sweater sleeve, blows her nose loudly. "Yeah, again, but this time it's for good, Henry."

"I'm sorry, Ma."

"I'm not," she spits vehemently. "He's a creep. A rat. Worse than a rat. He's a mouse."

A mouse is worse than a rat?

"Come on, Henry. Let's go out for some cheesecake to celebrate."

"Celebrate?"

"Yeah. Who needs a mouse like Bernie Warshovsky anyway?"

"I don't know, Ma."

"Just wait till I powder my nose. There's Tang in the fridge. Help yourself."

"No thanks, Ma."

"It's fresh." Her voice trails down the hallway to the bathroom.

Fresh Tang. Terrific. Does she always drink Tang? Or is even my mother preparing for a Y2K meltdown?

At Bagel World we are ushered to a table for two by a matronly hostess. Belle orders the fruit salad platter.

"I'm on a diet," she explains, although frankly, she doesn't look overweight to me.

I order a pumpernickel bagel with lox.

"Get an order of cheesecake, Henry," Belle says.

"I don't feel like cheesecake."

"So, you'll try it anyway. And an order of cheesecake," she tells the waitress.

"I don't want cheesecake," I say.

"We'll share. I want to try it. Just a tiny bite. I'm on a diet, you know. We'll take the cheesecake," she announces. "With extra strawberries, please."

The waitress leaves with our order.

Belle clicks her long red fingernails on the tabletop, a habit she has. My mother is fastidious about her nails — has a manicure once a week, wears rubber gloves to wash dishes, is determined to have soft, young-looking hands. She works in the makeup department at Eaton's, where she gets a discount. She never leaves the house without makeup, usually done a little garishly for my taste.

"I don't know what to do, Henry." She fishes in her sleeve for the Kleenex as fresh tears begin to fall.

If she would only stop talking, I could tell her about me.

Outside the restaurant, I hug my mother goodbye.

"Where you heading, Henry? I can drive you," she offers.

"I'm going home."

"So? I'll drive you." She takes my arm.

"All the way downtown?"

"Why not?"

"I thought you get nosebleeds south of Eglinton," I remind her. "That's what you always say."

"I never said any such thing. Come on." She steers me toward her car, a rusted, dented, mid-eighties four-door sedan. "It'll give us more of a chance to talk."

Oh boy. I've already decided not to tell her. How can I break my unbearable news to her, when she's all broken up over Bernie? I'll wait until they're back together again, and happy. Bad news is easier to take when you're happy. She talks non-stop all the way downtown. I nod, smile and answer uh huh at appropriate intervals until we arrive.

Just as we pull up in front of my building, the lobby door swings open and my father saunters out, looking handsome and rugged in his early American gangster suit, complete with black shirt, light-coloured tie, pinstripes, felt fedora, thick Cuban cigar. He strolls up to the car when he spots me in the passenger seat, does a double take when he sees my mother. I glance at her. She turns beet red at the sight of Solly.

"Well, well, well." He leans into my window to take a look at his ex-wife. "What have we here?"

"What are you doing here?" my mother asks Solly. "What's he doing here?" she accuses me.

"Well ..." I don't know where to start. I have no idea how long it's been since my parents have seen each other. Belle gets so upset at the mention of Solly's name, I haven't gotten around to telling her he's been staying with me. I want desperately to get out of the car and run upstairs to the safety of my apartment. Sitting between them, I feel ten years old.

"I thought you were in jail again," she accuses Solly.

"Where'ja hear that?" he asks, offended, as if it weren't true.

"Your mother."

"My mother?"

"Yeah."

"You been talking to my mother?"

"Solly, she lives two blocks away. In the Home. I stop in to make sure she's all right. Your sister-in-law visits her too."

"Faygie?"

"Who else?"

"Even though she's remarried now? To what's-his-name? What's that *shmendrick's* name?" he asks me.

"Uh ..." I strain for the name of Nomi's new stepfather. "Uh, Moe Bernstein?" I try, but I know that's not quite the right name.

Belle shrugs. "Your mother grows on people. So? Is it true?"

He stands, adjusts his tie, strolls around to the other side of the car and leans in close to Belle. They look deeply into one another's eyes. I get the feeling the old attraction is still there between them. I get the feeling I should leave, so they can be alone.

"Yeah," Solly admits, in a low, gruff voice. "I did a little time. But," he lowers his hat brim for emphasis, "that's all behind me now. Ain't that right, Henry?"

"Huh?"

"So, what are you doing here?" Belle confronts him, although I can see a slight smile playing at the corner of her mouth.

"Here?" Solly returns the grin.

"What are you doing at Henry's?"

"Oh. Well ... let's just say I'm ... uh ... whatchacallit? Temporarily between apartments right now. And our son ..." he winks at me, "is helping his old man out. Ain't that right, Henry?"

"Henry." She turns to me. "Why didn't you tell me he was here?"

"Why don't you ask him?"

"Solly?"

"I didn't think you'd care."

"Who said I cared? I'd just like to know what's going on. And how come your mother doesn't know you're staying here?"

"What? I must have told her a dozen times."

"Funny. She never mentioned it to me."

"I'm going upstairs. Thanks for the ride, Ma." I lean over, kiss her cheek and escape.

"Henry ..." she calls after me.

Minutes later, my father comes back upstairs. I'm in the kitchen marinating a boneless breast of chicken for dinner, chopping vegetables to stir-fry. I slice into an onion. My eyes burn and water.

"She still going with that *putz?*" Solly leans against the fridge.

"Who? Bernie?" Onion tears roll down my cheeks. I sniff, wipe at my face with the back of my sleeve as I quickly chop the onion into small pieces.

"Yeah. Bernie." He repeats the name disdainfully, like something extremely distasteful.

"I don't know. They broke up again." I toss the chopped onion into a bowl, rinse my hands and the knife under cold water.

"Is that so?" He seems unnaturally interested.

"But they always break up. And then get back together again. Excuse me." I push him out of the way, open the fridge and check in the vegetable bin for garlic.

"Is that so?"

"Why are you so interested?"

"Huh? Oh. Well, why shouldn't I be interested in who my wife is dating?"

"*Ex*-wife, Pop."

"That's what I said." He pops a piece of chopped celery into his mouth.

"You did not. You said wife."

"Whatever."

While the chicken marinates, I dial Albert's number in New York.

"Did you read it, Henry?" He's in a foul mood.

"I saw it."

"That despicable, rotten, bourgeois, capitalist, scumbag,

guppy, creep, sweater-fag, jerk —"

"Al," I interrupt his tirade. "Rick's in the hospital."

"The way he misquoted me ... I look like a quack."

"He's really sick, Al —"

"I oughtta come right back there and strangle him, then run him over in a sport-utility vehicle with faulty Firestone tires, then program his computer to blow up on January first, then tie him to the CN railway tracks, stuff matches under his toe-nails and light them one by one ..."

"*Really* sick, Al."

"What?"

"PCP. His fifth time. He might die."

"Oh."

"I saw him. He says it's not his fault."

Albert is not convinced. "Then whose?"

"His editor."

"Hmmph."

"He says he's really sorry."

"I bet."

"Are you going to call him?"

"We wouldn't have worked out anyway, Henry. Too different."

"Sorry, Al."

"I gotta go. I'm in the middle of a ritual."

"A ritual?"

"I'm flushing Rick Jackson from my life."

"Oh."

"Everything he ever gave me. Everything he ever touched is going down the garbage chute. Then I'm going to play Donna Summer's extended version of 'R-e-s-p-e-c-t' — our song, hah! One last time. And then the CD goes too."

"Okay, Al."

"Take care, Henry."

"Keep in touch, Al."

I go back to my chicken stir-fry.

I hang up the phone and lie on my back on my best friend Betty's lumpy living room sofa, where I have been sleeping ever since my lying, cheating creep-of-an-ex-lover Sapphire dumped me. Unceremoniously and abruptly. For a man. A tall man. A tall man with a shaved head. A tall man with a shaved head and a Chicago Bulls baseball cap. It is after midnight but I am wide awake. The new love of my life, Julie, is coming to San Francisco to visit. It's been a whole month since we've seen each other. Four months since we fell madly, truly, deeply in love, while I was in Toronto for my mother's wedding to Murray Feinstein.

I hear the tromping of heavy footsteps climbing the stairs. Betty must be returning from her date. I pull the blankets over my head. I don't want to talk to my roommate and whatever new woman she's bringing home tonight. I just want to lie here and think about Julie.

The door opens. One pair of footsteps. No giggling. No kissing. No whispering. I listen closely.

"Hey, Nomi. You up?" Betty drops her husky body onto the end of the couch. Her clothes reek of cigarette smoke. Her breath smells of beer. She lands on top of my legs.

"Ow," I complain.

"Move your legs," she orders.

I peek out from under the blankets as I pull my legs out from under her, then I hug my knees and lean back against the arm-rest. "You're alone?" I can't keep the surprise out of my voice. Betty is a babe magnet. She can get any woman she wants. Any day. Any time. Anywhere. She seldom comes home alone. In fact, dating a different woman every night is Betty's philosophy on life. She wasn't always this way. Once she was in love, with Donna, the lead singer of the Marlettes, an all-girl reggae band. But after Donna ran off with her drummer, without so much as a Dear Betty letter, Betty vowed never to fall in love again. She figures that way she's safe.

Betty sighs. "Yeah. I'm alone. Can you believe it, Nomi? I think I'm losing my touch. You want a beer?" She stands up, heads for the kitchen.

"Sure. Why not?" I can't sleep anyway.

She returns with two bottles of imported Canadian beer. Labatt's Blue. After suffering through Betty's cheap watery American beer for months, I have taken to stocking the fridge myself. With real beer. Betty is still dressed in her work uniform: black jeans, crisp white shirt, blue and red striped tie, Super Shuttle windbreaker and cap. She looks like an African-American Ralph Kramden. I half expect her to throw back her head and shout "Alice!" Betty hands me a cold beer and plops back down at the other end of the sofa. She takes a long slug of beer, then removes her cap, runs a hand over her freshly shaved scalp. Sighs.

"What's wrong?" I sip my beer. This is not like Betty. She's generally upbeat and positive, the kind of woman who takes the bull by the horns.

She sighs again. "I've lost my touch, Nom."

"What happened?"

"I went out with Mona tonight."

"Mona? You mean your new boss?" Betty's old boss retired last month after twenty years of service. The day she was intro-duced to her new boss, Betty had come home excited. "She's absolutely fucking gorgeous. Toney toney toney," Betty had said. "Boy would I like to do her."

"You went out with your boss?" I stare at her incredulously. I can't believe she actually crossed that line. "Like on a date?"

"I asked her out for coffee. She said yes. I don't even know if she's gay."

"You were going to bring her back here?"

"I thought about it." Betty loosens her tie, undoes her top button.

"So what happened?"

"We went for coffee. Then we had dinner. Some wine. We talked. Then I asked her if she wanted a nightcap. She said she had to be going. I walked her to the Muni station. She went home."

"This late?"

"No. It was more like eight o'clock. I've been playing pool at Patty's. Couldn't even find a girl there to bring home."

"Poor Betty."

"What if this is the start of a trend?" She leans forward, head in her hands.

I pat her knee. "I hardly think one night constitutes a trend."

"Don't tell anyone," she threatens. "If this gets around ..." She shakes her head.

"Your secret is safe with me. Don't worry."

We sip our beers.

"Guess who's coming to town?" I deliberately steer the focus to my life. Enough about Betty.

She eyes me suspiciously. "Who?"

"Guess."

She studies my face. Tilts back her beer for another sip. Stares at me some more. "Oh," she says. "Your hot little number from Canada."

"She has a name," I say, offended.

"Right. Judy."

"Julie."

"Right." Betty looks around her small apartment. "You planning on staying here?"

I shake my head. "I'm going to ask Patty. She has an extra room."

"You're both welcome to stay here."

"Not on your life, bud."

"Why?"

"Gotta keep her away from your clutches."

"Hey, come on, Nom. I have ethics. Principles. I would never go after a friend's girl. 'Specially not one of yours."

"Why especially not mine?"

She shakes her head. The answer is obvious to her. "How long will she stay?"

"A week."

Betty nods. "Wow. This is more serious than I thought."

A few days later, I am at work at my under-the-table job as a bartender at Patty's Place, a small neighbourhood pub in Bernal Heights. I'm a Canadian living illegally in San Francisco. I don't have a green card. I'm lucky to have a job. Patty hired me two years ago out of solidarity. She's Canadian too. Originally from Sudbury, she moved to San Francisco in the sixties to be a hippie and never looked back. I have to be careful. If the immigration authorities find out I'm here illegally, I could be deported on twenty-four hours' notice.

Patty's Place is not a fancy club. No DJ. No dance floor. Just an old jukebox in the corner. The floors are real hardwood, unpolished. A long oak bar runs the length of the room. There is a pool table near the door, a couple of tables with chairs and Patty's special collection. She loves picking up eccentric items at yard sales and auctions and hanging them on the walls of the pub. There's an old "Enjoy Coca Cola" poster, neon beer signs, a toilet seat, a fake Mona Lisa, a yellow-on-red sign that reads *Tables for Ladies*, a football helmet, several brown fedoras, a red feather boa, chrome handcuffs, and a black-and-white photograph of Craig Russell as Judy Garland. On the ceiling are five-foot-long posters of Marilyn Monroe and Janet Jackson, a limited edition poster of the Beatles and an original placard from Harvey Milk's election campaign of 1978. Her newest acquisitions are a Gay Freedom Day poster from 1982, a cover from a Crosby, Stills, Nash and Young album, and a menu from Polly's, a dyke-owned restaurant that closed a decade ago.

A customer orders a Tequila Sunrise. We don't mix many fancy cocktails at Patty's Place. Most people drink beer or Scotch on the rocks. I smile sweetly, then bend down and secretly consult an outdated bar manual Patty keeps under the counter. The phone rings. I wait for the fifth ring. Boss's orders — Patty thinks it makes the bar seem busier than it actually is. I grab the receiver, continue pouring various shots into the shaker.

"Patty's Place."

"What are you wearing?"

"Julie!"

"Answer my question."

"Uh ..." I look down. "Jeans, T-shirt, Docs."

"Ask me what I'm wearing."

"I'm at work," I whisper.

"I know, silly. I phoned you."

I turn my face to the wall. "What are you wearing?"

"Jeans, T-shirt, boots."

"Oh." I thought she was going to say a black lace negligee, or something equally tantalizing.

"Ask me where I am."

I smile. Just the sound of her beautiful sexy voice makes my heart palpitate. "Okay ... where are you?"

She hesitates for a minute. "Uh ... Duboce Street."

"What?"

"Wait a minute. We just turned onto Market."

"You're in San Francisco!?" I shout.

"Yep."

"Oh my God! I thought you were coming next week."

"I'll be there in ... how long?" she says to someone else. "Ten minutes."

Oh my God. Why didn't she tell me? I glance at my reflection in the bar mirror. I need a haircut. And a shower. And I've been wearing this T-shirt for the past three days. It's stained and wrinkled. "I work until nine tonight," I tell her. It's only seven now.

"I'll wait." She hangs up.

I turn around. The woman who ordered the Tequila Sunrise glares at me. I look down at the shaker and realize I have no idea what's in it. I dump everything into a glass with ice and hand it to her, turn my attention to the door. Julie will be here in ten minutes.

Exactly nine minutes later, the heavy oak door to the pub swings open, and Julie Sakamoto, the most beautiful femme dyke in the universe, saunters in. Her long black hair is tied back in a loose ponytail. Her dark brown eyes smoulder. She's wearing a skimpy, lacy white top tucked into skin-tight blue jeans. There is red nail polish on her nails, and her lips have matching lipstick. The scent of her spicy sweet perfume floods my senses. A wine glass slips out of my hand. I barely notice as it crashes into the sink. I run around the bar counter and take her into my arms.

"Nomi." She buries her face in my neck.

"Julie." I kiss her face all over, searching for her mouth. I find it and we kiss passionately, like the star-crossed lovers we are, right in the middle of Patty's Place. My arms are tight around the small of her back. Her hands are all over my face. It's like the kiss in *From Here to Eternity*. Desperate, scorching, frenzied. It's like we're rolling around on the beach while the tide comes in and soaks us. We're making a scene. The drinkers stop drinking. The pool players stop playing. All conversation stops dead. I open one eye. Everyone is watching us. Someone whistles through her teeth. Others hoot and holler and catcall.

"Atta boy, Nomi!" someone shouts.

"What a looker."

"Who is that?"

"She's gorgeous."

"Is that Nomi's girlfriend?"

"Oh Nomi. I missed you so much," Julie exclaims.

"I missed you too, babe." I stroke her luxurious long black hair.

"Awright, awright. Break it up. What the hell's going on here? Huh?" the gravelly voice of my boss, Patty, bellows.

I pull away from Julie reluctantly. I feel like I've lost my left arm. "Hi Patty. This is Julie."

"I figured that. What the hell's she doing here?" she asks me.

"Pleased to meet you, Julie." Patty removes her ever-present New York Mets baseball cap and bows, like the gentleman she is. A genuine, old-school butch, Patty wears black jeans, white button-down shirts, has her salt-and-pepper hair cut at the barber's and wears men's underwear and aftershave. And she practises good old-fashioned, fifties-style chivalry. She's handsome, charming, abrasive and sweet.

"You must be Patty," Julie giggles.

"Are you working or what?" Patty asks me, replacing her cap.

"Sorry, boss." I take Julie's hand and sit her on a high stool at the bar. I zip back to my side of the counter.

"Finally. Gimme a vodka, no ice," a surly dyke orders.

I pour Julie a glass of white wine and get back to work with a huge smile on my face. Out of the corner of my eye I can see her. It's the loveliest sight. I don't even mind working.

When my shift is over, I drive Julie to Patty's apartment on my motorcycle. Patty follows us in her jeep. She lives in a two-bedroom flat on 18th Street, right in the Castro. Has lived in this apartment for fifteen years. Even though the rents in the area have quadrupled three times over the last two years with the influx of Silicone Valley millionaires, who are buying up all the properties and jacking up the prices, Patty has one of those rare landlords with a conscience, so her rent is manageable. She installs us in the den, which is furnished with a hide-a-bed couch, a TV and a bookshelf filled with lesbian mysteries, Patty's favourite reading. Patty's dog Lulu, a huge overgrown Great Dane, stands on her hind legs, slobbering all over Patty. Julie squeezes my hand and moves behind me, eyeing Lulu warily.

"Don't worry," I tell her, "Lulu is harmless."

"Course she is. She's a lesbian," Patty says. "Hi Lulu. How's my baby?" Lulu's huge tongue licks Patty from chin to forehead.

"A lesbian dog?" Julie giggles.

"Sure she is. See? She didn't bark at you, did she?"

"No."

"If you were a man, she woulda taken a bite right out of you. Wouldn't you, baby?" Front paws back on the floor, Lulu wags her tail enthusiastically.

"Patty, she would not," I argue.

"What do you know about dogs, Rabinovitch?"

Patty wants to socialize, but I remind her it's been four whole weeks since Julie and I have seen each other, and she's only staying for eight days.

"Oh," grunts Patty. "I see." She grabs her jacket. "Guess I'll take Lulu out for a walk." On the word "walk," Lulu barks loudly. "Come on, Lulu." She clips a leash to the dog's purple-studded collar. "I can see we're not wanted around here." Lulu continues barking. Patty leads her to the door of the apartment.

I grab Julie's hand and pull her into Patty's den. To have a door that actually closes is such a luxury after staying at Betty's.

We stand in the middle of the room and stare at each other. Julie is so beautiful I feel awkward, shy. My feet are glued to the floor. I want to throw her down onto the bed and touch every part of her, kiss her all over, make love until morning. But I don't want her to think I only want her for her body. I sense that I should go slow. Get to know her again. After all, we barely know each other. I walk past her to the window.

"Boy, you should check out this view, Julie." Actually it's quite dark and you can't see much.

"Maybe later."

"Wait a minute." I point outside. "I think we can see Twin Peaks from here."

"Nomi ..."

"Oh. No. I think it's just a cloud."

"Nomi ..."

"You can see more from the living room. It faces south."

"Nomi ..."

"Huh?" I turn from the window. She has removed her shirt and stands facing me in her black lace bra.

"Come here." She holds out one hand.

I step forward and take her hand. She pulls me to her, presses her mouth on mine. We kiss. Her tongue pushes its way past my lips. I pull her close, my hands on her naked back. She moans. Pulls my T-shirt up, slips it over my head.

"Julie." I still can't believe she is here.

She fumbles with the buttons on my jeans.

"Wait," I say. "The bed."

I disentangle myself from her, toss the sofa cushions onto the floor and search for the handle on the hide-a-bed. Give it a yank. It's heavy. I feel a pain slice up my back as the bed springs out. "Ow," I groan.

"Nomi?"

I clutch at my back with one hand. "I'm okay. It's heavier than I thought."

"Did you hurt your back?"

"It's okay," I lie.

There are no sheets on the bed yet, but I don't care. I reach for her hand and pull her down. She is in my arms. We kiss. I reach for the zipper on her jeans. She slips out of them, tosses them to the floor. I have fantasized about this moment for a month. I am in a dream state. Julie is here, in my arms. We are here together. I can barely believe it's true. Julie takes my hand and guides it inside her panties.

In the morning, I get up to make us coffee. I find a note from Patty taped to the fridge. It reads: "If you come in to work today, I'll call Immigration on you." Thanks, Patty. What a pal. Lulu is nowhere to be seen. Patty must have taken her to the pub.

"I've got the day off," I tell Julie. She's sitting up in bed, looking out the window. I hand her a cup of coffee. She stares at it.

"What's wrong?"

"I don't usually drink coffee."

"Oh right. You drink tea. I'll make you some." I reach for her cup.

"It's okay, Nomi. I'll drink this. It's already made."

"No. Please, let me make you tea."

"Nomi. Sit down."

"You don't want tea?"

"It's okay."

"You sure?"

"I'm sure."

I slip back into bed beside her.

"You're right," she agrees. "It's quite a view."

I glance out the window. We can see the radio towers on Twin Peaks and the hills rising below. Brown scrub, dotted here and there with short green bushes and the occasional palm tree.

Julie puts her coffee down on the table beside the bed.

"What do you want to do today?" I ask.

"Is Patty at work?"

I nod.

"Lulu?"

"Gone."

She reaches for my face, draws me close. Kisses me. "Let's stay home."

"You don't want to see the sights?" I ask between kisses.

"There's plenty to see right here." She slides down in the bed, and brings me along.

Later that afternoon, we are napping, deep and peaceful in one another's arms. A stream of sunlight floods the bed. It's a beautiful, sweet moment. I hear the apartment door open. A knock on our door, then it opens a crack. Patty peeks in.

"Aw, for chrissake." She swings the door wide open. "It's two o'clock in the goddamn afternoon. Time to get the hell up." Lulu bounds into the room and jumps up onto our bed, excited. She wags her tail, bounding from me to Julie and back again, licking our faces with her huge, wet tongue.

"Patty! You just barge in here?" I try to sound indignant. "Lulu, would you quit that." I push at the dog, try to get her off the bed.

"Oh hell, I'm not looking," Patty says. "Now come on, you two. Get up. There's lots to do."

"There is?"

"You bet your ass. We're having a dinner party. We gotta clean up this place. You two can start on this room, then you can help me in the kitchen."

"Wait a minute, Patty," I say. "We're thinking of going out tonight."

"Like hell you are. The party's in your honour. I hope you like barbecue chicken. 'Cause that's what we're having." Patty leaves the room as abruptly as she entered. "Come on, Lulu." Lulu barks, then leaps down and follows Patty, her tail high in the air.

I smile at Julie. "Sorry about that."

She shrugs and throws the covers off us. "Guess we'd better get up, huh?"

"We don't have to stay, you know. I mean she didn't ask us if we wanted a party in our honour."

"I think we'd better stay. It would be rude, Nomi. She went to a lot of trouble. Come on." Julie slips out of bed and starts dressing.

Patty is a terrible cook. God knows why she volunteered to host the dinner party. An hour ago, she covered three pounds of chicken wings in a packaged sauce, scattered them on a baking sheet and shoved them in the oven to bake. Now the smell of burning meat permeates the apartment. Patty's smoke detector shrieks.

I run to the kitchen, fling open the oven. Smoke pours out. I reach for the oven mitts, pull the tray out, set it on the stove.

Patty rushes in, dragging the vacuum cleaner behind her by its long grey hose. "What the hell you doing to my chicken?" she hollers over the screams of the smoke detector and the roar of the vacuum.

"Rescuing it."

"What the hell happened?"

Julie runs in. "What's burning?"

I look at the oven dial. Patty had it set for 450. "Patty, the oven was up too high."

"What difference does it make?"

I shake my head. "Can you turn that off?" I shout.

"Calm down." She switches off the vacuum. The smoke detector screams on. The sauce has splattered and run all over the oven, causing most of the smoke. The chicken is overdone, but salvageable. "Patty. Can you shut that damn thing off?"

"Yeah, yeah." She leaves the room.

I check in Patty's fridge, find a bottle of barbecue sauce and spoon some onto the chicken to cover the burnt spots. The shrieking stops. Patty returns and stands hovering over my shoulder as I repair the chicken. "I think it will be okay," I say. "What else are you making?"

"Nothing. It's potluck. Everyone is bringing something."

"Oh." You should have had them bring everything, I think, but don't say it out loud. She is, after all, my boss. Patty restarts the vacuum cleaner. It's old and the muffler is broken. It sounds like a 747. She barrels around the apartment, knocking into table and chair legs as she runs the ancient vacuum over her wall-to-wall blue shag carpeting that was installed at least two decades ago. I follow Julie back to the living room to help her dust.

Chester arrives first. Lulu attacks her with love in the entrance-way. Out of all of Patty's friends, Lulu loves Chester best. She has brought dessert. A quart of double chocolate chip, mocha almond crunch, espresso ice cream. When I introduce her to Julie, Chester practically faints. She hasn't had a girlfriend in about five years, but if she had one, she'd be something like Julie.

"Keep your hands off," I warn. "She's mine."

Patty offers Chester a beer. Chester offers to help in the kitchen, but we all know she is an even worse cook than Patty.

"Why don't you just sit?" I suggest, pointing to the living room couch.

Chester sits on the couch. Lulu lies on the floor by Chester's feet.

Betty arrives a few minutes later with AJ and Guido. Betty's brought a pasta salad she picked up at the deli on the way over. AJ hands Patty a loaf of sourdough bread and a half pound of herb-flavoured cream cheese. Guido has contributed a case of Budweiser.

"Well, I can see why you're so head over heels," Betty says to me when I introduce her to Julie. "Pleased to meet you, Julie." She steps forward and shakes Julie's hand. I watch closely.

"It's a pleasure," says Guido, bowing to Julie, giving me the thumbs-up behind her back. Guido is a small woman who is a big, tough butch. She is almost as good a cruise machine as Betty. A thumbs-up from her is worth a lot.

"I know someone in Toronto," AJ says. "I met her at the Gay Freedom Day Parade last year. Let's see. I think her name was Deb. Do you know her?"

"Uh, Deb what?" Julie asks, amused.

AJ shrugs.

"Toronto's a big city," Julie says. "And Deb is a very popular name."

"Yeah," I add, "do you know how many Debs there are per capita, AJ?"

"Oh."

Robert arrives with his lover Spencer, fashionably late. Lulu growls at Spencer until Patty calms her down. Robert, a former celebrity drag performer, now in his mid-fifties, is my co-worker. An old friend of Patty's, he tends bar three days a week. Dressed impeccably in dark dress pants and white shirt, he has a turquoise sweater tied around his shoulders. Spencer, a few years younger and an investment banker, is slumming it tonight in tight black jeans, blue denim button-down shirt and shiny new white runners.

Robert air-kisses everyone, then heads straight for Julie, bends and kisses her once on each cheek. "My dear. My dear. Welcome to the family. Thank God you came along. We just about lost our poor Nomi for a while there," he says, humiliating me. I smile, as if it's a big joke. He swishes into the kitchen with Spencer on his heels. From the safety of Chester's feet, Lulu watches Spencer closely. "I sure hope you have a garlic press, Patty," Robert says. "The secret of my world-famous Caesar salad is to prepare the dressing at the very last second. The very last."

"What kinda press?" Patty pries open her cutlery drawer to search.

There are too many of us to sit around Patty's table, so we each grab a plate and find a place in the living room.

"All right," says Robert, once everyone is settled. "Now tell us everything. When did you meet? And where? What do you do in bed? Spare no details. When will the wedding be? Can I give you away, Nomi?"

I glance at Julie. She is laughing, thank God.

"Leave them alone, Robert. For chrissake, the poor girl just got here," Patty snaps. "How do you all like the chicken?"

"Terrific," says Betty skeptically, holding a burnt piece up in front of her, examining it.

"It's all right, Robert. We don't mind. Right, Nomi?" Julie says to me. She bites a tiny piece of chicken, then scoops up a large forkful of pasta salad.

I gulp. "We don't?"

"We met five years ago," Julie says. "Originally. But ..."

Everyone leans forward, eager to hear the gossip.

"... we both had other lovers at the time."

"And we ran into each other last winter, when I was in Toronto for my mother's wedding," I continue.

"Oh yeah. How's your mother doing?" Chester pipes up.

"Quiet, dear," Robert says to Chester. "We'll get to that later. Where did you run into each other?"

"It was at the Rose, a dyke bar in Toronto."

"Natch," says Robert.

"Nomi was so nervous."

"That's our Nomi," confirms Betty.

I scowl at her.

"We talked for a bit that night. And then we found out Henry had been gay-bashed."

"Her cousin ..." Betty fills in for the benefit of the others.

"You have a gay cousin?" Chester asks. "That's great. All my cousins are straight."

"If I had a gay cousin, maybe my grandmother would talk to me," says Guido wistfully.

"Oh," says Robert. "Is he the one who thinks the President invented AIDS?" He asks this with more than a hint of skepticism.

Julie looks annoyed. "Actually I'm working on that project with Henry."

"Oh," says Robert, stuffing his mouth with chicken, to keep his foot out.

"You guys should hear about that," Betty says. "It's fascinating. Really."

"And then what happened?" AJ loves hearing about true love. Or sex. Especially sex. She's been with her lover Martha for thirteen years, only she never brings her along when she goes out. Martha has been recovering from whiplash from a car accident for years, or so she says, and prefers to stay home after work with their three dogs and two cats. We all figure AJ and Martha stopped having sex years ago. AJ's usually on the edge of her seat when anyone talks about sex.

"I lured Nomi up to my apartment," Julie tells them.

I take Julie's hand.

"She was so sweet. So shy."

"It's always the femmes who make the first move," declares Chester.

"Not necessarily," argues Betty, who I'm sure makes the first move all the time, and no one would accuse her of being femme.

"I fell in love with Nomi that first night," Julie says, and my heart swells.

"So sweet." Robert clasps his hands together. "Isn't that sweet?" he asks Spencer.

"Like chocolate-covered macadamias."

"Who wants more chicken?" Patty says to the crowd. No one speaks up. "There's plenty. Don't be shy."

Still no one steps forward.

"I'll have some more," Julie smiles politely. "It's delicious, Patty."

Betty stares at Julie like she's crazy.

"What happened with the whole AIDS thing?" Betty asks. "Did your article ever get into the paper?"

Julie sighs. "Well, we waited for months and then finally a few days ago the article appeared in the mainstream daily paper, the *Toronto Star*, on page forty-seven or something, in the human interest section. Dr. Maxwell came out sounding like a lunatic. And Henry was portrayed as an angry AIDS victim-slash-left-wing radical troublemaker. Anyway, hardly anyone saw it."

"What article?" Robert-the-skeptic is suddenly interested.

Julie tells Robert about Albert Maxwell's theory about the origins of HIV. Albert tried to publish an article about his theory in the United States for years, to no avail. Finally, in desperation he went to Julie and Henry's ACTOUT Toronto chapter. Albert figured the Canadian media might be more willing to print the article than the American press, since he was naming the U.S. government as responsible for the whole mess. He planned to make his theory public in the hopes that someone would do something about it. Like push for more funding for AIDS research and compensation for people with AIDS. So far, the Canadian media haven't been much better than the American.

"All right, " interrupts Patty. "Let's talk about something else. Come on. This is supposed to be a party." Patty is touchy about AIDS. Her best friend, Tony, died back in 1990. She still misses him, and just talking about AIDS puts her in a melancholy mood. I try not to bring it up around her. Robert, who was out and cruising in the early seventies, is miraculously HIV negative. "Good," said Patty when he told her. "Stay that way, will you? Can't stand to see people die like that." "Whatever you say, boss," he had replied dryly. Robert has buried practically his entire social circle. It offends him when people who have lost one or two friends act like martyrs, but Patty is his boss, so he holds his tongue. Sort of.

Betty picks up the cue and starts talking about *her* new boss and how she hopes to lure her into bed one day soon.

"But you don't even know if she's gay?" Chester is amazed. She has a hard enough time just asking a woman to dance at the dyke bar, let alone cruising a boss who may be straight.

Betty shrugs. "I guess we'll find out."

"With men, it's easy," Spencer says. "I've never met a straight man yet who would turn down a blow job."

"Spencer!" Robert's hands fly to his hips. "We're in mixed company."

"We are?"

"Time for dessert," Patty announces. "Where the hell did I put that ice cream?"

"Uh oh," says Chester. She reaches under the coffee table for the tub of ice cream, which has been sitting there since she arrived three hours ago.

Everyone turns to her.

"It's right here." She opens the lid, peeks in. Melted, of course.

"I'm stuffed anyway," says Robert. "How about some cognac, Patty?"

"What? You mean my good stuff?"

"The very same. We do have a lovely guest of honour." Robert gestures toward Julie. "All the way from Canada."

"Oh, what the hell." Patty stands, goes to the china cabinet she inherited from Tony, and pulls out a bottle of Rémy Martin and some snifters. "Drinks all around?" she inquires.

"I think I'll have another beer," says Guido, who drinks nothing but beer.

"Suit yourself," says Patty, as she pours the first glass of cognac and with a flourish hands it to Julie.

In no time at all the week has gone by and it's Julie's last night here. Patty's working my shift for me. Julie and I have the apartment to ourselves. We sit on our bed, legs entwined, sipping glasses of white wine, feeling miserable about parting in the morning.

"Do you think you'll ever move back?" Julie asks.

I spill white wine on the bed sheets. "To Toronto, you mean?"

"Well, you don't have to act like it's poison."

Uh oh. She's offended. I wipe at the spilled wine with my hand. "Sorry. It's just that ... I don't think I could ever live there again."

"Why not?" Her big brown eyes are wide with concern.

"Well ... the weather. I hate the winter ... too cold. And I hate the summer. Last time I was there in the summer the humidity and the pollution were so bad, I felt like showering every other minute. My skin felt dirty. My throat hurt. I could barely breathe. I was miserable."

"It's not that bad."

"It's not?"

"Don't you want to be together?"

"You know I do ... what about ... here?" I take a large slurp of wine.

"You mean, what if I move here?"

"Yeah."

"Well, I like San Francisco ... but what would I do here? I can't get a job."

"You could do what I do."

"You mean work in a bar?" She says this with some distaste, as if it were the most disgusting thing in the world. Now it's my turn to be insulted.

"It's not bad."

She sighs. Deeply. "I can't just leave my job, Nomi. It's not just a job, you know."

She means like my job, which is just a job and not a career. Julie is the assistant director at the Asian AIDS Association, also known in the community as Triple A. She represents the organization at city hall meetings, provincial conferences and community forums. She's quoted in the news, has met with the mayor, the minister of health and the chief of police. In her job, she commands a lot of respect. Whereas I stand behind a bar and pour cocktails and pull draught in a crummy rundown neighbourhood pub.

"You mean like my job?" I say it out loud, then instantly regret it. Are we having a fight?

"Nomi ... that's not what I meant."

"Yes it is. It's exactly what you meant," I say angrily. What am I doing? I don't want to fight with her. I want to throw her back down on the bed and make mad passionate love for the rest of the night. And into the morning.

"I don't know why you won't even think about moving back to Toronto." She stands, walks to the window, her back to me. "You grew up there, after all."

"And that's exactly why," I shout, although I don't mean to. "I hate Toronto! I can't live there, Julie. I can't." I leap up off the bed and move toward her, touch her arm.

"What's wrong with Toronto, Nomi? It's a great city."

"No, it's not. It's dirty. And cold. And grey concrete."

"The last few winters haven't been so bad."

"Yeah, 'cause of global warming. And it's way behind in everything."

"Way behind?"

"Yeah. Music. Art. Fashion."

"Oh, you mean behind San Francisco?"

"Everywhere." What am I saying? Like I care about fashion?

"That's ridiculous, Nomi. Toronto has an incredible music scene. And theatre."

"Not that I recall. I hate it. That's all. I hate Toronto, Julie. I hate it!" I'm shouting again. Damn. Why is this making me so mad?

"Fine." She pulls away. "If that's how you feel." She plunks her wine glass down on the dresser, grabs her jeans and throws them on, angrily pulling up the zipper.

"Julie ... what are you doing?" A lump of fear rises in my throat.

She tosses on her sweater, the soft green angora I love on her. "I'm going out!" She hurls open our bedroom door and stomps through Patty's apartment to the front door, where she steps into her shoes, tosses on her jacket.

"Julie ..." I follow her to the door in my boxer shorts and undershirt. "What are you doing? Where are you going to go? You don't even know your way around San Francisco," I plead.

"So?" She opens the door.

"You'll get lost."

"Good!" She steps out into the hall.

"Julie ... come back inside."

"Good riddance!" she hollers, slamming the door behind her.

I pull open the door, my heart thudding in my chest. Our first fight. What did I say to make her so angry? A few minutes ago we were happily lazing in bed, our bodies entwined, staring lovingly into each other's eyes. How did it come to this?

"Julie," I yell at her disappearing back. "Come back. Where are you going?"

I have absolutely no idea what to do now. Should I follow her? Probably. I dash back to the bedroom, throw myself into jeans, shoes no socks, fling on my leather jacket, run out the door, down the stairs to the street. Damn. No sign of her. Which way would she go? I turn in all directions. Nothing. What should I do? I should probably stay put. She'll be back in a few minutes. How far could she go? She doesn't know her way around. She'll probably go for a walk around the block, cool down, then return. I trudge back up the stairs to Patty's apartment. I had no idea Julie was so passionate. What a temper. I find one of Guido's leftover Budweisers in the fridge, pop off the top, plunk down on Patty's living room sofa to wait.

I hear footsteps. She's back. I run to the door, fling it open.

"Oh, it's you," I say to Patty.

"Well, don't act so thrilled to see me, Rabinovitch." Lulu strains on her leash, jumps up, plants her front paws against my chest, slobbers all over me.

"Quit it, Lulu." I push her away.

"She's happy to see you. What's the matter with you?" Patty looks around. "Hey, where's Julie?"

"Beats me." I drop down onto the sofa.

"What's going on around here? You two have a fight?" Patty

fills Lulu's bowl with smelly, wet, lumpy dog food. Lulu eats ravenously.

I sigh. "What are you doing here? Thought you were working my shift."

"I *am* the boss, Nomi." She puts one hand on her hip. "I called Robert in to cover the bar. I'm spending quality time with Lulu."

"Oh."

"Don't worry, after she eats we're going to Golden Gate Park for a long walk."

"Good."

"Aw, cheer up, Rabinovitch. She'll be back."

"I hope you're right."

"Course I'm right. Where's she gonna go?"

"She was pretty mad."

Patty sits beside me on the sofa. Grabs my beer, takes a sip. "What did you fight about?"

"Patty ..."

"I'm only trying to help."

I sigh. "She wants me to move back."

"To Canada?" She hands my beer back to me.

"Toronto."

"Well, you should go then, Nomi. True love doesn't grow on trees, you know."

"I thought that was money."

"Love's harder to come by than money. You know that."

"I can't live there. I hate Toronto."

She shakes her head. "I know what I'm talking about, Rabinovitch." She stands. "Come on, Lulu. Come on, sweetheart." She speaks in a five-year-old's voice that nauseates me. "Come on, baby. Let's go to the park."

On the word "park," Lulu howls.

"You wanna go park?" Patty encourages her. She loves to make Lulu howl. "That's my advice, Nomi. Come on, baby."

Lulu barks as Patty opens the door and together they leave me to my misery. I glance at the clock for the fortieth time.

Julie's been gone twenty-three minutes and thirty-one seconds. My head aches with tension. Now, I'm worried. What if she's lost? What if she stumbles into a bad neighbourhood like the Tenderloin or somewhere and gets mugged, or shot, or worse? I should have run after her, even in my underwear. I pace back and forth. It's impossible to sit still. I check the clock. Only one minute has gone by. Feels like eternity. I can't just sit here doing nothing. I reach for the phone.

"I'll be right over," Betty offers.

"You don't have to come over," I say. "It's just ... I don't know ... I'm worried."

"You shouldn't tie up the phone, Nom. What if she's trying to call you?"

"Oh God, you're right." Abruptly I hang up on Betty.

Julie has a cellphone. I curse the universe because she didn't take it with her when she stomped off. It's sitting on the dresser in Patty's den. I pick it up, hold it by my face, as if I can will Julie to call me. It smells like her: sweet and sexy. I stand by the window and look out. Three teenagers roll by on skateboards, wheels bumping over the sidewalk cracks noisily. A man watches his dog defecate on the sidewalk, then he pulls a plastic bag from his pocket and scoops up the litter. A heavy bass beat emanates loudly from a sport-utility vehicle's CD player. I hear footsteps in the hall. I rush back to the front door. It swings open. My heart pounds. Oh. It's only Betty. My face falls.

"Here," she says, "I brought you something." She tosses a Häagen-Dazs ice cream bar at me. It's her favourite — vanilla crunch.

"I can't eat at a time like this." I fling it back at her.

She shrugs. "Suit yourself." She peels off the wrapper, takes a big, satisfying bite. "Just thought you should keep your energy up." She sits on the couch.

"What are you doing here?"

She glares at me like I've just hurt her feelings, which I probably have. "It's called friendship, Nom," she says icily.

"Maybe you've heard of it."

"I'm sorry, Betty," I say. "I'm just scared."

"That's okay. I know what you're like. Remember?"

I sit beside her on the sofa. "Thanks for coming over."

"Don't try to get back on my good side." She polishes off the ice cream bar. With her mouth full of melted ice cream and chocolate cookie crumbs, she lectures. "Anyway, you and Julie have only known each other a short time. You only just got dumped by Sapphire what? Two months ago?"

"Five."

"Okay, five. But don't you think you should slow down a little? You know? Play the field? I mean, I know Julie's a fox, but Nom, there's lots of other birds in the sky."

"Birds?"

"Babes."

"Who are you? Frank Sinatra? You call women birds?"

"It's a retro expression that's making a comeback, Nom. Where've you been?"

"On your living room sofa."

"Yeah, moping and pining. It's time you picked it up, girl-friend." She snaps her fingers in the air above her head. "You can't go around changing your life, moving across the world every time a new girl comes along. Look what happened when you moved here for Sapphire. Anyway, all femmes are crazy. You know that, Nom."

I'm just about ready to slug Betty. I have my right hand balled up into a fist and am just about to strike when the door bursts open. Julie stands in the doorway, one hand on the frame, looking sheepish. Betty thankfully stops lecturing. I stand and face Julie. I don't know what to do.

"Nomi," Julie whispers. I open my arms. She runs into them. We hold each other tightly. "Oh Nomi, I'm sorry." She kisses my forehead, my lips, my nose.

I go for her mouth, kiss her passionately. "No, babe, I'm sorry," I say between kisses.

"I'm too crazy. I have big feelings." She kisses me all over my face.

"No, it's my fault. I shouldn't have yelled."

"No. You're fine, honey. I get too mad."

"I love you."

"Oh God, I love you, Nomi."

Betty clears her throat loudly. "I'm gonna vomit." She squeezes her bulky frame past us through the door. "I'm outta here."

Julie runs her fingers through my hair. I wave to Betty as she leaves. For some reason, she stuffs her sticky ice cream wrapper into my open hand, then walks down the hall to the stairs, shaking her head as she goes.

In the morning, we walk to Castro Street. I'm taking Julie to my favourite breakfast place, a little greasy spoon called Welcome Home for bacon and eggs and grits. We cross 18th Street and head up the hill toward Market.

"Spare change, sir?" A thin man in soiled clothes sits on the dirty sidewalk beside the newsstand outside Walgreen's drugstore, holding a rusty tin can in my direction. I reach in my pocket for a quarter. It clinks against his stash of coins. We pass tastefully dressed gay urban professionals. Fags in leather. Others in jeans. Some hold hands. Others talk on cellphones or walk dogs. The street is lined with rainbow flags. A woman who looks older than she probably is lies sleeping in a doorway. Her hand-painted sign reads HOMELESS AND HUNGRY. I drop a quarter in the upside down baseball cap by her face on the sidewalk.

Directly in front of Lumberjacks, a fag bar that changes persona every couple of years — from leather to country, to sweater-fag to army motif and back again — we bump into my deceitful, underhanded, devious bitch of an ex-lover, Sapphire. She stops in front of Julie and me, with a huge fake smile plastered on her scheming, conniving face.

"No-mi ..." She stretches out my name, as if she's thrilled to see me.

"Out of my way, Sapphire." I try to drag Julie forward. I have no desire to stop and chat with my ex. Julie digs her heels in.

Sniffs the air, like a bloodhound. Smiles back at Sapphire.

"Nomi," Julie says, "aren't you going to introduce me to your friend?"

I take a deep breath and hope for nuclear war to start right this very second and put me out of this misery. "Julie, this is Sapphire. See ya, Sapphire. We're late." I make a second attempt to pull Julie away. But she resists.

"Sapphire," Julie repeats, wrapping an arm around my shoulder. "So good to meet you. I've heard so much about you."

Sapphire looks surprised, but in true bitch fashion, ignores Julie. "Nomi," she says, "I can't seem to find my double-headed dildo. Do you think maybe you took it by accident when you ... moved out?"

Someone starts up a loud motorcycle. I wish they would run over Sapphire.

I know she has said this deliberately to hurt Julie. Or maybe to hurt me. It's hard to tell. I struggle for a good comeback. Something witty and razor sharp. Something deadly. Like cyanide.

"Nomi doesn't need sex toys," Julie interjects, calmly and sweetly, kissing my face. "But I can certainly see why you would. Come on, babe." Julie licks the inside of my ear and steers me up the street. We leave Sapphire standing on the sidewalk with her mouth hanging open.

"Wow," I tell Julie, "that was great."

"Never," she advises, "underestimate the powers of a femme in love."

"Are you in love?"

"You know I am."

Liquid honey spreads through my chest.

In the restaurant, I ask for an intimate table near the back. We order breakfast specials and coffee for me, tea for Julie, and wait for our food to arrive. I reach across and take Julie's hand.

"So, what are we going to do?" Julie asks.

"Do?" Uh oh. She has that serious look on her face again.

Why do femmes always want to Talk About The Relationship? Why can't they just enjoy it?

"About us." She says this in a singsong way, as if I should have known what she was talking about.

"Us?"

A big sigh. "Nomi, I don't know about you ... but I'm having a hard time with this long distance thing."

"Oh." God, can't we just let it go for now? I moved here for Sapphire and look what happened. What if I move back to Toronto and Julie dumps me? What if I move back to Toronto and she dumps me for a man? A tall man with a shaved head? I can't do it again. There have to be other reasons to move. Why can't we just get to know each other for a while?

"Sooner or later we're going to have to figure something out. Make some decisions," Julie continues.

Oh boy. Are we going to have another fight? If I tell her what I'm really thinking, we sure will. "Listen Julie. You're right. But ..." I glance at my wristwatch. "You have a plane to catch. And we don't have to figure it out right now. Do we?"

"All right, ladies." Saved by our jovial wait-person, who carries our breakfast plates on his forearm. "Over easy with bacon, crisp." He lowers the plate onto the table in front of me. "And scrambled, with spicy sausage over here." He places Julie's breakfast in front of her. "And sourdough rye all around. Enjoy your breakfast, girls." He saunters off to wait on a hunky businessman who has just sat down.

Julie tastes a bite of her sausage.

"Is it good?"

"Great." She smiles.

I eat a forkful, wait for her to bring up our dilemma again, but she doesn't. She slips a foot out of her shoe and runs a naked toe up my calf to my thigh, smiles at me seductively and eats her breakfast.

I touch the side of her face tenderly, and eat mine.

HENRY'S DOCTOR

Before our ACTOUT meeting, I meet with my fellow activist and my cousin Nomi's current paramour, the lovely lipstick lesbian Julie Sakamoto. We decide to dine at Andy's on Church Street for overpriced burgers, gigantic chocolate milkshakes, wooden booths with plush red seats, dim lighting and young, buff, beautiful waitpersons. Julie has recently returned from visiting Nomi in San Francisco. She's a mixture of jubilance and sorrow. The trials and tribulations of long distance love are getting to her.

"I like San Francisco," Julie says, taking a bite of her Canuck Burger, a quarter pound of ground beef with Canadian back bacon and cheese. "But I couldn't live there."

"I adore San Francisco." I'm having a Californian, a hamburger topped with guacamole and alfalfa sprouts. "It'd be a great place to live."

"And she refuses to move back here."

"She's got a point."

"Hey. Whose side are you on, anyway?"

"It's a hard one, Julie. But you know what they say ..."

"What?"

"Love conquers all."

"I hope you're right."

We eat in silence.

"What was she like? When you were kids?" Julie asks.

"Nomi? Well, you know I'm ..." I count it out on my fingers. "I'm eight years older, so she always seemed like a little kid to me. And after my parents divorced, we didn't see Nomi's family as much as we used to. But ..."

"Tell me a story about her."

"A story?"

Julie sips on her milkshake.

"Okay. I've got one. How much time do we have?"

She checks her watch. "An hour. The meeting starts at seven."

"Okay. This story's called 'Nomi Ties One On.'"

"Hey ..."

"Don't worry. You'll love it." I sip my milkshake. The smooth sweet chocolate slides down my throat. "On Passover we used to go to our Bubbe and Zayde's — that's grandmother and grandfather in Yiddish."

"Zay-dee." Julie sounds out the unfamiliar word.

"Anyway, on Passover it's traditional to drink four cups of wine throughout the evening. Everyone, even the kids. Of course, when we were little, our wine glasses were the size of thimbles. On this particular Passover, I was twelve, so Nomi would have been uh ... four."

Julie giggles, presumably at the image of a four-year-old Nomi.

"Nomi was sitting right beside me at the table, and whenever she thought I wasn't looking she would steal sips from my wine. After dinner, my grandfather started telling the story of his great escape from Russia. We'd all heard his story many times before, but we never tired of hearing it. Except for my father. He was at the seder that year for the first time in six years, because he had been in jail. My parents were divorced at this point, so my mother wasn't there, just me and my father and my twin brothers, Larry and Moe."

"I didn't know you had twin brothers."

"Yeah, Larry and Moe."

"Larry and Moe? As in the three stooges?"

"Kind of. Actually everyone used to call my sister Curly, just to complete the set."

"Curly, Larry and Moe," Julie repeats. "Is that her real name?"

"No, her real name is Sherry. Curly's just a joke. Anyway, while we were all listening to my Zayde's escape from Russia stories, my father noticed that Nomi kept stealing my wine, and so he figured she liked it quite a bit. This amused him, because remember she was only four years old. So, he got up and plunked Elijah's cup in front of her."

"Whose cup?"

"Oh. Elijah is a prophet. And the custom is to fill a large cup of wine in the centre of the table for him. He's kind of like a spirit now, right? And he's supposed to drop in to every Jewish house during the seder night and sip from his cup of wine."

"Really?"

I shrug. "It's a custom. So, anyway, my father sat Elijah's cup in front of Nomi and told her he'd give her five bucks if she drank the whole thing. Her parents went ballistic at this. You know, it was a lot of wine for a four-year-old, and it was disrespectful to Elijah. But Solly has amazing powers of persuasion and he convinced them it would be okay, all in good fun. So she did it."

"She drank the whole cup?"

"Not the whole cup, but quite a bit."

"And what happened?"

"She giggled at everything for the next few minutes, then she laid her head down on the table and fell fast asleep. Her father had to carry her home."

"Was she sick the next day?"

"I don't know."

"That was terrible of your father."

"He has a strange sense of humour."

The ACTOUT meeting begins promptly at seven. The 519 Church Street Community Centre is an older, three-storey building right in the heart of the Ghetto. We're in a large room on the second floor, with scuffed hardwood floors, walls in need of a paint job, an ancient drip coffee machine on a table in the corner that also holds a stack of Styrofoam cups, a box of sugar cubes and a jar of Coffee-mate. Hard folding chairs are arranged in a large circle. The ceiling is high, with garish fluorescent lights. The only windows are at the far end of the room, overlooking a back alley. There are two hundred members of ACTOUT, but only thirty or so show up for meetings. The chairperson tonight is a young leather dyke named Raven. She's wearing loose green khakis, black leather jacket, studded leather dog collar. She has about sixteen silver earrings in each ear, a nose ring, a lip ring and a pierced tongue. Six or seven black and silver chains hang from her belt loop to her knees and back again. Her head is shaved bald.

Raven runs a tight ship. Even so, it takes half an hour just for the opening announcements: the Premier wants to shut down the AIDS hospice because of funding problems; there's a demo in support of Chinese refugees; the Green Party wants to know if we will co-sponsor a fundraiser to close down the Riverdale Zoo; Dr. Laura is speaking at the Sheraton Hotel in Buffalo and the Stop Dr. Laura Coalition is organizing a protest.

Then we get down to business. The main agenda item: Rick's article in the *Toronto Star*.

"I think we should picket his house," says Greta, a fifty-something lesbian feminist who has worked on every gay, lesbian and feminist collective known to womankind. Her political position on everything sits far to the left of the spectrum. Greta has a contrary opinion on everything.

"He's in the hospital," I announce.

"Oh shit," says Jeff, the fag in our group with the lowest T cells. About three. He just got home from his last hospital stay himself, a few days ago. "What for?"

"PCP," I say.

"Again?"

"His fifth time."

Jeff just shakes his head. His beeper goes off. He flips open his pink plastic pill container and downs a handful of pills without water. He's on the new treatments, the so-called AIDS cocktails. A lot of good it's doing him, I think.

"I still say we should picket him!" Greta shouts.

"In the hospital?" Julie asks.

"A die-in?" suggests Raven.

"Die-ins have been done to death," says Ed Leung, one of Julie's co-workers at Triple A.

"Ha ha," laughs Queen David, never one to miss pointing out a good pun.

Jeff coughs, then rubs the fingers of his right hand. He has persistent tingling in his fingers and toes, a side effect from the drugs.

"What does Albert say?" asks David-the-Former-Accountant.

There are eight Davids in the group. They are all identified by certain redeeming qualities, like David-the-Former-Accountant, David-the-One-to-Die-For-With-the-Piercing-Blue-Eyes-and-Bulging-Basket, David-the-Computer-Geek, David-the-Gym-God, Annoying David, Nice David, David from New York (who was in the original Gay Men's Health Collective and personally knows Larry Kramer), and Queen David.

"Albert's angry," I answer. "I spoke to him yesterday. He's livid, in fact."

"What does he want to do?" asks Sebastian, a former dentist who retired last year at the age of thirty.

"I don't know. He was too angry to think straight."

"Ha ha," notices Queen David.

"I'll call him again in a few days, I guess, and see what he thinks."

"Well, we can't picket the man in the hospital. It's in poor taste," says Nice David.

"So is betrayal," shouts Greta.

"We don't know that he betrayed us," Julie points out. "He told Henry his editor changed the article without his knowledge. Isn't that right, Henry?"

"That's what he said."

"As if we can trust his word." Greta sulks. She loves direct action: pickets, chaining herself to the Ontario Health Minister's office, die-ins, protests. She was involved in the first gay rights demonstration in Ottawa in 1969. She hasn't stopped protesting since.

"I think he was telling the truth," I say in Rick's defence.

"Hah," Greta challenges.

"We have to give him the benefit of the doubt," points out Nice David. "He didn't have to write the article in the first place."

"That's true," concedes David-the-Computer-Geek, who has no doubt worked out the mathematical probability on his palm pilot.

"I think we should just wait until next week's meeting," I suggest. "I'll talk to Albert again before then and see what he suggests."

"Is that a motion?" asks Raven, clearly disappointed. She's having a hard time being an impartial chairperson.

"I guess. Sure, it's a motion," I decide.

"I second it," says Ed.

"All in favour?"

Everyone but Greta and Annoying David raise their hands.

"All opposed?"

Greta's hand shoots up.

"Abstained?"

Annoying David, as usual, abstains.

"Motion carried. Next item." Raven moves along with the agenda. "REAL Women are holding their annual convention in Toronto next month. There's been a proposal to picket outside the convention centre, in protest of their homophobic and AIDS-phobic rantings. Any ideas for an action?"

"Yes," David-the-Computer-Nerd says. "I've got a great idea."

We all wait with bated breath.

"I can hack into REAL Women's listserve." David pushes his thick wire-framed glasses higher on his nose. "And we can bombard them with ACTOUT propaganda ... or I can infest their email list with a virus ..."

"Yes!" shouts Raven gleefully. "A virus!"

"Of course," Queen David rises to her regal feet, one hand on her hip, "it's beautiful. A virus. What shall we name it? Let's see ... how about Acquired Interior Decorator's Soirée?"

"Lovely!" says David-to-Die-For, his dreamy blue eyes flashing with mischief.

"I like it," agrees Ed.

"How about something ... I don't know ..." says Raven. "Something more revolutionary."

"I'll do a name search," suggests David-the-Computer-Nerd. And he whips out his palm pilot and logs on.

"I think responding to REAL Women is a big waste of time," gripes David from New York.

Computer David looks up, disappointed.

"Well," says Julie, in a conciliatory tone, "let's strike a subcommittee. Whoever is interested in this action can meet separately."

"Bravo," says Queen David.

"Okay," agrees New York David.

Computer David smiles, gets back to work.

I flash a flirtatious grin at David-the-Gym-God while we wait for the search results.

By ten o'clock I'm exhausted. I decline after-meeting drinks at Woody's, say goodbye to Julie, and head for home. Roger's on night shift. He won't be home until dawn.

I open the apartment door to find my father adjusting his tie in the hall mirror. He's all dressed up in a fresh suit, with a carnation in his lapel.

"Hiya, Henry. How do I look?" He opens both arms wide, like Al Jolson singing "Mammy."

"Great, Pop. Where you going this time of night?" I flop down on the living room sofa, slip out of my runners. I'm so tired, I could fall asleep right here.

"I'm meeting your mother," he says, like it's the most natural thing in the world. As far as I know the last time they met — other than their chance meeting the other day when Belle dropped me off — was over five years ago, before my father's latest jail time. They met for coffee. It was a disaster. They had a huge loud fight in Bagel World. My mother swung back her arm, swept the table clean, smashing dishes and cutlery to the floor in a shattered heap. Then she shouted obscenities at my father and stormed off, vowing never to see him again.

"You're what?"

"What's the big deal, Henry? A man can't have a simple drink with his ex-wife?" He pulls a small black comb from his back pocket and backcombs his thick grey hair.

"Pop, remember what happened the last time?"

"What?"

"You were barred from Bagel World for life."

"Nothing is for life, Henry."

"They had to call the cops."

"Yeah." He replaces his comb, turns to face me, laughing. "That was some night." He pinches my cheek. "Relax, Henry. You worry too much. Your mother and I are just going out for a couple of drinks."

"Couple of drinks?" I can't believe what I'm hearing.

"For old time's sake. Don't wait up. I might be late." He places his fedora on his head at a jaunty angle, tips the brim to me, swings open the apartment door and leaves.

My divorced parents are going out on a date. It makes no sense. Divorced people aren't supposed to go out for a couple of drinks. They're supposed to hate each other. They're supposed to never want to see each other again except to send or pick up alimony. Or share custody rights. Or fight in court. What is my mother doing? What's Bernie going to think? What is my father doing? Should I stop him? I'm exhausted just thinking about it. I struggle to my feet, stagger into the bedroom, strip, fall into bed. Sleep comes quickly.

I feel Roger slip into bed beside me. He wraps his arms around my belly, spooning me from behind, and kisses the back of my neck.

"Hi ..." I mumble.

"Go back to sleep," he says softly.

I cover his hands with mine, drift away peacefully.

A few hours later I slip quietly out of bed, shower, dress, kiss Roger goodbye. He rolls over in his sleep. He's on night shift for the next three days, then has three days off, then back to morning shift. I don't know how he does it — how his body adjusts — but he does. Roger's been a nurse for eighteen years. He likes his job, likes helping people. He doesn't like the politics, but he loves the work. And he's good at it. Gentle yet firm; strong yet kind. Roger could have been a doctor if he could have afforded medical school. Raised in foster homes, he was on his own at sixteen, put himself through nurses' college. Roger has no regrets. That's the kind of man he is: quiet, steady, content.

I watch him for a moment, then close the door and leave him to sleep.

Dr. Green studies the lab report while I sit on the white paper-covered examination table in my boxer shorts — black Calvin Kleins.

"I'm afraid your T cells have dropped again. Henry, have you thought about what we discussed? About going on protease inhibitors?"

Not this again. Yes, I've thought about it. The so-called AIDS cocktails. The gay rage of the nineties. Forget about Absolut martinis, strawberry daiquiris or Corona with a lime wedge. This year, gay men everywhere are sipping on Bottled H2O, chased with DDI, protease inhibitors and garnished with a slice of AZT. I, on the other hand, am a teetotaller. Dr. Green thinks I'm crazy not to take advantage of available treatments. But I don't agree.

As an activist, I've read every pamphlet ever produced on the new treatments, scoured every report released, and I'm not convinced. The side effects include joint pain, blood in urine, kidney stones, nausea, headaches, insomnia, gastrointestinal discomfort, diarrhea, mouth ulcers, fatigue, peripheral parasthesia, which is numbness or tingling in your hands and feet, and this is my favourite: taste perversion. I mean, what exactly is taste perversion? Does it mean if I go on the drugs I'll trade in my tasteful Hockney original for Elvis on black velvet? Will I give away my leather jacket and start wearing lime green polyester leisure suits? Will I serve Hamburger Helper for dinner with Baby Duck rosé wine? Will I remove our tasteful track lighting from the living room in favour of fluorescent tubes? Taste perversion in faggots. Terrifying.

And the instructions for taking the drugs are enough to drive you mad. Protease inhibitors are administered every eight hours. You're not supposed to eat two hours before taking a protease inhibitor and you have to wait one more hour before eating again. But if you're also taking DDI, it's recommended that you take them on an empty stomach and two hours before or after the protease inhibitors. Although with some protease inhibitors, eating a large, high-calorie, high-fat meal with the drugs may eliminate some side effects. Except with the nausea you won't feel like eating. Also, many of the protease inhibitors must be refrigerated at all times, so unless you want to carry around a thermal lunch bucket with ice packs, taking your drugs at the correct time means you must stay at home, or at least within walking distance of your refrigerator. There go overnights at your boyfriend's, or even stepping out anywhere in another part of town.

And here's the real kicker: most of the pamphlets are produced and paid for by the drug companies — the very corporations Albert insists were involved in the original experiments to create and test immune-system-destroying agents for germ warfare. Translation: their research funding helped invent AIDS and now they're profiting immensely by so-called treating it. But the treatments are so new and so toxic, we don't know what their long-term effects will be. AZT lost its effectiveness in most patients within a year and a half. It's likely the same thing will happen with these, the new generation of AIDS drugs.

"I've thought about it, Jeff," I tell Dr. Green. At this point we are on a first-name basis. "But I'm not convinced they're of benefit to me. Too toxic, for one thing."

He sighs deeply in the way only a mother, or a doctor with a large AIDS practice, can. "Okay, Henry. It's your decision, but at least let me give you a vitamin B shot, and I think you'd better start on a weekly dosage of aerosolized pentamidine. You can take the treatment right here in my office."

"Aw shucks, Jeff. Do I have to?" I bat my big brown eyes at

him like the flirt that I am.

He smiles, then speaks seriously. "With your lower T cell count, you're extremely susceptible to PCP, and I don't like the sound of that cough."

"You noticed that, huh?"

"We could do a bronchoscopy and find out for sure, but it's a painful procedure and I'd just as soon not put you through that."

"Thank you."

"But we might as well start the treatment as if you have PCP. Okay?"

"You're the doctor."

He peers at me over the top of his designer glasses. Usually I'm not so agreeable. Usually I argue. I debate. I ask for written statistics on any treatment he offers before even considering taking it. But I have seen the ravages of pneumocystis carinii, the pneumonia that frequently visits people with AIDS, and I'm scared. I don't want to end up in the hospital, hooked up to an oxygen tank, gasping for my every breath. The aerosolized pentamidine is used as a prophylaxis. It's been useful in keeping PCP away. I've heard from others that it's not so bad. It leaves a funny metallic taste in your mouth, but other than that, no adverse effects.

Seeing me in such a docile state, Dr. Green moves in for the kill.

"I think we should begin your first treatment right away. This morning. Okay, Henry?"

"Fire away."

"Do you want to grab a couple of magazines from the waiting room? I'll set you up with the nebulizer in my office. You have to sit there for about half an hour."

"What exactly do I have to do?"

"It's painless, Henry. I hook you up to a mask and you just breathe."

"I think I can handle that."

He smiles in victory. "You can get dressed first."

The examination table paper sticks to the back of my legs, ripping as I hop to the floor. Dr. Green squeezes my shoulder affectionately and leaves the room as I slip into my jeans.

NOMI'S SOCIAL DISEASE

I'm working the Saturday afternoon shift at Patty's Place, minding my own business, wiping down the bar for the hundredth time, when Betty bounds in, handsome and dashing in her Super Shuttle driver's uniform. She flirts with two women by the pool table, drops some change in the jukebox, takes her time selecting her songs, waves hello to Miss Polly Ester, a seven-foot-tall (in heels) female impersonator who hangs out at Patty's, then plops her substantial butt onto the bar stool directly in front of me.

"What time you off?" Betty asks.

I glance at the bar clock. "Half an hour."

"Good. Give me a Guinness, Nom. No head."

I glare at her. I don't need advice from Betty. I've been pulling draught all day. I know how to do it. I plunk her glass of beer with a quarter-inch head, as it should have, on top of a bar napkin in front of her. Dare her with a long stare to complain. She raises it to her lips, drinks enthusiastically, opens her mouth with a satisfied "Ahhh," places the mug on the bar. She has a beer moustache — white foam on chocolate brown skin. I don't bother saying anything. It looks good on her. But then, everything looks good on Betty.

"Start cleaning up now, so you're ready. We're leaving as soon as you're off shift," she announces.

"Where we going?"

She grins. "You'll see."

Outside the pub, I go to start up my motorcycle, a small red Honda Rebel 250.

"Leave your bike. Come with me. I've got the van," Betty says, pointing to her Super Shuttle van.

"Aren't you supposed to drop that off at the station?"

"Shhh. I'm still on duty. Come on." She grabs me by the arm and steers me to the bus.

I sit behind the driver's seat, shove my motorcycle helmet underneath. Betty slides the van into gear, speeds recklessly down the hill toward Mission. The two-way radio crackles and hisses.

"2-4-0, do you copy?" a desperate dispatcher pleads.

"Damn," curses Betty. Swerving past a double-parked news-paper truck, she scoops up the hand-held microphone. Speaks into it. "2-4-0."

"Where the hell you been, girlfriend?" the dispatcher whines in a hoarse voice.

"Engine trouble on the freeway. Had to change a spark plug."

"A spark plug?" I raise my eyebrows.

Betty glares at me in the rearview mirror. Puts a finger on her lips to silence me.

"You've got pickups. Do you copy?"

"Shoot." Betty reaches for a pen attached to the sun visor with elastic bands, furiously copies a couple of addresses onto a pad of paper affixed to a small plastic clipboard — the kind you buy from Wal-Mart — mounted just to the right of the steering wheel.

"Got all that, Betty?"

"Affirmative."

"I'm going to be at The Café later. See you there, Betty?" the dispatcher asks in a kinder, gentler tone.

"That's a 10-4, Rosie."

"Over."

Betty replaces the mike on its hook.

"Rosie?" I enquire.

Betty's mouth turns up at one corner, like she's got a secret.

"Rosie," she confirms. Then the smile fades. "Sorry, Nom. Gotta make some pickups. Pretend you're a customer, okay? Don't say anything. To anybody. Got it?"

"No way, Betty. Let me out. I'm not riding all the way to the airport and back."

"Cool out, Nom. It won't take long. Anyway, you'll thank me later." Betty glances over her shoulder to turn onto Mission, hits the accelerator hard, turns the wheel sharply and squeezes the van into traffic between a maniacal taxi driver and a hulking city garbage truck, tires squealing. I'm thrown against the window.

"Ouch," I complain.

"Do up your seat belt, Nom. I can't be held responsible."

"Let me out."

"Take a Prozac."

"Why will I thank you?" I rub my sore shoulder.

"You'll see. Quiet. Here's our first pickup." She double-parks the van in front of a beautiful multicoloured Victorian house on Delores Street in the Mission District. The elaborate trim has been painstakingly painted in three different shades of lavender. The front of the house is guarded by a single stately palm tree. The bus shelter out front is completely covered in white-lettered graffiti. The glass has a large crack running down its length. The sidewalk is littered with dog shit. Every inch of curb space is filled with parked cars. There is a motor-cycle perched on its kickstand on the sidewalk. Beside it an abandoned shopping cart lies on its side. Two young, attractive women wait by the side of the road, suitcases by their feet. Betty puts the van into park, swings open the door, hops down to help them with their luggage. I sit in my seat, fuming.

"Hallo," says the first woman with a thick British accent, as she steps up into the van.

"Hi."

"Nom, can you please move back a seat? Elspeth and Gwen would like to see the sights."

"Why not?"

I grab my helmet, move back one seat. The English tourists

sit directly behind Betty. I sit behind them. Betty pays more attention to the girls, especially to Gwen, who bears an uncanny resemblance to Julia Roberts, than she does to her driving.

Elspeth, feeling left out, turns around and speaks to me.

"Where are you from, love?" She smiles a toothy grin.

From? Oh right, I'm supposed to be a tourist. "Saskatoon," I lie.

"Oh. Is that in Australia?"

"Saskatchewan."

"Where?"

Our next stop is in the Castro. Betty pulls the van up in front of another beautifully restored Victorian on the crest of the hill on Diamond Street. It has been painted powder blue, with purple and pink trim. Over the third-storey window is an ornate gold carving mounted on the wall. Giant purple irises stand at attention in the tiny front yard garden plot. Clay pots filled with pink trailing geraniums spill down the front steps. From a second-storey balcony juts the requisite rainbow flag. A jumbo-sized drag queen with forty-three matching Samsonite suitcases struggles to climb aboard, clanging and smashing his luggage into the side of the vehicle and against Gwen and Elspeth.

"Ouch."

"Oops."

"Ow."

"Sorry, girls."

"Women," Elspeth corrects.

The queen lumbers regally to the second row and plunks her radiant, abundant frame onto the seat beside me. I scoot as close to the window as I can. Even so, her thigh touches mine.

She smiles at me, then fumbles in a carry-on bag, pulls out a round plastic compact case, the kind used by Hollywood starlets in the forties, flips it open and powders her nose.

"I will not arrive at the airport with a shiny forehead," she informs me.

"Heaven forbid."

"I'm acting in a film."

"You don't say?"

"An independent feature. It's being shot in Toronto, Canada." Of all places.

She snaps the compact lid shut, replaces it in her huge carry-on — I don't know how she's going to get it on the plane — and sticks out one manicured hand for me to shake. "I'm Gregory," she says, "although you may call me by my stage name, Miss Glorious Swan."

I take the proffered hand. "Charmed." She hardly looks like a swan. More like a killer whale.

Betty drives over a series of deep potholes. We bump madly along.

"Ouch! Careful, honey," Glorious Swan reproaches Betty with an outstretched hand, her movements reminiscent of Diana Ross and her Supremes singing "Stop in the Name of Love."

"Sorry, miss," Betty responds sweetly, then guns the motor, screeches the tires and races to our next stop. Miss Swan bumps into me rather indelicately as we lurch around corners, scream up hills and stop abruptly. Betty has pulled into the circular driveway of Beck's Motor Lodge on Market Street. I glance out the window as Betty helps the next passengers into the van. They look like Mr. and Mrs. Middle U.S.A. The man is dressed in a checkered suit with a bow tie. His huge potbelly sticks way out in front and his pants are held up by a belt just under his belly. He's in his late fifties, his hair is thinning on top, but he's grown it long on one side and combed it over the bald spot. A sudden wind picks up and blows the longer hair back to the other side. He looks like a used car salesman, or a Southern governor. His wife looks like she just walked out of a Family Values convention. Her polyester skirt and sweater set is pink. Her shoes are sensible. On her sweater front is a paper badge that reads, "HELLO, my name is MRS. DINGER."

"Wherever shall I put my bags?" Mrs. Dinger asks Betty with a thick Southern accent.

"Yes'm." Betty acts the part of the servant as expected of her. A true professional. Give the customer whatever they want. "I got 'em, ma'am."

"I don't see why we didn't call the airport limousine, Lyman,"

Mrs. Dinger tells her husband.

"G'wan now, missus. Get your sweet butt up inside the bus."
Mr. Dinger slaps his wife on the derriere. "Afternoon, miss," he
tips his hat to Glorious Swan as he prods his wife toward the
back seat.

"Why, charmed, sir," Miss Swan bats her glorious lashes.

The Dingers take their seats behind us. Betty hits the accelerator enthusiastically. We lurch forward.

"Oh my," declares Mrs. Dinger.

"Hush now, missus. That boy's a good driver. They always are."

I turn in my seat, gawk incredulously at our Republican
friends. "Who are?"

"Why, the coloured, of course."

"The coloured?" Never having been to the South, I am
astounded that this sort of racism still exists. Do people still use
words like that?

Miss Swan tugs at my sleeve, leans over, stage-whispers
loudly in my ear: "Scratch the surface of a Southerner, and you
will find deep in the farthest recesses of their hearts, a not-so-
secret longing for plantation days."

"My great-great-granddaddy was good to his slaves,"
defends Mr. Dinger, with a pointed finger.

"I'll bet." I glance toward the front to see how Betty is taking
this. She hasn't heard a word. She's been focusing on Gwen,
who gets up from her seat beside Elspeth and plops down on
Betty's lap, an act which does not go unnoticed by Mrs. Dinger.

"Why, I never," she says indignantly. "Why is that girl sitting
on our driver's lap?"

"Oh, I can explain that," I say.

"Please do." Miss Glorious Swan looks amused.

"Well ... that girl is from England, you see ... and she is prone
to motion sickness ... and unless she sits right up front with the
driver, she's liable to throw up at any moment."

"Oh my," says Mrs. Dinger.

"Why don't you sit on *my* lap?" her husband recommends.

"Stop that, Lyman." She swats his hand away.

"Come on, missy. We're on vacation."

"Oh, you stop that. Or I'll ..."

"You'll what?"

"Lyman, I'm warning you." The Dingers giggle like teenagers. I avert my eyes. I'm too young to see this blatant display of uncensored middle-aged heterosexuality.

"Here, honey." Miss Swan hands me a shiny silver flask. "Try this."

I unscrew the cap, take a swig. It's one hundred proof Scotch. Burns its way down my throat and into my stomach. "Thanks." I hand the flask back.

"Have another," she urges.

About a hundred years later, we finally arrive at the airport. Glorious Swan gives me her business card. "When I get back, we'll do lunch. Okay, sweetheart? On me. We'll go to Nob Hill. We'll have strawberry margaritas and nachos with extra guacamole. It'll be fabulous." She pats my hand affectionately.

I'm sure that it will be. Glorious swishes her ample body radiantly through the glass doors of the airport. Behind her, the Dingers insult an African-American pilot on his way inside, assuming he's a porter. Elspeth waits patiently while Gwen and Betty say their non-verbal goodbyes. I slump in the front seat of the van, wondering when exactly it was that I lost my mind and decided to become friends with Betty.

Finally she tears her lips away from Gwen's, waves goodbye and hops back into the van. There is red lipstick smeared all over her face, neck and collar.

"Now *that*," she pops the van into gear and we're off, "is one hot woman."

She stops the van in front of a Super Shuttle stop.

"Now what?" Why doesn't she just head back to town?

"I have to do one more round of drop-offs, Nom."

"What?" I glance longingly at the freeway signs directing traffic to San Francisco. "Why?"

"Rules, Nom. Once I'm at the airport, I can't leave with an

empty van. I have to drive people back to the city." From her shirt pocket she produces two chocolate Tootsie Pops, hands one to me.

"I thought we were going somewhere?" I snatch the Tootsie Pop.

"We are, Nom. All in good time. You sure are tense, girl." She unwraps her candy, stuffs it in her mouth, the white cardboard stick jutting out between her lips like a thin cigarette.

I growl at her and stomp to the back seat, where I lean against the window and pretend to be asleep.

The ride back in is more sedate: a couple of sweater fags returning home from a two-week vacation in Palm Springs; a yuppie couple with a small baby; and a businesswoman who works on a laptop computer the whole way home. People who live here are much easier to take than tourists. None of them mistake Betty for a boy. They tip well. Nobody bothers me. The traffic on the freeway is unusually smooth. We make it back to the city in record time.

"Okay," says Betty after the last passenger has been dropped off. "Ready for some fun?"

"Will you at least tell me where you're taking me?" I stumble up the aisle to the front seat.

"Not on your life, Nom."

To avoid a car running a red light she slams on the brakes. I am thrown against the window. "Ow."

"Sit down, will you, girl? I told you, I can't be held responsible."

"Okay, you can open your eyes now," Betty says. She's led me across a street and inside a building. I have foolishly agreed to close my eyes until we are inside. I can't see much. It's dark. We are at the bottom of a steep flight of stairs. At the top of the stairs I can see two women sitting at a table. There is a red light bulb above them, casting a blood-red glow down the stairway. I eye Betty suspiciously.

"Come on." She nudges me up the steps.

"Hi there," the woman seated at the table says cheerfully.

"Cover charge is twelve dollars each."

"Twelve dollars!?"

"Relax, Nom. I'm paying."

I grab her roughly by the sleeve. "Where are we?"

"Here you go." Betty hands thirty dollars to the woman, who makes change. Betty tips her generously.

"Why, thank you."

"Don't mention it."

I'm going to gag.

"Come on." Betty pulls me inside. It looks like an apartment that's been converted into ... into what? In the first bedroom, there is a couch and a VCR. Three women sit on the couch watching TV. On the monitor is a heterosexual porn flick, a male fantasy of lesbians. There are three "pseudo lesbians" — extremely skinny, straight women with long hair tied in pony-tails and stoned expressions — "fucking" each other with sharp, red fingernails.

"Ouch," I say.

"Let's sit down," says Betty.

"No way. I can't bear to watch." It dawns on me where we are. It's a sex club. "Where are we?" I snarl.

"Clit Club. Just opened. Cool huh?"

"Not really." I look down at my shoes. The linoleum floor is sticky with spilled Coke or beer or something else. I don't want to imagine what it might be.

"Okay, let's check out the rest."

"I'm leaving." I head for the stairs.

"Hey, I just paid twelve bucks to get you in here."

"That's your problem."

"Come on, Nom. You don't have to do anything. Let's just look around."

"You could catch a social disease just from walking on this floor, Betty."

"You *are* a social disease, Nomi. Come on. You must be curious."

"Not really."

We move to the next room. It's dark. My shoes stick to the floor.

A well-endowed femme approaches us. She is wearing a short leather skirt, garters and stockings, a dog collar around her neck and numerous studded wrist- and arm-bands. In her hand is a large black leather whip. She cracks it against the sticky floor. It snaps with a satisfying crack. She turns in our direction, sticks out one clawed fingertip and beckons us forward. The sickeningly sweet smell of too much cheap perfume wafts over to us.

"Come on," says Betty, practically drooling.

"Uh, n-no thanks," I stutter.

"Come on, Nom. Don't be a wimp."

"I won't bite," the femme hisses through bared teeth, "unless you want me to."

"I'll see ya later," I tell Betty.

"Both of you," the femme says. "I like two butches at a time."

Betty grabs my shirtsleeve for dear life, not about to let this sexual opportunity slide.

I pull desperately hard, hear my shirt rip at the shoulder seam. Betty hangs on tighter. I pull with all my might, until my sleeve rips clean through. I am freed from her grasp. I fall forward from the force, toppling onto the sticky floor with a thud. I don't wait to inspect the linoleum too closely. I scramble to my feet and run for the door.

"Nomi!" Betty calls, my torn sleeve still in her grasp.

Pushing off from the wall on both sides, I race down the stairs and outside in record time.

"Nice time?" I ask Betty when she arrives home two hours later. I'm feeling much better after showering. I'm reclining on the couch, eating take-out pizza and watching a rerun of *All in the Family*.

She shrugs. "It was okay."

"Just okay?"

"She was really set on having a threesome, so she roped in the very next butch who walked in the room."

"And?"

"I don't like threesomes. I like to be the centre of attention."

"Of course."

She removes her boots near the door, walks over and is about to sit on the couch.

"Oh no you don't!"

"What?"

"Betty, that floor was sticky."

"Oh yeah."

"It's a gay men's club, usually."

"Gross."

"I think you should strip over there. God knows what the hell was on that floor." I point to the door. My clothes are inside a green garbage bag, ready to go to the laundry.

"Good idea. Listen, Nom, I've been thinking." She unbuttons her shirt. "I think we should look for a two-bedroom. I mean since we seem to be living together and all ... we might as well be comfortable." She drops her shirt to the floor.

"You're probably right," I concede.

"I picked up a paper." Betty fishes in her back pocket for a copy of the *San Francisco Examiner*. "We can check the classifieds." She unbuttons her faded blue 501s, lets them fall to the floor by her feet. She removes her socks. In her loose flannel boxer shorts, she pads to the bathroom, tossing the newspaper at me as she passes.

I glance at the TV. Archie Bunker sits like a king in his chair.

"Stifle it, Edith," he says, puffing on a cigar.

"But Ar-chie ..." she squeals, "I got something I gotta get off my chest."

Go for it, Edith.

Archie turns and peers at his wife with naked disgust. "Aw jeez, Edith. Not in mixed company."

The studio audience roars with laughter.

Edith looks up at Gloria and Meathead, perplexed.

There aren't many apartments available in our price range in any area we'd want to live in. The first place we look at is advertised as a two-bedroom flat in Bernal Heights, not far from Betty's. When we arrive, we discover it's more like a studio apartment with a large closet. It's even smaller than Betty's current apartment. The next one is large enough but it smells damp, like mould. The next three are too close to the Tenderloin for my tastes. We'd have to pass by drug dealers and working girls, and trip over homeless people every day on our way in and out. There's only one more ad to consider and I absolutely, positively, unquestionably, indisputably, categorically, without a doubt refuse.

"Come on, Nom. We should at least look," Betty urges.

"Forget it!"

"Nomi."

"Not in that building. No way!"

"It's just a building."

"Sapphire's building."

"Come on, Nom. It's in our price range."

"No!"

"It's in the Castro."

"I said no!"

"Just one look."

"Betty, I'm going to hit you."

"I'm bigger than you, Nom. Don't be ridiculous."

"I'm serious."

"You'll hurt your hand."

"I don't care."

"Just one little look. Just to see."

"Absolutely not!"

"It's on the third floor," the landlord says as we follow him up the stairs in Sapphire's building.

Great. *Her* floor.

We walk past Sapphire's apartment. I sneer at her door and stifle the urge to kick it. At the other end of the hall, the landlord pulls out a large key chain loaded with keys, then fumbles for the correct one.

"It's on here somewhere," he assures us. "You look familiar." He squints at me.

I shrug, not willing to go into it.

The apartment is not half-bad. A little more expensive than we would like, but it has two full bedrooms, a decent bathroom and kitchen, a small balcony. And it's on States Street, just a stone's throw away from the Castro. A miracle, really. If only Sapphire didn't live here.

"It's perfect," Betty decides.

"Not perfect," I remind her.

"Okay. Except for that," she concedes.

"What? You were looking for two bathrooms? Not at this price," the landlord butts in.

"No. It's something else."

"You want it, you better decide fast. I got five other people looking at it today."

"Come on, Nom. I think we should take it."

"Go to hell, Betty." I push past her, leave the apartment.

"We'll be right back," she tells the landlord, following me.

I stomp down the stairs and out to the street with Betty on my tail. I keep stomping until I am outside Harvey's, a trendy bar and grill at 18th and Castro, named for Harvey Milk, San Francisco's first openly gay city supervisor, who was assassinated in 1978 by a homophobic fellow supervisor. The bar's clientele are mostly upscale gay men. I go inside, sit at the bar, order a vodka martini, straight up. On the sound system, k.d. lang is moaning about her cravings. Betty follows me inside, plops onto the stool beside me.

"See, Betty? You've driven me to drink."

"I'll have the same," she tells the bartender.

She waits until I have had the first few sips and the vodka is slip-sliding inside me, working its calming magic.

"It's not like you'd ever have to see her," Betty says.

"She'd be right there all the same." I finish my drink, knocking it back quickly, then suck on the olive.

"Two more," Betty calls. "It's just a building, Nom. You saw all the other places."

"Yeah, dumps."

"And look where we'd be." She gestures around the room.

"Right in the Castro. Didn't I hear you say just the other day that you'd love to live here again?"

"Yeah, but not that building."

The bartender removes our empty glasses, replaces them with fresh drinks.

"Just ignore her, Nom, if you run into her. You can do it."

"Yeah. I could."

"Thatta boy, Nom."

"But I don't want to."

"You don't want to ignore her?"

"I don't want to run into her."

"I bet it wouldn't happen that much."

I sigh. We drink our drinks. Maybe Betty's right. It *is* just a building. And it's the only decent apartment out there. It's not like we're going to find anything better. And I can't go on living on Betty's living room sofa forever. I have to get over Sapphire eventually. It *has* been almost five months since we broke up.

"Okay." I give in.

Betty practically chokes on her olive. "Great!" She leaps up, drops a twenty on the bar, grabs me by the arm and drags me back up the hill to talk to the landlord.

Later that evening I phone Julie.

"Betty and I went apartment hunting today," I tell her.

"Oh." She sounds disappointed. I'm not sure what's wrong.

"And we actually found a place."

"You did?"

"Yeah ..." Suddenly I'm nervous to tell her that it's in Sapphire's building. Earlier when I agreed to the apartment I never really considered how it would affect Julie. Now I have a sinking feeling she's not going to like it. "Boy is it hard to find a decent place in San Francisco these days. Everything is crazy expensive, or a dump, or it's really one bedroom even though they say it's two, or it's in the Tenderloin ..."

"The what?"

"The Tenderloin ... it's a really rough area."

"Oh."

"So, where's this place?"

"Uh.. it's right in the Castro."

"Oh. I guess that's good."

"Yeah. It's a great location ... and well, actually I've lived in the building before, it's a good building. Laundry right downstairs, good security."

"You've lived there before? When? I thought you'd only lived with Betty and with ... Oh ..." Her voice drops off.

Uh oh.

"Nomi ... are you moving back in with your ex?" she asks icily.

"No. Of course not. Not in with her. I'm living with Betty. It's just that — "

"What?"

"It's in the same building."

"As your ex."

"Yeah." Damn. Why did I tell her?

There is silence.

"Julie?"

Still nothing.

"Julie? Are you there?"

"I'm here." Quietly.

Oh shit. She's hurt. I can hear it in her voice. "Julie ..." I don't know what to say. "I mean ... Julie ... are you okay?"

A small sniffle. "Not really."

"Julie ... I mean ... it's just an apartment."

"Just an apartment?"

"It's got nothing to do with ... Sapphire."

"It's just in her building."

"Yeah. But that's just a coincidence."

"There are no coincidences, Nomi."

"Julie ... I mean ... I think you're overreacting ... just a little. I mean ... it's just a building."

"The same building as your ex."

"Yes."

"I can't believe you would do that, Nomi. How would you feel?" Her voice rises.

"It's not like I'm ever going to see her Julie. I mean, can you calm down?"

"No! I will not calm down!" she shouts. "I don't want to calm down. Why should I? I find out you're moving back in with your ex and you want me to calm down?!"

"I'm not moving in with my ex." I stand and walk to the window, phone in hand.

"I thought maybe *we* were talking about living together."

"We were?" Outside I see the piercing green eyes of a stray cat staring up at me from the street.

"Someday ..."

"Yeah, but not right away. I mean I have to live somewhere right now and Betty's place is getting too small." The cat opens its mouth wide, hisses at me from the street.

"So you have to move in with your ex?"

"No. Not with my ex. Julie? Are you listening?" I glare down at the cat.

"Yeah. I'm listening. You don't want to live with me. You won't even consider moving to Toronto. You want to live with your ex, Nomi? Go ahead. I mean, why are we even bothering?"

"Julie ..." I pace the floor to calm my racing heart.

"That's what I'd like to know. If you're not ready to have a relationship, then fine. Let's just say goodbye right now." She slams down the phone.

I pull the receiver from my ear and stare at it. I can't believe she hung up on me. I dial her number. It rings. And rings. And rings. I try again. She won't pick up and she's switched off her answering machine. The phone just rings. Damn.

I storm into Betty's room. I don't care that she's got a girl in there with her. I don't care that they are both naked. I barely notice. I don't care that they're listening to the extended version of Madonna's "Erotica." Betty and the girl are lying in bed. The girl has just drawn a happy face in whipped cream onto Betty's stomach. I hover by the edge of the bed, looking down at Betty.

Madonna whispers, *"I'd like to put you in a trance."*

"I told you it was a bad idea, Betty."

"Nomi! What are you doing in here?"

"I told you."

"Nom, we're, uh ... busy."

"She hung up on me."

"Can you please leave the room? I'm not alone." She gestures at the woman with her head.

"I can see that, Betty." I turn to the woman, say hello.

"Hi, I'm Crystal."

"I just had a huge fight with Julie," I tell Betty. "It's over. She hates me because we're moving in with Sapphire."

"We're not moving in with Sapphire."

"Who's Sapphire?" Crystal asks, scooping up a glob of whipped cream from Betty's belly.

Madonna sings on. *"Put your hands all over my body. Erotic, erotic, put your hands all over my body ..."*

"Well, Julie thinks we are."

"Who's Julie?" Crystal licks her finger.

"Well, did you tell her we're not?"

"Of course I did, Betty."

"And?"

"She won't listen. What am I going to do?" I sit on the edge of the bed, lean forward, hang my head in my hands.

"Don't sit. Don't sit on the bed, Nom," Betty urges. "I mean, maybe you didn't notice, but we are kind of busy in here."

I stand. "Sure, Betty. What do you care? You've got ..." I strain for the girl's name. "Crystal. You're covered in Cool Whip. You've got Madonna."

On cue, the Material Girl says, *"I don't think you know what pain is. I don't think you've gone that way ..."*

"You're having fun," I shout at Betty. "Why should you care about my problems? I'll just go and talk to someone who cares."

"Good idea, Nom. See you later."

"In your dreams." I slam the door behind me. It shakes on its hinges. I spend the night pacing the living room floor, collapse on the sofa at dawn and sleep restlessly.

The next day by noon I am racing my bike furiously up the hill to Patty's Place. I have to work today. In this mood, some bartender I'm going to be. I shove open the heavy oak door of the pub, my helmet under one arm, and stomp inside. Robert is behind the bar rearranging bottles of liquor and singing along at the top of his lungs to a scratchy Billie Holiday record.

"All of me. Why not take all of me? Can't you see I'm no good without you?" Robert croons, winking at me. I snarl at him.

Patty sits on a bar stool, the black account book open in front of her. She is counting receipts.

"Go home, Robert, it's my turn for punishment," I say bitchily.

Patty looks up from her calculator. "Stay where you are, Robert. You," she points to me, "outside. On the double."

"Take my lips, I want to lose them," Robert belts, twirling around behind the bar. *"Take my arms, I'll never use them ..."*

I follow my boss to the small patio out back. It's a wooden deck with cedar trellising, crowded with potted geraniums and nasturtiums, and flanked by a mature avocado tree on one side and a bright purple bougainvillea on the other, its branches climbing gracefully up the wall. The pungent smell of rotting garbage from a dumpster in the alley wafts over the sweet scent of flowers.

"Okay, Rabinovitch. What's the problem?" Patty pulls out her package of Marlboros, taps it on her palm, slips out a cigarette.

"There is no problem." I fold my arms across my chest.

"Come on. Let's hear it." She lights her cigarette, looks deeply into my eyes with concern. This breaks down my defences. My eyes fill with tears, damn it. Last thing I want to do is cry.

"Julie broke up with me." The tears overflow, run down my cheeks.

"What?"

"Last night on the phone." I wipe at my face roughly with the back of my hand.

"Oh boy. What did you do now, Rabinovitch?"

"Who said I did anything?" I grab Patty's pack, pull out a cigarette and hold it between two fingers, even though I don't smoke.

It feels good in my hand.

"Come on. Whadja do?" She stares at the cigarette, probably wondering what I'm planning on doing with it.

I sigh. "Yesterday Betty and I put a deposit on an apartment in Sapphire's building." I puff on my unlit cigarette like a pro, and blow invisible smoke from my mouth. No wonder people smoke. It forces you to breathe.

"You what?!" Patty takes a deep drag of her real cigarette.

"You don't have to yell, Patty."

"You are even dumber than you look, Rabinovitch. For chrissake." A steady stream of smoke billows out through her mouth.

"Gee, thanks for the support."

"Sapphire's building? Have you lost your damn mind?" Patty flicks ashes into the fifties-style chrome floor ashtray that sits like a centrepiece in the middle of the patio.

"Patty, you know what the rental situation is like in the city." I copy her, flicking "ashes" from my unlit cigarette onto the floor.

"Sure, but still ..." She removes her Mets cap, runs her fingers through her hair.

"Well, I didn't think ..."

"Yeah, that about sums it up."

"Are you going to help me or not?"

"You're beyond help."

"Terrific. Are you finished? I'm going to work."

"No, you're not. Not in that mood. I got enough trouble getting customers in the door."

"What am I going to do, Patty?"

"Hold on. I'm thinking." She puffs on her cigarette while I pace around the small patio, puffing on mine. "Did Betty already give notice on her old apartment?"

"Yeah, yesterday. Why?"

"Maybe she can take it back. I bet it's not rented yet."

"You think I should go and find out?"

"No!" she shouts. "You stay here. You've done enough damage already. Go in the restroom and soak your head. Cool down.

Then I want you to get to work. Just let me handle everything. All right, Rabinovitch?"

"What are you going to do, Patty?"

"I said I'll handle it. Now scoot. And gimme that." She snatches the cigarette from my lips and pushes me toward the restroom.

Thankful that somebody else will fix my problems, I go.

Inside the door Robert is still singing.

"You took the part,
That once was my heart,
So why not ... take all of me?"

HENRY'S MISSION

In the subway station I stop at the kiosk to buy a pack of cinnamon gum. My mouth tastes like I've been sucking on a large piece of tinfoil. The aerosolized pentamidine leaves a strong metallic taste on the tongue. Why is the cure almost as bad as the disease? Where's my spoonful of sugar to help the medicine go down? Where is Mary Poppins when I truly need her? I scan the crowd for Julie Andrews. All I see are people on their way home from work, mothers with small children, students carrying huge knapsacks on their backs and scruffy teenagers with their pants falling down. No cute guys anywhere. No beautiful, kindly governess with a crisp English accent floating down from the sky with an outstretched umbrella and tightly laced calf-high boots, waiting to take my hand and lead the way.

Oh, a spoonful of sugar helps the medicine go down, the medicine go do-own, medicine go down, I sing softly to myself as I emerge from the station into a bright sunny April afternoon. Spring has finally come to the hinterlands. It has been an unusually cold and snowy winter. In January we had the worst blizzard in decades, snow piled as high as the roofs. "When I was a child, I had to walk ten miles to school in the snow. Barefoot," we'll tell our children in thirty years. As if I'll still be here in thirty years. As if I will have children to tell. Although why not? Maybe some lesbian will ask Roger to go behind closed doors with a copy of *Blueboy* in one hand and his swollen manhood in the other, and emerge with a tiny jar of semen, loaded with Roger's spermatozoa, with which she will impregnate herself, using a turkey baster, and nine months later Roger and I will become co-fathers. The child will visit us every Sunday afternoon. I'll give him cooking lessons and Roger will teach him how to knit. On Thanksgiving we'll all get together as a family. One child, two mothers, two fathers, several assorted aunts and uncles, a twenty-pound turkey, my home-made sourdough herb stuffing, a smart bottle or two of dry French Cabernet Sauvignon for Roger and me, and a case of imported beer for the lesbians. A modern nuclear family.

The late afternoon sun shines warmly down on me. I tilt my face up to catch every bit of its golden rays, slipping out of my leather jacket and slinging it over one shoulder. To my annoyance the complete soundtrack of *Mary Poppins* runs through my mind as I walk. That's what happens when I start singing from a Hollywood musical. Once I start, I can't get it out of my head. I am up to *Supercalifragilisticexpialidocious* when I arrive at the hospital. *Even though the sound of it is something quite atrocious.*

"Morning, Henry," Shirley chirps as I approach the seventh floor nurses' desk.

I glance at my watch. "It's five o'clock, Shirley."

"Already? Darn. I haven't even had lunch yet. Can you cover for me while I slip downstairs to the cafeteria?" She brushes a swirl of grey-brown hair off her forehead.

"Sure," I shrug. "What should I do? Give someone an enema? Empty a few bedpans?"

"Would you, love?" Shirley winks at me, pushes her glasses up on her nose, finishes writing something on a chart on a clipboard. "Roger's doing the rounds. Do you want to sit back here and wait for him?" She gestures to a chair behind her, inside the nurses' station.

"No thanks, Shirley. I'll go look for him."

She looks over her bifocals at me. "Are you okay, Henry?"

I flash her my best Brad Pitt smile. Charming yet vacuous. "Sure."

A bell sounds, the signal that a patient has pushed a call button. Shirley glances at the patient board. "Not Devon Shields again? Good Lord." She smiles painfully at me. "He's got dementia. Thinks he's at Studio 54. Whenever I answer his call button, he orders a gram of cocaine and a large vodka, no ice."

"Sounds like a good idea to me."

She gives me a stern look.

"Want me to answer that one? I know Devon. We used to trick together ..." Shirley looks horrified. "That is ... I know him ... from the ... community."

"Well, it's against regulations ..." She raises her eyebrows, considering the idea.

"How could it hurt?"

"I guess you're right." She glances at the board again. "Room 712."

"Got it." I walk down the hall.

"Thanks, Henry. Gina, where's that roll of white gauze I requisitioned this morning? We're all out up here," she barks at a young nurse who has just rushed inside the station.

At the doorway of room 712, I hover for a minute, looking in. Devon Shields used to be a perfect ten. A gym faggot with gorgeous biceps, legs of a runner and a flawless washboard stomach. About a hundred years ago we had a one-night stand — well, make that a one-hour stand — inside the tearoom of the Jewish Community Centre gym on Spadina. God knows what a nice gentile boy like Devon with his blond hair, blue eyes and Gregory Peck cleft was doing working out with members of the Hebrew persuasion, but there he was, in all his *goyisha* glory, waiting to be jumped on by a descendant of Abraham, namely me. In the relative privacy of a cubicle, we took turns administering oral sex to one another, while older gents and teenage boys tromped in and out to use the urinals. A few months later, I joined the new fitness club on Church Street and lost track of Devon. Last time I ran into him was over a year ago, at a fundraiser for the Persons With AIDS society. He'd dropped twenty pounds, and his blond hair had thinned considerably. He had survived four hospital stays and was rapidly going blind from CMV, learning how to walk with a white cane. If he has dementia now, he's at the end of the line. I take a deep breath for courage, then enter his room.

Devon is sitting up in bed, "watching" a television that is not turned on, laughing hysterically at the "funny parts." I sit on the hard vinyl chair by his bed. The room smells of antiseptic and something rank and decaying. Death.

"Hi Devon." I announce my presence.

"Finally. You got the stuff?" he snaps.

"Sure," I play along.

"Give it here." He keeps his eyes on the television and sticks out a sweaty palm.

I place an invisible gram of coke in his hand.

He raises his arm, licks his palm. "You can't fool me."

"I can't?"

"No. That's not a full gram." He laughs.

I lean over his bed. Peer into his blind eyes. "Devon? Do you really have dementia?"

But he's laughing wildly and doesn't seem to hear me. He laughs until he begins to choke. I stand and hit him on the back. His face is turning red. He's gasping for breath. I push the nurse's call button.

"Come on, Devon, quit fooling around," I snap at him desperately.

Roger rushes in, looks surprised to see me. Gently, he pushes me out of the way, grabs an oxygen mask from a hook on the wall, expertly slips it over Devon's mouth, turns on the tank, rubs Devon's back softly as the coughing subsides and Devon settles back against his pillows, breathing hard.

"What are you doing here, Henry?" Roger leaves the oxygen mask in place, adjusts the tank levels.

"I just came in to say hi."

"You came to see Devon?"

"I came to see you."

He glances at his watch. "I just started my shift."

"Did you have lunch yet?"

"It's too soon."

"Coffee break?"

"Henry, we're kind of short-staffed today."

I glance at Devon. He seems to have passed out. Sleeping soundly. "I'm scared, Roger."

"Scared?"

"That I'll end up like him."

"Oh."

"I don't know if I can do it, Roger."

He takes me by the elbow, moves me toward the window. The bed beside Devon's is vacant. Roger closes the curtain between us and Devon. He steers me to the empty bed, sits beside me. "What's going on, Henry? Something Dr. Green said?"

"I flunked my latest test results. My T cells are leaving me. In droves, Roger. Packing their bags and catching the first plane out of here."

"Henry." He strokes my back with his big, strong hands.

"Roger ... what happens when ... ?" I can't say it.

"What happens ... ?" he prompts gently.

"When I'm like that?" I gesture toward poor Devon.

"Henry ... you're not going to end up like Devon."

I wonder whose denial is fiercer, mine or Roger's. "But it could happen ..."

"I don't believe that, Henry. You haven't been sick yet."

"What about you-know-what?" I say, referring to the one KS lesion that Dr. Green found a few months ago.

"Kaposi's sarcoma can be a chronic manageable skin cancer ..." he rattles off with his nurse's ease.

I cover both ears with my hands, like the six-year-old I am. "Don't use the 'C' word, Roger. Bad luck."

He frowns, says something. I can't hear him, so I lower my hands. "What?"

"I said, whatever happens, we're in this together, Henry. Do you hear me?"

"We are?"

LOVE AND OTHER RUINS   91

"Come 'ere, you." He folds me into his big, strong arms and holds me.

Just holds me.

I walk into the apartment to the sounds of vacuuming and Frank Sinatra blaring from the CD player. My father hasn't heard me enter. He's singing along with Frank at the top of his lungs, vacuuming up a storm, wearing my frilly pink Doris Day apron over his dark trousers and white button-down shirt. With his muscular frame, he looks like Julia Childs without her wig.

"But more ... much more than this ..." he bellows out the finale, eyes closed, arms outstretched, "I did it *my* way."

His singing isn't half bad. A little out of key, but strong and clear. I applaud enthusiastically. What else can I do? He opens his eyes, smiles.

"Henry!" he yells over the vacuum motor. "I didn't know you had any good music here. I found that tape in a box full of other great singers. Judy Garland and Barbra Streisand. I didn't know you had music like that."

"Pop, I'm a male homosexual. Of course I have Judy and Barbra."

"Huh?"

"Also Peggy Lee, Ethel Merman and Bette Midler."

"Betty who?"

"Pop, will you shut that off? I can't hear you."

"What?"

I reach over, switch the vacuum off. Frank moves on to his next selection.

There's a somebody I'm longing to see,
I hope that she turns out to be
Someone who'll watch over me.

Violins and a cello swell.

"Pop, I appreciate the effort. It looks nice in here, but what are you doing?"

"It's a mess. What'sa matter?" He reaches under the apron, which completely covers his chest, and pulls out a cigar stub from his shirt pocket. He slips the stub inside his mouth, unlit. "A man can't clean up once in a while without attracting attention?"

"No ... I guess not ..."

"Besides ... your mother's stopping by."

"What? Why's my mother stopping by?"

"I'm taking her out for a late lunch."

"Again?"

Frank continues singing:

I'm a little lamb who's lost in the woods
I know I could,
Could always be good
To one who'll watch over me.

"Pop? Are you dating my mother?"

"Dating?" He removes the cigar stub, waves it around in the air. "Dating? I don't think I'd call it that."

"Then what exactly would you call it?"

He considers my question. Frank moves on to selection number three. A duet with his daughter, Nancy.

And then I go and spoil it all by saying something stupid like I love you ...

By way of an answer, my father grabs me in his arms and leads me around the dance floor. Like the good bottom I am, I follow. I even let him dip me. He laughs from deep in his belly. It's contagious. I laugh with him. He brings me back to standing position and we both double over laughing. I'm not sure which part is the funniest — dancing in the living room with my father to Frank Sinatra? The sight of him in my frilly Doris Day apron? Or the fact that my father is dating his ex-wife, my mother? I laugh so hard I start to cough from deep in my chest. I can't stop. It's a horrible dry racking cough. I stumble to the sofa and drop down onto it, coughing my guts out. My father stops laughing and leans over me, hitting me hard on the back, as if that would stop the coughing.

Finally it subsides. He peers into my eyes. "That don't sound so good, Henry," he says.

No kidding.

The buzzer sounds.

"You okay now?" He walks over to the intercom. "Come on upstairs, Belle." He talks into the speaker. "Henry wants to say hello."

I don't want to say hello. I want to crawl into bed and hide.

When my mother knocks, Solly walks over to the door, still dressed in my apron.

"Uh, Pop," I warn.

"Yeah, what?"

"Uh ..." I point to the apron.

"Oh jeez. Thanks, Henry." He rips the apron off, crumples it into a ball and stuffs it inside the hall closet just as he opens the door for my mother.

After they leave, the phone rings. I hesitate. I don't really feel like talking to anybody right now, but it could be Roger.

"Hello?"

"I'm glad you're home," Albert says briskly. "I have incredible news. You won't believe it."

"What?"

"I can't say. Not over the phone. You know ..."

"Oh, right." Albert is convinced we are both still being watched and our phones are bugged. Four months ago Albert and I were both attacked and beaten on the street, on the same day. He was in New York. I was in Toronto. He's sure it was intentional. Professionals sent by the FBI or CIA. The Department of Defense. We're not sure which agency. To scare us off of our mission to expose the truth about HIV.

"I'll be in touch. Don't worry."

"Is everything okay, Albert?"

"Better than that. Gotta go, guy."

I grab my leather jacket and head for Triple A, where Julie works. In the past, Albert has sent messages to Julie there, or through Julie's co-worker Ed Leung. I assume he's doing the same today.

I find Julie working late, at her desk in the far corner of the noisy, crowded office in a three-storey walk-up off Church Street. Most of the office is a mess: papers scattered on desks, empty take-out cartons and coffee cups, overflowing wastebaskets. In stark contrast, Julie's corner is immaculate. Her desk is sparsely covered with one thin, neat stack of white papers, a pencil holder with exactly one pencil, one red pen, one blue, one black marker, one sleek stapler, a pair of scissors and a black Scotch Tape dispenser. There are no sticky notes on her keyboard or monitor, as there are on other computers. No empty coffee mugs or take-out food wrappers. No piles of files or boxes of disks. No newspapers. No personal items. In the afternoon when Julie leaves work, she clears her desk of all files and papers, dusts its surface and covers her monitor with a pale blue patterned cloth. Noise from other workers carries across the office. From behind a temporary partition, a woman in the next cubicle yells at someone from the Ministry of Health over the telephone.

I plunk down into the chair opposite Julie. It's only then that I notice she looks down in the dumps.

"Hi Henry," she says.

"You don't look so good," I say.

"I don't?" She opens a desk drawer, pulls out a tiny round compact, snaps open the lid, checks out her face in the mirror.

"No. That's not what I mean. You're beautiful as always, Julie. It's just that you look … I don't know … sad."

"Oh." Wistfully, she replaces the compact in her drawer. "It's Nomi."

"What's she done now?"

"I don't know what to do." Huge tears form in her big almond eyes and roll down her cheeks, splashing on her pristine desk.

I sit up, reach over, stroke her arm. "About what, Julie?"

She pours out her sad little heart. Late last night she had a big fight with Nomi. Bottles were thrown — figuratively (the fight was over the phone). Hair was pulled. Names were called. They broke up. It was terrible, Julie says. I can't quite figure out what the fight was about. Something about Nomi moving back in with her ex, although I can't imagine why she'd want to do that.

"Sapphire's a bitch anyway, Julie."

Between sniffles. "You met her?"

"Didn't have to. Everyone who's anyone knows she's a full-time loser," I say in my best bitchy fag impersonation. I'm trying to make Julie laugh. Best remedy for the blues. It works.

Her face brightens momentarily, then gloom descends. "It's over, Henry." Fresh tears roll.

"Over? Are you sure?"

She says nothing, simply nods gravely, splashing the desk.

"But do you love her?"

"I'm crazy about her."

I stand, rub Julie's shoulders from behind. "Then fight for her. She doesn't want Sapphire. She wants you. Nomi's just ... well ... she doesn't make the best decisions sometimes. Believe me, she's nuts about you."

"I don't know ..."

"Come on, Julie. She told me."

"But ..." Her big brown eyes are pained.

"What, sweetie?"

"I don't have blue eyes ..."

"What?"

"Or long legs."

I look at her carefully, not sure what this is about.

"Or long blonde hair."

"Julie ..."I say gently. "What makes you think Nomi wants blonde hair?"

She looks at me hard. "The usual reason."

What's the usual reason? I study Julie. Then her mood switches back to melancholy.

"Henry, I just don't know what Nomi sees in me. She could have anybody."

"But she wants you."

She studies me. "You think so?"

"I know so. Why don't you call her, kiss and make up?"

"I can't. Not now." She glances at her watch. "God, I have a dinner meeting in five minutes." She reaches for the compact again, this time to repair her running mascara.

In a low voice, I say, "Albert phoned today."

"Oh God, I almost forgot."

"What?"

"He sent a message through Ed. We're to be at his apartment at nine this evening. Albert's contacting us there."

"I thought so."

"Meet me there?" She stands, grabs a thick file from a desk drawer.

"Chin up, girlfriend."

With time to kill, so to speak, I duck into This Ain't the Rosedale Library, a community bookstore on Church Street. I browse the magazine section for a while, finally settle on a copy of the *Advocate*, pay and mosey across the street to the Second Cup, where I order a double latte. I choose a prime spot on the concrete steps outside, where I can sip my coffee, read and boy-watch all at the same time. Nobody sits at the tables *inside* the Second Cup — nobody who is *anybody*, that is. Located right at the corner of Church and Wellesley, the outdoor steps are the perfect place to socialize. Especially at this time of year, after a long, cold winter. Everybody wants to be outside. To see and be seen.

"Hi guy," says Simon as he snuggles on the step beside me. I haven't seen Simon all winter. He used to be active in my ACTOUT group. He looks thin and tired, weary.

"Simon." I throw an arm over his shoulder. "Where have you been?"

He gives me a long, hard look. "Didn't you hear?"

Oh God. My belly drops to the ground. I know instinctively what he's going to say. "No. What?"

He sighs, sips on his coffee. "Steven died at home. Like he wanted to."

"Oh God, Simon. I didn't know."

He stares at me. "Where have *you* been?"

I squeeze him closer to me. "Navel-gazing, I guess. I'm sorry, Simon. I would have come for a visit."

"I haven't exactly been in the mood."

"Well, I could have cooked you dinner. Done your laundry. Rubbed your back."

"What about Roger?" He bats his eyes shamelessly. Simon is an attractive man. If not for Roger, who knows?

"Not that kind of back rub. When did he die?"

"Just after New Year's. He wanted to make it to the millennium. He was only one year off. He'd just turned thirty-eight."

My heart freezes. My age exactly. Is this a sign? From God? In fear, I gulp at my latte, burn my tongue.

"I've been kind of hibernating since then. I quit my job to take care of him. Now I don't know what to do."

I say nothing. What's there to say? His lover of ten years died at thirty-eight. I hug Simon to me. We drink coffee in silence and watch the parade of boys walk by in the warm evening air.

Julie is already at Ed's place when I arrive. He lives on Alexander Street, a block from my apartment. He's on the sixteenth floor facing south and has a view of the downtown core, high-rise concrete office buildings and the giant grey penis, the CN tower. Toronto's idea of scenery.

"We're sitting on the balcony. It's still warm. Glass of wine?" Ed takes my arm, escorts me through his tastefully decorated apartment. I don't know Ed well, but Julie trusts him implicitly, and he seems devoted to the cause.

"Do you have any ginger ale?"

"Club soda?"

"Sold."

I sit by Julie on a green plastic patio chair. Lean over and kiss her cheek. "You look a little better," I tell her.

"Thanks. I feel better. You're right. I'm just insecure. What would Nomi want with her ex anyway?"

"Exactly."

"I'm going to call her later tonight."

"Atta girl."

"If she still wants me."

"She wants you."

Ed hands me a beer glass filled with bubbling club soda. A lime wedge garnishes the glass. He's holding the receiver of his portable phone. Ready for the call.

"Thanks."

I glance at my watch. Nine o'clock exactly. The phone rings.

"Hello?" Ed answers cautiously. "Yes. Right. Thanks. You too." He hands the phone to me.

"Hi," I say.

"You're not going to believe what I've got." Albert sounds like he's going to burst with excitement.

"I'm listening."

"Sitting right beside me is Professor Jonathan Garrick. Does that name sound familiar to you?"

"It does. But I can't place it."

"Jon worked on the original experiments. In Maryland. In the seventies. Do you hear what I'm saying?"

"Oh my God. He's there? With you?"

"What?" Julie asks quietly.

"Yes," continues Albert, "and he's willing to ... testify."

"Testify?"

"Figure of speech, Henry. I mean he's willing to tell the whole story. The truth. He's willing to go public. Do you know what this means?"

"Oh my God." This is incredible. This is exactly what we've been waiting for. If Professor Garrick goes public, the world just has to listen.

"What is it, Henry?" Julie is about to climb out of her skin with curiosity.

"Hold on," I tell Albert. "One of the scientists on the original experiments is there with Albert," I whisper to Julie and Ed. Just in case someone on the next balcony is listening.

"Oh my God," says Julie.

"Fantastic," says Ed.

"This is unbelievable," I tell Albert.

"A dream come true."

As I open the door to my apartment I hear voices. My father's home. And someone is with him. I kick off my runners in the front hall. Inside the living room, my mother sits on the sofa. Solly sits beside her, one arm draped around her shoulder protectively. Belle is crying. She holds a wadded-up piece of Kleenex in one hand. When she sees me, a fresh torrent of tears flow.

"Henry," she wails. "Why didn't you tell me?"

What? Tell her what? I look at my father, who shrugs.

"How long have you been sick?" my mother manages through sobs. "Why didn't you tell me? I'm your mother." She blows her nose loudly.

I glare at my father.

"Sorry, son. I thought she knew."

"Why would I know?" my mother complains. "Nobody tells me anything around here."

I feel about five years old. The whole scene is horribly familiar: my mother crying, my father apologizing. The only difference is when I was a child, she was usually crying over something Solly had done.

"Ma." I stand in the middle of the living room, silently begging her to stop crying. "I tried to tell you. I tried just the other day, but you don't make it easy."

"You can talk to me, Henry. I'm listening. You can tell me anything." She clicks the fingernails on one hand against her thumbnail.

"Ma, it's not that easy."

"Why? All my friends say I'm a good listener. Aren't I a good listener, Solly?"

"Yeah, sure ya are, sweetheart." He glances at me.

"Ma, I tried to tell you."

"Henry, where were you just now? You shouldn't be running around so late. You have to take care of yourself. Maybe you should come back home. I'll take care of you."

"Ma, I am home. Roger takes care of me."

"But I'm your mother."

"And he's my lover."

She purses her lips. "A lover's not a mother."

"Ma, Roger's a nurse, remember?"

"Of course I remember. Where is he? I haven't seen him in such a long time. Such a nice boy," she tells Solly.

"Yeah, he's a swell guy." Uncomfortable with all the lover talk, Solly stands and heads for the liquor cabinet, reaches for his bottle of Jack Daniel's. "I need a drink. Anyone else?"

"Maybe a little white wine," Belle says.

"I'll get it." I find an opened bottle in the fridge, pour a glass for my mother and a glass for myself.

"Now Henry." Belle pats the sofa beside her. "I want you to sit right here and tell me the whole story. From the beginning."

"The story?" I sit beside her, but not too close.

She sips her wine. "How did you get it? Oh my God, you didn't get it from Roger, did you? Henry, you should have been more careful."

"Ma, Roger's negative."

"Negative?"

"He doesn't have it."

"Oh."

I gulp down a large swallow of wine.

"So, how then?"

I stare at my mother. Where should I begin?

NOMI'S PHONE CALL

I'm restocking the beer fridge. The bar is half empty. Too early for the evening crowd. It's mellow. Almost pleasant. People have stopped in for a drink after work or to play a game of pool. To sit at the bar and unwind from their day. Patty trundles in, looking proud of herself. She hops onto her bar stool at the end. Pulls out a cigarette. Lights it.

"It's all fixed, Rabinovitch," she announces.

"Fixed?" I pour her a cup of coffee, black with a packet of Sweet 'N Low, just how she likes it.

"Betty talked to the super. He hadn't rented out her old place yet, and she's lived there so long, he gave it back to her. So you don't have to move in with Sapphire. It's all fixed."

"I wasn't going to move in with Sapphire. Is anybody listening?"

"That's the thanks I get?" Patty blows smoke across the bar.

"Oh. Right. Thanks. How was Betty about the whole thing?"

She shrugs. "On to the next thing. You know Betty." She looks around the bar. "How'd we do?"

After work, I push open the apartment door slowly. I'm worried Betty's going to be angry. She's slumped in her usual spot, on the sofa — my bed — channel surfing. I try to sneak past her into the kitchen.

"Sit down, Nom," she says. "Look." She points at the TV screen with the remote control. "It's Ellen's coming-out episode."

"I've seen it."

Betty gives me a look. "Yeah. But how many times?"

"Six or seven."

"That's all? What kind of a lesbian are you? Come on, sit down."

I plop onto the sofa. It's the scene where Ellen is in a hotel room with the scrawny guy, her old friend.

"Men, men, men," says Ellen. "Boy, do I love men."

"You're not mad at me?" I ask Betty.

"Shit, girl. No. I thought you were mad at me."

"No."

"Good. Now shut up. I want to see this."

"Show me the money," says Ellen, pushing the guy onto the big double bed and pouncing on him.

"How many times have *you* seen this?" I ask.

"Shhh," says Betty.

We watch the show. Ellen and the guy start making out. Then something goes wrong, and Ellen jumps up and kicks the guy out into the hall. A commercial comes on.

"Oh. Almost forgot." Betty says. "Your girlfriend called."

I leap up. "Julie?"

"Who else?"

I dash into Betty's bedroom to use the phone in private.

"Hey!" she calls after me, "don't you wanna see the part where Ellen comes out?"

But I'm already dialing Julie's number.

Julie and I fall all over ourselves apologizing.

"I'm too sensitive," she says.

"No. I was wrong," I counter. "Anyway, we're not taking the apartment."

"Oh Nomi. You don't have to do that."

"Yes, I do. It was a stupid idea anyway. I didn't mean to hurt you."

"I know."

"I'm sorry, Julie."

"I know."

I take a deep breath to loosen the lump of fear in my throat.

"What are you going to do, then?" Julie asks.

"Huh? About what?"

"Where are you going to live?"

"Oh. Here. At Betty's. We're just staying here."

"I don't want to lose you, Nomi."

"You're not going to lose me."

"This is harder than I thought."

"I know." The phone beeps. Call waiting. I hate call waiting, but it could be for Betty. She made me promise to always answer in case one of her many babes is trying to reach her. God forbid she misses a call. "Julie, can you hold on for a second?"

"Ok-ay." She sounds annoyed. Who can blame her?

I flick the button down once. "Hello?"

"Hello, Nomi?"

It's my mother.

"Hi Ma, listen, I'm on the other line. Can I call you back later?"

"Sure, Nomi. I'm only your mother. Why talk to me?"

"Ma. Come on. Don't be like that."

"I've been trying to reach you."

"I'm on the other line, Ma. I'll call you back."

"Who knows if I'll be here."

My mother the drama queen. "Ma ..." I'm conscious of Julie waiting on hold.

"Fine."

I'm not going to fall for my mother's tactics. "I'll call you back soon."

"Fine." She says this as if she is on death row.

I hit the phone button twice. "Julie?"

"I was just about to hang up. Who was it? Your other girl-friend?"

"My mother. Julie, you're my only girlfriend."

"Are you sure?"

"What do you think?"

"What are you wearing?" Julie asks in a sultry voice. I slip farther down on the bed, stretch my legs out. This is what you do when you're in a long-distance relationship. You have phone sex. We'd probably have on-line computer sex too, except Julie's only computer is at work and lacks privacy. And I don't have access to a computer at all.

"Black leather chaps," I lie. "And a tight black tee." Really I'm wearing baggy blue jeans and a stained denim shirt, an old one Betty tried to throw away, that is about five sizes too big for me.

"Ask me what I'm wearing" she urges.

"What are you wearing?" I glance at the bedroom door, which unfortunately has no lock, and hope like hell Ellen's coming-out show is enthralling enough to keep Betty in the living room for a while.

"Black negligee," Julie answers. "Lace, with a low ... low neck-line. And Nomi ..."

"Yes." She is turning me on.

"No panties."

"Oh God." My hand finds its way between my legs. "Tell me more."

"I'm wet for you, Nomi."

The phone beeps. "Shit."

"Don't answer it, Nomi."

"Shit."

"Please, baby ..."

"Sorry. I promised Betty. She's expecting a call. Shit. Don't go away. Please, babe. Please ..."

She sighs. "All right."

I push the button. "Hello!" I bark.

"Nomi ... I'm waiting."

"Ma!" I shout, "what are you doing? I said I'd call you when I'm finished."

"I thought you forgot about me."

"Who could forget?"

"Nomi, I need to talk to you."

"I'm hanging up on you, Ma."

"Fine. I can see I'm not important enough."

"Goodbye, Ma." I hit the button. "Julie." There is silence but no dial tone. "Julie?"

"I'm here, Nomi."

"Where were we?"

"I was just slipping out of my negligee."

"Oh God. Where are you?"

"In the bedroom."

"Take it off slowly," I instruct. "And describe it to me."

"I'm slipping off the top part ..." Julie says. "My breasts are exposed. My nipples are hard."

I sink lower on Betty's bed, getting back in the mood. "Yes ..." I urge.

"I'm touching my nipples. Squeezing them."

"Julie ..." I undo the top button on my jeans.

The door swings open. Betty bursts in, the remote control clutched in her hand.

"You gotta see this, Nom. It's the best part, you know, where Ellen has a crush on Laura Dern."

"Betty!" I leap to my feet. "Can't you knock?"

"It is *my* room, Nomi." She is offended. "Oh." She understands. "Why didn't you tell me you were having phone sex? Hi Julie, how's it going?" she yells in the general direction of the phone receiver. She turns on her heel. "Well, I guess you couldn't care less about Ellen. Lucky for you I'm taping this." She closes the door behind her.

"Julie?" I say into the phone.

"Nomi, why don't you just call me tomorrow?"

"I'll call back later."

"It'll be too late here. I have to go to sleep."

"It's okay now. Betty won't come back."

"What about your mother?"

"I won't answer if it beeps again."

"What about the call Betty's waiting for?"

I sigh. Deeply.

"Goodbye, Nomi. Call me tomorrow."

"I love you," I say tentatively.

Her voice softens. "I love you too."

She loves me. The second I hang up, the phone rings again. I pick it up. "Hi Ma."

"How did you know it was me?"

"Psychic, I guess."

"Nomi, are you involved in one of those psychedelic cults down there in California?"

"Yeah, Ma, the cult of annoyed daughters."

"What?"

"Ma, it's not the sixties."

"Don't tell me they don't have cults nowadays. I read the newspapers. I'm in the know."

"I'm sure you are, Ma."

"I keep up."

"Why did you phone me? What's wrong?"

"Oh Nomi ... everything."

"Everything? What do you mean everything?"

She lowers her voice to a near whisper. "It's Murray Feinstein."

"Murray? What's the matter?"

She takes a breath and sighs. Loudly. "I guess I got used to living alone."

"What's he doing?"

"Lots of things."

We're getting nowhere fast. "Well, can you name some?"

"Sure. I can name plenty."

"Like ..."

"Like he leaves the toilet seat up."

"Still?"

"I ask him and ask him. He can't remember one simple thing. I'm not used to that."

"Didn't Dad used to do that?"

"Well, it's been two years since your father, may he rest in peace, passed away ... it's nice not to worry about falling in."

"Just lay down the law, Ma. You have rights in the relationship."

"Also, he throws his dirty socks on the floor."

"His socks?"

"I'm supposed to pick them up."

"Ma, that's no good. You don't have to take that. You have rights." I want to kill Murray Feinstein. Who does he think he is?

"What can I do? He's the man."

"Ma, this is the nineties. It's almost the year 2000. Women don't have to take that kind of shit anymore." My voice rises in anger. I've given her this advice repeatedly. It's a little frustrating.

"Oy Nomi, you know I don't like that kind of language."

"What? Oh, sorry. You know what I mean."

"What can I do, Nomi?"

"Did you tell him you don't like it?"

"I told him. I told him."

"And?"

"He smiles and shrugs."

"That's it?"

"Like a little boy. Maybe he thinks it's cute."

"Cute?" I rack my brain for advice. What can I say? It's not like I have any experience living with men — unless you count my brothers. "I have an idea."

"What?"

"Hang a sign."

"What?"

"A sign. Over the toilet."

"A sign?"

"Yeah. A sign that says, 'put down toilet seat.' That way he can't say he keeps forgetting."

"That's an idea."

"And one in the bedroom."

" 'Pick up your socks'?"

"Yeah. What do you think?"

"You think it's okay, Nomi?" My mother is a product of the fifties. Doris Day mentality. Women are supposed to clean up after men. Even if it's driving them mad.

"Course it is, Ma. You're not his servant."

"Well, Nomi. He's the breadwinner."

"Aren't you still getting a monthly cheque from Dad's insurance?"

"Yeah, but Murray pays for a lot more. It's only right that I do the cooking and cleaning."

"Okay, Ma, but you don't have to put up with things that bother you."

"I knew you'd say the right thing, Nomi. You always do."

"It's supposed to be a partnership, Ma."

"What is?"

"Marriage."

"It is?"

"Isn't it?"

I hang up the phone, slip out of the bedroom and into the living room. Betty is sitting on the edge of her seat. Ellen is in an airport waiting room sitting beside Laura Dern. Then Ellen follows Laura into the passenger lineup, and with the flight attendant's microphone an inch from her face, unbeknownst to her, Ellen tells the entire waiting room, "I'm gay."

Betty glances at me. "You go, girl," she tells Ellen.

Ellen realizes her blunder, turns three shades of red. Laura hugs her. The commercial break comes on. My eyes glaze over. All I can think about is Julie.

SUMMER 1999

NIGHT SWEATS AND OTHER EVIDENCE

HENRY'S VISIT TO THE TEAROOM

R oger is on day shift. He slipped out of bed early to head for work while I continued sleeping. It's hot for June. The air in the apartment is humid. I wake up sweaty and tangled in the sheets. In my briefs I stagger sleepily down the hall. My feet stick to the hardwood floor. My only thought is coffee.

"There you are. 'Bout time you got up," my father shouts from his place at the dining room table, where he sips coffee from a mug. There's still half a pot. Thank God. Like me, he's mostly naked — too hot in the apartment for clothes — wearing loose white boxer shorts and nothing else. His slight belly protrudes over the waistband of his shorts. He's in pretty good shape, though, for his age.

I glare at him, pour myself a cup, notice the greasy frying pan sitting in a pool of brown water in the sink. The only thing Solly eats in the morning is fried kippers. He douses them liberally in ketchup, then fries them until they're almost burned and the whole apartment smells of sea salt, burnt ketchup and fish. I sink into the chair opposite him, reach for the sugar.

"Hurry up, Henry. We're going to visit your grandmother this morning."

"What?" I dump a spoon of sugar into my coffee, a shot of half-and-half from the carton.

"Sure, I thought we'd take in lunch after. We'll take a taxi. I can't stand taking the subway all the way uptown."

"A taxi? You know how much that'll cost?" I raise my cup of coffee, blow to cool it. The aroma calms me. It's a dark roast, full-bodied and rich.

"Not just any taxi. Lou's driving us." Solly crunches on a piece of burnt fish.

"Oh."

Lou Greenberg owns his own cab. He has some kind of deal with my father. I really don't want to know what their agreement is, but Lou seems to be available to drive my father places whenever he's called upon. I take my first sip. The coffee works its magic, waking my senses, unclogging my brain.

"Have some kippers." Solly holds up a plate with two burnt fish. "There's lots."

"Uh, no thanks." I slurp my coffee. The bright morning sun streams through the balcony door, into the sweltering apartment.

"Henry, you gotta eat." He helps himself to another whole fish.

"I'll have toast." A bead of sweat forms on my upper lip.

"Okay, but hurry up."

"Pop ..." I'm a little annoyed. "Don't you ask me first if I want to go and visit Bubbe? How do you know I'm even free?" I wipe my lip with my napkin.

He speaks with his mouth full. "Awright, awright. So I don't got the uh ... whatchacallit ... ? Etiquette of royalty. For chrissake, I'm your father."

That explains something?

"So you'll come?"

Why not? One thing is sure: time spent with Solly is always interesting. "Okay." I push back my chair, toss two pieces of sourdough rye into the toaster.

"Good." He belches loudly.

I've taken one bite of my toast when the buzzer rings.

"That's Lou. Hurry up, Henry." Solly's dressed now, in white trousers and a turquoise and yellow Hawaiian-style shirt, so loud it makes my eyes hurt. Perched on his head is a beige straw fedora. His summer hat.

"Okay. I'll meet you downstairs." I grab my toast, head for the bedroom to get dressed.

"Hiya, Henry," Lou says when I slip into the back seat of his cab. Solly takes the front passenger seat. Lou's dressed as usual in a plain white short-sleeved, button-down shirt, dark pants and his signature 1940s-style newsboy cap.

"Hi, Lou." I lean back against the vinyl seat and crank the window down as far as I can, which is only halfway. There is no air-conditioning in Lou's cab. Lou's owned the cab for thirty years. This car is at least ten years old and its body is rusting in places. The interior vinyl is worn and ripped. His cab licence and photo are mounted in a cracked and yellowed plastic folder on the back of the front seat. The photo is over twenty years old. It shows a younger, thinner Lou, when he still had hair on his head.

"Awright. Awright. Cut the small talk, fellas," my father complains. "Let's hit it, Lou."

"Sure, Solly." Lou puts the car in gear and hits the accelerator hard. My stomach lurches. I reach for my seat belt. My father is the leader in his group of friends. They've been friends since boyhood, growing up in the Kensington Market area. Fiercely loyal, it was Lou, Meyer and Stan who kept Solly going when he served his first six-year sentence when I was a little boy. They visited him regularly. Brought him care packages with kosher salami, kippers fried in ketchup and burnt, the way he likes them, Cuban cigars, cigarettes, books, copies of the *Canadian Jewish News*. And the racing form. Small luxuries that made him feel like a person even while he was an inmate.

I'm only half-listening to their conversation as we drive north on Avenue Road. Solly and Lou are reminiscing — their favourite activity after poker.

"No. No. It was Stan who passed out at his stag party," my father insists.

"Stan. Are you sure? I thought it was Meyer." Lou cuts off another cab, then leans on his horn harshly.

"It was Stan. I remember because it was Meyer who wrapped the stripper's whatchacallit?"

"Boa," Lou provides. I smile, wonder how Lou Greenberg knows about feather boas. My, my.

"Yeah, boa." My father continues the story. "Wrapped it around Stan's neck, and took the picture."

Lou shakes his head. "I coulda sworn it was Meyer."

"I'm telling you, it was Stan."

"Well …" Lou is reluctant to give in. "If you say so … but … I thought it was Meyer."

"Stan." Solly gets in the last word. "I'm telling you, Lou, your memory's going. We'll have to reserve you a room at the old folks' home soon." My father guffaws loudly at his own joke.

Lou is not laughing. In the rearview mirror, I see terror in his eyes. Has my father hit a nerve? "I got a good memory," Lou insists. "Don't worry about that."

"Stop the car!" Solly shouts suddenly.

Lou hits the brakes. My body is thrown forward. The seat belt catches me across the chest, the strap digs hard into my ribs, winding me. I lean forward over my knees and cough, gasping for breath.

"Jesus, Lou. You trying to kill us?" Solly turns around in his seat. "You okay, Henry?"

"Yeah," I spurt through coughs. Breathe in. Out. In. Out.

He stares at me with concern. It's unnerving.

"I'm fine, Pop. It's the seat belt." I cough more.

"How'd you get a driver's licence!" he barks at Lou.

"You told me to stop, Solly. You said." Lou throws up his hands defensively.

"Lunatic."

"Solly, you said to stop. I stopped."

"It's okay guys," I rally. "I'm okay."

"You're okay?"

"Yeah." I clear my throat, then smile to prove it.

"Awright." Solly opens his door. "Wait here."

"Pop, what are you doing?" I rub my chest. It might be bruised.

He shakes his head, as if it's obvious. "Can't show up without flowers." He steps out, slams the door. Lou and I watch him walk to a convenience store with flowers displayed in white plastic tubs. Solly picks a large bunch of bright yellow daisies, checks in his trouser pockets. Gestures for me to roll down my window.

"Henry, can you spot me? I'm short on cash," he yells.

Again? "Sure, Pop." I undo my seat belt, get out of the car, one hand on my chest, hand him ten dollars.

"I'll just pick up a fresh cigar while I'm in the store. You need anything?"

A new father, I think; one who has his own money. "Yeah, get me a pack of Smarties."

"You wouldn't rather have a nice cigar?"

"No."

He shrugs. "It's your life."

Lou drops us off outside Sholom Aleichem, Home for the Jewish Aged.

"You sure you don't wanna come in?" Solly asks Lou.

"I'll come back for you, in what? An hour? I gotta grab a couple of fares in the meantime. Make some money." Lou wipes the back of his sweaty neck with a white cotton handkerchief.

"Okay. Don't forget about us, Lou. You know I can't stand taking the bus up here."

"I know, Solly."

"So you'll come back in an hour?"

"Don't worry. I'll be back."

"In an hour."

Lou nods his head emphatically, like one of those felt dogs people set in the back windows of their cars. Nod. Nod. Nod. "An hour," he assures us.

"Awright." Solly closes the door. "Good."

Lou hits the gas. I wonder why my father hates taking the bus uptown. He doesn't seem to mind using transit downtown.

Inside the Home, we spot Bubbe. She always sits on the same chair in the lobby, near the window, third chair from the left, staring into space. Her eyes have gotten so bad she can't read anymore. She doesn't like television. She claims that all the other residents are senile, so what's the point in making friends?

There's nothing left for her to do but sit and stare. It breaks my heart every time I come here, seeing what's become of her life: sitting on a plastic-covered chair in a lobby, staring into space, hoping your family will come visit today and break the monotony.

She spots me. Her face brightens.

"Herschel. Is that you?" Bubbe calls me by my Hebrew name.

"Hi Bubbe, it's me. And look who else." I move aside for my father to approach.

"M-A," he shouts, spelling out her name as is his custom. "How are you?"

"Why don't you come see me no more? I'm waiting. You're so busy?" She scolds, but she's smiling, happy to see her son. Bubbe has selective hearing. Sometimes she seems to hear fine; other times you have to shout at her.

"I'm here now, Ma. Look, we brought you something." From behind his back, Solly produces the daisies.

"What's that? Flowers? What do I need flowers for? I'm an old lady."

"So?"

"Who needs it?" She pretends to be angry, but I can see she loves the flowers.

"We'll put them in your room," Solly says.

"They'll die."

"Not for a few days. Come on, M-A. Be nice."

She turns to me. "Henry, you'll go upstairs and put them in my room?"

"Sure. Is it open?"

"They won't let me lock it. Any meshuggener could just walk into my room. That's why I gave all my jewellery to your Aunt Shell."

"You gave it all to Shell?" Solly seems surprised.

"To hold for me."

"I'll hold it for you," he offers.

Bubbe shakes her head. She knows from experience that Solly would hold the jewellery long enough to get to the nearest pawnshop or poker table. "Henry, you'll ask at the desk for a jar."

"You mean like a vase?"

"That's the one."

I wander to the nurses' desk. It's hard not to get depressed. The residents of the Home are mostly women, with just a few men. Bubbe is right. Most are senile, in advanced stages of Alzheimer's or other diseases that steal the mind. Many sit in wheelchairs, staring into space. One woman shouts in Yiddish. Another woman beside her is crying softly. A man wearing a yarmulke sways back and forth, praying quietly to himself.

The Home is air-conditioned. The lobby is cool but underneath there's the smell of urine, antiseptic and the undefined scent of old people, a cross between mothballs, decay and cheap cologne.

"Mrs. Goldberg," a young nurse shouts loudly. "Open your mouth. Open it." The nurse is trying to feed Mrs. Goldberg her medicine. Mrs. Goldberg shakes her head, and like a small child, clamps her mouth tightly shut. Her white-yellow hair is long and swept up on top of her head in a tight bun. She wears a blue flowered housedress. Somebody has tied an adult-sized bib around her neck. She wears stockings rolled down to her ankles and no shoes. Her eyes have a crazed look.

"Mrs. Goldberg, do we have to go through this every day?" The nurse taps one foot on the polished linoleum floor.

Mrs. Goldberg grins emphatically, then burps. The nurse seizes the opportunity and slips the spoonful of medicine into her mouth. Mrs. Goldberg looks stunned, frowns at the taste of the medicine. A small drop dribbles from the corner of her mouth.

"Yes?" a harried desk nurse asks me.

"Oh, I was wondering if I could borrow a vase?" I hold up the flowers.

"For those?"

I nod. She shakes her head, annoyed, opens a cupboard, pulls out a medical-looking glass container. "Will that do?"

"I guess."

"It's best to bring one from home," she lectures.

"Next time," I promise. I take the jar and head up the stairs to Bubbe's room.

Bubbe first moved into the Home three years ago, with my grandfather, Zayde Avram, who had Alzheimer's. She wasn't exactly ready for an old folks' home at the time, but she couldn't take care of him by herself any longer. So they ended up here. He died a few months later and Bubbe just stayed. They'd already given up their apartment and all their furniture, except the two dressers and a chair that they brought here. They'd slept on side-by-side twin beds. After Zayde died, Bubbe refused to let them move his bed out. It's still there now, pushed up beside hers. It has no sheets or blankets. The bare mattress shouts the absence of my grandfather. I don't know how Bubbe can stand to leave it there. When I die, I hope Roger gets rid of all my stuff. I don't want him to be depressed looking at it.

In Bubbe's bathroom I fill the jar with water, unwrap the flowers and arrange them. On her dresser there are framed photos of her children and grandchildren. I notice that my cousins are featured in pairs, with their husbands, wives, even boyfriends and girlfriends. There's a picture of Nomi by herself. Same for me. My heart flutters. There's a picture of my brother Larry, with some girl he dated once or twice. I can't even remember her name. And a similar one of his twin Moe, with an equally short-term girlfriend. Roger and I just celebrated our fifth anniversary, and he's nowhere to be seen on my grandmother's dresser.

"I thought I saw you across the lobby." A soft voice interrupts my thoughts. In the doorway stands Dov, a gorgeous young Israeli orderly who works at the Home.

"I haven't seen your handsome face around here for a while." He flirts, in his cute Israeli accent, then swishes his lithe frame toward me.

"Dov, how nice to see a sister up here, just when I'm feeling sorry for myself."

"Oh?"

I gesture to the photos on the dresser. "Oh, you know. Good old ho-ho-homophobia."

Dov peers closely at the photos, instantly understands. He kisses each of my cheeks. "Poor Henry. So you still have that hunky boyfriend?"

I nod.

He shakes his head. "All the good ones are taken. What can you do?"

"I'm sure glad to see you." I smile.

"Oh ..." He bats his long lashes.

I slap his hand playfully. "Stop. You know what I mean."

"Sure you wouldn't be interested in ... visiting the tearoom?" He nods toward the bathroom. In spite of myself, my dick springs to attention. If I wanted to, I could take him up on his suggestion. Roger and I have a handy little agreement. Anonymous quickies are permitted. But in my grandmother's bathroom? At the Home? What if someone walks in? And does this really qualify as anonymous?

"Hmmm?" Dov persists, moving his eyes down my body, resting on my crotch.

I grab his hand, haul him inside the bathroom, double lock the door.

Twenty minutes later, we kiss goodbye and I take the elevator back downstairs.

"What the hell took you so long?" Solly blurts.

"Had to make a phone call," I lie.

"Lou'll be back soon. Visit with your grandmother," Solly orders, then stands.

"Where you going, Pop?"

"Have to make a phone call too."

I raise my eyebrows in disbelief. For a brief ridiculous second I imagine my father going for a quick blow job in the bathroom. But of course, he walks to the pay phone near the front doors and grabs the receiver.

"Herschel." Bubbe takes my hands in hers. "Tell me what's new. I never see your brothers. Do you see them?"

"Well ..."

"That's what I thought. It's not right. You should see your brothers."

My twin brothers Larry and Moe are five years younger than me and we're polar opposites. They're straight as two thick planks, Conservative with a capital C — they actually voted for the Reform Party. They're probably the only two voters east of Calgary to do so. They know their big brother is a flaming homosexual but they're not exactly lining up to join Parents and Friends of Lesbians and Gays, if you know what I mean. My father is actually more mellow about my sexual orientation than my brothers are.

"Do you hear me, Herschel?" Bubbe persists.

"I hear you, Bubbe." In the background I can hear my father talking loudly on the phone, arguing with someone. At the far end of the lobby, a large-screen television is switched on to a daytime soap opera. A handful of residents sit watching.

"You only got one brother."

"Two, actually."

A woman two chairs down turns toward me and smiles brilliantly. To be polite, I smile back.

"Oh my," the woman says, pulling a black shawl tightly around her. "Oh my."

"Once they're gone, that's it," Bubbe says. "How's your sister?"

"She's fine." My sister Sherry, on the other hand, is a saint. A couple of years younger than the twins, she's straight too, but Sherry doesn't have one judgmental bone in her body. She's always been easy with my lifestyle. She gets along great with Roger. Sherry loves everybody. Even Larry and Moe.

Bubbe leans in so her face is an inch from mine. "Does she have a boyfriend?"

"I don't know," I answer honestly. I haven't seen Sherry for a while.

"She should be getting married soon. How old is she?"

"She just turned thirty."

"You see? She's an old maid."

"Bubbe ... uh ..." How do I explain this? "She's not ready to get married."

"It's because of your father, isn't it?"

"What do you mean?"

The black-shawl woman grunts. She's trying to stand, trying to pull herself up, hands on the armrests. I wonder if I should help or just leave her be. She groans loudly.

"He's a jailbird," Bubbe continues. "He left your mother high and dry when you kids were little."

"Sherry does all right."

"So she probably hates men."

"She doesn't hate men."

"Who can blame her?"

"Bubbe, she doesn't hate men."

"If I hadn't met your Zayde when I did ... who knows? All the other men were bums."

What is she saying? Is she trying to tell me she would have been a lesbian if she hadn't met my grandfather? I peer at my grandmother with new eyes.

"Sherry doesn't hate men," I repeat.

The shawl-woman makes it to a standing position. On shaky legs, she shuffles directly over to me. She reaches forward and takes my face in her two hands.

"Oy Shlomo. Eet's you. You came back," she tells me. "Eet's a miracle," she tells the rest of the room.

"Uh," I say, trying to pry her hands from my cheeks.

She moves forward and plants a sloppy, dusty wet kiss on my lips.

Bubbe swats her. "Go away. You're meshuge," she tells the woman. "She's crazy, Herschel. Make her go away."

Thankfully the woman drops her hands. I stand. It's safer that way. She grabs my right hand in hers, raises it in waltz position. Her other hand rests on my shoulder.

"Remember how we used to dance, Shlomo? Ta da da da da ... da ... da ... da ... da." She hums. She's surprisingly strong for her age, which I guess to be about eighty. She drags me around the "dance floor," humming exuberantly. There is nothing to do but follow her lead. An old man in the corner claps his hands in time. Several other old ladies swoon at the sight of us. Mrs.

Goldberg smiles and stands in front of her wheelchair. She takes a few steps toward us, then loses her balance and topples over onto the floor. A nurse rushes to her aid. Shawl-woman is beside herself with joy. She pulls me closer. Her large, pendulous breasts push against my chest. She smells of sweet-old-lady cologne and mothballs.

My grandmother shouts, "Stop it! Leave him alone. Herschel, make her go away. She's meshuge."

I glance in the direction of my father, who has turned to see what the commotion is all about. He puts down the phone and laughs full-bellied. Thanks, Pop.

"Ta da da da da ... da ... da ... da ... da." Shawl-woman belts out the tune for all she's worth. Something catches in her throat and she coughs, leaning her weight on my shoulder as she chokes. I pat her on the back.

"You okay?" I search frantically for a nurse. Last thing I need is some old woman dying on my shoulder. The only nurse in sight is the one helping Mrs. Goldberg, who lies stretched out on the floor.

My knight in shining armour, Dov, appears from out of nowhere.

"Mrs. Rosenfeld," he scolds. "I told you, no dancing in the lobby. Come on, let's get you back in your chair." He winks at me. "I didn't know you could dance."

Together we help Mrs. Rosenfeld back to her chair. She plops down into it hard. Dov rubs her back.

"There. All better now?"

"Go away," she tells him. "Who needs you?"

She's forgotten all about Shlomo and me. Thank God.

"Go away," she repeats.

"You okay?" Dov asks me.

I smile. "I've had worse dances."

"She's meshuge," Bubbe tells Dov.

"Yes, Mrs. Rabinovitch. She has Alzheimer's. Like your husband had."

"My husband had the Old Timers," she agrees. "I still miss him," she tells me, her eyes filling with tears. "Sixty-five years we were married. I can't believe he's gone. I miss him. What can I do?"

"I know, Bubbe." I take her hand. "Thanks," I tell Dov.

He whisks away to tend to other duties.

A nurse announces over the loudspeaker that there will be finger painting commencing in the arts and crafts room. Finger painting? For seniors? I shudder at the horror and humour of it all. Is that what we come to in the end? Back to finger painting?

Bubbe and I sit in silence for a few minutes. She doesn't participate in any of the Home's programs. She thinks they are for the crazy ones, not for her.

"Look at your father, Herschel." We both turn toward the pay phone. Solly is still arguing with someone on the phone, waving his arm in the air, his unlit cigar stub clutched between thumb and forefinger.

Bubbe leans in close. "Tell me, doll. Is he working?"

"Sorta," I lie.

"He's working?" She's shocked. "Where's he working?"

"He's kinda in ... uh ... public relations," I strain.

"What?"

"It's kinda hard to explain."

"What, Tatelah? Speak up. I can't hear you."

As if on cue, Solly hangs up, saunters back over, sits beside Bubbe. Checks his watch. Bubbe turns to him. "Is it true, Solly?"

"What's that, Ma?"

"You're working?"

Solly looks about ready to choke. "Working?"

"You have a job?"

He glances at me. I smile innocently. "Yeah, sure. I got a job, Ma."

She pats his hand. "Okay, Solly. Okay."

Mrs. Rosenfeld has recovered from her coughing fit and has noticed my father. She lowers her shawl, exposing her brightly flowered housedress, and bats her eyes at him.

"Shlomo?"

NOMI'S BAD HAIR DAY

The morning sun streams into the living room and across my face, waking me. Last night I tended bar until closing, then cleaned up. Got home at four, too wired to sleep. With the three-hour time difference, it was far too late to call Julie. I'm taking on extra shifts to pay for all the long distance calls. Julie wants me to visit her in Toronto, but I can't afford the plane fare right now. She's getting impatient. We're constantly talking about our relationship, but we're still at an impasse. On Betty's couch, with the sound down low, I watched *I Love Lucy* reruns until five. I'm exhausted, not ready to face the world. I pull the covers over my head, sink back into a deep sleep. I dream of Julie. We are in her apartment in Toronto. Alone. Holding hands across the table at a candlelight dinner. She feeds me a forkful of pasta. The front door to her apartment bursts open. Betty drives inside the living room in her Super Shuttle van, knocking furniture and dishes all over the place. The racket is deafening: glass shattering, wood thumping, engine revving, Betty's booming voice above the din.

"Wake up, Nom. Time to get up."

"What?" I open my eyes. The real Betty leans over, shaking me.

"Time to get up. We'll be late."

"What?" I look around the room for broken dishes, for Betty's van. Oh. A dream. Thank God. What a mess. "What time is it?" I reach for my watch on the end table by my head.

"Time for coffee. Here." She thrusts a hot cup into my hand. It burns my finger.

"Ouch."

"Come on, Chester's picking us up in fifteen minutes."

"What?"

I squeeze my eyes shut, open them, focus. Betty's all decked out in her leather pants, a leather chest harness that exposes her breasts, silver nipple rings, motorcycle boots, leather cop hat. She's packing. There's a red handkerchief stuffed in her back left pocket — I never remember the handkerchief codes, so I don't know what that one stands for — studded leather wristband, a series of silver chains strung from her belt to her back pocket, and a small black whip slung through her leather belt. Betty's not officially an s/m dyke; she just likes to try a different look every year. This year she's going for leather. I have to admit, she looks fabulous.

"It's Gay Freedom Day, Nom," she says. "Remember?"

"Oh yeah." Patty's organized a float this year, and a booth for after the parade. I'm scheduled to ride on the float and then work a couple of shifts at Patty's booth. Yesterday it seemed like a good idea to catch a ride with Betty and Chester and get to the parade grounds early. Now, I'm not so sure. I sit up, sip my coffee. I'm tired and my head hurts.

"I'm done in the bathroom," Betty informs me as she sits heavily at the end of the sofa, leather pants creaking, chains rattling.

"What?"

"Go ahead, Nom. Get ready. We're leaving in ten minutes." She shifts in her seat, removes the whip from the back of her belt. "Ouch," she complains.

"Ten minutes?"

"Chester's picking us up here. It's Boys' Night Out." Betty tests the whip, cracking it in the air.

"It's hardly night." I gulp more coffee.

"Okay, Boys' *Morning* Out." She cracks the whip again.

I glare at Betty, grab my coffee, stagger to the bathroom.

Chester arrives right on time. For the occasion, she's wearing black leather chaps over blue jeans, a white tank top and a black leather vest. God knows where she got all the leather. Chester's more of a Gore-Tex-and-flannel kind of dyke. *Plaid* flannel.

"Looking good, girl." Betty spins Chester around to see from all angles.

Chester beams.

"Where'd you get all that?" I slip a T-shirt over my head. It's from last year's parade. Black with red lettering that reads "Gay by Nature, Proud by Choice." I step into a pair of black cutoff shorts.

Chester shrugs. "Stormy Leather."

"You actually bought all that?"

"Sure. Why not?" Chester looks down at herself.

"I don't know." I button up the fly of my shorts. "Just never seen you in leather."

"Don't you like it?" Chester looks crushed.

"Never mind her," Betty tells Chester. "She's a grump."

"I didn't get in until four." I defend my surly mood.

"Yeah, and then you watched *I Love Lucy* till five."

"I thought you were sleeping."

"Who could sleep with all the racket?"

"It was down low."

"Not low enough."

"Sorry."

"Bad enough I had to sleep alone ..." Betty says, then stops.

"Wait a second." Chester is shocked. "You were alone last night?"

Betty glares at Chester. "Yeah. So?"

"Nothing. Just never heard of you sleeping alone before," Chester concedes.

Betty removes her cap, runs a hand over her scalp. "I'm losing my touch," she says miserably.

"Betty ..." I step into my Docs, bend to tie the laces. "It's only the second time ..."

"Quiet." Betty clamps a hand tightly over my mouth. "Don't say it out loud. I don't want to jinx myself."

"Second time. Wow," says Chester.

"Shut up," Betty warns.

I knock Betty's arm off my mouth and stand up. "Okay, I'm ready. Let's go."

We pile into Chester's pale blue 1980 Honda Civic. It's rusty and falling apart, but it's the perfect size car for San Francisco. It can fit into the smallest parking space, or in a pinch, onto the sidewalk. Chester drives like a little old lady, steering wheel gripped tightly in two hands, crawling along slowly. She never runs a red light, won't turn left into traffic. She'll go around the block and make three right turns to avoid a left. She won't pass. She stops for pedestrians. She actually slows down when the light turns yellow. Cars behind us continually honk at her to hurry up, but Chester doesn't care. She ignores them all and creeps along slowly. It makes Betty crazy. But Chester won't let anyone else drive her car, claims it's only insured for her. Personally, I don't care. It's kind of relaxing. I lean back in my seat and think about Julie. I wish she were here beside me in the back seat, on our way to the San Francisco Gay Freedom Day Parade, with my best friends in the front.

The streets close to the parade route are all parked up. Chester circles the block slowly seven times.

"Go for the sidewalk," Betty instructs.

"You think it's okay?" Chester is leery.

"Sure. They never ticket on Pride Day," Betty assures her. "There." She points to a small space on the sidewalk ahead.

"Okay ..." Chester isn't entirely convinced but she goes for it anyway. Her car lumbers slowly over the curb and up onto the sidewalk, where she fits it between two motorcycles, pulls up the handbrake, turns off the ignition. The Honda's engine gurgles to a stop, belching a sickly blue-grey cloud of exhaust into the air. Passersby glare at us: rabid polluters. I smile from the back seat, innocently.

It's ten-thirty when we leave the car and walk three blocks to the beginning of the parade, where floats and contingents are lining up. It's going to be a hot day. The morning fog has been burned off by the sun. I'm glad I wore shorts but wish I'd brought a hat. My head already feels hot. I don't know how Betty and Chester are going to stand the heat in all that leather. There is a festive tone to the crowd all around us. Music blasts from all directions as people on floats and marching contingents jockey for position. Spectators stake out good spots along the parade route. A steady bass beat from a boy-bar float thumps heavily, vibrating from under the sidewalk like a slow, insidious low-level earthquake. We pass by a large group of leather dykes, who smile admiringly at Betty and Chester. They ignore me. Maybe I should have borrowed something leather from Betty. At least I thought to wear black — even if it's one hundred percent cotton. Betty saunters over to the dykes, her flirtatious grin plastered on her face. Chester and I wait awkwardly.

"Hi," a long-legged woman in beaded cornrows, a tight leather miniskirt, black fishnet stockings and not much else, says to Betty.

Wasting no time on small talk, Betty backs Miss Mini up against the brick wall of a building, runs one hand up her fishnet stockings and dives in for a kiss. Miss Mini throws her arms around Betty's neck and they kiss wildly, as the group of leather dykes cheers them on and whistles. I don't know if Betty is previously acquainted with Miss Mini or if we are witnessing a spontaneous pickup. Either way, it's spectacular. Real-life dyke drama. In the flesh.

Chester watches wide-eyed, shaking her head. "How does she do it?"

I shrug. "You know Betty."

"Yeah. Boy."

"Yeah. And she's worried about losing her touch."

"Wish I could lose my touch like that."

Miss Mini winds one leg behind Betty's. Hands grope everywhere. They look like they're about to fall to the dirty sidewalk at any second, rip off all their leather and fuck madly right here on the street, moaning and screaming their ecstasy for all the world to see. One of Miss Mini's friends — a butch dressed in leather shorts, high-top runners, black tank top, leather cap — waltzes up behind Betty and grinds her crotch into Betty's backside. Betty glances back. The look in her eyes can only be described as horror. Betty pushes hard at the butch, who stumbles backward.

"Hey."

Betty untangles from Miss Mini. Whispers something in her ear.

The butch stomps closer to Betty. "Whadja do that for?"

Miss Mini reaches into her cleavage, extracts a black marker, writes something on the inside of Betty's palm, kisses Betty lightly on the mouth and smiles. Betty turns and saunters back toward me and Chester.

"I don't do threesomes," Betty tells the butch over her shoulder.

"I oughtta deck you one," the butch tells Betty, although it's a ridiculous idea. Betty is three times her size.

"No need. I'm outta here." Betty smiles at the small butch and joins us. "Well," she tells us, "great parade so far. What do you guys think?"

"Terrific," I grunt.

"You're inspiring," Chester gushes. "I don't know how you do it."

"Come on, guys." In a great mood, Betty throws an arm around each of our shoulders and steers us down closed-to-traffic Market Street in search of Patty's float. Patty, Robert and I spent the last couple of days decorating Patty's black Jeep Cherokee. On either side we taped a large sign that reads "Patty's Place," with a drawing of her signature pink martini glass with an olive. Robert and Spencer covered the rest of the jeep in sequins and glitter. "To make it festive," Robert justified.

"Looks like a goddamn drag queen's dressing room," Patty complained.

"It looks festive," Robert repeated.

Patty splurged on the rental of a small flatbed trailer, which is attached to the back of her jeep. On the flatbed, we anchored a portable bar with stools, and a mini-pool table. Guido, a whiz with electronics, hooked up a huge set of speakers to the jeep's CD deck. Just like the larger bar floats, we'll be pumping loud music throughout the parade.

"'Bout time you slackers showed up. I've been here since the beginning of time," Patty barks, cigarette dangling from the side of her lip, as we approach the float. For the occasion, Patty wears a leather vest over her white T-shirt and black jeans. "Come on, you guys. Hop up."

Guido's already in her position in the driver's seat of Patty's jeep. Patty stands behind the bar. Betty and I take our positions on bar stools. Chester is going to pretend to play pool. Robert and Spencer stand by the cardboard jukebox, where they will dance. AJ's supposed to play pool with Chester, but she's late.

"Goddamn it," Patty curses, jumping from the flatbed. I watch as she walks to the side of the jeep. The sign on one side has fallen off. "Damn tape won't hold. We need some of that invisible fishing line to tie it down. Rabinovitch!"

"Okay, okay. I'm going."

"Here." Patty reaches into her wallet, hands me twenty dollars.

I trudge back up Market Street toward Castro, hoping like hell that Cliff's Hardware isn't closed for the parade. Behind Patty's float I pass the dykes of colour contingent, the Native American group and Black and White Men Together. The AIDS groups go on forever: The Shanti Project, Open Hand, AIDS San Francisco, AIDS Oakland, AIDS Sacramento, AIDS East Bay. The men's bars have extravagant floats that dwarf Patty's little rented flatbed, filled with dozens of cute young men wearing next to nothing, ready to bump and grind to the disco lined up on their portable CD players attached to huge speakers. There is a city cable car with a sign on front that reads "Diesel Dykes." Lesbian bus drivers in uniform dangle from the sides. Behind the Diesel Dykes stands a small group of butches carrying a sign that reads, "Women who have trouble getting into women's washrooms ..." A sexy red convertible filled with femmes in slinky dresses, garters and stockings follows behind under a banner, "... And the women who love them."

The Gay and Lesbian Business Association contingent are dressed in skimpy shorts with ties around their necks and briefcases by their sides. They are practising their parade plan — using the briefcases like batons and dancing in unison like a Broadway chorus line. I smile at them as I pass. My early morning funk is lifting. I'm starting to feel excited about the day.

I return with the fishing line just in time for Guido to tie Patty's sign in place, and the parade begins. AJ runs over at the last second, hops up onto the float and joins Chester at the minipool table. She is out of breath from running. From my position at the bar on the float, I throw down Patty's Place matchbooks. The energy from the crowd is infectious. I join Betty and the others as we bop on the float to Guido's mix tape of dance music.

"Oh my God!" Betty's eyes go wide. She's spotted someone.

"What?" I crane my neck, try to find whoever she sees in the crowds.

"It's Mona," Betty says.

"Mona?" Chester questions.

"Her boss," I explain. "Where?"

"Oh my God. Over there." Betty points down to the street spectators, and moves behind Chester. I've never seen her nervous around a woman before.

"Which one is she?"

Betty peeks out from behind Chester. "The gorgeous one."

"Which one?"

"There," Betty says, "with the red balloon. She's wearing turquoise spandex."

"Oh." I spot a thirty-something woman with a round face, big brown eyes, high cheekbones, cropped kinky hair. She is quite lovely. Betty peeks out at her from behind Chester as we pass. I've never seen her like this. It's unnerving.

"Oh God," Betty groans.

"You really like her, huh?" I suggest.

"Oh boy, Nomi. What am I gonna do?"

"Didn't you say she's straight?"

"Yeah."

I shake my head. "She don't look so straight to me."

"You think?"

After the parade I volunteer for the first shift at the booth.

"Okay," Patty agrees, "I'll spell you off in a couple hours, okay?"

"Sure."

"I gotta see what the competition is up to," Patty says as she heads toward the row of booths.

"See you later, Nom." Betty waves, eyes everywhere. She's on the lookout for Mona, or Miss Mini or any number of women she currently has the hots for. AJ, Guido and Chester tag along behind, hoping no doubt for a taste of Betty's leftovers.

The time goes quickly behind the booth. I pour mini-mugs of dealcoholized beer, which I hand out to people and tell them about Patty's Place. Lots of regulars stop by for the free drink.

"First time Patty's ever offered anything free," one of them grumbles.

"There's always free peanuts at the pub," I remind her.

"Oh yeah." She helps herself to another near-beer.

In the background, on the lawn outside City Hall, I can hear political speeches being delivered. Every now and then the crowd cheers. There must be half a million people at the parade this year. The streets and the lawn of city hall are packed. There are huge lineups everywhere. For the porta-potties. At the food booths. For the pay phone. Men have stripped out of their shirts. Some women are topless, breasts bared to the wind. The scent of sunscreen floats in the warm air. Every now and then I smell the sweet skunky aroma of marijuana, mixed with tobacco smoke. Patty's booth reeks of beer, even though it's fake. Eight-foot-tall-in-their-heels drag queens wander by, sweltering inside ball gowns and makeup.

Carla, an attractive femme who sometimes hangs out at Patty's, bellies up to my booth. The scent of her perfume wafts over me.

"I'll have a martini, Nomi." Carla flashes serious brown eyes at me. "Hold the olives," she adds.

"Oh. Sorry, no real drinks today. Just fake beer."

"Oh." She picks up a mug, sips. "So," she leans over the counter, close to me. "How are you, Nomi?"

Is she flirting with me? "Okay." I grab my rag, wipe down the counter.

"You look very ... handsome in that ... T-shirt."

"Oh, this?" She *is* flirting with me. "It's from last year."

"Well, it looks great on you."

"Thanks." What am I going to do? I can't have a woman flirting with me. Where's Betty? Maybe she can take Carla off my hands. Where was Carla when I needed her? Where was she last year, before I met Julie, after Sapphire dumped me and I felt like the biggest loser on the face of the earth. Where was she then?

"So, what time are you off shift?" She reaches forward, touches my arm.

How am I going to get rid of her without being rude?

"Uh, never really."

"What?"

"I'm never really off shift." What am I saying? It doesn't even make sense.

She looks at me strangely. "What do you mean, Nomi?"

"Oh, you know." I furiously wipe the counter again. "Work work work. Always working." Oh God. I'm such a nerd. I don't have a clue how to pick up a woman. Or how to get rid of one.

"You're working at the booth for the whole day?"

"Yep. That's me." I turn my back to her, busy myself with straightening the empty booze bottles on the shelf.

"Oh." She drains her drink. "Well, I guess I'll see you later then."

"What was that?" I pretend to be deliriously interested in a fingerprint on the mirror, which I wipe meticulously.

"I said, maybe I'll see you later."

"Uh huh." I keep my back to her. In my peripheral vision I see Carla wandering off. She looks sad and confused. I replay the scene in my mind. Did I say something to lead her on? God, I'm a heartbreaker, without even trying.

When Patty relieves me an hour later, I'm exhausted. The lack of sleep has caught up with me. I wander back to Chester's car. The lock on the passenger side is broken, so her car is never locked. I crawl into the back seat, open the windows wide to let in some air, curl up and fall asleep. The thumping music and sounds of people talking and laughing don't bother me. I sleep right through it all.

I wake up a few hours later feeling somewhat refreshed. The whole afternoon has passed. It's almost six o'clock, time for my last shift at the booth. I lean forward in the car, tilt the rearview mirror toward me. My hair is flattened down on one side of my face and sticking straight up on top. I spit into my hand, try to puff up the flattened part and smooth down the top. It's not working. I need hair gel. Mousse. Brylcreem. Olive oil. Anything. Oh God. I look like Eraserhead. Frantically, I pop open Chester's glove compartment. There's a map of Los Angeles, a tire pressure gauge, a pack of cinnamon gum. I take a piece of gum for my breath, unwrap it, pop it into my mouth. It's hard and stale, but the spicy cinnamon is a welcome relief from the jungle breath I woke up with. Come on, Chester, don't you keep an emergency tube of gel in your car? I find a plastic spatula — why does she have a spatula in her car? A book of New Age spiritual affirmations, a tampon and a coupon for Mr. Muffler that expired three years ago. No gel. No mousse. No luck. I spit into my hands again and furiously run them through my hair, trying my best to look human. It's a little less flat on the side. It still looks pretty bad, but I give up and walk toward Patty's booth. I'm not sure if I'm imagining it, but it seems like people are staring at me.

Robert is standing behind the booth, flamboyantly pouring a mini-mug of fake beer for a large man, who is wearing leather chaps with nothing underneath. His big white butt protrudes proudly from the back of his chaps. I avert my eyes. Last thing I want to see fresh from my nap is a large man's naked butt. As I approach the booth, Robert's hand flies to his mouth. He stifles a laugh.

"Good God, Nomi. What rock did you just crawl out from under?" he blasts. Several heads turn in my direction.

"What?" I squeeze my way in behind the booth, beside him. There's not much room for both of us.

"Your hair, my dear. Oh, it's a fright. An absolute fright."

"I fell asleep." Self-consciously I rub my hands through my hair.

"No, no. You must let me," Robert shrieks. "Sit down, girlfriend."

"It's okay."

"Don't be ridiculous, Nomi. Sit," he orders. "Excuse me, honey," he tells the leatherman.

"I'll see you later, Robert." The leatherman wanders off.

"Now, let me see. Let me see." Robert looks me up and down, shaking his head as if I've done something terribly wrong. He bends and fishes in the large leather bag he always carries. "Ah, here we are." He pulls out a can of hair mousse. Of course he would have some.

"Thank you," I tell him.

"Not at all, Nomi. I just don't know what you'd do without me."

"You got that right, Robert."

He fusses with my hair, massaging in the mousse, fluffing and arranging my hair. It feels good. I close my eyes and sink into the feeling.

"What the hell's this?" Patty's voice booms. I open my eyes. "A massage parlour? What are you two characters up to now? Can't I leave you alone for a second?"

"Puh-lease, Patty. You should thank me." Robert is offended. "Nomi was having a bad hair moment. Do you want her representing the pub looking like a lesbian Eraserhead?"

So I did look like Eraserhead. Terrific. I'm so embarrassed. I feel my cheeks flush.

"She really looked that bad?" Patty asks.

"Worse," Robert confirms.

Patty leans across the counter, peers at me. "Whadja do? Fall asleep?"

"Yeah."

"Well, no sleeping on the job," she announces.

"I was off shift," I defend myself.

"There," Robert declares. "You're gorgeous now, Nomi."

"Well, let's not go overboard," Patty mutters.

I stand. "Thanks, Robert."

"Don't mention it, Nomi. There's not much of that dreadful imitation beer left, Patty," Robert says.

"What?" Patty squeezes behind the counter beside me. With the three of us back here, it's ridiculously crowded. "There should have been enough for the whole day."

"People were thirsty in this heat," Robert says.

"They're supposed to be samples. We're not here to quench people's thirst." She bends down, checks the dwindling supply.

"Nomi! There you are." Betty rushes over, holding her cell phone up in front of her. "It's for you, Nom. Your mother."

"What?"

She says it's an emergency." Betty hands me the phone.

"Hello, Ma?"

"It's your grandmother, Nomi," my mother says gravely.

"What?"

"She's been rushed to the hospital."

"Oh no. What is it?"

"Who knows? Old age. Heart attack, maybe. She collapsed."

"She collapsed?"

"Right during bingo."

"Oh my God."

"And her card won."

"What?"

"She stood up, yelled BINGO and then she collapsed."

"Oh my God."

"She won a makeup bag."

"What?"

"At bingo."

"Oh."

"Can you come right home? We don't know what's gonna be." This is my mother's euphemism for "your grandmother's probably dying."

"Um, I guess." I can't really afford a plane ticket, but I'll just have to charge it to my credit card.

"Murray will pay for your flight."

"He will?"

"Of course. Your brothers will pick you up at the airport."

"Okay." In a daze, I hang up the phone, hand it to Betty. I feel scared. Sad. And at the same time excited, aware that if I go to Toronto I'll be able to see Julie. My chest is ready to explode from all the feelings.

"Nom?" Betty peers at my face.

"It's my grandmother. I gotta go home," I tell Patty. "As soon as I can get a flight."

HENRY'S PARENTS

It's another sweltering day in the city. The humidity level is through the roof. I showered last night before bed and was sweating again five minutes later. In the night I woke to drenched sheets and panicked, worried I was having AIDS-related night sweats. But Roger was sweating just as heavily. We had the bedroom window wide open, but it didn't help much. Earlier, Roger pulled two fans out of our storage locker downstairs. We set up one in our bedroom, gave the other to Solly. We're going to need another for the living room. The air is so still, it's thick.

Tomorrow is the Gay Pride Day march. I'll be marching with ACTOUT. Everyone's going to be there. Julie, all the Davids, Greta, Raven, Ed, Simon. Even Roger has agreed to march with us. We're expecting a lot of attention this year because of the article in the *Star*. Today I'm planning to rest up. The lesbians are taking over Church Street today in the annual dyke march. I can already hear them from the street, yelling and chanting.

Solly and I sit across from each other at the dining room table. He's eating his morning kippers. I'm sipping my first coffee.

"What the hell's all that noise?"

I stifle a laugh. "The Dyke March," I say with an air of seriousness.

"What?"

"You heard me."

He stares at me, stands, goes to the window, looks out. There probably isn't much to see on Alexander Street, other than small groups of dykes making their way to Church Street. "Do you people march for everything?"

"Just about."

He sits back down across from me. "When's Roger off shift?" he asks.

I stare at him, wonder what's up. He's never shown any interest in Roger's work schedule before.

"Uh ..." I think about it. "Seven."

"Good," says Solly. "'Cause I made reservations for eight o'clock."

"What?"

"We're all going out for dinner. It's high time."

"We?"

He shakes his head. The answer is obvious to him. "You and Roger. Me and your mother."

"What? What's going on with you and my mother?" Are they still ... dating? This is starting to get a little ridiculous.

"Calm down, will ya, Henry. You get that from your mother, you know?"

"What?"

"The two of you. Nervous wrecks. You gotta learn to roll with life's punches."

"I know how to roll."

"And wear a tie. We're going to a nice place." Solly stands, clears his dish from the table, plops it in the sink. "Up the street. It's called Alice's, or something like that. I made reservations."

I eye him suspiciously. "Who's paying?"

He smiles. "You are."

"I have no money."

"Don't worry. I'll pay you back. In a few weeks. I'm expecting a windfall." He stuffs a cigar in his mouth, stands by the balcony door.

"A windfall?"

"That's right. And don't ask me about it, 'cause I can't tell you anything more. I only told you so you wouldn't worry so much about the money." With one foot on the balcony, the other in the living room, he lights his cigar.

From the street we hear a chorus of women. "Two four six eight. How do you know your mother's straight?"

"My mother's straight!" Solly yells down to them. "What the hell kind of thing is that to say?"

"Pop, go outside with the cigar."

"I am outside."

"All the way." I cough and wave my hands at the thick, putrid smoke pouring into the apartment.

"See?" He steps outside. "Just like Belle. Excitable." He closes the sliding door. "My mother's straight!" he yells again.

"I'm tired, Henry," Roger whines as I pick out a nice tie for him to wear. "I don't want to go out."

"Just for dinner, Rog. Please." I decide on the blue tie with a subtle diamond pattern.

"And I have to get up early again tomorrow."

"We won't stay out late. I promise."

"Shirley was off sick today, and if she's out tomorrow, that means I'm covering front desk." I untie the string on Roger's uniform, slide his pants to his ankles.

"I know. But listen, we have to go."

He steps out of his pants. I toss him his dress slacks. Dutifully he puts them on. "Why do we have to go?"

"I gotta find out what's going on with Solly and Belle. It's driving me crazy." I find a good shirt for Roger in the closet.

Roger zips his fly. "Why don't you just ask them?"

"What? Don't be crazy. I can't just ask them." I hold out his shirt. He slips his arms in. I button it for him, slide the tie under his collar. Roger puts his hands on my butt.

"Why don't we let them go out without us? We'd have the place to ourselves." He kisses my neck.

"Hold still." I knot his tie.

There is a knock on the bedroom door. "Come on. Hurry up in there," my father yells.

Roger removes his hands from me.

"Okay, Pop. In a minute."

"I have to be in bed by eleven," Roger warns.

"I know." I grab our jackets. Hope like hell the restaurant is air-conditioned.

The front door to Slack Alice's on Church Street is wide open when we approach. In the front section, a chorus line of topless, rowdy dykes in tight black spandex shorts bump and grind on top of the long black veneer bar. On the sound system, Melissa Etheridge is screaming for someone to bring her some water. It looks like the dancing dykes could also use some hosing down. My mother and father stop in their tracks just inside the bar and stare. I catch Roger's eye and try not to laugh.

"What the hell's this?" Solly turns and asks Roger and me. "It's obscene."

"It's the Dyke March party, Pop. Maybe we should go somewhere else," I suggest.

"Oh, let's stay." My mother surprises me. "Look," she says, pointing, "it's quieter in the back."

"You wanna stay?" Solly is as surprised at my mother's sudden liberalism as I am.

"Come on, Solly. It's Pride Weekend. Get in the spirit," she tells him.

I stare at her. How did my mother know it was Pride Weekend?

"I read the paper, Henry," she says, reading my mind. "I read books. I watch 'Ellen.' I'm not as square as you think I am." She saunters past my father and marches up to the maître d' to enquire about our table.

"Henry was always delicate," Belle tells Roger when we are seated at a table in the back. "Even as a little boy." The dykes are still dancing on the tabletops up front, but it's actually quiet enough to have a conversation back here.

A hunky waiter serves us homemade sourdough rolls to start. We're waiting for our salads. Solly is drinking a Jack Daniel's on

the rocks. Belle is sipping a whisky sour. Roger and I are drinking red wine — a Chilean Cabernet Sauvignon, very dry.

"Ma." She's embarrassing me.

"He never liked sports," Belle continues, buttering a roll.

"I'm not surprised," says Roger, taking my hand under the
table.

"He preferred to cook."

"Well, I'm glad. He does all the cooking in our house." Roger
squeezes my hand.

"Listen, now we know better. But in those days, we thought
he wasn't normal." Belle bites into her bread. "We were worried
what he would become."

"In those days," Solly continues, "it was terrible to be a queer.
The worst thing."

"It's still not a picnic, Pop," I say.

"But," Roger steps in, "we've got it a lot better than the generation before us."

"That's for sure."

"We didn't know any better." Solly drains his drink, looks for
the waiter.

"What we're trying to say to you boys is ..." Belle says.

"We're sorry," Solly finishes her sentence.

"Sorry?"

"Yeah, you know." Solly spots the waiter, snaps his fingers.

"That we've never done this before," Belle says.

"This?"

"Invited the two of you to dinner."

I take a big gulp of my wine. It's not that I don't appreciate their
sentiment, but the whole scene is overwhelming. Sitting here with
my hand in Roger's under the table, across from my parents, who
seem to be together again after twenty-five years of divorce.

"We appreciate it, don't we, Henry?" Roger says.

"Yeah, I guess." I reach for a dinner roll.

Belle stares at me. "Why are you eating with your left hand,
Henry?"

I glance at my right hand entwined in Roger's on his lap.

"Uh, 'cause my right hand's busy," I tell her.

"Oh." She gets it, stuffs a huge piece of bread into her mouth.

"There you are, Solly." A voice booms across the restaurant, even over the dyke commotion up front.

We all turn. It's Lou Greenberg, dressed in his rumpled work clothes. Dark trousers, short-sleeved white shirt. Cap.

"Lou," Solly says. "What the hell you doing here? We're having a family moment."

"I know, Solly. I'm sorry. Evening, Belle." He tips his cap. "Hiya, Henry." He nods to Roger. "It's an emergency."

"What'sa matter?"

"Your sister got the dispatch to phone me. On account of I always know your whereabouts, Solly."

"I know that, Lou," Solly says, annoyed.

"She's been trying to reach you since eight."

"Awright already, Lou. Get to the point."

"It's your mother."

"My mother?"

"She collapsed."

"What?"

"Oh my God," says Belle.

"Come on. I'll drive you to the hospital," Lou offers.

"I have my car," Belle says, standing.

"Uh ..." Lou says, looking around as if for the first time.

"What'sa matter, Lou?"

"Is this like a strip joint?"

"Never mind, Lou. Get moving." My father stands, pushes Lou toward the front.

In a daze we all stand and rush to the front of the restaurant, just as the waiter arrives at our table with our second round. Roger hands the hostess some cash to cover our drinks, and we follow Lou outside.

Bubbe is lying unconscious on a gurney in the hallway of the emergency ward. It's a busy ward, with doctors, nurses and orderlies rushing purposefully by. Worried relatives loiter around patients lined up against walls and in the hall. Every few minutes, a nurse or doctor is paged on the PA system. Two paramedics race down the hall with a person on a stretcher. I stand by Bubbe and watch her. She looks even tinier than usual. Her white hair is messy. She is hooked up to an IV drip. There is a heart monitor attached to her chest. The monitor shows a steady green line that beeps once every couple of seconds. I glance at Solly. He looks worried. His younger sister, Aunt Shell, has been here for a couple of hours.

"We don't know what happened," Aunt Shell says. "I'm glad you're here, Solly. Belle ..." She surveys my mother suspiciously, wondering what the hell is going on. "I wasn't expecting to see you."

"We were out for dinner," Solly explains.

"Oh." Aunt Shell looks at me, trying to figure it out. She probably hasn't seen Belle in years. "Henry." Aunt Shell kisses my cheek.

"You remember Roger," I prompt.

"Course I do." Aunt Shell surprises me by leaning in and kissing Roger's cheek.

A doctor approaches.

"I'm her son," Solly tells him. "What happened?"

The doctor consults his clipboard. "We're not sure. Her heart is strong and steady, so we've ruled out heart attack. Possibly a stroke."

"Oh my God," says Belle.

"Could be she just fainted."

"Fainted?"

"She's not in any immediate danger," the doctor assures us. "We're moving her to a room shortly."

Roger steps forward. "I'm a registered nurse, doctor. Is there anything else you can tell us?"

The doctor surveys Roger for a second, nods, then consults his clipboard once more. "I've put her on a saline solution. She's terribly dehydrated. As if she hasn't had any water in weeks. Does she drink water?"

We glance at each other, shrug.

"As you can see, we're monitoring her heart. I've scheduled a CT scan for tomorrow. We've taken blood. She's on a catheter. A nurse will be collecting urine for testing. Keep a watch on her vitals. That's all we can do for now."

"Of course. Thank you, doctor," Roger says politely.

The doctor nods and strides off.

"What the hell did he say?" Solly asks Roger.

"A CT scan. That's how they can tell if she's had a stroke. It's like an x-ray of the brain. The blood test is routine. They'll check her for infectious diseases, any blood problems. Watch for any changes in her condition."

"You see?" Aunt Shell says. "I'm always telling her to drink more water."

"How come she's out here in the hall?" Solly cuts in.

"Staff shortages, probably. It's the same everywhere," Roger explains.

"She won't drink any water," Aunt Shell continues.

"I'll move her to a room myself." Solly grabs the end of the bed as if to push it.

Roger gently touches his arm. "Let me see what I can do," he offers.

I smile at him in gratitude.

"All she drinks is coffee. Coffee, coffee, coffee."

"All right, Shell."

"Morning, noon and night."

"We get it, Shell."

"I've been telling her for years."

"What's the difference?"

"You gotta drink water. Am I right, Henry?"

Roger approaches the nurses' desk.

Outside Bubbe's hospital room, we wait as two nurses move her from the gurney to a bed. As they leave the room, one points to a sign on the door.

"Two visitors at a time only, please. This is Intensive Care."

The second they turn the corner, we all rush into the room. Bubbe is still unconscious. No one knows what to do. Aunt Shell sits on a chair at Bubbe's bedside. My father sits beside his sister. I stand on the other side of the bed, between Roger and my mother. We watch the heart monitor and wait. There are three other women sharing Bubbe's room, separated by pull-across curtains. Bubbe's bed is by the door. Against the wall sits a nurse's cart, filled with green hospital gowns, sheets, blankets, latex gloves — maybe I should steal some for Julie, I know how crazy lesbians are for latex gloves — wooden tongue depressors, washcloths, bottles and jars of Vaseline and body lotion. The air smells of disinfectant. I shiver involuntarily. I've been in too many hospital rooms lately. Wonder if the next time it'll be mine.

When my twin brothers rush into the room a while later, I am shocked to see them. My parents both look surprised too. Larry and Moe are not known for being family-minded.

"We came as soon as we could," Larry says.

"I had to wait for my assistant manager to show up," says Moe. He manages a sleazy video arcade on Yonge Street. Larry is an insurance agent. In their early thirties, the twins are both unmarried, decidedly heterosexual, average-looking men with the beginnings of potbellies, thinning hair and bland personalities. Belle approaches her sons and kisses each on the cheek, leaving bright red lipstick marks in her wake.

"Hiya, Pop," Larry says. "Henry," he nods at me.

"You guys remember Roger," I say.

Roger sticks out his hand. "Hi, Larry." How he can tell them apart is beyond me. I can, but I've known them their whole lives. Most people can't. My brothers are the kind of twins who finish each other's sentences, have the same haircuts and the same mustaches they've had since they could grow a decent one at eighteen. Although they don't wear identical clothes, they dress in the same style: off-the-rack, ill-fitting suits with too-tight trousers, pinstriped shirts and garish ties. I notice each one has the beginnings of a bald spot on the top of his head. My father and I both have full heads of hair.

"Boys," says Aunt Shell, "it's been too long. You should call your aunt once in a while."

"Well ..." begins Moe.

"We're pretty busy ..." interjects Larry.

"With work and all," finishes Moe.

"Yeah," says Larry. "Work."

"Still, you can have a little time for your family," Aunt Shell counters.

Larry and Moe shrug.

"What happened to her?" Larry asks.

"She collapsed," Aunt Shell reports. "During bingo."

"At the Home?"

"Yeah, and she won."

"What?"

"Bingo. She won."

"That's terrible," says Moe. And for once in my life I agree with my brother.

"Did anyone call your sister?" my mother asks suddenly.

"I called. I called," confirms Aunt Shell. "And your sister-in-law," she tells Solly.

"Faygie?"

"I thought her kids should know. Just because Harry's not here ..." Aunt Shell doesn't finish her sentence. Nomi's father Harry died suddenly two years ago, of a heart attack. He was my father's kid brother.

"There she is," Solly announces as Sherry runs into the room.

"I just got the message," Sherry says, out of breath.

"It's okay, sweetheart." My mother opens her arms to hug my sister.

"I was out at a movie with a friend," Sherry says.

"A boyfriend?" my mother asks hopefully.

"A friend, Mother," Sherry returns with an edge. "What are you doing here?"

Belle gestures toward Solly. "We were out for dinner."

Sherry looks at me, confused.

"Hi, Henry, Roger." Sherry kisses each of us.

"Hi, kiddo." My sister's always been the best in our family at treating Roger right.

"Hi, Dad." Sherry walks around to the other side of the bed and kisses Solly on the cheek. He's not really her father. Sherry was conceived while Solly was in jail the first time. Belle claims the father left town the second he found out she was pregnant. She never heard from him again. All Sherry knows about him is that his name was Stanley, he was a minor league pitcher and, in Belle's words, "he had big bedroom eyes, but when it came right down to it, he was a louse." When Solly got out of jail, Sherry was a little kid. She just started calling him Dad along with me and Larry and Moe. Solly never told her to stop. I don't think she even found out the truth until she was a teenager.

We all turn and watch Bubbe sleep. Solly reaches into his pocket and slips an unlit cigar stub into his mouth. One of the twins pulls a bag of mixed nuts from his jacket pocket and passes it around. I share a pack of Smarties I bought earlier. Belle rummages in her purse until she finds a stainless steel emery board, which she uses to file her nails. Roger walks to the end of Bubbe's bed and studies her chart. It is standing-room only at this point. A nurse bustles into the room and practically faints when she sees how many people are crowded around Bubbe's bed. She stops just inside the doorway, her eyes wide and fierce.

"This will not do," she states. She points to the sign on the door, tapping it with one long finger for emphasis. "Only two visitors permitted at any one time. This is Intensive Care, people." She commands respect with the stern tone of her voice. We all stare at the floor, guilty.

"I've got some paperwork to do tonight anyway," Larry offers. "You coming?" he asks Moe.

"Yeah. My ride." He points at Larry, shrugs.

"I've been here a while," Aunt Shell says. "I left Jerry at home." She squeezes past Solly toward the door.

"I better be going," Roger says. "I'm on early shift," he explains.

"Henry, Roger, you boys need a lift?" my mother offers. "I've got to get home."

"I'll drop them off," Larry says.

Everyone stares at him. It is unusual for Larry to be generous.

"I'm going right by there," he explains.

"Okay," I agree recklessly, although it could be a big mistake. "What about you, Pop?"

"You go ahead. Think I'll stay for a while," he says.

Belle looks disappointed, but she plasters on a fake smile as we all leave the room.

Sherry takes the seat beside Pop, a vigil of two.

NOMI'S STEPFATHER

The plane to Toronto is so full I get a middle seat. I'm crammed in between a beer-bellied salesman and a hulking college student. Both have firmly planted their arms on the middle seat armrests. There is nowhere to rest my arms. Do they think I have no arms? The feminist in me feels like making an issue of it, or at least slugging them. But I opt for a more subtle approach. I squeeze my elbows against theirs, try to pry them apart a little bit, so there's an inch of armrest for me. The guys barely notice. I shove my face into a bestseller I picked up at the airport newsstand and vow to ignore everyone except the flight attendant for the whole trip.

We sit on the runway for forty-five minutes before the pilot announces we are next in line. I throw away all manners, push my way farther onto the armrests so I can grip the edges, and prepare for takeoff. I'm a nervous wreck. I don't like flying, especially takeoff and landing. I don't like the queasy feeling in my belly, and frankly, I don't see how such a large, heavy metal object can possibly stay up in the sky. My imagination works in overdrive. Images of crash scenes flash through my mind as the engine revs. I can picture us tearing down the runway, lifting off just a few feet, only to have the tail end catch on the tarmac. The plane flips over and lands hard on the roof, crushing most of us on impact. Another image bombards me. We take off and rise thirty thousand feet in the air, only to crash into another plane and plummet to earth at a breakneck speed. The potbellied businessman grabs onto me for dear life, screaming for his mother. The college student passes out, and his two-hundred-and-fifty-pound body lands on top of me. I'm trapped under his weight, unable to move as we spiral to earth.

"Put your seat up, please." I'm snapped out of my daydream by the flight attendant.

"What?"

"In an upright position, please. For takeoff. Excuse me." She leans over the businessman and hits the button to pop my seat upright.

"Sorry." I smile.

Takeoff isn't nearly as dramatic as in my fears. As I grit my teeth, the back of my head smashed against the chair, the armrest gripped tightly in my hands, we lift off gently and smoothly into the afternoon sky. As the plane levels I release my grip.

"Scared of flying?" the businessman asks me.

"A bit," I admit.

"I travel all the time. You get used to it. I'm in sales," he tells me.

Oh no. I hope he's not going to talk to me for the whole flight.

"Do you live in Toronto?" he asks.

"Nope." I give him the shortest answer possible to discourage small talk. The college student stares out the window.

"I'm from Toronto. Well, Mississauga, really, but that's almost Toronto. I sell vitamins. Big market in San Francisco. Those California fruits and nuts are crazy for vitamins."

"Really?" Oh great. Do I detect a note of homophobia?

"Sure. They lap it up. I do a lot of business there."

"Well," I tell him, "I'm a California fruit."

"What? Oh. Oh. Listen, I'm not prejudiced or anything."

"Course not."

"I didn't mean it like that," he backpedals.

"Right."

"I know a lot about people, you know. You got to in my line of business."

I need a drink. I crane my neck, searching for the flight attendant. When will the drink cart arrive?

"For instance ..."

Oh God. I have to stop him. "Listen," I say holding up my book, "I'm going to read now."

"Oh. Oh sure. Go ahead."

Mr. Vitamin shuts up, leafs through the in-flight magazine he finds in the seat pouch. Looks around. "That a Mac?" he asks the man across the aisle, who is working on a laptop computer. "Or a PC?" Why don't people like this bring a book?

When the drink cart finally arrives, I order a vodka and tomato juice to settle my nerves. While we're flying over Ohio, I get a funny feeling in my belly. I'm convinced my grandmother has just died. I glance out the tiny airplane window. It's completely dark outside. I can only see the reflection of the college student in the window, but as I'm staring, I see a shadow pass by, and I'm positive the shadow is my grandmother's spirit. My eyes fill with tears. They drip silently down my cheeks. I should have left sooner, I berate myself. I should have gone to the airport last night as soon as my mother phoned, or even early this morning. If only I could have said goodbye. I've always been close to Bubbe. We've always had an emotional bond. Like she can look right into my soul and know what's going on. It's one of my biggest regrets about living in San Francisco. Especially since Bubbe now lives in the Home. If I lived in Toronto I could visit her more often. If I lived in Toronto, I could be with Julie. We could even live together. Not at first. It would be better to live separately and date for a while first. Maybe that's what went wrong with Sapphire. I moved to San Francisco and moved in with her right away.

By the baggage area in the airport, I feel a sense of doom as I see my brother Joshua walking toward me. I don't want him to confirm what I already know — that my grandmother is dead. I take a deep breath and walk toward him. I stand on tiptoes to hug him. Josh is eight inches taller than me, really good-looking, dark eyes, curly hair, a perfect body, like a Greek god. Josh plays guitar in a rock band. He's barely making a living, but his band is starting to get more gigs in clubs. They're working on their first CD.

"Nomi, I'm so glad you made it," he says, smiling.

"Is she ... ?" I can't bring myself to say it out loud.

He shakes his head. "Still out cold."

"You mean she's still alive?"

He nods. "Unconscious."

"Oh good. Can we go see her now?"

Josh frowns. "Visiting hours are over at eight."

It's eight-thirty. I knew I should have come sooner. "You don't think we could sneak in anyway?"

"She's in Intensive Care. The nurses in that ward are like sergeant majors. There's no way we'd make it."

"No way?"

"You should see the nurses. You can go in the morning. Anytime after eight. Come on, let's get your bags." He nudges me forward.

I hold up my knapsack. "This is it."

"Great. Then let's get out of here."

It's hot and muggy in Toronto. I strip off my leather jacket, toss it into the back seat of the car, my other brother Izzy's car — a late-seventies model Pontiac, a big boat of a car, rusted in places, but it runs like a charm. A mechanical whiz, Izzy has rebuilt the engine several times with spare parts he's found in junkyards or picked up cheap from mechanics' shops.

"Where's Izzy?" I ask Josh.

"Oh, Mom's air-conditioner was acting up. He's looking at it for her." Josh turns off the highway onto Dufferin.

"I guess Murray isn't much of a handyman."

"No. Doesn't seem to be."

"What do you think of him so far? Is Ma happy, do you think?"

Josh shrugs. "You know she's always complaining. So it's hard to tell. It's like she isn't happy unless she's unhappy."

"Yeah."

"How about you, Nom? You still seeing Julie?"

"Julie," I say dreamily.

"I guess that's a yes?"

"The long distance thing is killing me," I confess.

"Yeah, must be hard. I've never done it."

"It's torture, Josh."

"So? What are you going to do?"

I shake my head. "I don't know."

He smiles at me. "Poor Nomi. Why don't you just move back here?"

I stare at my brother. "Not you too."

"What?"

"Everyone thinks I should move back."

"Well, maybe everyone's right."

"How about you?" I change the subject I don't want to deal with.

"What?"

"Still seeing Maria?"

He smiles. "Yeah. She's great."

Josh turns onto my mother's street and into the driveway of her house. He points to the window where my mother stands frantically waving. "Ready?"

I take a deep breath. "Let's go."

"Get inside," my mother orders as soon as we're at the door. "Hurry, close the door. The air-conditioning's back on. Izzy fixed it. Oy, it's so hot. Is it this hot in California, Nomi? Let me look at you. You look tired. Are you okay?" My mother ushers us inside.

"I'm fine. Just tired from the plane. It's a long trip."

"How long?"

"Five hours. Plus a three-hour time change."

"Okay, so, you're here now. Come inside. Murray!" she yells down the hall. "They're here! He's in the bathroom," she tells us. More information than I want. "He spends a lot of time in there." Terrific. Now I feel even more uncomfortable. My mother married Murray last winter, two years after my father died suddenly of a heart attack. I'm not used to my mother living with another man. Why did I say I would stay here? I should be staying with Julie. I must be out of my mind.

"Where's your suitcase? In the car?" Ma asks.

"This is it." I hold up my knapsack.

"That's it?"

"That's it."

"Okay, come into the kitchen. I'll make tea."

"It's too hot for tea. How about something cold."

"Anything you want. Come inside and look in the fridge. Murray!"

Josh and I follow my mother into the kitchen. The first thing I notice is a sign taped to the wall above the sink that reads, "Put dishes in sink." I smile. She must have taken my advice. I can't wait to see the bathroom sign.

My brother Izzy trundles up from downstairs. His hands and face are dirty from working on the air conditioner. "Hey Nom."

"Hi, Izzy."

He leans over to hug me.

"Uh, why don't you wash first," I suggest.

He looks at his hands, as if only just noticing how dirty they are. "Oh. Right." He walks toward the hall.

"Use the kitchen sink. Murray's in the bathroom." My mother says this as if it's a terrible burden. I'm sure I'm going to hear about this later.

I hear a toilet flush, then a moment later Murray wanders into the kitchen, a section of the daily newspaper folded under his arm. He smiles broadly.

"Hello, Nomi. How are you?" He moves toward me awkwardly, kisses me on the cheek.

"Fine, Murray. How are you?"

"Couldn't be better." He beams at my mother.

At least *he's* happy. Murray plunks down at the head of the table. My father's place. My heart lurches into my throat.

"I have to call Julie," I say.

"You just got here," my mother complains.

I shoot her an evil look.

"What did I say?"

I escape to the room I will be staying in — my childhood bedroom. My mother hasn't changed it much since I left home. The same bed, dresser and small desk. Some time ago, she removed my posters of Bette Midler, Janet Jackson, Madonna and *The Rocky Horror Picture Show* and replaced them with two tasteful paintings by my father — portraits of my mother. The paintings are still up. I'm surprised Murray didn't insist they come down. Guess he's not the jealous type — a point in his favour. I plop my travel bag on the floor, grab the phone, dial Julie's number, flop out on the bed.

"When did you get in? Can't you come over?" Julie entices.

"I want to, but it's late. I just got here. I should visit with my mother. And Murray."

"Then I'll come over there," Julie threatens.

"No. You can't. Not tonight."

"Nomi, I miss you. I want to see you."

"I know, babe. Tomorrow. Okay?"

"Breakfast?"

"Well ... I should go to the hospital in the morning. I want to see Bubbe. And we don't know what's going to be. How about lunch?"

"Right. How is she?"

"I got in too late to see her. Josh says she's still unconscious."

"Are you worried?"

"On the plane I imagined she was dead."

"Poor Nomi."

"But she's not. I'm going to see her first thing in the morning. I'll come downtown after that."

"Pick me up at work. I miss you, Nomi."

"I miss you too," I say.

"You'd better."

Roger and I climb up into the back seat of Larry's brand new forest-green SUV. The shiny clean back trunk area indicates he doesn't really need a truck. It's for show. And, I'll bet, to prove how butch he is. Moe has the identical truck in red. Moe hops into the passenger seat, fiddles with the CD player. Loud rock music fills the car.

"Uh, can you turn that down?" I tap Moe on the shoulder.

"What?" He turns in his seat.

"It's a bit loud."

"Oh." He turns the knob. The music fades down.

Larry pulls out into traffic. He switches on the air-conditioning. Cold air blasts through the vents. I take Roger's hand.

"Why do you drive a truck, Larry?" I can't help asking.

"What?" He glances at me in the rearview mirror. "It's not a truck, Henry. It's an SUV."

"Okay. Why do you drive an SUV?"

"I need it."

"For what?"

"I don't know. Carrying stuff for work."

Work? He's an insurance agent, not a lumberjack, a farmer or a carpenter, someone who might actually need a truck. "What stuff?"

"You know. Paperwork, files."

"You need a truck for paperwork?"

"Sometimes there's a lot."

"I bet."

My stomach growls. I remember we left the restaurant before dinner arrived. "I'm starving," I tell Roger. "How about you?"

"Same," he agrees.

"You guys want to stop somewhere?" Larry asks.

I lean forward. "You mean a restaurant?" I can't believe he's asked.

"Yeah, like a pizza or something." Larry glances at Moe, who seems deep in thought. Or as deep as Moe can get.

"Yeah, pizza's okay. What do you think, Rog?"

Roger shifts uncomfortably, probably at the thought of prolonging this visit with my brothers. "Whatever you want, Henry. But ..." he glances at his watch. Ten-fifteen. "Somewhere fast. I'm on early shift," he says for my brothers' benefit.

"How about Pizza Palace?" Moe suggests. "That okay with you guys?"

"Sure." I squeeze Roger's hand in silent thanks. How often are my brothers nice? I have to seize this moment. It might not happen again.

Larry glances at me in the mirror, catches my eye. "As long as you guys can act normal. Okay?"

"Normal?" My stomach tightens. Same old Larry. What was I expecting?

"Yeah, you know. No holding hands or anything."

"Oh. You mean like this?" I hold Roger's hand up in the air.

Larry nods. He seems happy that I understand.

"Well," I say, "I don't think I can do that, Larry."

"Henry ..." Roger placates me. "It's okay. We don't have to."

"Just take us home, Larry, okay?" I say, angry.

"Hey, what'sa matter, Henry?"

"Larry didn't mean anything," Moe explains.

"Oh no?"

"Come on, Henry. You know, one of my customers might see me."

"What? And think maybe you're a big old fag too?"

"Me?"

"Hmm? Is that what you're so afraid of, Lar?"

"No. What do you mean?"

Once I've started I simply can't stop goading my brothers. I lean forward onto the back of their seat. "I mean, how old are you guys now? Thirty-two? Why is it that you're not married yet? Hmm? If you're so straight."

I feel Roger stiffen beside me. Roger hates scenes. I, on the other hand, adore them.

Larry slams on the brakes. I bang my chin on the seat back. "Ouch."

"Shut up Henry. Just shut up," Larry spits.

I rub my jaw. Feel around my mouth to make sure I haven't broken any teeth. Wonder if I should sue him.

"Jesus, Henry." Moe turns around in his seat to stare at me. "What a thing to say. Jeez."

"Touched a nerve, did I, boys?"

"Shut up," says Larry.

"Yeah," agrees Moe.

"Henry ..." Roger says, trying to calm me.

"I have just one question for you guys. What century do you live in?"

Larry opens his mouth, shoves his foot in farther. "Come on, Henry. What's so terrible? We just want you to act normal for an hour. That's all. So we can eat without everybody staring at us and thinking we're queers too. Right, Moe?"

"Yeah."

"We go to Pizza Palace all the time, see?"

"Come on, Roger." I take his hand, open the car door. "I've heard enough."

"Where you going, Henry? I said I'd drive you home."

"No, thank you." I step out. "Roger." Roger sighs, opens his door and steps down.

A wall of heat slams against me.

"Henry. Come on, don't be like this," Larry pleads.

I shut the door hard, grab Roger's hand and start walking. We're on the side of the Allen Expressway. There's no sidewalk. Cars speed by at eighty kilometres an hour. It's not exactly safe for pedestrians. Roger nudges me in front of him so that we are walking single file on the narrow shoulder. Larry moves his car forward slowly, driving alongside us. Sweat forms on my lip and under my arms.

"For chrissake, Henry. Get in," Moe shouts out the window. "You'll be killed."

"No thanks. It's safer out here," I holler back, my jaw set.

"Henry. Come on. Larry's sorry. Aren't you, Larry?" Moe turns to our brother.

I sneak a look at them from the corner of my eye. Since when did Moe become the mediator? Usually he backs Larry up, unconditionally.

"Henry ..." Roger says, "we should let them at least drive us to the subway. It's not safe."

He's right, of course. But I can't admit it. I say nothing.

Roger understands. He opens the car door. Larry stops and we slip in. "Just drop us off at the Eglinton station, Larry," he says.

"I can take you home," Larry pushes.

"You've done enough already."

"Damn them," I shout, slamming our apartment door. "Why do they get to me so much?"

Roger strips as he walks down the hall to our bedroom. "'Cause they're your brothers."

"So?"

"Family does that to us."

"Not you. Your family doesn't." I kick off my shoes, let them bounce against the wall.

"What family?"

Roger just has his mother. She was fifteen when she had him. He's in touch with his mother now, but not often. He has no brothers or sisters and he's never met his aunts and uncles. He has grandparents he met once when he was in nursing college.

"Your mother."

"Henry, my mother's far more dysfunctional than your family."

"But not as crazy."

"That's not true. She's just not ... as dramatic as your family."

Of course he's right. I stomp into the bedroom after him.

"What about dinner?" I ask.

"I'm too tired. Let's go to bed."

Roger lets his pants fall to the floor, slides down his briefs, crawls into bed.

"Good night," he says.

"That's what you think," I answer, peeling out of my clothes and joining him.

After morning coffee, Solly and I head for the subway. He tried in vain to get Lou to drive us uptown, but Lou had to drive a regular fare to Oshawa and wouldn't be able to take us until the afternoon. Solly is in a sullen mood as we enter the Wellesley station, pop our tokens into the slot and push through the turnstile. It's another sweltering day. Inside the subway station, it is hot, muggy and smelly. I try to breathe as little as possible and I pray for an air-conditioned car. The train that approaches has all its windows shut. A good sign.

On the lovely and cool subway car, the farther north we go, the more upset Solly becomes.

"Pop, what is it?"

He turns in his seat, glares at me.

"What's so bad about taking the subway uptown?"

He breathes deeply, blows the air out through one side of his mouth forcefully, as if it were smoke. He reaches into his shirt pocket for his cigar stub.

"Pop?"

"Okay." He glances out the window as the train bursts out of the dark tunnel into the daylight. Summer trees sway in the wind. "Let me tell you a story."

"Okay." Now we're getting somewhere.

He scratches his upper lip. "When you were a little boy, I had a crummy job, working for your Great-Uncle Moe at his fish shop in the market. Your Uncle Moe was a *meiser oisvorf*, you know what that means?"

"A cheapskate?"

"That's right. Your brother's named after him. I don't know why your mother did that. We lived in a small apartment on Dufferin Street near College. Okay, it wasn't a palace, but I was young. Times were tough. I was doing the best I could."

"I'm sure you were, Pop." I pat his arm.

"Yeah, well, your mother didn't see things that way. See? She wanted to move uptown to the suburbs."

"Wasn't that what everyone wanted back then?" I say, trying to see my mother's side.

"Yeah, yeah, I know. That's what she said at the time. That's all I heard from her. 'We gotta move uptown. We gotta move uptown.' Only I didn't have the kinda money that would take, see? 'Cause your mother wanted to buy a house, not rent a crummy apartment. I needed more money. So, I went and asked your Uncle Moe for a raise. You already know the story, right?" He glances at me sideways.

"Yeah. He said he'd give you a raise when you started working harder, then you told him to fuck himself, and you were out of a job."

He grins at me. "You remember?"

"Yeah."

"Okay, so you remember the next part, right?"

"You went to the Italian pool hall on College where you ran into Sid Walensky — "

"Aw jeez, Henry," he cuts me off. "Do me a favour. Don't speak that name."

"Sorry, Pop. I forgot." Solly hates to hear the guy's name out loud. "You ran into the *yutz* of all time ..."

"That's better."

"And he got you messed up in that insurance scheme."

"He set me up and I did time while he got off scot-free."

Walensky set it up so when they were discovered, my father

was the fall guy. It was the event that changed his life, ruined his marriage, and rendered him virtually unemployable.

"Anyway," Solly continues, "after I finally got out on parole, six lousy years later, your mother was renting in the building she's in to this day, and I got a room on Dundas Street. I came to visit you kids every Sunday. You remember that?"

"I remember."

"Well, I didn't have a car, so I had to ride the TTC all the way from Dundas and Dovercourt to Finch and Bathurst. The ride wasn't so bad. That's not it, Henry."

The train rumbles through the dark tunnel. Solly stares at his own reflection in the window. I wait for him to finish.

"The second Sunday I'm free, I'm sitting on the goddamn Bathurst Street bus and guess who walks onto the bus?"

"Who?"

"Guess. Only don't say his name."

"Oh no."

"That's right. The *yutz*. Walks right over to where I'm sitting. 'Don't even think about it,' I said to him. The *yutz* was going to sit right beside me. I woulda killed him with my bare hands, 'cept there was a lot of witnesses and I'm not that stupid. So, I got off the bus at goddamn St. Clair and waited for the next one. I was shaking with anger, Henry. I swear, I coulda killed the *yutz*."

"I'm glad you didn't."

"So now you know."

"What?"

He looks at me like I'm stupid not to have understood. "Why I can't stand the Bathurst Street bus."

"Oh."

"Every time I'm on it, I flash back to that day, Henry. You understand?"

"Sure, Pop."

"All right." He takes a deep breath, blows it out through his mouth.

N O M I ' S   L O V E

I force my mother out of bed early. I want to be at the hospital as soon as visiting hours begin. To my surprise, Henry and Uncle Solly are already in Bubbe's room, sitting at her bedside. Henry's face lights up when he sees me.

He stands to hug me. "Hey, Cuz." He releases me, takes a good look. "Hi Auntie Faygie," he says to my mother.

"Henry. Let me see you." She stands back to survey him. Henry just about curtsies for her. "You look good. Did you gain?"

She means weight.

He shrugs. "Maybe a little."

But I don't think so. I think he lost weight. He looks skinnier to me.

"Hello, Solly," my mother says to my uncle.

"Faygie." He nods. "Good of you to come."

"Listen, she was my mother-in-law for twenty-eight years. That doesn't stop just because Harry died. Am I right?" she asks me.

"Sure, Ma."

"Still," Solly says, "no one expects you to — "

"Never mind what anyone expects. I'm here because I want to be here."

"Whatever." Solly relents. "How's ah ..." He strains for a name.

"Murray?"

"Yeah."

"He's fine, thank you."

"Good."

All this formality is going to kill me. "How is she?" I move closer to Bubbe, beside my uncle.

"No change. When did you get in, Nomi?" Uncle Solly throws an affectionate arm over my shoulder. "How was the flight?"

"Last night. How long has she been like this?"

"Since yesterday morning."

It's sad. Bubbe looks like she's aged a hundred years in the six months since I was last here.

A matronly nurse bustles into the room at a crisp pace. She stops in her tracks, takes a long look at me, then moves her eyes over Solly, Henry and my mother.

"People," she says sternly. "What did I tell you yesterday?" She points to the door.

I don't know what's going on.

"Sorry, Ma'am," Uncle Solly says politely. "They just got here."

The nurse unhooks Bubbe's chart from the bottom of the bed, checks the IV drip, glances at the heart monitor, opens Bubbe's eyelids with a thumb, peers into them, writes something on the chart.

"Only two visitors at a time," Henry explains for my benefit.

"I'm going to go to the cafeteria for a coffee. You coming, Henry?" Uncle Solly asks.

"No, no, Henry should stay," my mother offers. "I got a million things to do. Nomi, I'll pick you up in an hour?"

"Ma, I told you. I'm going to see Julie after this."

"Pardon me." She is offended. "I forgot."

Convenient, I think, but don't say it out loud.

"So I'll see you for supper?" she asks tersely.

"I'll phone you and let you know."

"O-kay," she says, put out. "I only thought you came here to see your grandmother. But if your friends are more important than your family ..."

"Ma, Julie is not just a friend. We've been over this." I look to

Henry for help.

"All right, pardon me. I forgot. Nice to see you, Solly. Bye, Henry." My mother gathers her purse and leaves.

Solly winks at me and follows her out. The nurse finishes up and moves on to the next patient.

"Hey, Cuz," Henry says. "Great to see you." We hug again.

"You too."

"Have you seen Julie yet?"

"I'm meeting her for lunch."

"How's it going?"

"Great. But the long distance is so hard."

"I know. She misses you."

"What did she say?"

"She's crazy about you. What are you going to do, Nomi?"

"God. I don't know. What would you do?"

"Good question. San Francisco's such a great town. The Castro Theatre, Fisherman's Wharf, the bougainvillea, Pride Parade, all the bars ..."

"I have friends, a job."

"But no Julie."

"I wish she would move there," I tell him.

He shakes his head. "I don't think that's going to happen, Cuz."

"I know. What am I going to do?"

"I guess you'll have to figure that out sooner or later."

"I know, Henry. In the meantime, it's killing me."

"You know what they say, Nomi."

"What?"

"Whatever doesn't kill you makes you stronger."

At the Asian AIDS Association I take the stairs three at a time, my heart pounding in my throat. At the top, I round the corner and stand in the office doorway. Julie sits at her desk, talking on the phone. She sees me. Her face lights up. I hover in front of her desk.

"Okay," she says into the phone. "Yes. No, that's fine. What?" She motions her hand around in a circle, urging the person on the other end of the line to hurry up. "No, no, really it's fine. Yes.

Yes. Yes. Yes. Same as last time. That's correct. Yes. Okay ..." she says with finality. "Okay, fine, we'll see you then. What? No, no. Really it's fine. Okay. See you next week. Yes, goodbye." She slams the receiver down. "Nomi!" Julie screams. She jumps up from her seat, runs to my side of the desk, throws herself into my arms. I hold her tightly. Our lips meet.

"Julie." I kiss her passionately.

Applause begins with one set of hands somewhere in the office. Others join in until the clapping thunders throughout the room. We are being serenaded with a standing ovation.

"Bravo," someone shouts.

I guess we are making a bit of a scene. We separate just a little. I bow. Julie curtsies.

"Everyone. This is Nomi!" Julie shouts.

Her co-workers wave at me; some yell out hello.

"I'm so glad you're here," Julie tells me. "Come on. Let's get out of here."

We make love everywhere in Julie's apartment. The first time in the hallway, just inside the door. After that, in her bed, and later in the bathtub where we lie under a blanket of bubbles.

"Did you ever think you'd end up with someone from out of town?" I ask Julie.

"You're not exactly from out of town, Nomi."

"Well ..."

"I never really thought about it." She scoops up a handful of bubbles, places them on my chin, like a beard.

"I never thought I'd move to San Francisco only to fall in love with a woman who lives in Toronto." The bubble beard slips down, plops back into the water.

"Are you in love?"

"You know I am." I scoop up some bubbles, place a dollop on each nipple.

"Keep that up and you know where we'll end up."

"Back in bed?" I lean over, kiss her. She throws her arms around my neck. She tastes a bit like soap and bubbles.

Julie breaks away. Looks at me seriously. "Oh Nomi, what are we going to do?"

I look into her eyes, as if the answer was hidden there. "Let's just enjoy this time together. How about that?"

"I guess."

"Tell me about your family. Why did your sister move to Japan?"

She shrugs. "You'd have to ask her."

"You're not close?"

"Not especially."

"She's older than you, right?"

"Four years. She didn't even tell anyone she was going until the night before. We hardly ever hear from her. It's like she's just gone. Abandoned us."

"Are you out to her?"

Julie looks at me hard. "Are you crazy?"

"Homophobic?"

"That's putting it mildly."

"How about your brother?"

"Wayne? He's okay. You know, he's a guy. A straight guy. I see him once in a while for dinner. But we don't talk about anything much."

"Is he married?"

"To his job."

"What's he do?"

"He works at a dot com company. He's making money hand over fist. At least he helps my mom out with money. At least he does that much."

"And your mom?"

"What about her?"

"Are you out to her?"

Julie kisses me lightly on the lips. "I don't think there's even a Japanese word for it."

"But she speaks some English. Right?"

"Sure, but not a word like lesbian."

"So she doesn't know about me, then."

"Not yet."

"Do you think you'll tell her? Can I meet her while I'm here?"

"Oh God. I don't know. I mean, I don't know what she would do."

"Just say I'm a friend."

"She's too smart. She'd figure it out."

"Good."

"Yeah, and then you'll leave town and I'll have to deal with her. No thanks."

"What if I was staying?"

She smiles in a sad way. "But you're not, Nomi."

Julie's phone rings. We listen to it ring three times, then her answering machine switches on. We hear Julie's outgoing message then the beep.

"Hi." I recognize the voice, but I can't place it. "The umbrella opened. The crow flies at midnight." Click.

I stare at Julie. I feel like I'm in the middle of a James Bond movie. "The crow flies at midnight?" I repeat.

Julie is already standing, drying herself off with a large pink towel. "Come on, Nomi, get dressed. We have to go to Ed's."

"Who's Ed? And who was that?" Stubbornly, I sit in the tub.

"Oh my God," Julie reaches for her bra from the floor where we flung it earlier. "Where's Henry? We need him, too."

"He might be at the hospital."

Julie hooks her bra. Steps into her panties. "We'll have to page him."

"Why? Julie, what's going on? I don't understand."

"Come on, Nomi. Get dressed. I'll fill you in on the way there."

HENRY'S SCIENTIST

I'm all in a flap. My hair's a fright when I arrive at Ed's apartment and my heart is racing. We've been waiting for this breakthrough for a long time.

"Henry, come on in. You're out of breath. Did you run?" Ed opens the door.

I pant. Breathe. Pant. "Yes." Lean forward on my knees to catch my breath.

"I'll get you some water. Come and sit." Ed steers me into the living room. Julie has dragged Nomi along. She waves. Albert stands when he sees me. He, too, looks dishevelled. He must have just got off the plane from New York. His wavy salt-and-pepper hair is messy. His usual tweed jacket is rumpled. His face is dark with a five o'clock shadow.

"Henry." He grabs my arm. "I'd like you to meet Dr. Jonathan Garrick."

Dr. Garrick stands and we shake hands. "Please," he says, "call me Jonathan."

Dr. Garrick is in his late fifties. His grey hair is balding on top, cut short on the sides. He has a neatly trimmed grey beard, clear blue eyes and full lips. He looks more like a college professor than a scientist. But he's ours. All ours. Our very own scientist. Imagine.

Ed returns with my water. I sit. My palms are clammy.

"Why don't I let you tell them?" Albert suggests to Jonathan.

Jonathan takes a deep breath. He rubs his ring finger. His hands are tanned. There is a white patch of skin where a ring used to be.

He sips his water. "I used to work for the Department of Defense. I've left now, thank God, but I started there in 1969 when Nixon was president." He looks at Albert. "There's so much to tell."

"Can you say what you told me?" Al prompts.

"Okay," he takes a breath. "It's really because of the internet. I'm a newshound. Especially around AIDS. I picked up your article in the *Toronto Star* on the web. I was thrilled to see it there. You know, someone talking about the truth ... even though you were obviously misrepresented."

"Thank you," says Albert.

I like Dr. Jonathan Garrick already. I lean forward, listening.

"I was involved, you see. In the original experiment."

"Experiment?" My heart is in my throat.

"To develop immune-system-destroying agents for germ warfare," he recites.

"To invent AIDS?" I interject.

"Precisely."

I knock back the rest of my water, glance at Julie, who nods her head slowly. Nomi sits wide-eyed, as if up to this moment she hasn't quite believed us and it's all becoming horribly clear. I remember that moment. It was over a year ago when Albert first attended our ACTOUT meeting and told us his theory. At first, I thought he was nuts. Or at least one of those absent-minded professors, out of touch with reality. Later, after reading the reams of research he had, I believed him.

Al looks positively vindicated. "And you're willing to be quoted?"

"I don't work for the government anymore. I suppose they're not going to be thrilled with me. It might even get nasty, but ..." Jonathan stops.

"But?"

"I can't remain silent any more. Too many lives have already been lost."

"So," Julie says, "we need to enlist a reporter again."

"Rick?" I suggest. Why not? We've already worked with him.

"Forget it," Al says bitterly. "The traitor."

"Al, it wasn't Rick's fault," I say.

"Hah."

"He said his editor butchered his piece. I believe him. I saw him the day it came out," I explain.

"You're so naive, Henry."

"Come on, Al ... I know you're sore."

"He betrayed us."

"His editor betrayed him."

"Well then," says Al snidely, "who's to say he won't do so again?"

"Well ..." It's a good point. "Let's at least talk to him."

"But Rick's in the hospital," Julie reminds us. "Do you think he's up to it?"

"He's out," I say.

"What?" Even Al is interested.

"I phoned his place yesterday. Phil the nurse was there. Rick's home. He's weak, but he can sit up, and he can write."

"I don't know ..." Al won't give in.

"Why don't we go and see him?" I suggest.

Albert sighs.

"Come on, Al. For the cause," I urge.

"Oh, all right. But don't expect me to be nice."

"Oh, we wouldn't."

"No," agrees Julie, "not at all."

"I'll see you guys later," says Ed. "I've got a meeting."

Nurse Phil motions for us to come inside. We trudge into the living room. Rick lies on the living room couch in his green silk pajamas and robe. The bedside table is littered with pill bottles. He is hooked up to an IV drip. There is an oxygen tank with a mask by the couch, alongside many other little reminders of his illness. He eyes Al suspiciously as we tromp into the living room.

"Hello, Henry, Julie. I don't believe we've met," he says to

Nomi and Dr. Garrick. He doesn't acknowledge Al.

"This is my girlfriend, Nomi," Julie says.

"And this," I put a protective arm around Jonathan, "is Dr. Jonathan Garrick."

"He's a scientist," Julie says. "He was there. In 1969. At Fort Detrick when they invented AIDS."

"My God!" Rick stares at Jonathan.

"I worked at the Biological and Chemical Warfare Department in the 1970s," Jonathan clarifies.

"He wants to make a statement," Julie tells Rick. "Are you up to it?"

Rick sits up straighter. "Of course." Rick pushes a button, speaks into an intercom on the bedside table. "Philip?"

"At your service," Nurse Phil's voice echoes through the tinny speaker.

"Can you please fetch my tape recorder and a fresh tape from the shelf in my office?"

"No problem."

"Just a minute." Al steps closer to Rick. "How do we know you won't screw us up again?" he says meanly.

Rick sighs, although it's hard with his shallow lung capacity. "It wasn't my fault, Albert," he spits through clenched teeth.

"So you say."

"It's the truth. Look, it didn't work out between us, okay? But we can still work together."

Al snorts.

"Can't we?"

All heads turn to Al.

"Look, I'm sorry, all right?" Rick offers. I can tell he's not the sort of man to apologize lightly. This is hard for him.

"He's sorry, Al," I prompt.

Al folds his arms across his chest, closing up.

"Look, Albert, let's just cut the bullshit, all right? This is an extremely good day for me. I can talk. I can breathe. I can write. Don't waste this opportunity. Anyway, who else will do this for you? Hmmm?"

He's right. We all know it. Even Al knows it.

"What's going to be different this time?" Al asks Rick.

Rick breathes a few short, shallow breaths. "Everything."

"Like what?"

"Let's just say, this time I'm going to ... shall we say ... circumvent usual procedure."

"What does that mean?"

"I don't have anything to lose."

"And?"

"I've been practising my editor's signature."

"Really?" I'm surprised. Rick is a straitlaced, conservative guy. Plays by the rules. If he's planning to do what I think he's planning ..."You're going to forge your editor's signature?"

"Let's not talk about it," Rick cuts me off. "Let's just say I'll get it to the printers without editorial revisions this time. How's that?" He directs the question at Al, who remains unmoved.

Julie touches Albert's shoulder lightly. "Al ..."

"Oh, all right. Stop pestering me."

"Good."

"Just don't expect me to be friendly."

"We wouldn't."

"Fine."

"Good."

Phil slips into the room with Rick's tape machine. It has a small clip-on microphone and a headset.

Rick addresses Jonathan. "Can I tape this?"

"Yes. Of course."

"Good. Clip this to your shirt." He hands the microphone to Jonathan. "Now, is this on the record?"

"Yes."

"Good. Can you state your full name, city of residence and occupation, please?"

"I am Dr. Jonathan Theodore Garrick. I live in Boston, Massachusetts. I am a biological scientist and currently on the faculty of the Department of Biological Sciences in the Medical School of Harvard University in Boston."

"You have a statement to make?" Rick prompts.

"Yes."

"Why don't you start from the beginning?"

Jonathan nods, rubs his ring finger. "In 1969 I was employed by the Department of Defense. I was on staff at Fort Detrick, a laboratory under the joint auspices of the National Institute of Health and the World Health Organization. It was my first appointment out of medical school. I was excited to work at such a prestigious organization. I thought we were doing important work. I thought our goal was to discover the root of viral infections so we could create cures. I believed we could eradicate disease completely by the turn of the century. It was an exciting time. Nixon was president. The Vietnam war was in full swing."

He hesitates.

"You must understand I was a junior researcher. I wasn't privy to ... the broader scope of the department's work. I was simply given tasks to do, and I did them and reported to my boss. I didn't piece together that this was the agent we had created until AIDS started appearing in the early eighties."

There is a collective gasp in the room when Jonathan admits on the record that he had a part in creating AIDS. This is it. How can anyone dispute the theory now? We've got an eyewitness report.

"How do you know?" Rick asks.

"In the seventies the department's bio-warfare program intensified, particularly in the area of DNA and gene splicing research. We were working with the National Cancer Institute. Cancer virologists had learned to jump animal cancer viruses from one species to another."

"Wait a minute." I can't help but interrupt. "Isn't that what they say? That HIV jumped species from green monkeys?"

"Precisely," says Jonathan. "It's true probably, but not in the way you would imagine. Not in Africa, not in ... the wilds. In America. In laboratories. Intentionally, you see? We were splicing chicken viruses into lamb kidney cells. Baboon viruses were spliced into human cancer cells. The combinations were endless.

There were several deadly man-made viruses developed. And new forms of cancer, immunodeficiency and opportunistic infections were produced when these viruses were forced or adapted into laboratory animals and into human tissue cell cultures."

Rick sits up straighter on the sofa. "You admit that deadly man-made viruses were developed in the lab?"

"Yes. That was the whole point."

"Can you give us an example?"

"All right." Jonathan studies his fingernails, picks at a cuticle. He seems somewhat uncomfortable. "In ... oh ... it would have been ... 1974, I worked on an experiment. Newborn chimpanzees were taken away from their mothers at birth and weaned on milk obtained from virus-infected cows. Some of the chimps sickened and died with two new diseases that had never been observed in chimps. The first was a parasitic pneumonia known as pneumocystis carinii pneumonia ..."

"Oh my God. PCP," I say.

"That's right."

"So in the 1970s you were intentionally moving animal viruses into human cells?" Rick asks.

Dr. Garrick nods. "I'm afraid so. It was common in the mid-seventies for virologists to alter animal viruses by inserting them in other animal species and into human tissue cells in culture."

"And this was under the auspices of the Department of Defense?" Rick asks.

"Yes, but the Center for Disease Control, The National Cancer Institute and the large pharmaceutical companies were involved as well."

"I knew it!" I shout. "I knew it. Damn it. The drug companies were in on it. I knew it."

"So you're saying AIDS didn't jump species from green monkeys in Africa?" Rick probes.

"The first AIDS cases were uncovered in the U.S. in New York in 1979," Jonathan says. "Not Africa."

"You see?" Albert is beside himself. Jonathan is supporting everything Al has theorized about the origin of AIDS. "Doctor ..."

"Please call me Jonathan."

"Okay. Jonathan, can you tell us exactly how HIV began in the gay community?"

Jonathan takes a sip of water, hesitates.

We all wait in silence.

"You've heard of the hepatitis B experimental vaccine trials?"

"See?" Al leaps up from his chair, paces the room. "So it was through the vaccine trials, then?"

"In my opinion," Jonathan admits.

"What do you know about the trials?" Rick asks.

Jonathan sighs. "I'm sorry," he says.

"You're sorry?"

"I'm sorry I didn't do anything to stop it. We were sworn to secrecy. Well, I wasn't directly. I wasn't supposed to know. But I have eyes. Plus I, shall we say ... accidentally leafed through a report I wasn't supposed to see."

"A report?"

"Look, a basic tenet of scientific research says a hypothesis is nothing more than a theory until it's tested on a control group. A cohort. Do you know what that means?"

"I think so," Rick says, "but for the record, can you explain anyway?"

"In the dictionary it would say a group of persons with a common statistical characteristic. In science it means a control group."

"Gay men?" I can't help myself; I know I shouldn't interrupt. I should just sit quietly and listen, but it's too exciting.

"I'm sorry," he says again. "It wasn't an accident, of course. They could have chosen other groups. They considered mental health patients, pregnant women, Native Americans. You see? All marginalized groups of people. People with no political power."

"But they picked gay men?" I ask.

Jonathan smiles weakly. "I'm sorry ..."

I wish he would stop apologizing. It's giving me the creeps.

He sighs. "You see, they decided to pick a control group of people who ..."

Albert nods his head. "Go ahead and say it, doctor. We can

take it."

Jonathan shakes his head. "They picked homosexuals ... sorry ... gay men in order to avoid serious legal and logistical problems."

"Damn," I say.

"Was it intentionally put into the hepatitis B vaccine? Or was it an accident?" Rick asks.

"What do you think?" Jonathan replies.

"For the record, can you answer the question?" Rick asks.

"I think it was intentional. I think the hepatitis B experimental vaccine was a cover-up for the real experiment. The Department of Defense, the National Cancer Institute and, most importantly, the pharmaceutical companies did not spend millions of dollars to save the lives of gay men from hepatitis. Their motives were far more sinister, I'm afraid."

"What were their motives?" Rick asks.

"Each organization had a different motive. The Department of Defense was searching for a weapon. I don't think I need to spell out what the pharmaceutical companies were searching for."

"For the record?"

"Money."

"Money?"

"A new disease requires new drugs."

"The National Cancer Institute?"

"Ah yes. Well that's where it gets a bit more complicated."

"Go on."

"Nothing more than a cover for the government. To appear ... benevolent."

"Goddamn it," I say. "I knew it. Damn it." I stare at Jonathan. I think about all of the men I've known who have died. I remember my own HIV status. I feel a hot rage bubbling in my gut. "Why didn't you do anything?"

"I'm sorry," Jonathan says.

"Stop saying that." It's driving me crazy.

"How could this happen?" Julie asks angrily. "You call yourself a scientist? How could you stand by and let it happen, Dr. Garrick?

All these years ... so many people have died."

"I'm sorry. I wish to God ..." he stops.

"Is this why your wife left you?" I ask on a hunch, glancing at his recently bare ring finger.

He looks at me, shocked. "My wife?"

"Is this why she left you?" I repeat. I don't care if it's mean. I want him to hurt. "Because you let it happen?"

He looks me in the eye.

"Is it, Doctor?"

"Yes."

"Is that why you've come to us now?" I am relentless.

He looks at each of us. "Yes."

"So if she hadn't left ... ?"

"I don't know," he admits. "Yes," he decides, "I would still be here."

I'm not sure I believe him. I stare at Jonathan skeptically.

"Thank you, Doctor," Albert says.

"You're thanking me?"

"Why are you thanking him?" Julie asks.

"For coming forward now," Albert clarifies.

"I wish to God I'd done it sooner," Jonathan offers.

Nomi says nothing. Her eyes are wide.

Soon a full two hours have gone by. Rick has had to flip the tape once and call Phil for a second tape. We've gone through four pots of coffee, a tray of cookies and a pitcher of water. Jonathan looks exhausted, but relieved. The rest of us are a mixture of horrified and satisfied. He didn't tell us anything we didn't already suspect, but the cold-blooded viciousness has shaken us. The United States government purposely set out to create and test AIDS on Africans and gays. It's exactly what Al's been saying all along. Rick shuts off the tape recorder and we sit in silence. Jonathan pours himself another glass of water.

"I'm going to need one of you to transcribe the tape," Rick says. "I don't have the strength."

"I'll do it," offers Julie.

"No, I'll do it," I say. "You've got company." I gesture to Nomi.

"Yeah," Julie agrees, "but your grandmother is in the hospital."

"Oh damn." Nomi jumps up. "Can I use your phone, Rick?"

"Course." He points to a phone across the room. "It's cordless. If you need privacy, you can take it into the den."

"It's okay. I just need to call the hospital," Nomi says as she dials. "Hi, Ma? Is that you? You're back there? What? Oh no. Okay. Yep. Right away." She hangs up the phone, turns to me. "Henry, we've got to get back there. My mother says Bubbe's taken a turn for the worse."

"Oh no."

"I'll drive you," Julie offers. "Al, where are you and Jonathan going to stay?"

"I suppose we'll check into a hotel."

"Don't be silly," Rick interrupts. "Why don't you stay here? Plenty of room."

"Here?" Al looks horrified and pleased simultaneously. Maybe there is hope for Al and Rick after all.

"That way I can continue talking with Jonathan. I'm sure there's many details we haven't touched yet."

"That's true," Jonathan confirms.

"Then it's settled. You can have the guest room," he tells Jonathan. "And Al, you can use my room. I'm sleeping in here now anyway."

"I don't know," Al hesitates.

"Oh puh-lease, Albert. Can we stop the hysterics? It's getting tiresome. If you prefer, you can have the den. That's where Phil is staying. He can move to my bedroom. It's up to you."

"That'll work."

"Fine."

"We should go," Nomi prompts.

"We'll talk to you all later," I say on our way out.

"Go. You don't want to be late," Rick pushes. He's probably fine-tuned to the untimeliness of dying.

Julie takes Nomi's hand. I follow them out the door and down the hall.

NOMI'S SILENT SCREAM

Julie drives her fire-engine red Toyota hatchback with ease. I sit in the passenger seat beside her, one hand resting on her thigh. Henry's slouched in the back seat. I'm numb with shock. I hadn't wanted to believe Al's theory. I never told Julie; I didn't want to offend her. She's been working on exposing the theory for so long. But until today, I was skeptical. It's not that I'm naive. I just couldn't believe the government could be that callous. I feel shaken to the core. The whole world looks different to me now. And on top of it, Bubbe's really dying. I've been lucky to have known my grandmother this long. She's lived a long life. But the thought of losing her still hurts. Like a big chunk has been torn from my heart. I feel lost and vulnerable.

Julie pulls into the parking lot at Branson Hospital. "I'm coming with you," she announces.

"What?"

"I'm not leaving you at a time like this, Nomi." She shifts the car into park and opens her door.

"Okay." I'm nervous about bringing Julie upstairs to meet my family, especially my mother, but I know there's no arguing with a femme once her mind is made up.

"It'll be okay, Cuz," Henry assures me, stepping out of the back seat.

I take Julie's hand and we enter the hospital.

Everyone is crowded into Bubbe's room. Solly sits by the head of her bed. Aunt Shell is beside him, with her husband Jerry. Aunt Belle is there, with the twins and Sherry. My mother and my brothers Josh and Izzy are all there. Even Lou Greenberg hovers near the doorway. It's quite a scene. The nurse rushes in, shakes her head when she sees the crowd, adjusts a few dials on Bubbe's machinery, then exits in a bustle. I guess Bubbe must really be dying or Nurse Ratchet would surely have kicked all but two of us out of the room.

As we enter, everyone looks up and stares at Julie. I stand beside her, numb and overwhelmed. Joshua comes to my rescue. He pushes past my mother.

"You must be Julie. I'm Josh, Nomi's brother. I've been dying to meet you." He offers a hand to shake.

"Everyone, this is Julie," I say. "My girlfriend," I add.

"Hi Julie," Sherry waves.

"Nice-looking girl." Uncle Solly nods his head.

"I love your hair." Belle moves forward, touches Julie's long hair.

The twins grunt a hello. Izzy waves from across the room.

My mother says nothing.

"Ma, this is Julie," I say.

My mother cracks a fake smile. "Hello."

Julie sticks out a hand. My mother shakes it limply. "I'm very glad to meet you," Julie says politely.

"And we're thrilled to meet you," Josh offers on my mother's behalf. "Someone's gotta watch out for Nomi."

"She does," I confirm.

Julie smiles.

My mother raises her eyebrows, like she's heard just about enough. I am embarrassed by her behaviour and feel protective of Julie. I expected my mother to be awkward, but not rude. I've rarely brought a woman home to meet my family. My mother met Sapphire once, but that was in San Francisco, our turf, not hers, in our very gay world, far away from my mother's home and family. Is she ashamed of me? I glare at her.

"What?" she asks.

"Nothing." I take Julie's hand and pull her closer to Uncle Solly and away from my mother. I'll deal with her later.

"Where you been?" Uncle Solly asks Henry. "We've been trying to call you."

"A meeting."

"Now?"

Henry shrugs. "She was stable this morning. How could I know?"

"All right, Solly," Belle defends Henry. "He's here now."

Bubbe makes a noise. We all turn to look. Her breathing is laboured.

"Doesn't sound so good," Solly says.

"Oh," Sherry moans, her eyes big and sad.

"Listen," my mother says, "she lived a long life."

"Ninety-two to ninety-seven," Henry says.

"Really?" Julie asks.

"Yeah," Henry says, "that's how old she is."

"Ninety-two to ninety-seven?"

"Yeah. Somewhere in there. Right, Pop?"

"Yeah, sure. That's right," Solly confirms. "We don't know exactly how old she is. She'd never say."

"That's right," I remember now. "It's because she was born in Russia and they didn't have birth certificates like they do now. She only knows she's the second girl."

"After Aunt Rose," Henry adds.

"Yeah, well, it's a crock." Solly grins, looks down at his mother affectionately.

"You mean she really knows?" I ask.

"Yeah, sure."

"Then why?"

"Why? My father was a couple years younger. And in those days it was a crime for the woman to be older. She was ashamed."

"So she lied about her age for seventy-five years?"

"Pretty much."

"Wow," says Izzy, no doubt trying to work out her age math-ematically based on probabilities.

"It makes sense to me," says my mother.

"Sure," agrees Aunt Belle. "The man should be older."

"And taller," my mother adds.

"I don't think it matters," Josh-the-Renaissance-man counters.

"Ninety-two to ninety-seven," Henry repeats with wonder. Henry's worried he won't make forty.

I smile at him empathetically.

Bubbe sucks in a long raspy breath. It sounds watery. She exhales the breath long and slow. Then she stops breathing. We collectively hold our breaths for a moment, watching. I breathe in deeply, willing Bubbe to breathe with me. She does not. She is still. And silent.

"Oh my God."

"Is she?"

"I don't know."

"Someone check her pulse."

"How do you do that?"

"Get the nurse."

"Nurse!"

"Check her pulse."

Solly bends one ear over Bubbe's mouth. He sits up, shakes his head.

"Oh no."

"Push the nurse's button!"

"It's too late."

"Where's the button?"

"On the wall. Over there."

"I can't see it."

"It's too late."

"Push it."

Sherry starts crying. Aunt Shell joins her. Henry's eyes get misty. I feel a huge lump in my chest. Julie squeezes my hand tightly. Izzy studies the heart monitor screen. Belle shakes her head. My mother frowns. Josh's lower lip trembles. The twins stand stiff, stoic.

"What day is this?"

"The fourteenth."

"That's funny. Zayde died on the fourteenth also."

"Of September."

"And this is June."

"But it's the fourteenth."

"True."

"The shivah's at Faygie's house," Aunt Shell announces. "We decided."

"Why not your place? You're the daughter," Solly asks.

"We're doing renovations. The house is a mess."

"I don't mind," my mother pipes up.

"It's not right," Solly argues. "It should be at her daughter's."

"Or son's," Aunt Shell counters. "Why don't you do it?"

"Me?"

"Henry, do you have room?"

"Well, I'd have to ask Roger."

"I've already offered," my mother shouts above the din. "I can do it. The shivah was at my house when Avram died."

"But Harry was still here."

"You're remarried now. What will your husband think?"

"He doesn't mind. I already asked."

"You see? He doesn't mind."

"It's my pleasure," my mother reiterates, a little inappropriately, I think.

"Then it's settled."

A sudden loud sound, a snore, belches out of Bubbe's mouth. Followed by a cough. We turn and stare at her. She coughs again, clears her throat, opens her eyes.

"Oh my God."

"It's a miracle."

"She's alive."

"M-A?"

"How could it be?"

"She was dead."

"Shhh."

"She had no pulse."

"Quiet, she'll hear you."

"It's a miracle."

"She was dead."

"M-A?"

Bubbe looks around the room, from one to the other of the family gathered at her bedside. "What's for supper? I'm starving."

I can't help it. A laugh slips out of my mouth. It spreads to others. And we're all laughing. Comic relief. Fear. Shock. Who knows? Bubbe focuses her eyes on Julie.

"Who are you?" she asks. "The nurse?"

I step forward. "No, Bubbe. This is Julie. My girlfriend."

Bubbe stares at Julie. "Girlfriend? Is she Jewish?"

"What's the difference?" Solly says. "We're just glad you're feeling better."

The nurse returns and notices that Bubbe is awake. She pushes her way up front.

"Well, you're awake."

"Who are you?"

"I'm your nurse. You gave us quite a scare, Mrs. Rabinovitch." The nurse fiddles with the IV. Checks the heart monitor. "Are you hungry?"

"Yeah, doll, can you bring me a piece of toast maybe?"

"I can bring you a whole dinner."

"Kosher?"

"No problem." The nurse writes something on Bubbe's chart and is about to leave. "Oh, now that she's doing better, you'll have to clear this room. Only two persons — "

"We know," Uncle Solly interjects.

In the hallway, my mother stops me. "Nomi, you'll come back with me. Murray and I want to have dinner with you."

"Well, I was planning on spending time with Julie."

My mother digests this information. "All right, so you'll bring her with."

"What?" I didn't expect my mother to come around so

quickly after her bad behaviour earlier.

"You heard me. So you'll both come. All right?"

"Well ..." I'm not so sure I'm ready to forgive her. Or to put Julie in a situation that might be awkward.

"Thank you," Julie steps in. "We'd be delighted. Wouldn't we, Nomi?"

"I guess," I relent.

"Good, so come on. I'm parked in the back."

"Julie's got her car. We'll meet you there, Ma."

"All right. You'll come right over?"

"Don't worry. We're coming. We're coming."

"It's north on Bathurst," I tell Julie. She steers the car into the left turn lane. "Are you sure you're okay with this? I'm sorry about my mother."

"It's okay."

"No, it's not okay. You didn't deserve that."

"I didn't take it personally, Nomi. She would have been like that if it was me or some other girl you were with."

"You're the only girl I want." I reach over and take Julie's free hand.

"Good answer, Nomi."

"Thanks for doing this."

"I want to."

"You might not feel that way when you meet Murray."

"Why?"

"He makes my mother look progressive."

"Oh."

"Yeah." I lean over the stick shift, kiss the side of her mouth.

"Okay, girls," Murray announces after the introductions have been made. "How's about we go out for Chinese?"

"That okay with you?" I ask Julie.

"Sure."

"There's a new restaurant at the plaza we want to try out."

"You mean we're not going to Spring Gardens?" My family

has been eating out at the same local Jewish-style Chinese restaurant for decades. I'm shocked to hear we might be going someplace else.

"It's the same menu," my mother says.

Great. Sweet-and-sour chicken balls, honey garlic chicken wings, vegetable chow mein, consommé soup, all the blandest, sweetest items in Cantonese cuisine. I prefer spicy Szechuan myself. But my mother will eat nothing spicy at all.

When the food arrives, we load up our plates.

"Do you eat this kind of food at home?" my mother asks Julie.

"Ma, Julie is Japanese, not Chinese," I explain.

"What's the difference?" my mother says between bites of chicken fried rice.

"Ma!"

"What did I say?"

"Ma, think about it. That's like saying Polish culture is exactly the same as German. Or Italian."

"It is? I thought the Orientals were all the same." Murray adds this helpful little comment into the racist discussion we are having in front of the love of my life. I want to fall into quicksand and be swallowed into the centre of the earth.

"That's it." I stand. "Come on, Julie. You don't have to listen to this."

"What did we say?"

"Nomi, calm down, you're making a scene."

Julie takes my arm, pulls me back down into my chair. "It's okay, Nomi, they don't mean any harm."

"You see, Nomi?" my mother says.

"Julie, how can you say that? I'm sorry you had to hear that."

"It's okay. I've heard worse."

"I'm sure you have."

"Your parents probably have never actually met an Asian person before, have you?"

"He's not my parent," I grump. I refuse to take responsibility for Murray Feinstein. Just because my mother married him doesn't mean I have to have anything to do with him. Now that I know how racist he is. Murray looks hurt. But I don't care. It's the truth. What a *putz*.

"There's a lot of difference between Japanese and Chinese culture," Julie patiently explains. "Our food is different. Customs. Language. Everything."

"Who would have thought?" my mother muses.

"I'm sorry, Julie," Murray says. "It's true. I'm ignorant."

"That's okay." Julie lets them off the hook.

"Pass around the chow mein," my mother says. "There's plenty. Did everyone get?"

We pass around the food, eat in silence. I don't know how much more of this I can take.

"I've always thought you people were very lucky," my mother says, through mouthfuls of sticky red, sweet-and-sour chicken balls.

"Ma, I think we've heard enough."

"No, it's okay. How do you mean, Mrs. Rabinovitch?"

"Oy. I'm Mrs. Feinstein now." She looks lovingly at Murray.

"I'm sorry," says Julie. "I forgot."

"Never mind," my mother says. "I'm not used to it myself. Anyway, please call me Faygie."

"O-kay ..." I know Julie is uncomfortable with that suggestion. "Faygie, what do you mean we're lucky?"

"The Asians are lucky because you don't age," my mother the genetic-expert announces. "You all look so young."

"Thank you," Julie smiles.

"The Japanese are small. That's what I think. They're much smaller than the Chinese. The Chinese can be big, even fat. I've seen some fat ladies ..."

"Ma, can you pass the rice? We need more rice over here."

Julie giggles. I sigh dramatically and eat more rice.

"I've never eaten Japanese food. It's that raw fish, isn't it?" Murray gets back into the conversation.

"Sushi, you mean. But we have other dishes. Teriyaki salmon and chicken."

"That sounds good."

"It's delicious. Why don't you come over for dinner one night while Nomi is here. I'll cook you a Japanese dinner," Julie offers. I choke on a deep fried chicken bone.

"A real Oriental meal," Murray surmises. "With fortune cookies and everything?"

"Uh, we don't have fortune cookies."

"That's the Chinese," my mother corrects him.

"I think it's just about time for cookies now." I call the waiter over with the bill.

"Oh look," my mother says, reading her fortune. " 'You are popular and charming.' What's yours, Murray?"

"Mine says, 'Watch for fallen rocks.' What do you think that means?"

"Fallen rocks?"

I peer over Julie's shoulder. Hers says, "You are well loved."

"That's the truth," I whisper to her. Mine reads, "Beware the tall stranger." I glance at Murray. He is kind of tall.

"Well." Murray pulls out his Diner's Club card, plops it over the bill. "That was great, girls. How's about a game of Scrabble?"

"Uh, thanks Murray, but I'm going with Julie back to her place tonight."

"Nomi. Really? I was hoping you would stay by me. I hardly get to see you," my mother pleads.

"Ma, I was just here for your wedding."

She shrugs. "What can I say? I miss you. I'm a mother."

"Well, sorry, Ma. But Julie and I need to spend some time together too. We don't get enough time."

"I know." My mother leans forward, addresses Julie. "Why don't you stay with us too. Then we can all be together."

"Ma, I don't think ..."

"We'd be delighted," Julie says.

I stare at her. "We would?"

Back at my mother's house, we sit around the kitchen table, the Scrabble board between us. It's Julie's turn. She's a genius at

Scrabble. I'm barely functional. Julie adds an *e* and a *d* to Murray's word, *guard*, to become *guarded*. The *d* lands on a triple word score.

"What's going to happen with Bubbe now?" I ask my mother, stalling for time. It's my turn. I have both *q*'s, an *x* and a *j*. The only vowels I have are *e*'s and *i*'s. I don't have a clue what to do with this.

My mother sighs. "I guess she'll go back to the Home now."

We contemplate that in silence while I strain for a Scrabble word. I feel depressed. What kind of a life is that? To live your so-called golden years in a second-rate old folks' home where you spend your days sitting on a plastic-covered chair in the lobby, doing nothing, staring into space.

"When I get to that state," my mother says, "just put me to sleep. Like you would for a sick dog."

"Ma, we can't put you to sleep."

"I'm putting it in my will, Nomi. I don't want to end up in a Home."

"I'm not putting you to sleep, Ma. And you mean a living will."

"I mean put me to sleep. Whose turn is it?"

"Mine. I don't have anything."

"Let me see." Julie leans over, studies my tiles.

"Hey, is that allowed?" Murray asks.

"No, it's not allowed," my mother confirms.

"Sorry." Julie pulls back.

"I'm serious, Nomi," my mother says. "I can't live in a Home like that. I can't do it."

"Ma ..."

"So just put me to sleep. Like a dog. They do it for dogs, don't they?"

"Ma, you're not a dog."

"I'm warning you, Nomi."

"Ma ..."

"You can live with us, Faygie," Julie announces.

"What?" I can't believe Julie just said that.

"Thank you, dear."

"I'll take care of you, Faygie." Murray seems hurt.

"That's nice, Murray. But I'll outlive you. Men always go first."

Murray's face falls. "Is that true?"

"Course it's true. Nomi, put down a word already."

"I pass. I have nothing." I grumble.

"You have an *e*." Julie prods.

"So?"

"Look on the left side."

"Huh?" I do as I'm told. The word leaps out. *Gap*. "Oh." I add my *e* on the end. Seven points. Better than nothing.

The rest of the evening is actually pleasant. My mother makes tea. We play out the game. We manage to make it until bedtime without any more racist remarks.

"Well," I say, stretching, "think it's time for bed."

"Oh. Okay," my mother says. "I thought I'd put you in your room, and Julie can sleep in the den."

"Ma ..."

"What'sa matter?"

"Julie is sleeping with me. Don't be ridiculous."

"Oh ... I just thought ..."

"No. You didn't think." My stomach tightens in anger. "What if I was Josh? Would you make Maria sleep in the den?"

"Yes, I would," my mother insists.

"You would not."

"Until they're married, you can forget that."

"But if he lived out of town ... ?"

"Same thing. I treat all my kids the same."

She's infuriating me. We could just leave. I could take Julie's hand and we could walk out the door and sleep at her house. It would be more fun. "Ma, Julie is sleeping with me." I stand, grab Julie's hand. "Good night." I pull Julie up and toward the hall.

"Good night," Julie says. "Thanks again for dinner, Mr. and Mrs. Feinstein ..."

"Call us Faygie and Murray," my mother reminds her.

Julie smiles.

"Good night," I say, dragging Julie to the bathroom.

Then finally we are blessedly alone in my room. I switch off the overhead and light some candles. We strip and climb into bed. Julie falls into my arms. We kiss. She runs one hand up the length of my body. I freeze.

"I can't."

"What's the matter, Nomi?"

"I can't make love in this room."

"Why not?"

"It's my childhood bedroom."

"So?"

"My mother is in the next room. With Murray."

"Maybe they're doing the same thing."

"I don't want to even think about that."

"Okay, then let's just sleep."

"Are you sure?"

"Yes, Nomi."

"Good night."

I hold her to me tightly. Kiss her forehead.

"I don't know what I would have done," I say to Julie.

She strokes the side of my face. Kisses it. "Done?"

"You know, if Bubbe had died before I got here. When I was on the plane, I thought for sure she had."

"It would be hard, but ..."

"What?"

"I was away when my father died," she says.

"When was that?" The candlelight plays across Julie's face. I can see the grief in her beautiful eyes.

"It was three years ago."

"Where were you?"

"At an AIDS conference. I was in New York. I flew back as soon as my mother phoned, but ..." Her eyes well up with tears.

I wipe her tears with my thumbs. Kiss her face. "That must have been hard."

"I felt so bad. Like, why wasn't I here?"

"You probably didn't know, right?"

"He'd been sick for a while, but I didn't know."

I hold her tightly.

"I've never talked about this." She looks at me intently.

"I'm glad you trust me."

"Can I?"

"What do you think?"

"What are we going to do, Nomi? I want to be with you. Really be with you."

I don't know what to say.

"Don't you?" I can hear fear in her voice. She's afraid of my answer.

"Course I do."

"Then?"

"I really like San Francisco. And I have friends there."

"Don't you have any friends here?"

"Well, not many. Not like there. I mean, there's Stein, but ..."

"Stein?"

"We've known each other a long time. I haven't seen her since I moved."

"Nomi, that's not good."

"I know."

"Tell me about Stein."

"How about later?" I lean over and kiss her.

My hand wanders over her back. She moans as I stroke her gently. Her lips find mine. We are kissing again. Deeply. Silently. Falling into the abyss of our lust for each other. We can't hold back. I push her over onto her back, touch her everywhere. She moves under me.

My mouth finds her nipple. Julie moans quietly. We are riding a five-foot wave in the middle of the ocean. Its power lifts us, carries us away from the shore. We are alone in the world as the swell rises. Julie's hand pushes its way inside me. I rock in rhythm with her. As the undertow drags me under the surface and my orgasm rips through me, Julie thrusts one hand over my mouth to contain my scream. I come all over her hand. Silently. The world outside this room is nothing. There is no Murray. No mother. No one but Julie and me.

FALL 1999

AN AUTUMN CHILL AND OTHER HAZARDS

HENRY'S COLLAPSED LUNG

I'm wearing nothing but a flimsy towel tied around my waist as I walk into the Barn, a dark bar on Church Street filled to the brim with big burly leathermen, fading queens and stud muffins. I'm looking for Roger but I can't find him through the crowd. I'm drawing quite a bit of attention, dressed as I am. An older fag, lined face as leathery as his chaps, throws a heavy arm over my shoulder, leans forward and kisses me with thick wet lips. I push at his chest. Where's Roger? The phone starts ringing like mad. Why doesn't someone answer? It rings louder. I open my eyes, sit up, lunge for the receiver before it wakes Roger, who is in a deep, exhausted sleep in the bed beside me.

"What?" I whisper gruffly into the phone, crawling out of bed over Roger. He got to bed at seven this morning, after working night shift. He needs his beauty sleep. With the phone, I creep into the hallway and quietly close our bedroom door.

"You're not going to believe it." It's Albert, calling from New York.

"Good news or bad?" I clear my throat. My chest feels congested.

"The best. Have you seen the Toronto paper?"

"Roger got in late. I haven't checked."

"Well, listen to this. Here's the headline. Front page. Did I mention?"

"Front page?"

"Front and centre. It's the top story."

"Okay. What's the headline?"

"'U.S. Government Invented AIDS. Scientist Blows Whistle.' Can you believe that?"

"Just barely." I cough.

"Then it goes on to detail everything we've been saying. Jonathan is quoted throughout. He sounds like the expert he is. They didn't cut a line from Rick's original. They left in Jonathan's memories of working at Fort Detrick, of the pressure to invent an immune system-destroying agent, the complicity of the pharmaceutical companies and the money they stood to make, how they slipped it into the hep B vaccine, and how the President knew about the whole thing."

"They left that in?"

"Everything. It's all there. It's a special three-page report. And it says there will be more to follow in the next couple of days. This is it, Henry. We've done it."

"Oh my God." I sink onto the hardwood floor. "We need to celebrate, Al."

"Later, Henry. We've got lots to do."

"Right."

"We have to monitor all the news stations, CNN, the internet news. Everything. We need to see who covers it next. And we need to send out new press releases. Maybe the story will be picked up by some of the network shows. I spoke to Jonathan already. He's all set to go on air and be interviewed if anyone asks. Can I count on support from your ACTOUT group?"

"You got it. I'll call an emergency meeting this morning and split up all the work."

"Thanks. I knew I could count on you."

"No problem, Al." I breathe in. The air catches in my throat. I cough, deeply.

"Henry, that cough doesn't sound so good. Have you seen your doctor?"

"I see my doctor all the time, Al. I'm inhaling pentamidine three times a week. I feel like a junkie. But it doesn't seem to be working this time."

"Don't burn yourself out, Henry. Spread the work around, okay? I don't want you ending up in the hospital. What kind of a celebration are we going to have then?"

"I hear you."

"Good."

At six o'clock I'm posted at the living room TV in Queen David's lavish home in the east side, switched to ABC, waiting for the evening news. Queen David has five television sets in the house. Julie is in the bedroom tuned in to CBS. Ed is stationed in the kitchen on NBC. Queen David is in the master bedroom watching CITY TV. "I just love the local news. So quaint," he gushes. The TV in the guest room is being manned by David-to-Die-For. He's going to switch between CTV and CBC. Al in New York is covering CNN. Computer David is searching the web for news items. New York David volunteered to track down copies of any out-of-town newspaper he could get his hands on at the magazine stores on Yonge Street. Annoying David is scanning international stations on a friend's short-wave radio. Ed ran around all day borrowing VCRs and is hooking them up to Queen David's TVs so we can tape everything. Even Greta is helping. She's tuned into CHUM Radio.

Julie phoned Nomi earlier and asked her to watch the San Francisco news. Her friend Guido has a satellite dish and can pick up stations in northern California, Oregon and Washington, and as far south as Mexico City. Al has enlisted help from ACTOUT New York and they have members covering all the major eastern stations. Queen David put on a pot of coffee earlier. There is pizza on the way. It's going to be a long night.

At six o'clock, it starts. It's the top story on NBC, ABC, CBS, CTV and CITY TV. There is a brief mention on CNN with a promise of a full interview with Dr. Garrick later this evening. Queen David's phone starts ringing at five after six with reports. I squeal with delight when Dan Rather says he put in a call to President Clinton at the White House and has so far not received a response. The President is going to have to make some kind of statement. I can see his speechwriters madly at work as we speak. I can't wait to see what he will say. Of course, he's right in the middle of the Lewinsky scandal and can scarcely afford another problem. On the other hand, he may relish this opportunity. After all, it was the Nixon administration that approved the study, not his. It's obviously not his blunder. The Republicans must be squirming tonight. This can't look good on them.

All the excitement is going to my chest, which is already tight. I'm sipping a cup of herbal tea with lemon, but can't stop clearing my throat. It's getting harder to take a deep breath. It feels like my lungs are collapsing. I keep it to myself. I don't want to impersonate Patient Zero on such an incredible night. Too drama-queen for my tastes. Being the son of my Jewish mother, I prefer to suffer in silence. Don't worry about me. I'll sit in the dark with a cracker.

At seven we gather in the living room to report and eat pizza. Queen David sets out his good china and pops the cork on two bottles of champagne, real French champagne.

"Only the best for such an occasion." He pours the bubbly into fabulous crystal flutes and passes them out.

We toast each other, and especially Jonathan Garrick. Without his testimony, none of this would be happening. I sip lightly on my champagne. Despite the festivities, my head is pounding. My forehead is hot. I should go home to bed, but it's too exciting. Julie sits beside me with her pizza.

"You don't look so good," she says to me quietly.

I smile bravely. "I might be coming down with something."

She touches my face. "You're burning up, Henry. Let me drive you home."

"Not yet. I really want to be here."

She sighs. "Okay, you let me know when."

"What's the plan after this?" asks David-to-Die-For.

"We wait for requests from the media," I say.

"Jonathan is all set to be interviewed live. Al will go on the shows too," Julie adds.

"I'm the local media contact. Al's handling the U.S.," I say.

"Are you sure you're up to it, Henry?" Julie asks. "I can do it if you want."

"Aren't you feeling well?" David-to-Die-For asks.

"I'm fine," I insist.

"You do look a little peaked, dear," Queen David observes. "Can I get you something? A Tylenol, perhaps?"

"Sure. A couple, please. I want to do it," I tell Julie. "If I get overwhelmed I'll divert some of the calls to you. Okay? Don't treat me like a patient. Please. Then I'll really start to feel sick."

The phone rings.

"Buckingham Palace," Queen David says into the receiver. "Yes. Isn't it glorious? A true victory. Bravo, Albert. Bravo." He passes the phone to me. "Here you go, love."

"Isn't it great?" Albert says.

"Amazing."

"Listen, I just got a call from CITY TV. That's in Toronto, isn't it?"

"Yep."

"They want to interview someone from ACTOUT right now. Can you do it?"

"Me?"

"Sure. You know the details."

"Uh ... no. Not me. I'm not really up for it. How about Julie?"

"What?" Julie asks.

I turn to her. "Can you do an interview for CITY TV?"

"Now?"

"Yeah."

"I guess. Are they coming here?"

"I don't know." Into the phone I say, "Where?"

"I believe at their studio." He rattles off the contact information. I jot it down on a pad Queen David has by the phone, hand it to Julie.

"Call later and fill me in," Albert says. "This is too good."

We hang up.

"Come on, Henry," Julie says. "I'll drop you off at home on my way, okay?"

"Okay." I don't really want to leave. I want to be here to celebrate our victory. But I should lie down. Everyone is planning to stay and do it all over again for the eleven o'clock news. I'll have to watch the news from bed, where I can lie down in relative quiet. I hope my father is not home. I don't think I could take any more excitement.

In Julie's car I lean my head against the headrest, open the window slightly. It's warm for September, but you can already feel the fall chill in the night air. We pass by several green bags of rotting garbage on the street in front of restaurants and stores. The stench makes me gag. A fine layer of sweat breaks out all over my skin. Fever again. Every muscle in my body aches, even my skin and my teeth. I concentrate on breathing. It feels like my lungs are pinching smaller and smaller with every breath.

"Henry, I'm worried," Julie says.

"Me too," I admit for the first time.

"Is Roger home?"

"He's on night shift. Won't be back until morning. But I'll be okay. Really. My father's probably there."

"I have my cell phone. Call me if you need anything. I don't care what time it is. Okay, Henry?"

"Yes, Mother." I offer a smile.

Julie tries to insist on riding the elevator with me to my apartment, but I assure her I'm fine on my own. As I open the front door of my apartment my mother stomps out, red-faced, mouth pursed, cigarette burning between two fingers.

"I should have known," she tells me. "Same old Solly. What was I thinking? A man doesn't change overnight, does he, Henry?" She puffs on her cigarette, blows smoke all over me. I cough, wave it away.

Great. This is just what I need right now. A hysterical mother.

"No. Not Solly Rabinovitch. Hah. To think I trusted him. Again. What an idiot I am. Henry?" She stares at me.

"What?"

"You look tired. Are you feeling well?" She reaches up, puts a hand on my forehead. "Oh my God. You're burning up. You have a fever."

"It's okay. I'm getting into bed. Can you put out the cigarette, please?"

"Henry. Maybe we should call the doctor."

"Ma, it's 1999. It's not like doctors still make house calls."

"Then we should take you to the hospital. Solly!" She grabs my hand, hauls me inside my apartment. "Solly, we're taking Henry to the hospital. Look at him." My father sits in the big armchair sipping Jack Daniel's.

"What are you talking about?"

"I'm fine." I say. "I'm going to bed. Ma, the cigarette?"

She stubs it out on a saucer filled with butts she must have used earlier. I glare at Solly for allowing her to smoke in the apartment.

"Henry?" my mother says softly. "You're sure you're okay?" She looks frightened. I lean over, kiss her on the cheek.

"I'm fine." I cough.

"Just as stubborn as your father," she says.

"Belle ..."

"Don't Belle me, Solly. I'm still mad at you." She scowls at Solly, then smiles sweetly at me. "Good night, sweetheart." She marches past me, out the door.

"Goes to show you, Henry," my father says. "Never go back. I don't know what we were thinking. But you know, Henry, your mother's crazy about me. Always has been. Always will be."

"What's she so mad about?" I plunk onto the sofa, remove my runners.

Solly sighs. Takes a sip of his drink. "She wants a commitment. I don't see why we can't just relax and enjoy the moment. You know what I'm saying?"

"What kind of commitment?"

"How the hell should I know?"

I lean back into the sofa. Try to take a deep breath. It catches in my throat. I'm out of breath from my walk down the hall.

"I don't know why she's so upset." He sips his drink.

I nod, breathe rapid short breaths.

"All I said was, 'What for, sweetheart?'"

"What for?" I repeat.

"Yeah. Then she went ballistic, started screaming, threw her drink in my face. A nice martini I made her. Then she stomps outta here."

I listen, nod, breathe.

Solly turns his head, looks at me for the first time. "You look terrible. What'sa matter?"

In between breaths I say, "Not ... feeling ... good."

"You gotta get in bed. Come on." He places his drink on the coffee table, helps me up. I lean on his arm down the hall. Like a little boy I let him remove my shirt. He helps me slide my pants off and puts me to bed. I feel like crying.

"Maybe I should call Roger," my father suggests.

"Just need sleep," I say, although he's probably right. I just can't bear the thought of going back outside, even if it's to get to the hospital.

"I don't know."

"It's okay."

"All right," he says, but he doesn't sound convinced. I just want him to turn off the light and leave me alone, but he sits in the armchair by the window, facing the bed. "Your Bubbe's gotta go back to the Home tomorrow. The doctor says she's fine. Lou's gonna pick me up in the morning. We'll take her back, settle her in. Guess you don't wanna come?"

"Think I'll sit this one out."

"Yeah, sure."

I close my eyes. Breathe. Sleep overtakes me. I feel safe, in bed, with my father watching me. As I drift off I hear him humming faintly. I recognize the tune. It's an old Yiddish lullaby my grandfather used to sing. It's so comforting I actually fall asleep.

NOMI'S GREAT IDEA

I throw open the doors to Patty's Place and walk outside. It's a brilliant September afternoon in San Francisco. We haven't had fog for days. It's been hot and sunny, even in the evenings. We are getting our summer now, after a rainy July and August. Cortland Avenue, the heart of Bernal Heights, is filled with lesbians. I wave to Esther, the woman who owns Bernal Books, a neighbourhood bookstore across the street from Patty's, as she arranges books on shelves. A lesbian couple in business suits walks past. A bus stops by the curb, its exhaust pouring out the back pipe. The sidewalk cafés are full of patrons sipping the latest in Californian espresso drinks and Italian pastries, all the rage since Starbucks came to San Francisco. People are walking around in shorts and T-shirts, basking in the warmth. The sky is turquoise. There are thin wispy clouds high in the sky. Palm trees flutter in the slight breeze. The sun burns through the ozone layer down on us mortals. I worry that I don't have any sunscreen on.

I slip into my leather jacket but leave it unzipped, stuff my gelled hair into my helmet, fasten the strap under my chin. My bike starts up first try. I stand beside it while it idles. A group of boisterous lesbians heads my way up the sidewalk. When they are within a block I recognize them. Betty, Chester, Guido and AJ. My gang.

"Hey Nom, wait up," Betty shouts.

"What?" I yell over the din of my motor.

"We came to pick you up. You off work already?"

"Patty let me go early. What's up?"

The gang huddles around my motorcycle. "We figure a celebration is in order," Betty announces.

"Celebration?"

"Sure. Aren't you excited?"

"About what?"

"The AIDS conspiracy thing." Betty says this as if I'm really dense to have missed the point.

"Oh."

"Aren't you happy for your girlfriend? And your cousin? Isn't this the big breakthrough they were waiting for?" Betty persists.

"Yeah ..."

"So we're having the West Coast Lesbians in Support of Julie Celebration."

"The what?"

"You heard me. It's a new group. We're the founding members. Switch off your bike. We're going to Patty's." Betty reaches over and turns my ignition off. My bike sputters to a stop.

"Hey."

"Come on, Nomi, it'll be fun," Chester says.

"I just came from Patty's. I worked all afternoon."

"First round's on me." Betty throws an arm over my shoulder and steers me toward the door.

"Since when did you become so generous?" I remove my helmet and allow her to lead me back inside the darkened pub.

"Since she's in love," Guido answers.

"What?" I stare at Betty. She hasn't been in love, hasn't even toyed with the L-word since Donna.

"I'm not in love," Betty insists, but a hint of a smile gives her away.

"Sure she is." Guido shakes her head. "Head over fucking heels."

"She is? What did she tell you?" I pump Guido for the info.

"Hey, I'm right here. Don't talk about me as if I'm not here."

Betty heads for the bar, leans her arm heavily on the counter. "Gimme a Guinness, Patty. No head."

"No head, my ass." Patty grabs a beer mug and pulls the draught, makes sure there's a good two-inch head on it. She looks up, notices me. "What the hell you doing here, Rabinovitch? I thought I told you to go home early."

I shrug, helpless to affect my own destiny. "Give me a vodka martini. Straight up with a twist."

"Martinis are made with gin, Rabinovitch." Patty despises vodka martinis. Says they're imitations, like no-name cola. "You should have the real thing, or nothing at all."

"Fine." I don't really care. Vodka or gin, they both taste like rubbing alcohol to me. I just like martini glasses — so elegant and sophisticated. They make me feel like a grown-up.

"Give me a Bud." Guido orders her usual watery American beer.

"I'll have a Jameson's, on the rocks," Chester says.

AJ orders a gin and tonic. No lime.

We take up five stools at the bar, sit elbow to elbow like guys. Betty, me, Guido, Chester, then AJ.

"So?" I face Betty, martini in hand. "Who are you in love with?"

"I am *not* in love." Betty sips her Guinness.

"Come on, Betty. We saw the way you looked at her," Guido counters.

"Yeah. Your boss." AJ is amazed at Betty's prowess, as always.

"I am not in love with my boss," Betty repeats.

"Mona?" I ask. "What happened?"

"Nothing happened."

"But it will," Guido predicts. "It will. We know you, Betty. Come on."

"Yeah."

"That's right."

"We'll see." Betty plays it coy. Lifts her mug in the air. "So? How about that toast? Boys?"

We all lift our glasses high.

Betty begins her speech. "The first official gathering of the West Coast Lesbians in Support of Julie would like to propose a toast in honour of the AIDS conspiracy thing being splashed all over the news."

Kind of a lame toast, but we clink glasses and drink exuberantly. I feel happy and sad at the same time. Julie would love this. I wish she were here.

"Okay," says Betty, "who wants to play Ms. Pac Man? Dollar a game."

Patty still has an old Ms. Pac Man machine from the eighties. It's probably the last one in civilization. It actually works. But then Patty oils and maintains all her video games and pinball machines weekly. Two of the pinball machines are over thirty years old and still work like a charm.

Guido takes Betty's challenge. As they head for the game, I walk toward the rest room. A notice on the bulletin board at the back of the pub catches my eye. It's a job posting. ASIA, the Asian Society for the Intervention of AIDS in Vancouver, is looking for a program co-coordinator. The posting makes me think of Julie, but then everything makes me think of Julie. It's not until I'm sitting on the toilet that the idea strikes me. Vancouver. I've never actually been there, but I hear it's beautiful. And it's on the west coast. No winters to speak of. Couldn't be that much different from San Francisco. No palm trees, of course. But probably no fog either. On my way back to my seat at the bar, I snatch the posting from the bulletin board.

"What's that?" Chester asks.

I ask Patty to fix me a second martini. "Job posting."

Chester looks over my shoulder. "Program co-ordinator? You don't know anything about that, Nom."

"Thanks for the vote of confidence." I snarl.

"Well, it's true."

"Not for me. For Julie."

"Oh." Chester reads on. "Vancouver. Hey, that's in Canada, right?"

"Ten points." It never ceases to amaze me how ignorant

Americans are about Canada. "It's in B.C."

"D.C.?" asks AJ.

"No. *Bee*, Cee."

"Oh. Is that in Maryland?"

"Canada, stupid," Chester tells AJ.

"All the way up there?"

"Vancouver is about an hour or two north of Seattle," I guess.

"I was in Seattle once," AJ announces. "Rained the whole time. Rain, rain, rain. Nothing but rain."

"Really?" Hmmm. Maybe Vancouver's not such a good idea.

"Rain, rain, rain." AJ repeats.

"Aren't there mountains there?"

"Yep. Mountains and rain. Lots of rain."

"Would you stop saying that?" She's starting to annoy me.

"I bought a T-shirt there," AJ continues. "It said ..." she thinks hard. "Wait a minute, I'll get it ..."

"I've never been farther north than Oakland," Chester decides. "It must be cold in Seattle."

"Oh, it was," AJ confirms. "Now what did that shirt say?"

"But there's no snow?" I grasp at straws.

"No, just rain."

"You already said that."

"You wouldn't believe how much rain."

"Say that one more time and I'm going to kill you."

"Nomi, would you take a pill? Why are you so upset about the rain in Seattle?" Chester asks.

"Who said I was upset?"

Patty places my martini in front of me. I grab it and take a large swallow.

"You just threatened to kill AJ," Chester points out.

"Yeah and I meant every word."

"I know what it said," AJ blurts. "It said, 'Seattle Rain Festival. January 1 to December 31.' Isn't that funny?"

"Hilarious."

Patty reaches forward and snatches the job posting out of my clutches. Reads it carefully. Nods her head. Looks me in the eye. "Damn good idea, Rabinovitch. Best idea you've had in years. Remember what I said." She returns the posting to me.

"What?"

"Love. It doesn't grow on trees."

"Isn't that money?" AJ asks.

"No," Patty says. "Everyone knows love's harder to come by than money. You want another beer?" she asks Guido.

"Sure."

"How about a Miller?" Patty grabs the empty Budweiser bottle.

"No. A Bud."

"Nobody wants the Miller. If you have a Miller, I'll give you a discount."

"How much of a discount?"

"Fifty percent off." Patty grabs a Miller from the beer fridge.

"Fifty percent? In that case, give me two."

"I hope you're not driving." I stare at Guido as Patty sets down two bottles of beer in front of her.

"I'm not even walking. You guys are carrying me home."

"In your dreams."

After my second martini I get a ride home and call Julie.

"Vancouver?" she repeats. "I've never even been there, Nomi."

"Me either. But think about it."

"Yes ..."

"Oh God, Julie, don't do that."

"Do what?"

"Use your sexy voice. How can I talk about serious matters if you're going to get sexy?"

"Sorry."

"There you go again."

"Don't be a nut, Nomi. If we moved to Vancouver, where would we live?"

"I don't know. We'd find a place. Maybe if you got the job, they'd help you."

"Would you really leave San Francisco?"

"Sure."

"Really?"

"Julie, I miss you too much. We have to do something."

"Then why not move here?"

"I like being on the coast."

"You've never even been to Vancouver."

"I know. But I know I would like it."

"What about all your friends in San Francisco?"

"They'll come and visit. I'll visit them."

"You'll miss them."

"Not as much as I miss you."

"What would you do?"

"Same thing I'm doing now. There's bars in Vancouver, right?"

"I don't know ..."

"Why not?"

"Well, my mother, for one thing."

"Oh."

"Who would take care of her if I left Toronto?"

"Your brother?"

"Fat chance."

"Oh, and your sister lives in Japan."

"Right. There's just me."

"Oh."

"Nomi. Don't be upset. It's a good idea."

"It is?"

"Sure. Fax me the posting. I'll apply for the job. Let's see what happens."

"What about your mother?"

"I don't know. Let me think about it."

"Really?"

"Sure. Fax it to me. I'll apply."

"You're going to get it."

"Let's just see what happens."

HENRY'S VALLEY
OF THE DOLLS

I open my eyes to be assaulted by harsh fluorescent ceiling lights. My mouth is covered in a plastic oxygen mask, the elastic strap digs into my chin. I hear the sounds of my own breathing — short, shallow, raspy. My chest aches. It feels like my lungs have fully collapsed, like I am breathing under water. Every breath bangs against my ribs painfully. My hands and feet are cold. There is tingling in my fingers. There are razor blades in my throat. It is impossible to swallow. My tongue is parched, like a thick, dried-out sponge resting against scratchy teeth.

I vaguely remember getting to the hospital. I fell asleep with my father sitting in the chair in my room. I had bad dreams: my feet are in a bucket of concrete. Two thugs throw me off a pier into the lake by the commercial docks. I plunge down to the bottom of the freezing lake like a rock. I flap my arms, try to swim back up, but it doesn't work. I sink like a stone. I try to breathe. Water rushes into my mouth, my lungs. Who said that drowning is a peaceful way to die? All I feel is terror. The need to breathe. Violent assault against my lungs. Bursting. Raging. Black spots in front of my eyes. My hands and feet are freezing. Eyes wide, struggling for the surface.

"I'm here, Henry. Hang on." Roger held my cold fingers in his warm hand as the paramedics attached the oxygen mask to my face. I remember the sting of a needle in my forearm, the IV tube. The rush of euphoria, numbing drugs. I couldn't speak.

No words. Trying to breathe. Roger's face alert and terrified. I remember the siren, the bounce of potholes on the road, under my back. Lying in the back of the ambulance. Roger rode to the hospital with me. Held my hand the whole way.

I shift in the bed, turn my head to the side. Pain slices up my side. Roger is sitting on the hard chair by my bed, watching me. He smiles. I breathe.

"Good news," he says quietly.

What could possibly be good? I'm in the hospital. I can't breathe. My hands and feet are numb. I can't speak. I can tell without a mirror I'm having a bad hair day. I have jungle breath. And I missed the eleven o'clock news. I was supposed to be monitoring CITY TV. I wanted to see Julie's interview. I hope Queen David taped the show. I feel like crying. Defeat runs through me like a tainted blood transfusion. How could I end up in the hospital again? And what could possibly be good?

"It's pneumonia." Roger beams.

Why is he so happy about that? I nod. I figured it was PCP. My first bout. Usually the beginning of the quick decline from HIV positive to full-blown AIDS. I've watched so many friends go through the drill. Asymptomatic. Maybe a couple of minor ailments like thrush, or herpes, or shingles, or intestinal parasites, or the heartbreak of psoriasis, or the beginnings of a bald spot, or occasional impotence, or bad breath or athlete's foot gone astray. And then suddenly they're rushed to the hospital with pneumocystis carinii pneumonia and it's all downhill from there. The beginning of the end. The storm after the calm. Break out the dancing, boys. I'm Barbara Hershey dying at the end of *Beaches,* leaving my firstborn daughter to Bette Midler to raise in my absence. I'm Tony, dying in the arms of Maria. I can hear the soundtrack from *West Side Story* playing in the background. *There's a place for us, somewhere a place for us, hold my hand and we're halfway there …*

"Not PCP, Henry." Roger interrupts Tony and Maria's touching duet.

I'm too weak to talk. What? I ask with my eyes.

"Just regular pneumonia." Roger seems happy about this. Has he finally gone round the bend? Since when is pneumonia something to celebrate?

"Don't you get it? It's not PCP."

I swallow past the lump of coal in my throat.

"Regular pneumonia is easier to treat. It's not as aggressive as PCP. And it's not a symptom of full-blown AIDS." Roger seems genuinely happy about all this. When I can speak again I'm going to recommend a good psychiatrist to him. If it isn't a symptom of full-blown AIDS, what is it a symptom of? Half-baked AIDS?

"You should be on your feet again in a couple of weeks." Roger is practically gushing. "You've probably had walking pneumonia for weeks now. I should have made you slow down."

"Roger." I move the mask away from my face.

"Don't." Gently he repositions the mask. "Just breathe, Henry." He takes a deep breath to show me how it's done.

As if I don't know. And if I only follow his example I'll be breathing again. But will I ever set the world's one-hundred yard dash record? Will I make the Olympic track team? Will I win a gold medal for my country? And will I ever play the piano again?

"It could be a lot worse," Roger repeats. "You're going to be fine. It's a good thing your father was there. Never thought I'd say that, but if he hadn't been there ..."

He trails off. Was it that bad? Is he saying I would have died if my father hadn't been there? Perished, in the absolute prime of my youth? Would Roger have come home to find me expired?

"Solly phoned me at work. Do you remember the ambulance?"

Sort of. I nod. He came home early? It must have been bad if Roger left work early. Normally Roger is little Miss Eager Beaver. Takes on extra shifts. Helps Shirley at the front desk without being asked, as if he's going for the Miss Congeniality award.

"After you fell asleep, your breathing got worse. Solly was scared. I phoned an ambulance as soon as I saw you. There was no circulation in your hands or feet. Your lips were blue, Henry."

A new fashion statement perhaps. Blue lips.

"He's here. In the cafeteria. He's pretty shaken up."

That makes two of us.

"He did the right thing, Henry. It's a good thing he was there. You should have phoned me earlier. How long were you feeling like that?"

I shrug. I didn't realize things had deteriorated. I thought I could handle it.

"Are you hungry?"

I shake my head. I feel queasy. What kind of drugs do they have me on?

"Do you feel sick?"

I nod.

"You could have a Gravol, if you want. The sulpha drugs they have you on can make you feel nauseous."

I nod.

"Hang on. I'll be right back." He leans over, kisses my forehead. My Prince Charming. I feel like Sleeping Beauty. He dashes out of the room. I check in with myself, try to figure out what I'm feeling, besides sick. Relieved? Depressed? Sad? All three? I guess Roger's right. It is good news. Sort of. It could be worse. But what does it mean? If it's just plain old garden-variety pneumonia, am I still merely HIV positive with symptoms? We used to call it ARC. AIDS-related complex. We used to believe that ARC didn't necessarily lead to AIDS. Just like heterosexual sex doesn't necessarily lead to pregnancy. Smoking doesn't necessarily lead to lung cancer. You're asymptomatic HIV positive if you have certain low-grade infections. It's full-blown AIDS if you have PCP, KS or CMV. It's so tiring. Honestly. All these rules and regulations. It's like the hanky code, or the agreement you sign when you join a new gym. No cruising in the sauna. No spitting in the pool. No urinating in the whirlpool. No loitering in the shower room. PCP equals AIDS. Silence equals death. Action equals life. Roger says I should be on my feet in a couple of weeks. Is he just being optimistic? Am I a real blond or is it Clairol? Only my hairdresser knows for sure. At this rate will I make it to the millennium? Or will I join Simon's lover Steven in the great beyond? If I die, will I go to heaven? Or hell? Or Miami Beach? Just as I'm about to fall deeper into my neurotic thoughts, Solly saunters into my room, sidles up to my bedside, peers at me.

"You look better," he decides. "Jeez, Henry, you scared the crap outta me." He's eating a broiled hot dog in a bun, covered in sweet relish and hot mustard. The smell makes me want to puke.

"Pop," I move the mask to the side. "Nauseous," I manage, while struggling for breath.

"Huh?"

I lift one heavy hand and point at the hot dog.

"Oh. Sorry, Henry. Hang on a second," he says, as if I'm going anywhere. He leaves the room. I breathe. He returns sans hot dog. "Jeez, Henry. Not doing so good, huh?" He sits beside my bed. "You had some kinda nightmare. Thrashing around on the bed. I thought you were suffocating. Jeez, I haven't been around many sick people. Didn't know what the fuck to do, so I called Roger. He sure knew what to do. Had you in an ambulance in no time. Tell you what? Next time I don't feel so good, I'm calling Roger. That guy woulda made some doctor. Hoo boy. What a guy."

I watch my father in amazement. This is the first time he has ever spoken so highly of Roger. Maybe some good does come out of everything bad.

Roger returns, smiles at my father, who smiles back. A regular mutual admiration society. Roger hits the switch that tilts the back of the bed up so I'm in a sitting position. He hands me a small blue pill. He gently moves the mask from my mouth. I take the pill with the water he offers. He fluffs the pillows behind me.

"I don't think I've ever spent so much time in hospitals," my father announces as I wait for the Gravol to take effect. "Between you and your grandmother. I hadda send your brothers to take her back to the Home this morning. Can you believe that?"

Sure. Why not? Isn't it about time Larry and Moe started taking on some family responsibilities?

"I better go up and see how she's doing, now that we know you're gonna live."

I nod. He's exhausting me. I want nothing but to sleep.

"Good idea," Roger tells my father. He can probably see I

need the rest.

"Okay then. I'll come back later." My father stands. "I'm telling you, one hospital to the next. I shoulda been a doctor, I been in so many hospitals lately." He leaves without saying goodbye.

Roger smooths my hair back. "You rest now. I'm going to be right here."

"No," I say into the mask. "Sleep." He's been up all night and now all day. He needs his sleep, too.

"It's okay. I booked off the next couple of days. I'll sleep later." He slouches in the chair. I close my eyes. The Gravol is making me drowsy. It's hard work to breathe. My chest aches with every breath. Feels like I'm going to bust apart. When I open my eyes again, Roger is dozing in the chair. It's a comforting sight. I allow myself to drift off.

I can barely believe my eyes when I wake to see Queen David in full drag, a jumbo Bette Midler as she was in *The Rose*, standing at my bedside. Julie sits in the chair. She looks like she hasn't slept all night. There are dark circles under her eyes. Other than a hint of lipstick, she is uncharacteristically without makeup. The second Queen David notices I'm awake, he breaks out into song, minus a proper introduction.

Some say love, it is a river
That drowns the tender reed.
Some say love, it is a razor
That leaves your soul to bleed.
Some say love ...

He looks good for a two-hundred-and-fifty-pound female impersonator. He's even got the gravelly voice down pat. But his wig is slightly askew and his large belly jiggles with every note, over the top of his turquoise spandex. The Divine Miss M would be horrified. Either that, or delighted. I laugh, then cough, splitting my lungs in two.

"Stop," I mumble into my plastic mask. I clutch my aching chest and look around for Roger.

"Your boyfriend's not here," the queen informs me. "I sent

him home for sleep before he ends up in the next bed over."

"Henry." Julie leans closer. "I feel so bad. I should have brought you here myself instead of dropping you off at home."

"It's okay." I breathe in. My chest opens, just a little bit.

"God, Henry, I would never have forgiven myself ..." Julie's big brown eyes fill with tears. She means if I'd up and died that night.

"It's okay ..."

She quickly composes herself, wipes the tear under each eye with a deft motion of her index finger, pinkie held high. Do femme lesbians imitate drag queens? Or is it the other way around?

"How do you feel?"

I shrug. "Run over."

"Run over by a truck?"

I nod.

"You should have seen Julie on the news," Queen David spurts. "She was simply divine. The next Miss Connie Chung."

"Yich." Julie shakes her head.

"What's wrong with Connie Chung? She's fabulous," the queen announces, one hand on a hip, the other outstretched, like Carol Merrill on *Let's Make a Deal.*

"Why compare me to her? Because we're both Asian?"

"Oh." Queen David realizes his blunder. "Because you're both Divine." He says it with a capital "D."

Julie sighs. "We taped it for you, Henry. For later." Julie pulls a videocassette from the huge black purse she always carries.

Too bad there's no VCR. I'd love to see it right now.

"You wouldn't believe it, Henry. The whole thing's been on every news program all last night, and all day today. President Clinton is making a televised statement tonight. Can you get your TV hooked up? It's on at eight."

I don't see why not. Roger can do anything. I nod.

"I'll come back and watch it with you here," Julie offers. "Oh, I guess visiting hours are over by eight."

I move the mask. "It's okay," I croak. I mean it's okay, Roger can probably sneak you in, but she thinks I mean it's okay, she doesn't have to come.

"Oh, well, I guess I'll watch at home."

"No, you must come to my house, Julie," Queen David says. "I'll phone around. We'll all watch it together. I mean ..." He stops, realizes it will be everyone but me. "I'm sorry, Henry."

I smile, but really I'm crying inside. Maybe I'm just a big baby. I'm lucky to be alive. I should be happy. But I feel sad. After all the hard work we put in to expose the truth and I can't be there with the gang to watch and celebrate. It's bittersweet. No. That's not right. It's just bitter. There's nothing really sweet about any of this. Even our victory is hollow in a way. It's terrifying, really. We haven't changed a thing. So many people have already died. There are still thirty million people worldwide who are infected with HIV. All of those people will eventually die. More people are getting infected every day, especially in Africa and Asia. We've exposed the evil truth, but does anybody care? I feel a deep and lingering depression somewhere in the centre of my belly. If this keeps up, Roger will have to prescribe Valium. I'll become Jacqueline Susann and enter the *Valley of the Dolls*. Uppers, downers. Prozac. Lithium. I'll pop them all. Anything but feel. I smile at Julie again. Hum a few bars inside my head of the old Judy Garland standard. *Smile, though your heart is aching. Smile. Smile. Smile.*

At precisely eight o'clock, Roger and I are posted in front of my TV-on-a-stick. It is attached to the wall behind my bed, right beside the oxygen outlet. There is no external speaker and only one set of headphones. Roger insists he doesn't need to hear the sound. President Clinton looks puffy. I know, on television you gain fifteen pounds, but he looks positively obese. The stress has probably sent him running to Krispy Kreme Doughnuts every hour on the hour. He dons a sombre expression, but his eyes are laughing. I suspect he finds this amusing, a welcome diversion from his own sordid scandals. In the face of government-sponsored bio-warfare, people have developed sudden and total amnesia. Monica who?

"... and as President of this graht nation ..." Is it just me, or is his Southern twang more pronounced than usual? "I am appalled and shocked at the allegations. To suggest that the Government of the United States would have a hand in this kind of biological warfare during peacetime is a serious, serious contention. But it is one which we must take seriously. And as President of this graht nation I am determined to get to the bottom of this. My staff has requisitioned through the Freedom of Information Act all of the related files from 1969 and on. I ask the American people and the world to extend a measure of patience as my staff work their way diligently through the documents. As soon as possible my administration will make a further statement as to the legitimacy of the alleged charges. In the meantime, I ask my fellow Americans to stand in solidarity with the government through this difficult episode."

It's stunning, really. My eyes fill with tears that run down my face. They're tears of relief more than anything. If the President feels pressured to acknowledge our charges, something has to be done. This is more than we'd hoped for. Why then, do I feel so sad?

"It's for you, Rabinovitch. Your girlfriend." Patty hands me the phone receiver. I walk to the opposite end of the bar. The phone has a twenty-five-foot spiral cord so we can talk on the phone from any end of the counter. "And keep it quick. It's long distance, you know."

"Julie?"

"I can't do it, Nomi."

"You can't?"

"Vancouver. The job. I've thought about it."

"Oh." My heart sinks.

"I just can't leave Toronto. Not now ..."

"Okay."

"There's my mother, for one thing. She's practically all alone. And ACTOUT. My work there. I mean with everything going on. You know, all the media attention."

"Yeah, it's been all over the news. You looked great on *20/20*." Julie's become the Canadian spokesperson. I'm a little worried for her. I keep thinking about last year when Henry and Albert were assaulted over this.

"And Henry ..."

"Henry?"

"His health."

"Right." Henry's in the hospital. I haven't spoken to him yet;

he's too sick to talk on the phone. Roger says he's getting stronger every day. If I had the money, I'd fly out to see him.

"So you're not disappointed?"

"No. I mean yes. I mean, it was kind of a crazy idea."

"Not that crazy ... it's just ..."

"What?"

"Not a good time. You know."

"I know."

"I love you."

"You do?"

"What'sa matter with you, Rabinovitch?" Patty asks while I'm washing another load of glasses. I guess I've been washing the same glass for an extended period of time, lost in thought.

"Nothing."

"Like hell. I know you better than you know yourself."

Probably true. I shrug.

"What happened?"

"Nothing happened."

"On the phone with your girlfriend," she pushes. "What happened?" Patty pulls a cigarette out of her pack, lights it. The city passed a no-smoking rule in all bars and restaurants, but Patty doesn't care. She'd rather smoke and be charged the fine. "I'm paying the rent around here," she says to the smoking rule.

"We're not moving to Vancouver," I say.

"Why the hell not?"

"I don't know. She's not ready to leave Toronto."

"Why not?"

"Her mother. Her job. ACTOUT. Henry."

"Oh."

She studies me.

"I don't know what we're going to do."

She blows smoke in my face. "Rabinovitch, you amaze me."

"I do?"

"The answer's obvious."

"It is?"

"Course it is, kid."

"Okay, Patty. I'll bite. What's the answer?"

She shakes her head. "You have to move *there*, knucklehead."

I stare at her.

"Back to Toronto."

What if she's right? "Toronto?"

"It's the only way."

I sigh. "What if I did? What would you do without me?"

She shrugs. "Find a replacement."

"Am I that easy to replace?"

"Hell no. Finding someone who's a bigger pain in the ass than you's going to be hard."

"Thanks."

"Don't mention it. Aren't those glasses clean yet?"

"Oh." Slowly I stack the glasses on the rubber dish drainer, one at a time.

After work I go for a long motorcycle ride, up and down the streets of San Francisco. I end up at Fisherman's Wharf, park my bike. I buy an order of deep-fried oysters from a booth and walk out along the long concrete peer. At the end I sit dangling my feet over the water, eating my oysters. Beside me two men are fishing. I don't know how they can consider eating fish from the bay. The water's got to be completely polluted with all the gasoline-spewing boats running up and down the bay, ferries, floatplanes, not to mention the city sewage that is emptied into the water on a regular basis.

I imagine moving back to Toronto to be with Julie. If I leave San Francisco, I'll miss this. Fisherman's Wharf. Deep-fried oysters. Not that I come here often. This is only my third or fourth time in three years. But I'll miss it. The ocean, I'll miss. After three years on the West Coast, I can't imagine living away from the ocean. It does something to you. Maybe it's the negative ions, the milder climate, the ebb and flow of the tide. I don't know what it is, but it has a calming effect on me, on the city itself and the people. I'll miss this crazy city. The community.

And I'll miss everybody. Betty especially. What will I do without Betty? And Patty, and the rest of the gang. Best friends I've ever had. Life just won't be the same without them.

And what if Julie and I don't live well together? What if we grate on each other's nerves? What if our habits are so completely different we can't live together? What if I annoy her? Her apartment is so neat. I don't know if I can be that neat. What if she doesn't like my taste in paintings? Or posters? Or if we can't agree on how to arrange the furniture? What if I uproot my life, move thousands of miles away only to find it's a big mistake? God. Patty was right. I do worry a lot. What if Julie finds out I worry so much and it drives her crazy and she leaves me for a man with a buzz cut, baggy pants and a baseball cap? A man who never worries. If she does, I'll have to kill her, like I wanted to kill Sapphire. Then what? Then I'll spend the rest of my days in a maximum security penitentiary alongside other ruthless killers. I'll be in such a state of disgrace even my own mother won't speak to me.

It's been three and half years, but it seems like I've always lived in San Francisco. I moved here to be with Sapphire. Is there a pattern here? Do I always move to be with a lover? What does that say about me? A serial monogamist with a twist. With every new relationship I leave town? Am I immature? Am I running from my problems? Burning my bridges? Moving on just as I'm getting to know people here? Or is it all just a strange coincidence? I know we all have a type, but this is ridiculous. What's my type? A woman who lives in another city?

On the other hand, what if Patty's right? Maybe Toronto wouldn't be so bad. Maybe Julie and I are so much in love that living together will be great and I won't care what city I'm in. We'll be the perfect couple. I'll change the light bulbs. She'll wash the dishes. I'll do the cooking. She'll do the laundry. I'll mow the lawn. She'll arrange the furniture. It'll be a marriage to die for. A local lesbian folksinger will write a song about us. We'll inspire younger dykes to get hitched. My life will be so fabulous, San Francisco will be but a fond memory. I'll even forget about Betty and the gang. Julie and I will live happily ever after, back in my home and native land. O Canada. My money will be worthless but I'll have health care again. There will be less graffiti and no guns. I won't have to worry that the teenager sitting beside me on the bus might have a semi-automatic weapon hidden inside his coat.

I wish my father could have met Julie. He would have liked her. My father never met any of my lovers. I had barely come out to him before he died. I remember a conversation we had when I was ten.

"One day you'll get married, Nomi," he told me. I was sitting on a high stool behind him in his studio in the basement, watching him paint. He was working on a landscape from a photo he'd taken at the shore of Lake Ontario. In the background was an industrial pier with a tanker; in the foreground, wooden boxes. "I'll give you away at your wedding," he said.

"Give me away?" I was horrified. Was my family going to dispose of me as soon as possible? Where would I go? To another family? Onto the streets? I started to cry. "Don't give me away, Daddy. I'll be good."

He put down his paintbrush, turned to me. He was trying not to laugh. I could see it in his eyes. "No, not like that, Nomi. No one's giving you away."

Tears of terror streamed down my cheeks.

He walked over to me, put his arms around me. "Don't worry, Nomi. It's just an expression. It's what happens at your wedding. I forget how sensitive you are. It's okay. No one's giving you away."

I sobbed into his arms, inconsolable.

Maybe if I move back to Toronto I could go back to school. Get a student loan. Do something with my life other than sling drinks. I could take a computer course, web design, interactive chat-line networking, e-commerce, internet options. Open my own dot com company, trade it on the stock market and become an overnight millionaire. My mother would be proud of me. I could buy her a new car. I could buy a house. Julie and I could become homo-owners. Every Saturday we'd shop at Homo-Depot for light fixtures, drywall and furnace filters. I'd move

Bubbe out of the old folks' home and into our house. We could have a rainbow picket fence in the front yard, a gas barbecue in the back. We'd buy white plastic lawn furniture at Canadian Tire. We'd adopt a cat from the SPCA, a dog from the animal shelter, and after a year or two we would think about having kids. We'd have long debates on whether to go with a known donor dad or anonymous sperm from a bank. Our friends would all disagree with our decision. Someone would write a scathing editorial in our local gay paper. My mother would be thrilled and horrified simultaneously. Julie, of course, would be the one to get pregnant. I would be the proud dad.

Over the bay the sun is starting to sink, a bright orange glow over the horizon, reflecting gold diamonds onto the water. I should head for home before rush hour begins. I pop the last oyster in my mouth, crush the paper container and start up my bike.

Back on Betty's sofa, with my shoes kicked off, I dial the long distance number. Stein picks up the phone on the first ring.

"Hi, it's me."

"Nomi? Where are you?"

"San Francisco."

"Well it's about bloody time you phoned. Nobody is that good in bed."

"What? Oh, you mean Sapphire. We broke up."

"Already?"

"It's been four years since we got together."

"It has? Are you sad? Are you broken-hearted? Are you in therapy? Do you miss me? When are you coming home?" Stein asks in her usual rapid-fire style. I'd forgotten about that. She never leaves time for you to answer one question before she asks the next.

"We broke up almost a year ago. I'm over it."

"So fast? That doesn't sound like you."

"Well ... that's because I'm in love with someone else now."

"That *really* doesn't sound like you. Bouncing back in less than a year. How long were you single after Monica?"

"That was different."

"Two years? Or was it three?"

"She broke my heart."

"Don't they all?"

"I don't want to talk about Monica."

"Okay, why don't we talk about how come you didn't phone me for four years."

"You know why."

"Oh, come on. You didn't even like Carol. You said so yourself. You said she annoyed you."

"That's not the point."

"You couldn't stand the sound of her voice."

"It's the principle of the thing."

"I only dated her once."

"It was enough."

"Okay, Nomi. I'm sorry."

"Well ... I'm sorry too."

"For what?"

"Not phoning you all this time."

"So why are you phoning now?"

"I'm thinking about moving back."

"Here? You hate Toronto."

"I know."

"Okay, what's her name?"

"You know her." Stein works at the AIDS Committee of Toronto. She's worked with Julie on organizing the Dyke March and other events.

"Who is it?"

"Julie Sakamoto."

"Julie Sakamoto!? Are you serious? She's fucking gorgeous. You're in love with Julie?"

"Head over fucking heels."

"Does she know?"

"Does she ever."

"And she's in love with you?"

"Well, don't sound so shocked."

"How did you score Julie Sakamoto? I can hardly believe this. I want all the details, Rabinovitch. Hang on. Let me get a cigarette."

"You started smoking again?"

"Don't ask."

I tell her all about it. Stein's the only friend from Toronto I think I can stand right now. We've known each other forever. I first met Rivka Stein in third grade of Hebrew School, when we were eight. Our class was in the basement of the synagogue. The windows at the side of the room were at ground level, facing out to the back parking lot. Our teacher, old Mr. Schecter, was sitting up front quoting from the Talmud when Stein leaned over and whispered in my ear that I should follow her. Mr. Schecter didn't seem to notice when Stein opened a window at the back and climbed outside. I followed her, tumbling out the window onto the sidewalk, skinning my knee slightly. We ran around playing hide-and-seek and tag for an hour, before casually slipping back inside for the end of the lesson. I don't know if Mr. Schecter didn't see or just didn't care.

The next week, two of our classmates got a detention for talking in class. The protest was Stein's idea. We had just learned about Moses and Pharaoh and getting the slaves out of Egypt. Stein ran back inside to the Hebrew School office and finagled several pieces of bristol board and markers from the secretary. In our eight-year-old handwriting, we scribbled slogans like "Let My People Go," and we marched back and forth in front of the windows to our classroom, singing and chanting, until Mr. Schecter let the kids in detention leave. After that Stein and I were inseparable. We grew up together and then within months of each other, in different cities, independently came out. She'd moved to Vancouver to go to school. I'd stayed in Toronto. Her coming out letter to me was hilarious. She was so scared to tell me. I called her back right away.

"So you're a dyke," I said, all serious.

"Well," she was scared. "A gay woman."

"Come on, Stein. Reclaim the word. It's okay. Dyke. Dyke. Dyke."

"Don't be such a creep, Rabinovitch. You're a homophobe. That's what you are."

"No I'm not. It's impossible."

"Why? You think you're above it?"

"Because I'm a dyke too."

"Get out."

"Really."

"Are you just copying me?"

"Don't be a fool, Stein. I've been going to the Rose for months now."

"The Rose?"

"It's a dyke bar on Parliament."

"Really?"

"Really."

We were back on track as friends. Just like we'd never stopped. That's the kind of friendship we've always had. I guess if I move back to Toronto at least I'll have Stein.

Betty's entered a drag king contest. She's forced me to be her assistant. She needs help with her costume. She's doing retro-hip-hop-cool. Baggy pants that fall halfway down her butt, humongous T-shirt with a slogan, high-top runners and woolen toque — the type of hat that is currently cool among the under-twenty set, but was absolute-nerd when I was twenty. We're going to glue sideburns and a goatee to her face with spirit gum. Her crotch will be stuffed with a large silicon dildo. I point out that with such baggy trousers it's hardly necessary, but Betty disagrees.

"It's the principle of the thing, Nom. You can't do drag without a dick."

She's got a point.

The show is being held in a minuscule club on 18th, near Valencia. There is barely room for fourteen people, but they're going to stuff in two hundred sweaty lesbians once the evening gets rolling. It will definitely be a fire hazard, and if an earthquake hits tonight, we're all doomed. You wouldn't know we were inside a death trap by the exuberant mood of the drag kings, their makeup dykes, stagehands, the director and assorted club staff. At the last second, Guido decides to sign up for the contest also. She's doing Frank Sinatra. She's going to wear a black pin-striped suit with a matching felt fedora, white shirt, tie, handkerchief in breast pocket, carnation on lapel, men's dress shoes. She's going to lip-synch to "My Way." The silicon dick she's stuffed into her pants is so large, she looks like Mick Jagger in a suit. What is it about dicks that even lesbians want big ones?

We're crowded into a tiny makeshift dressing room backstage. Betty's perched on a stack of beer cases. Guido keeps tying her tie, then untying it and starting all over again. Either one side or the other is too long. She can't find the midpoint. I'm struggling with the spirit gum to affix Betty's sideburns. The glue is all over my fingers. I reach for a sideburn, position it on Betty's face.

"So?" Betty says. "Did you hear the news?"

"What news?" Guido asks.

"Nomi's moving to Canada with her girlfriend."

Guido stops tying, turns to stare at me. "Really?"

"What?" I press the sideburn against Betty's skin. "I am not. Who told you that?"

Betty's eyes connect with mine in the mirror. "Patty. Hey, not so hard."

"I just said I'm thinking about it."

"Wow, Nomi." Guido turns back to the mirror to work on her tie. "We're sure going to miss you."

"You are?" I pick at the glue on my fingers.

"Sure. Who are we going to make fun of if you're not here?" Guido says.

"Gee, thanks a lot."

"Well, there's always Chester," Guido realizes.

"Or AJ," Betty adds.

I grab Betty's second sideburn from the dressing table. I didn't know I was so expendable. Feels like I was never here. My face falls. Betty notices in the mirror.

"We're just kidding, Nom. You know I'll miss you like crazy." She punches me on the arm to prove it. Butch bonding at its finest.

I smile weakly to cover the fact that I feel like crying. The sideburn is stuck to my fingers. "Pull." I hold it out to her.

She yanks hard. The sideburn tears free, taking a layer of my skin with it.

"Ouch."

"These were expensive, Nom," Betty complains, affixing the second one herself.

I have to admit, with the facial hair, she looks like a young rapper dude. If her lip-synch is good she might even win first prize — a gift certificate at Good Vibrations for a vibrator of her choice. As if Betty doesn't already have enough vibrators.

"Now the goatee," she orders.

I comply, feeling a little sad. Who's going to order me around in Toronto?

HENRY'S EX-BOYFRIEND TAKES CHARGE OF THE DECLINING SITUATION

I'm home from the hospital, resting on Roger's black leather couch in the living room, where it's easier to reach the phone, the remote control, the bathroom and the kitchen. Playing the part of the Southern invalid, I ring for my supper, allow others into my sacred kitchen, send out my laundry and wait for the latest doctor's report. Roger was right. Plain old garden-variety pneumonia isn't as bad as the other kind. The dreaded kind. PCP. The AIDS kind. I only spent three days in the hospital, which is short for someone in my delicate condition. Roger wanted me to stay in the hospital longer — probably so he could keep an eye on me. But I insisted. I know I do better at home. One more day of soggy fish sticks, cubed carrots and red Jell-O and I was going to die of starvation. Now that I'm home, Michael's here for the Henry's Home From the Hospital Cook Fest. Michael is my best friend in the whole world, not including Roger. Or Julie. Or Queen David. Or David-to-Die-For, if only he'd disrobe once in a while and let me gaze upon his washboard stomach, bulging pectorals and what I'm sure must be a twelve-inch uncut penis.

Michael is an ex-trick. We had a sordid three-day affair several hundred years ago, when we were barely out of our youth, and then in true fag tradition we became best friends. We met — of all places — in the tubs, in New York. It was during the time I was living in the Big Granny Smith, in 1978. I'd run away with my high school sweetheart, Morris Silverberg, after my mother walked into my bedroom and caught me down on my knees with Morris' cock in my mouth. Morris only lasted for a couple of months in New York. After his father found us, Morris went back home and I stayed on my own. Michael was just visiting, his first time in the city that never sleeps. I don't know what drew me to Michael. Perhaps it was his deep brown eyes. Maybe it was his Semitic nose, so like my own. Maybe his curly black hair. Then again, it might have been his fully erect, nine-inch member, straining against his rented white towel. I moved up one bench in the steam room, sat perilously close to Michael. Without a word, he took my hand and placed it on Exhibit A, and like the professional faggot I am, I wasted no time doffing his towel and taking said exhibit in my mouth. After a rather explosive steam room romp, we exited stage left, and I dragged him home to my tiny apartment in the lower east side.

On my modest income as a busboy, I lived among the lesbians and new immigrants in what used to be a tenement building and had probably housed my ancestors escaping Czarist Russia at the turn of the last century. Talk about finding your roots. My junior bachelorette studio apartment had most likely once been an unfurnished room, without bathroom or kitchen, the only window opening onto an airless wind shaft, housing a family of sixteen, plus four or five boarders. There was probably one toilet down the hall to service the entire floor. Sometime after the war, most of New York's tenement buildings were redesigned into one-bedroom and studio apartments to accommodate a sea of single men home from overseas and ready to take on the city's postwar boom.

In my apartment there was room for a sofa bed, a dresser, a desk and bookshelf in the main room. The kitchen was just inside the doorway, a narrow alleyway with a small fridge, stove and white enamel sink. An old-fashioned claw-footed tub took up the rest of the kitchen. The small bathroom just off the kitchen had a plain white toilet and sink. The building was heated with steam rads that rattled and moaned, day and night. The boiler was switched on October first and turned off precisely on March first whether it was freezing or not.

"You live in the lower east side?" Michael had asked incredu-lously as I schlepped him up the stairs of my four-storey walk-up.

"Me, four thousand lesbians and lots of little old ladies," I replied, ripping the shirt from his sculpted chest with one hand as I searched for my apartment key with the other. I wasn't sure whether to be offended or curious. Was he remarking on the lower-class status of my neighbourhood? Was he hoping for a west village fag? Or an upper west side interior decorator? "Why?" I asked rather defensively as I opened the door and pulled him inside.

"It's great. Amazing. I mean, this is where all the Jews lived at the turn of the century. The immigrants. Right?"

With a single deft motion I pulled open my sofa bed and pushed Michael down onto it. "Yes. My next door neighbour is a seventy-five-year-old grandmother who grew up here."

"Wow." Michael sat up, looked around the room. "This is history."

"So's this." I reached for his crotch, undid the top button on his tight blue Levi's.

He swatted my hand away, walked to my one tiny window, pushed aside the drape. I had a view of some other guy's win-dow, and the alley. Below was a mess of rotting garbage and other assorted items: a soiled mattress, several car batteries, empty liquor bottles, old newspapers, used condoms, cigarette butts and rats.

In between the history lessons, Michael and I had a tumul-tuous three-day affair. Then the sex fizzled out and we remained friends. Michael went back to the tubs, where he had sex with five or twenty other beautiful men, followed one or two home, brought several to the tiny hotel room he was renting near Times Square, then returned home to Toronto, his vacation over. We kept in touch, and when I moved back to Toronto in 1986, we resumed our friendship. Michael is my real brother, sold to gypsies when he was a baby. We're two peas in a pod. We have the same taste in music, men, clothes and art. We come

from similar families — unstable, dysfunctional Jewish subur-
banites. We have the same values. The only place we differ is
politics. Michael is so apolitical he doesn't even vote — unless
the candidate is to die for, and then he'll only make the effort out
of fashion sense, not civic duty.

We've seen each other through hard times. I brought him
back from the brink after Garth, a hunky stockbroker Michael
dated for three years off and on, left him. Michael was in love
with Garth. One day Garth decided that Michael wasn't suc-
cessful enough. Their relationship wasn't good for his career.
Michael is a window dresser. He makes good money, just not
good enough for the Garth types of the world. Michael was
crushed. He vowed to throw himself from the Bloor Street
Viaduct after Garth dumped him. I rushed right over with a
bottle of Jack Daniel's and we roasted Garth all evening. I
stayed with Michael for a week, by his side the whole time, until
he got Garth out of his system.

Michael is HIV positive. Like me, he has been mostly well,
positive but asymptomatic for years. Right now he's in the
kitchen making a big pot of chicken soup.

"It's in our heritage, Henry," he announced earlier this afternoon when he arrived at my apartment with a shopping bag
full of supplies. "I'm even making matzo balls. Gotta fatten you
up. You've gotten entirely too svelte, my dear. Remember when
we used to say ..."

"You can never be too thin." I finish his sentence for him.
Sometimes I can read Michael's mind.

"How about some nice ginseng tea? I stopped at a Chinese
herbalist on my way from Kensington Market." He fluffs up the
pillow behind my back.

"You went to Kensington Market?"

"Is there any other place to shop for chicken soup ingredients?
I mean Henry, please, it's the veritable hotbed of our ancestors."

Michael is a history buff. He's travelled all over the world and
he loves to find out the history of a place. He's particularly fasci-
nated with the neighbourhoods of Jewish immigrants. Michael

never knew his grandparents. His parents are Holocaust survivors, both the sole remaining members of their entire extended families.

"You are so lucky," Michael has told me, that I knew my grandparents.

In the kitchen Michael puts the kettle on to boil. From my position on the sofa I can see him through the kitchen doorway. He's standing by the counter, chopping celery.

"The secret to my fabulous chicken soup," he shouts through the doorway, "is parsnips." He holds one up for me to see.

"What are you going to do with that? Insert it in some inappropriate orifice?"

"You are so crude."

He plops the parsnip onto his cutting board and in a deft motion, chops it in two.

"The thing I don't understand," Michael's knife slices through the parsnip quickly, like an experienced prep cook, "is why you didn't phone me sooner."

"I don't know."

"I know why." He adds the parsnip pieces to his soup. "De-ni-al." He sings the word slowly to the tune of "Do Re Mi," from *The Sound of Music.*

"What?"

"You heard me." He chops another parsnip. "I mean, what was Roger thinking?"

"He didn't know. It got worse kinda suddenly."

"Does it hurt?"

"Only when I breathe."

"Where's your father today? Not in?"

"Visiting my grandmother at the Home."

"How's she doing?"

"Much better."

"Well, guess what I have?" Michael pokes his head into the living room.

"Oh, let me see. So many ailments to choose from."

"Not including yet another vicious herpes outbreak, in an

area I'll refrain from naming out of common decency, I have a lump in my breast."

I turn to look at him. "You're kidding, right?"

"I wish I was." Michael stirs the soup. The full aroma of chicken boiling permeates the air. The windows are fogging up.

"Seriously?"

"Can you believe it? It might be breast cancer. And all this time, I thought I was a boy."

"Can men get breast cancer?"

"A tiny fraction. I have to get it taken out."

"What if it is?"

"You're the executor of my will."

"They can treat it, though."

"Oh sure. Chemo. I just don't know if I want to lose all my hair. I don't think I can do bald."

"Come here, Michael."

He puts the lid on the soup, sits on the floor in front of the couch, leans back.

I run my fingers through his hair. "Look what we've become. We're a couple of old ladies."

"Sharing arthritis stories."

"You think you've got arthritis? You should see my impetigo. What is impetigo, anyway?"

"I don't know. Maybe we should move into the Jewish Home for the Aged with your grandmother."

"Do you think they'll take us?"

"We'll have to brush up on our Yiddish."

"We could claim early onset Alzheimer's. What do you think?"

"I forget."

"When's that soup going to be ready? It smells great."

"An hour. Let's watch trashy daytime soap operas while we're waiting." Michael reaches for the TV remote and switches it on.

With one hand, I massage his neck. It's riddled with tension.

NOMI'S CHOSEN FAMILY

I have the day off work. Betty left this morning for an early shift, so I have the apartment to myself. The day after tomorrow is American Thanksgiving. It's a much bigger deal in San Francisco than in Canada. Everyone celebrates Thanksgiving in America. Everyone. Patty's got the largest apartment, so she's hosting again this year. AJ usually spends Thanksgiving with Martha's family, who live in toney Marin County, half an hour's drive from San Francisco. The rest of us spend the holiday together. Chester's from the Midwest and has no family in the Bay Area. Same for Patty and me. Betty's mother and sister live in Philadelphia, too far to travel to. Robert's father lives in the East Bay, but he disowned Robert decades ago. Guido's from Philly, like Betty. Sometimes someone brings a date, but usually it's just us. Just Family.

Last year at this time I was still with Sapphire, mere seconds away from our big demented breakup, and like a fool I brought her to Patty's Thanksgiving dinner. This year, I'm going solo. Next year I might be in Toronto with Julie, if it works out. This might be my last Thanksgiving in San Francisco. I'll probably go to Patty's with Betty, and she never brings a date to Thanksgiving dinner. That way she can watch the football game after dinner. Betty doesn't usually watch sports — only on Thanksgiving. It's tradition. She used to watch it with her father, before her mother divorced him. It's a nostalgic thing for her. Me, I can't stand any kind of sports. I usually sit in the other room and heckle.

I promised Patty I'd stop by the bar this afternoon and help her plan for the big event. I eat a quick bowl of Shreddies, get dressed and grab my helmet. The phone rings. I hesitate. It's probably for Betty anyway. But what if it's Julie? On the fourth ring I lunge for the receiver.

"Hello?"

"What are you doing home in the middle of the day? Why aren't you working at the saloon?" my mother asks

"It's a pub, Ma. And I have the day off."

"On a Wednesday?"

"I worked over the weekend. What is this? The Spanish Inquisition?"

"Why didn't you tell me your cousin was in the hospital? I just heard."

"He was only in for a couple of days. He's much better now."

"Why didn't you tell me? I would have gone."

"I don't know, Ma. I figured you were busy."

"Not so busy I couldn't pay a visit. It's only nice."

"Sorry. I guess I just forgot."

"All right."

"So, what's up?"

"Nothing's up. I just wanted to say hello to my only daughter."

"Ma, there's always something up with you."

"Well, it made me sad, thinking about Henry. He's a young man and he's dying."

"He's not dying, Ma."

"Didn't you say he has AIDS?"

"He does, but ... these days, with drugs, AIDS can be a chronic manageable disease, like diabetes." I rattle off the jargon, although I don't believe it myself.

"Is that true, Nomi?"

"I hope so. Ma, it's expensive to talk now. It's prime time."

"All right, but Nomi, are you being careful?"

"What do you mean being careful?"

"You know what I mean. I'm worried, Nomi."

"Ma. Remember we already had this discussion."

"We did? I don't remember. Tell me again."

Oh boy. I take a deep breath. "Lesbians are a low-risk group. You should worry more about Josh and Izzy."

"Why? What have they done?"

"Nothing. It's just that AIDS is more prevalent in the hetero-sexual world than among lesbians." I hope I know what I'm talking about.

"Still, you can't be too careful. Are you using condoms?"

For what? My double-headed dildo? "Ma, please don't worry. I'm careful, okay."

"You kids are too promiscuous. That's how this all started."

"Ma. That's not true. And I'm not exactly promiscuous. I've had a total of five girlfriends in twelve years."

"So many?"

"I'm hanging up, Ma."

"All right. I'm only your mother."

"Goodbye."

"You'll call me on Friday night?"

I hang up the phone.

I have some time to kill before I'm due at Patty's Place, so I go outside, hop on my motorcycle and head to the Castro. Inside A Different Light Bookstore I run into AJ. She's standing at the magazine rack, studying the centrefold in *On Our Backs*, the lesbian sex magazine. It's a photo of a particularly voluptuous femme, naked except for high heels and jewellery.

"Does Martha know you're here?" I whisper into AJ's ear, then instantly regret it. She drops the magazine, spins around, a look of terror on her face.

"Shit, Nomi. You scared me."

"Take it easy, AJ." I bend down, retrieve the magazine. "You sure are jumpy. How come you're not at work, anyway?" AJ is the administrative assistant in a reiki therapist's office. She's been there for years and hates her job, but she's afraid to quit because she has health insurance through her employer.

She looks at me intently.

"What's the matter?"

"I got canned." Her bottom lip quivers. She's close to crying.

"Oh no."

"This morning." Her eyes fill with tears.

"Come on. I'm buying you a drink."

"Now?" She looks at her watch. It's barely noon.

"Now." I throw an arm over her shoulder and steer her out of the store and up the hill. The Café, a second-storey mixed gay and lesbian bar, is open. I park AJ in a dark corner of the bar and go up to fetch us two beers.

"Okay," I pass her a beer. "What happened?"

"I'm redundant."

"That's what they said?"

"Yep."

"After six years?"

"Eight."

"You've been there eight years?"

"Yep."

"And suddenly you're redundant?"

"That's what they said."

"Did something happen?"

She shrugs, takes a long swallow of her beer.

"Something lately?"

She shrugs again.

"Think, AJ. Maybe you can sue them or something."

"Who cares. Maybe it's for the best."

"Yeah. Maybe."

"Martha's going to kill me."

"It's not your fault, AJ."

"Doesn't matter."

I take a long sip of beer. "Is everything all right with you and Martha?"

Again she shrugs.

"Come on, AJ. Just tell me what's going on."

"Nothing. Everything's fine. She's just ... uptight about money. We split everything right down the middle. And now ..."

"You do?" That's crazy. Martha is a tax accountant. She must make four times as much money as AJ.

"Well, you hated that job anyway," I remind her.

"Yeah, I did." She polishes off her beer.

"You'll get another job," I reassure her.

"Gonna have to. You want another?" She stands, grabs her empty bottle.

"Sure. No, make it a club soda."

"Wimp."

"I'm driving."

AJ heads for the bar.

Two hours later, I drag AJ with me to Patty's Place. There's no way she can be left alone today. She's drunk, after drinking three beers and two Jameson's. In her inebriated state, AJ's gone from angry to resentful to belligerent to melancholy. I've brought her back to laughter by making fun of her former boss. She weaves beside me. I decide against riding her to Patty's on my Honda. In her condition, she might fall off. I leave my bike where it's parked and walk AJ to the bus stop on Castro Street.

AJ runs for the bathroom the second we walk in the door of Patty's Place.

"What the hell's the matter with her?" Patty asks.

"Got fired today."

"Aw shit. Poor kid. Martha's gonna kill her."

"That's what she said."

"Well, it's true. We might even be talking about divorce here."

"Really? Martha would dump her over this?"

"You don't know Martha, do you?"

"Not really."

Patty leans in close, speaks low. "Martha leaves receipts on the fridge when she buys milk or bread, or whatever. AJ has to pay her back exactly half of whatever she spent."

"You're kidding."

"Like sixty-two-and-a-half cents."

"And a half?"

"Right down the middle."

"After all these years?"

Patty just nods her head sadly.

"That's crazy. Are you sure?"

"Believe me, Rabinovitch. I know what I'm talking about."

Patty was right. Martha blew a tube when AJ went home later that day and broke the news to her. After thirteen years, you'd think the woman would have a little compassion. AJ doesn't know what's going to happen but she packed a small bag and is staying at Patty's for a while. She said she wanted to give Martha a chance to cool down, but we're all secretly hoping AJ decides to leave her for good.

We set our minds to Turkey Day planning. Behind Patty's back, we collectively decide not to let her do any of the cooking. Last year she forgot to take the turkey out of the freezer the day before to thaw it out. She tossed it into the oven frozen solid. Even cooking it all day at five hundred degrees, the meat wasn't ready to eat on time. We tell Patty she's off the hook with cooking, on account of hosting.

Guido offers to roast the turkey at home and bring it over. Guido's a bland cook but functional. You can always add more salt and pepper later. Betty and I are bringing potatoes and Brussels sprouts that we're going to cook at Patty's. AJ's in charge of pulling together a salad. We almost didn't give her a task, but then we figured we should give her things to do, to take her mind off her troubles. Betty insisted the salad be organic and fancy, with exotic ingredients like arugula and mustard greens. Chester's bringing a couple of pumpkin pies and ice cream. Robert and Spencer are bringing wine and dinner rolls.

It's going to be quite the feast.

HENRY'S BEST FRIEND GETS PICKED UP

I'm lounging on the sofa watching an old *M*A*S*H* rerun on TV. Hawkeye is building a monument to the dead from an oversupply of tongue depressors. Here at home, Michael is in the kitchen spooning his split pea soup into freezer jars. The windows are fogged up from the soup simmering on the stove all afternoon. It smells like my Bubbe's kitchen used to smell when she lived in her apartment and still cooked. The pneumonia is gone from my lungs. I'm still a bit tired, but I'm feeling almost human again, ready to go back into the world. Roger thinks I should take it easy a little bit longer, but I'm going stir-crazy just sitting around, watching TV and listening to Michael cook.

There's an ACTOUT meeting tonight and I'm bound and determined to get there. I might even drag Michael with me, although that would be an amazing feat.

"Why don't you come with me?" I try innocently.

He pokes his head in between the pass-through. "Have you lost your mind, dear?"

"I think you would really like David-to-Die-For."

"Who?"

"He's only the most gorgeous specimen you've ever seen," I entice.

"David-to-Die-For?"

"That's his name."

"Officially?"

"It's a long story."

"Tell me about him." He tries to say it casually, like he couldn't care less, but I know I have Michael hooked.

"Dark hair, broad shoulders, dark eyes, bulging basket." These are the magic words. Michael sidles out from the kitchen and plops onto the couch beside me.

"How bulging?"

I shrug. "You'd have to see for yourself."

"Tease." He flicks me with his dish towel. "Why do you want me at the meeting, anyway? You know I despise meetings. Unless, of course, they're meetings of the flesh."

"I don't know," I answer, and it's true. I don't really know. Maybe I want him to see that part of my life. Maybe I want all my friends involved in the cause. Maybe I just don't feel like leaving the house alone.

"Bulging basket," he contemplates, going back to his soup.

The apartment door swings open and Solly rushes inside in his trench coat. He hangs his fedora on a hook, smiles at me as he passes, heading toward his room with a mysterious crumpled brown paper bag. I notice a flash of green inside. The colour of American money. He emerges a moment later, stops in the living room and studies me for a long moment.

"You look better," he decides.

"Must be Michael's cooking."

Michael pokes his head through the kitchen doorway. "Hi, Solly."

"How's it going, Michael? Smells good. You're some cook, huh?"

"Are you having dinner with us, Pop?" I ask.

"Uh, no. I got a whatchacallit? Some business to attend to."

"Business?"

"I'll see you later, guys." He grabs his hat from the hook, and leaves us to our own devices.

You would think I'd survived a war or something the way everyone carries on when I enter the meeting room at The 519.

Queen David approaches first. He's wearing leather, perhaps in honour of impending winter.

"Henry, you look fabulous," he gushes, pulling me in for a tight bear hug.

"Liar." I've lost about fifty million pounds, my clothes are literally hanging off, I'm pale and I'm having a bad hair day.

Julie is right behind Queen David. "Henry." She hugs me gently. "Did you get my message?" Julie phoned earlier to offer me a ride to the meeting if I needed one.

"I did. Thanks. But I leaned on Michael and hobbled down Church Street. As you can see, we made it here just fine."

Queen David leans forward. "And who, pray tell, is your lovely friend, Henry? Hmmm?"

"Oh, this is Michael. He's sitting in tonight."

"Not *the* Michael?" Queen David probes. I've talked about my friend Michael to my other friends many times.

"In the flesh."

Queen David curtsies. Michael smiles, while nudging me in the ribs. I know it means he wants me to point out David-to-Die-For, who happens not to be here yet. I cross my fingers that he shows.

Greta walks in. "Henry!" She seems genuinely happy to see me. "I didn't know you'd be here."

"I didn't want to miss another meeting."

"Hi, Henry." Simon gives me a squeeze. He's started coming to meetings again. "Hi, Michael," he says. Simon knows everyone who's anyone.

Michael leans forward, kisses Simon.

To my horror, I discover that Annoying David is chairing tonight's meeting. It's bound to take twice as long. He's not a good chair. He has no chutzpah. Doesn't have a clue how to stop people from going off on tangents. Michael is going to kill me. Annoying David calls the meeting to order. I drag Michael to a seat. Computer David sits on Michael's other side. Damn. I was hoping to leave that seat open for David-to-Die-For. New York David enters the room, followed by Raven, Ed and a few others.

Michael gives me a look, because no one fitting the description of a Greek god is anywhere to be seen.

"He's not here yet," I tell him. "Sometimes he's late," I add, although it's a lie. David-to-Die-For is never late.

Annoying David goes through last meeting's minutes item by item, instead of just asking for a motion to pass the minutes as a whole. It's excruciating. Finally, out of sheer mercy, Queen David says, "I have a motion that we accept the minutes in full." It's seconded and passed. Annoying David moves on to announcements. Michael glares at me, then yawns. Raven announces that a lesbian sex party was raided by the police over the weekend. The organizers were charged with keeping a common bawdy house, an archaic law still on the books. Probably dates back to prehistoric times. Once a year, a group of local lesbians rent a gay male bathhouse for a private party, and every time it gets raided. It's 1981 all over again. That was the year the cops raided men's bathhouses in Toronto and galvanized the community.

"I think we should picket the cops, " Raven suggests. "Naked, wearing only bath towels."

"Splendid," shrieks Queen David, who would need an enormous bath towel to cover his bulk.

Michael stifles a laugh. I poke him in the ribs.

"Hah!" mocks Greta. "We'd be crazy to show up in towels. What if they pepper spray us?"

"She's got a point," Simon says.

"We'll wear towels over our combat clothes," Raven suggests.

"Oh dear. That would look hideous," Queen David points out. "I remember the old days, when protests were art."

"I remember getting kicked in the stomach by the cops," Greta says.

"When was that?" Raven asks.

"Before you were born," Greta guffaws.

"What does this have to do with AIDS activism?" New York David asks.

Greta glares at him. "Ever heard of solidarity, buster?"

I glance at Annoying David to see if he's even thinking of

containing this discussion. He sits motionless.

"How about we strike a sub-committee?" Julie suggests. "To hash out the details."

"Bravo," Queen David declares.

"Sure," Greta sulks. "When it has to do with lesbians, why take up meeting time?"

"Unless, of course, we'd rather discuss it here," I say to placate Greta.

"I think a sub-committee's a good idea. More efficient use of time," Computer David points out.

"A sub-committee's okay," Raven says.

"Hmmph," complains Greta.

"I'm sure we can count on the whole group for support, though. Right, guys?" Julie pushes.

"You bet," I say.

"Count me in on that sub-committee, honey," Queen David announces. "I've got the perfect towel."

Finally we move on to the main agenda item — the conspiracy. After President Clinton's original statement, we have heard nothing but silence and stall tactics from his administration. The media attention, however, has been fabulous. Jonathan Garrick was interviewed on every major news show and by every major paper in Canada and the States. It's been talked about on every show. He appeared on Oprah, Rosie, even Sally. He's become a household name. Everyone looks to me for the news. I haven't talked to Albert since my untimely hospitalization. I look to Julie.

"Well," she hesitates, "Albert's ACTOUT New York group has formed a coalition with AIDS organizations all over the States. They're using the momentum from all the media attention. They want to sue the government."

"Sue?" Greta asks. "Who? The President? He's too busy raping young interns."

"It was hardly rape," New York David points out.

"I'd like him to rape me," Queen David says.

"God, me too," admits Simon.

"That's disgusting," Greta responds.

"ACTOUT New York? So what about us?" I ask Julie.

She shrugs. "Albert says thanks for everything."

"So we're history? They don't need us anymore?" I feel crushed.

"Apparently not."

"We're just lowly Canadians?"

"Looks like it."

Annoying David moves on to the next item: fundraising. We're all volunteers, but we still need to pay rent on the meeting space and for a phone line and answering machine. We have a dreadfully dull discussion about where to look for more funds. I sit half-listening, silently fuming over being unceremoniously dumped by Albert and ACTOUT New York. Michael closes his eyes. I guess he's planning on a short inconspicuous nap.

"Sorry I'm late." David-to-Die-For rushes in.

I nudge Michael in the ribs. He opens his eyes, sees David-to-Die-For, sits bolt upright in his chair. Smitten. I knew it. David-to-Die-For sits across the circle, beside Greta. Michael starts making googly eyes at him instantly.

"Have you no shame?" I whisper.

"None whatsoever," he practically drools.

The fundraising discussion drones on. I have to admit watching Michael in action is far more interesting than listening to accounting details. He stares at David-to-Die-For until David notices. David glances across the room at Michael and smiles. Michael's eyes bore into David's. David looks at me, then back at Michael. Is he interested? I look at Michael. His gaze has lowered and fixated on David-to-Die-For's crotch. David shifts in his seat, adjusts his jeans. Is that a slight erection I see? I don't know how Michael does it. He communicates the whole world through his eyes. It's amazing. Like poetry. The second the meeting is called to an end, Michael bolts out of his chair and is by David-to-Die-For's side, whispering in his ear.

"Feel up to a coffee?" Julie asks me.

"Sure. Just wait a second." I saunter over to where Michael is putting on a debauched display of cruising David-to-Die-For.

"I see you've made alternate plans," I say.

"I was just meeting your charming friend." He bats his eyes at me.

"So you're going to join ACTOUT?" David-to-Die-For asks Michael.

"Wouldn't miss it for the world."

I practically faint at this. "Call me tomorrow," I tell Michael, squeezing his shoulder.

"You'll be all right on your own?"

"Julie's taking charge at this point, Michael. You're free to pursue other interests."

"Have a beautiful night, Henry," Michael twitters, heart and loins aflame.

I'm just about to gag.

"I'm trying to talk Nomi into moving here," Julie tells me.

We're drinking herbal tea at the Second Cup. Inside. It's too cold for the steps. It's crowded in the coffee shop. There are people on either side of us, inches away.

"But she's so stubborn."

"She loves you," I remind her.

"But does she love me enough?" Julie asks sadly.

I don't know what to say. I don't know what I'd do if Roger wanted to move somewhere else. I guess we'd figure out something. But then Roger and I have been together five years. Julie and Nomi are just starting. Everything is so much more tenuous at the beginning. You don't know if it's going to last or not. "What if you find a job for her here?"

"I don't think Nomi cares that much about a job, really. It's not like she has a career or something."

"No."

"The crazy thing is, I can see why it would be hard for her to leave San Francisco, Henry. She has good friends. It's beautiful there. The weather's good. There's something going on all the time. Much more exciting than here."

"Toronto's not so bad," I say a little defensively.

"To Nomi it is."

"Why don't we just kidnap her?"

Julie smiles.

"We'll fly to San Francisco," I elaborate on my plan. "We'll find her, tie her up, stuff a sock in her mouth and drag her back, kicking and screaming."

Julie laughs. "Henry, I wish it was that easy."

"Maybe it is."

DECEMBER 1999

THE END OF THE TWENTIETH CENTURY
AND OTHER MILESTONES

NOMI'S BIG MOVE

"You're doing what?" Betty leaps up from the sofa and screams down at me.

"Going to Toronto," I repeat.

"You're really moving there?" Betty begins to pace. She's more upset than I imagined.

"Not moving there. Just going to stay for one month."

"And then you'll move there," Betty declares.

"I don't know."

"You will. I know you. Isn't that what you said when you came here for one month to get to know Sapphire?"

"Don't speak that name out loud," I order.

"Sapphire. Sapphire. Sapphire," she goads.

"I'm warning you," I threaten lamely.

"Well, it's true. That's exactly what you said. And now what is it? Four years later and you're still here. If you go to Toronto, we've lost you, Nomi. That's a fact." Betty stomps into the kitchen, yanks open the fridge.

"You haven't lost me."

"Oh yes we have." Betty returns to the living room, a bottle of beer in hand. I notice she doesn't offer me one. "We lost you the moment you met Julie."

"I'm coming back," I insist. But I don't know if it's true. I really don't know anything anymore.

"Well, at least I'll have the place to myself again." Betty paces the living room.

"I'm coming back. Don't give away the sofa."

"Good thing we didn't move into that two-bedroom," she says, totally ignoring me. "I'd have to kill you if we had. Do you have life insurance?"

"Betty ..."

"Well ... I'll be thinking of you when I see on the news there's been a ten-foot snowstorm in Canada. What are you going to do for a coat? Isn't it cold there now? Who moves to Toronto in the middle of December? Thought you hated winter."

"Would you stop it, Betty? What are you so sore about?" I get up, go for a beer.

"Who said I was sore?"

"You're acting like I'm doing something to you."

"You are."

"I am?"

"You're leaving me, Nom."

"Just for a month."

"Just when I need you the most."

"You do?"

She stops pacing, stares at me with one hand on a hip. "If you'd ever stop navel-gazing for a minute or two you'd know."

Uh oh. She's right. I have been preoccupied with my own problems lately. And Betty was so good to me after Sapphire dumped me. "I'm sorry."

"Hah."

"What's going on?" I sip on my beer.

Betty plunks back down on the sofa. "She's driving me crazy, Nom."

"Mona?"

"Who else?"

"What's she doing?"

"Nothing."

"Nothing?"

"Nothing. She won't go out with me. I've tried everything.

Changed my cologne. Done my laundry every two days, so my shirts are always clean. Grown my hair." Betty removes her ball cap to prove it. On her shaved scalp are tiny tufts of the beginnings of hair. Betty hasn't had hair since she cut off her dreadlocks and shaved her scalp last winter.

"Wow." I walk over, run my hand over her head. "You are serious about her."

"I've asked her out for coffee. To the movies. For a drink. You know what she says?"

"What?"

"No."

"You're kidding?"

"She says no."

"Gee."

"No woman has ever said no to me, Nom."

"Ever?" This is too much. I knew Betty had a way with women, but I didn't realize she had never been said no to. I can't remember all the women who've said no to me.

"Until now." Betty leans forward, head in hands.

I sit beside her, rub her back. "Poor Betty."

"You oughtta stay for good, Rabinovitch," Patty tells me.

I'm washing the sinkful of glasses she's left me from the afternoon shift. "I'm just going to try it out," I insist.

"What for?" She lights a cigarette. "Come here, Lulu." Lulu bounces up from her basket in the corner, wagging her tail. She stands by Patty's side, rubbing her face in Patty's hand.

AJ's sitting at the bar beside Patty. She still hasn't found another job. Martha didn't take her back like we all expected. They're officially broken up after thirteen years. AJ's been living in Patty's spare room. All her stuff is still at Martha's house. Martha's holding it ransom until AJ pays her share of the rent from last month. Cheap till the end, Martha is. The bitter end.

"How do I know we can even live together?" I ask Patty.

"You love her?" Patty asks through the smoke.

"Yes, of course I do."

"Love wasn't built in a day, Rabinovitch," she lectures.

"Wasn't that Rome?"

"No. It's love. What's one month gonna prove? You love somebody, you love them. You gotta take the bad with the good. In sickness and in health, kiddo. Oh, I forgot to mention, we're outta red wine. Anyone asks for a glass, try to sell them the white."

"You mean that case from B.C. that nobody likes?"

"It's from California."

"No, it's not."

"It is now. And don't you forget it."

"You want me to lie?"

"Won't need to. I already changed the labels."

"You what?"

"Will you pipe down and stop gawking. I'm trying to make a living here, Rabinovitch."

"All right. All right. What do I care? It's *your* liquor licence."

"Sure, what do you care? You'll be living high on the hog in Hogtown anyway." She laughs uproariously at her own joke.

"What's Hogtown?" AJ asks.

"Toronto," I answer.

"What?"

"Kind of like a nickname."

"Not a very nice one."

"No, I guess not."

"Time for Lulu's late afternoon walk," Patty announces, hopping from her stool. "Come on, Lulu."

"I've never been to Canada," AJ tells me.

"Never?"

"Not unless Victoria counts," AJ says in all seriousness.

"Victoria counts. It's on Vancouver Island." I stare at her.

"Oh." She swills the rest of her Budweiser. Since Martha kicked her out, AJ's been drinking a lot.

"When did you go to Victoria?"

"That time I was in Seattle with Martha for her accountants' convention. I took a boat to Victoria. I thought I was still in America."

"Didn't you have to go through Customs?"

"I forget. It was pretty. Lots of flowers. I walked around for a while, then I took the boat back to Seattle. I was supposed to meet Martha for dinner, but she didn't show up. I waited for her in our hotel room all evening. She came in at one o'clock, half drunk. Said she forgot we had plans. She had dinner with a colleague. That's what she calls people she works with — Colleague, with a capital C. I shoulda known then."

"Known what?"

"What a creep she is. I wasted the whole evening waiting for her. I was starving by the time she showed up."

"Maybe you should have ordered up some food when she didn't show," I suggest gently.

"I shoulda dumped her ass years ago. Give me another beer, will you, Nomi?"

I reach into the fridge for another Bud.

"Why didn't you guys just tell me to leave her years ago?" AJ asks.

"Why didn't you guys tell me to leave Sapphire?" is my answer.

"Cheers." AJ holds up her beer, takes a long swallow. "What'sa matter with us, Nom?"

"What do you mean?"

"Butches. Why do we put up with crazy femmes?"

"Love?" I suggest.

"Love. Hah!" AJ counters. "They're all crazy as loons. The whole whack of them."

"Who?"

"Femmes, Nomi."

I grab the broom to sweep under the tables, readying the bar for the evening.

By the time Betty and Chester show up at Patty's Place, AJ's on her fifth beer. I've decided I'm not serving her another. She may hate me now, but she'll thank me in the morning. Betty looks a little happier than she did earlier — more like herself. Chester's all excited about something. They plop down on stools on either side of AJ.

Betty orders her usual. "A Guinness, Nomi. No head."

"Make mine a Jameson's," Chester says.

Why do they even bother? It's always the same. "Why don't you guys just sit and wait. I know what you want."

"Just testing," Betty says. "Guess what happened to Chester."

"What?" I grab a beer mug, fill it with Guinness.

"Wha' happened?" AJ slurs.

"You tell them," Betty says to Chester.

"I got a date." She beams.

"What?" We all stare at her. Chester hasn't had a date in eons. I can't even remember the last time. Probably at the turn of the last century.

"For New Year's Eve." Chester's positively glowing.

"No kidding." I plunk Betty's beer in front of her.

"Con-gra-gu-lashuns." AJ holds up her beer in a toast.

Betty slaps Chester hard on the back. "Ain't that something?"

I pour Chester an extra large shot of whisky, place it in front of her. "So?" I ask. "Who's the lucky girl?"

Chester blushes. "Aw, you guys don't know her."

"Come on. Tell us."

"Her name's Delilah."

"Yeah ... ?"

"She was just hired at the library."

"You work with her?"

"Not directly. She works in the kids' section."

"What's she look like?"

"Well ... she's tall."

"Tall?"

"Yeah. Six feet. Maybe more."

"That *is* tall."

"She has broad shoulders, a strong jaw, piercing blue eyes."

"Yeah ... ?"

"Tell them the interesting part," Betty pushes.

"I don't think so."

"Come on," Betty nudges Chester.

"What interesting part?"

Chester hesitates. Looks hard into my eyes.

"Tell them."

"She's an MTF," Chester says.

"No kidding?"

"She's a man?" AJ blurts.

"Used to be."

"A man?"

"She's an MTF. Post-op."

"Wow."

"Have you seen him, I mean her, naked yet? What's her pussy look like?" Betty asks.

"Don't be so crude, Betty." Chester is offended.

"What did I say?"

"We haven't even gone out yet. Course I haven't seen her naked."

"I've always wondered," Betty continues. "I mean, can they make it look like a real one?"

"It *is* real," Chester says.

"You know what I mean."

"I never thought you of all people would be prejudiced," Chester accuses Betty.

"Who said I'm prejudiced? I'm curious. Aren't you?"

"I'm gonna become an MTF," AJ announces.

"You mean an FTM," Betty corrects.

"FTM," AJ agrees. "Tha's what I said."

"You are not," I say.

"I decided today," AJ says.

"That's crazy," I tell her. "You don't decide something like that in one afternoon."

"I'm through with women," AJ says. "Every last one of them."

"That's not a good reason, AJ."

"Even me. I don't want to be a woman anymore. Too much trouble. Hey Nom, fill 'er up." She waves her empty bottle at me.

I grab her bottle and oblige by filling it with water, hoping she won't notice.

"I guess I'm a little curious." Chester swings the conversation back to her date. "But that's not why I asked her out. I mean it's not like we're going to do anything on the first date."

"You never know," Betty says. "It's New Year's Eve, after all."

"It's just a date."

"The end of the millennium. Might be the end of the world."

"You think?"

"I for one plan to have sex with two thousand women that night, in honour of the year two thousand," Betty announces.

"Two thousand." Chester whistles through her teeth. "Sex? With every one of them."

"My goal is to kiss two thousand women," Betty clarifies.

"What about Mona?" I ask.

"Forget about it," Betty spits.

"What happened?" I lean close to Betty.

"You know why she won't go out with me?" Betty swills her beer.

"She's het, right? Didn't you say she was married?"

"Hah. Give me another Guinness, Nom. No head."

"She's not straight?" I refill Betty's glass.

Betty takes a long swallow. "All this time she's been seeing Rosie, the dispatcher. That's why she won't go out with me. She's leaving her husband for Rosie. The traitor. Anyway, I'm through with love. Look where it gets you. I was messed up for half a year over Mona. Think of all the women I missed in all that time."

"It's not like you didn't date some," I remind her.

"Yeah, but not up to my usual quota. I've got a lot of catching up to do."

"That's our Betty." Chester slaps Betty on the back.

"Look where it got you," Betty says to me.

"What?"

"Love."

"Where did it get me?"

"Back to Canada. I'm telling you, Nom, there's lots of birds in the sky. Why waste yourself over just one of 'em."

"She's in love," Chester says.

"Love. Hah," AJ snorts. She tips back her beer bottle filled with water, takes a long swallow. "What the hell is this? Miller Lite?"

"Bud Light," I lie. "We're all outta regular Bud."

"Oh." She drains half the bottle.

"Well, I can't wait to meet your date," Betty tells Chester. "You're bringing her to Patty's New Year's Eve bash, right?"

"Where else?"

"I don't have a date," AJ says forlornly. "First time in thirteen years I don't have a date for New Year's Eve."

"Aw, me either, AJ," Betty says. "Stick with me. Why don't you go for a record too?"

"Me?" A look of terror crosses AJ's face. She probably hasn't kissed anyone but Martha in thirteen years.

"Sure. Why not?"

"You want me to kiss two thousand women?"

"Let's not go overboard," Betty suggests. "Why don't you start off slow."

"Good idea," Chester says.

"Why don't you start with one," Betty offers, "and see what happens."

AJ likes this idea. She actually smiles for the first time all month.

"Gee, I won't be here," I realize. I'm leaving for Toronto on the twenty-ninth, so I can spend New Year's with Julie.

"We'll miss you, Nom."

"You will?"

"Course. What did you think? Right, guys?"

I know I'm going to miss them.

HENRY'S BOYFRIEND'S
GREAT IDEA

"In a way it's for the best."

Roger reclines on our sofa while I clear the dinner dishes. First time I've cooked in weeks. We've been eating Michael's prepared delights out of the freezer. Swanson TV dinners à la Michael. I finally convinced Roger I'm fit as a fiddle. Okay, a dying fiddle, maybe. A slightly warped, on-its-last-legs fiddle. Not ready to run the marathon, perhaps, or leap tall buildings in a single bound, climb Mount Everest or go to a homosexual nightclub and do designer drugs and dance to disco until dawn. But certainly fit enough to lean against the counter in my very own kitchen and sauté mushrooms, garlic and fresh scallops in white wine sauce, boil spinach, whole wheat pasta al dente, and lightly steam fresh broccoli with just a tiny hint of lemon.

"Why is it for the best?" I dump the dishes in the sink, turn on the hot water, squirt dish soap into the basin.

"Things could heat up."

"That's the point," I say.

"They want to sue the President? I mean, come on, Henry. The government's not going to take it lying down."

I swirl the water in the sink to make it suds up. "I know."

He gets up off the sofa, enters the kitchenette. "Do you?"

"I understand the risk."

Roger leans his beautiful butt against the kitchen counter, facing me. Sighs deeply. "I don't want to see you get hurt again.

Like last year."

"That's not going to happen," I insist, although I have no way of knowing that.

"How do you know?"

I shrug, place the wine glasses and dinner glasses into the sudsy water, reach for the dishrag.

"See? You don't know. Damn it, Henry." He scratches the back of his neck.

I cough. Mostly for effect. I've discovered one way to get Roger to agree with me is to make him see me as sickly. Vulnerable. "Roger ... when we were working on exposing the whole thing, I felt alive. It was like ... I don't know. Justice?" The word feels funny in my mouth. Justice. Like our scraggly group of AIDS activists in little old Toronto could actually go against the Eagle — the mighty U.S. of A. No wonder our national animal is the beaver. Who would be scared of a beaver? Why couldn't we have picked the grizzly bear? Or cougar? Something fierce and power-ful. No, we had to pick the beaver: a large rodent that can swim, has buck teeth, an oversized tail and a talent for building dams out of twigs. What does this say about our national identity? That we're small and insignificant, but productive? That we under-stand how to harness energy using natural resources? That we can't afford decent dental care? No wonder Americans don't respect us. An eagle could swoop down and snatch a beaver in its sharp claws in a matter of seconds, break the beaver's neck like a dry twig, tear the flesh from its back and demolish every trace of it in thirty minutes. Then burp, satisfied, until the next day, when it craves more. "I just don't want to be a beaver anymore," I tell Roger rather cryptically, if I do say so myself.

"What?"

"I'd rather be a grizzly bear," I say.

"Henry, do you feel all right?"

"I'm fine."

"A grizzly bear? You mean like the basketball team in Vancouver?"

"Like a bear in the woods. Fearless. Angry. Coming out of

hibernation in the spring to a new day."

"Maybe you'd better sit down."

"I don't need to sit down. I'm fine."

"You're not making sense."

"I thought after we got this far, they'd want us to keep going."

"You mean Albert?"

"Yeah, and his group in New York."

"But Henry, you don't need to do everything. You helped get the article printed. The story broke. The whole world knows. Isn't that enough?"

"This is my life's work, exposing this thing. I can't stop now. It's the only thing that is keeping me going. My work."

"The only thing?" He looks hurt.

I touch his face. "No."

"But the work comes first."

"You have your work, Roger."

"Yes."

"And I have mine."

He nods.

"Don't take it away from me, Roger. Please."

"What do you mean, you're a grizzly bear?"

"It's hard to explain."

"Try me."

He stands behind me, wraps his arms around my belly and squeezes. I lean back into him. We stand like that until the dish-water grows cold.

We're sitting around the dining room table. It's Roger's first day off in three. He slept in, luxuriously, showered and came into the kitchen for breakfast. He's still in his bathrobe. Solly's already had his morning kippers, three or five cups of coffee and his morning cigar out on the balcony. He's gone to the store and for a walk, made several phone calls and is almost ready for his lunch.

"So?" Solly says. "What are you boys doing for New Year's Eve?"

"Oh. We don't know," I answer.

"You don't know?" Solly can't believe it. "You don't know?"

"That's what I said."

"It's only the fucking biggest New Year's Eve of our lives. The goddamn whatchacallit millennium and you don't know? Come on, Henry. You can do better than that."

"Okay," I challenge, "what are you doing?"

He smiles to himself. "Only taking a lovely young lady I met last week to the Royal York for dinner and dancing."

"What young lady?" I demand.

"Her name is Emma."

"Emma? What about Belle?"

"Henry, your mother's not speaking to me."

"She's not?"

"Ever since the night you took sick. Don't you remember?"

I think back. I have a vague memory of my mother stomping out of the apartment. But Solly and Belle always fight like that. I didn't think it meant they were calling it quits. Again. "Oh."

"Don't worry. Belle's crazy about me. Maybe one day we'll try it again. Maybe not. Who knows?"

"Just exactly how young is the young lady?" I interrogate Solly.

"Who knows? Thirty. Twenty-nine. You think I asked?"

"Pop, that's disgusting. She's young enough to be your daughter."

"It's just a date, Henry. Don't take it so seriously."

"She's younger than Sherry."

"I ain't marrying her. I'm taking her to dinner."

"And where are you going to get that kind of money? The Royal York Hotel?"

"That's what I was just about to tell you, if the interrogation is finished." He snorts.

"Tell us what?"

"I came into some money I been expecting."

"Money?"

"So I can pay you boys some back rent for your hospitality

and so on." He reaches into his trouser pockets, pulls out a huge wad of cash and starts counting off twenties. "That oughtta cover it." He hands me a wad. I flip through the cash. Must be three thousand bucks.

"Pop." I push it back toward him. "That's too much."

"Never mind. It's not like I'm a piece a cake to have around the house, huh?" He guffaws at his own joke, pushes the money back to me.

I take the money, count it carefully this time. Three thousand exactly.

"Anyway, I gotta move on now, boys."

"Move on?"

"Yeah. I got a whatchacallit? Previous engagement south of the border."

"What kind of an engagement?"

"The less asked the better, Henry. You get my meaning?"

"Pop. You're not going to get into any trouble again, are you?"

"Trouble? Me? What the hell you talking about? I'm the picture of reform here. Completely rehabilitated. What I'm doing is perfectly legit."

"Then how come you can't tell me what you're doing?"

"How come? How come?" He reaches over the table, slaps my face lightly. "Sometimes a man's gotta keep his cards close to the chest, Henry. That's all I can say."

"But where will you be?"

"Don't worry so much, Henry. I'll leave you the phone number in Florida."

"You're going back to Florida?"

"Just for a couple of months."

"Pop?"

"Yeah, what?"

"Don't stay away so long this time. Okay?"

"A few months is all."

"I'll miss you."

"Go on."

"It's true."

"Aw jeez, Henry. Don't soak the carpet or anything."

"When are you leaving?"

"Day after New Year's."

"So soon?"

"Jeez, I thought you'd be happy to get rid of me."

"What makes you say that, Solly?" Roger asks.

"Huh?"

"I've grown kind of fond of you, actually," Roger admits.

It's a touching moment, if a little awkward. I don't know whether to laugh or cry.

"Same here," Solly says. And then, because he doesn't have a clue what else to do, he playfully punches Roger in the arm. Roger beams. He never knew his own father, and his experience with father figures was mostly negative. Solly's as close as he's ever had to a father. Roger reaches over and punches Solly back.

"What *are* we going to do for New Year's?" Roger asks me later in bed.

"I haven't even thought about it ... I mean I wasn't sure for a while ..."

"What?"

"You know ... that I'd be home even." From the hospital, I mean. For a while I wasn't sure I'd make it.

"I'm glad you are." He takes my hand.

"I'd be happy just staying home. With you."

"Are you sure?"

"I don't think I could handle the crowds."

"Me too. Maybe we should have a small dinner party."

"You want to?"

"It'll be your father's last night here."

"He's going to the Royal York Hotel. Remember?"

"Maybe he could change his plans."

"Who else would we invite?"

"Didn't you say your cousin will be in town?"

"Yeah."

"So let's invite Nomi and her girlfriend."

"Michael?"

"Course."

"My sister?"

"Sure. And the boys."

"Which boys?" For a second I think he means Larry and Moe.

"Any beautiful boy we know who's free that night. You can never have too many beautiful boys around."

"What will we serve?"

"I'll leave the menu up to you, Henry."

"Okay."

"But get help. Promise me?"

"Okay. Michael will help. And Solly. Julie. Queen David loves to help plan a party."

"Good. It's settled, then."

"What'll we call it?"

"Call it?"

"We have to have a title. Let's see. Henry and Roger's millennium Bash? Nah, too boring. Queers of the Century?"

"Party of the Century?"

"Return of the Village People?" I try.

"I know. Liberace's Revenge," Roger says.

"What?"

"It's perfect. We'll make everyone dress in rhinestones and glitter. We'll round up candelabras and throw them all over the apartment. We'll play nothing but Liberace music."

"It's great, Rog, but can we stop at the music?"

"Okay. We'll play a Liberace song once every hour and on the stroke of midnight."

"Now you're talking."

"Do you think I have time to grow sideburns?" He strokes the sides of his cheeks.

"Let's go to sleep, Roger."

He tackles me. There'll be anything but sleep for a while.

NOMI'S PARANOIA
RUNS RAMPANT

Something is going on behind my back. I can feel it. Last night I walked into the apartment and Chester was sitting beside Betty on the sofa. The second I opened the door they quit talking and acted all funny, being nice and friendly, asking me how my day was, fetching me a beer. Betty hardly ever fetches me a beer.

I open the door to Patty's Place for my evening shift and the same thing happens. Robert and Patty shut up the second I walk in. Even Lulu looks up from her basket and watches me enter.

"What's going on behind my back around here?" I ask.

"Nothing, Rabinovitch. Don't be so paranoid," Patty snarls back at me. "We've got a lot of work to do around here. Good thing you're early."

"What work?"

"We gotta come up with a New Year's Eve theme," Robert says. "We're going to decorate."

"Theme?"

"Yes, Nomi dear," Robert says in a patronizing tone. "Every party needs a theme."

"It does?"

He shakes his head. "So cute."

It's too crowded behind the bar with Robert and Patty both back there, so I lean against the counter on the customer side, pour myself a glass of water from the pitcher.

"How about Hawaiian?" I suggest.

"Hawaiian what?" Robert asks.

I shrug. "Just Hawaiian. Everyone wears loud shirts and sun hats."

"That's pretty lame, Rabinovitch."

"It's hideous," says Robert.

"It is?"

"I was thinking of something more elegant," Robert says.

I look around the pub. I don't see how elegant would work at Patty's Place. Robert gets a faraway glassy look in his eyes, and stares off into some unknown distance. "*Swingtime*," he says.

"What?"

"1936. Fred Astaire and Ginger Rogers."

"A movie?"

"Not just a movie," he clarifies. "A classic. Art deco. Top hats and tails, glittery gowns. It's perfect for New Year's Eve. For the millennium."

"You mean everyone dresses up like Fred Astaire?" I ask.

"Or Ginger Rogers," Robert says. "It'll be fabulous."

"I don't know." Patty pulls out a cigarette.

"Don't worry. I'll design the decor. All you girls have to do is help hang it."

"Well ..." I can see Patty weakening. We always go with Robert's decoration plans. He is, after all, the fag. And we are two butch dykes without a decorating bone in our bodies.

Robert removes his apron, squeezes past Patty. "I have so much to do. I'll need at least a hundred dollars, Patty." He holds out one hand.

"A hundred bucks?! Last year we decorated for fifty."

"Patty, it *is* the millennium," Robert persists.

"Hell of a way to start a new year," she grumbles, but hits the no-sale key. The cash drawer clicks open. She removes the money, hands it over.

'Thank you." Robert snatches the money, turns on his heel and heads for the door.

"Bring me the receipts," she hollers at his back. "Hundred

bucks," she mutters. "What day did you say you're leaving, Ravinovitch?" She pulls the scheduling calendar off the wall, perches her bifocals on the end of her nose.

"The twenty-ninth," I tell her for the hundredth time.

"Cutting it pretty close, isn't it?" She peers at me over her glasses.

"Close?"

"If it was me, I wouldn't fly so close to the millennium," she announces.

"Why not?"

"Y2K, Rabinovitch. Don't you read the papers?"

"You think my plane will crash?"

She considers it for a minute. "Nah, I'm just saying if it was me, I'd drive."

"All the way to Toronto?"

"Better than crashing."

"I thought you just said you didn't think my plane would crash." I hadn't really thought about it when I booked my flight. But every time I tell someone the date, they get a funny look in their eye and remind me of Y2K. What if they're right? What if my plane goes down in a fiery ball over Lake Erie? What if this trip to Toronto is really a trip to my untimely death? Maybe I should call it off? Maybe I should drive? But who wants to drive across the mountains in the winter? That could be more dangerous than flying. And isn't Y2K supposed to happen at midnight on New Year's Eve? I'm travelling on the twenty-ninth. Two full days before the big event. Surely computers will hold out until the thirty-first?

"Your last day is on the twenty-seventh," Patty informs me. "You got that?"

"It is?"

"Night shift."

"Okay."

"Don't bother coming in during the day. Take the day to pack," she orders. I stare at her. Since when does she plan my personal itinerary? It's not like I have all that much to pack. Just a small suitcase with clothes. I am coming back. I don't care what they say.

Hours later Robert returns, arms laden with shopping bags. He spreads out his purchases on a table near the back. He's bought plastic black top hats, cardboard sequined tiaras to give out on New Year's Eve, the usual tacky whistles and noisemakers.

"And the pièce de résistance." He unveils an original framed poster of *Swingtime*, featuring a tuxedo- and top hat-clad Fred Astaire dancing with Ginger, who is decked to the nines in a long, sparkling evening gown. "This one's mine. Just on loan for a few days, Patty."

"What do I want with that?"

From another bag Robert pulls out plastic bags full of confetti. "We'll scatter this everywhere," he says. He also has glittery little stars that will be thrown on the bar and tables and rolls of silver sequined ribbon to hang on the walls. "It doesn't look like much on the roll," Robert says, "but when it's hung the effect is actually quite glamorous."

"Hmmm," says Patty, obviously not convinced.

Robert unpacks a slew of clear glass candleholders. "One for each table. With a candle inside, it almost resembles real crystal," he tells us. "And these ... " he produces a matching set of crystal vases, thin, the type to hold one rose at a time.

"You got all this for a hundred bucks?" Patty is impressed.

"Not exactly, dear."

"What?"

"These are mine. On loan." He holds up one of the rose vases. "And Spencer donated a few dollars to the cause."

"Spencer?"

"Yes. After all, he'll be my date. You don't actually think he'd attend the lesbian party of the century unless I promised him it would be fabulous."

"Amazing." Patty picks up a tiara, studies it, places it on top of her short-cropped hair. She looks ridiculous.

After my shift, I open the door to Betty's apartment and it happens again. Just as I enter she says into the phone, "Gotta go. Bye." Then, "Hey, Nom. You're home early."

"No I'm not."

"Oh. Say, you want a beer?" And she does it again. She goes into the kitchen and fetches me a beer.

"Am I dying or something?" I ask, pulling off my shoes in the hallway.

"What?" She hands me a beer.

"Why are you being so nice to me?"

"What? No reason," she says indignantly. "Can't a person be nice just because?"

"What's going on around here?" I plunk down on the sofa.

"Going on?"

"Every time I walk into a room, everybody stops talking."

"Don't be ridiculous." She sits beside me.

"So it's my imagination?"

"You said it, not me."

"Hmmph."

The phone rings. "I'll get it." Betty leaps up, grabs the phone. "Oh hi. No. I'll call you back. That's right. Okay. Bye." She hangs up.

I glare at her suspiciously.

"What?"

Betty turns on the TV. It's showing *The Simpsons*, a rerun we've both seen at least twice. I wander into her bedroom and dial Julie's number.

"Four more sleeps," Julie tells me.

That's how many more nights until I'll be in Toronto. "Do you think my plane will crash?" I ask.

"What? Why would it? Nomi?"

"You know. Y2K." I say it dramatically, as if the whole world is doomed.

"I don't believe that."

"You don't?"

"No. I think the computer industry made the whole thing up, just to make money from all us frightened people who don't know any better."

"But what if it's true?"

"You're not travelling on New Year's, Nomi. Nothing's going to happen on the twenty-ninth."

"Promise?"

"Cross my heart."

"Don't say the rest," I interrupt.

"What are you wearing?"

"Tight black jeans, leather jacket, nothing else," I lie.

"I'm slipping off my negligee, Nomi."

"Oh God."

I have a premonition the second I reach for the door to Patty's Place. It's my last shift before I go to Toronto. I'm actually looking forward to it, probably because I won't have to work for a while. A chill travels up my spine. I feel an adrenaline rush through my body. I yank open the door. It's completely dark in the pub, but I can make out shapes of bodies. I wonder if there has been a mas- sacre — a gang-style shooting, all the regular patrons of Patty's Place mowed down by machine gun fire. Except they're standing. Someone lights a match. I back up, toward the door.

"Surprise!" a million voices shout. Lights go up. Flashbulbs flare suddenly. "Surprise!" they shout again. Someone thrusts a cake under my face, a huge cake with the words, "Bon Voyage Nomi," written across it in blue icing. Everyone is there. All my friends, regular bar patrons, people I've never seen before. Lulu's barking up a storm. Someone has thrown in a tape. It's k.d. lang singing "Auld Lang Syne." I feel the tears well up in my eyes.

"Surprise, Nom." Betty sidles up beside me.

I grab the Guinness from her hand and drink. "So, this is how come everyone's been talking behind my back."

"Yeah, and let me tell you, Nom, you didn't make it easy." She snatches her beer back.

"Sorry," I grin. But I'm not. I'm not sorry at all.

I agree to accompany Solly on his last visit to my grandmother before he blows town, as he calls it. Roger's still on
his three-day weekend, so he decides to tag along. At the
appointed time, Lou buzzes from downstairs. We pile into his
cab. Solly in the front seat, Roger and I in the back. It's cold. A
light snow is falling. I zip up my ski jacket, pull on my gloves.

"You remember Roger," I tell Lou.

He glances in the rearview mirror, tips his hat. "Oh yeah,
sure. Hiya, Roger."

"Hi, Lou."

Lou hits the gas and we lurch off up Church Street.

"There sure are a lot of fairies around here." Lou uses the
archaic expression.

Roger and I just about lose our breakfast. I wink at him, then
lean forward over the seat back. "What do you mean fairies, Lou?"

He glances at me. "Oh, not like you, Henry. You know what I
mean." He tries to backpedal his way out of this.

"Whadja expect, Lou?" Solly interjects. "We're on Church
Street." My father's been staying with us long enough now to
have acclimatized to the neighbourhood.

"Oh," says Lou, "I forgot." We head northward. Dirty snow-
banks line the streets, accumulated from the last few days of
snow and traffic.

"Ya *putz*." My father playfully slaps Lou on the head.

I guess it's the best we can expect.

Lou drops us off in front of the old folks' home. At the front entrance, Solly punches in the five-digit code to open the door. They have it set for 1-2-3-4-5. The lock is not to keep intruders from getting in, it's to keep the old people from wandering outside and getting lost. Bubbe sits in her usual chair in the lobby, staring into space. It's almost as if she had never been in the hospital, except that she looks more drawn, just a little more hunched, as if she lost some of her strength in the ordeal and hasn't regained it. I can relate. I feel the same. I've mostly recovered from the pneumonia, but it's left me feeling generally fatigued. Or maybe it's just the virus. Slowly replicating inside my veins, calmly destroying my few remaining T cells, one by one.

Bubbe's face breaks into a huge smile when she recognizes Solly. He leans forward and kisses her cheek. I do the same. Roger stands beside me. Bubbe leans forward and stares at him.

"Who are you?" she demands. I guess that's one of the advantages of being ninety-two to ninety-seven. You can cast aside all social conventions and just be yourself.

"You remember Roger," I tell her. "My roommate." I use the standard lie I've been using for years.

"Your boyfriend?" she asks.

I smile. "Yeah, Bubbe. My boyfriend." Does she get it? Did I somehow come out to her last time I saw her? Or did she absorb the information by osmosis when Roger helped her get settled in the hospital on the day she collapsed? I strain my memory, try to remember if we gave any clues.

She grabs Roger's shirt, pulls him closer to get a good look at him. "So?" she says to Roger. "Are you married?"

So much for coming out to her.

"No," Roger lies. "Not married."

"He lives with Henry." Solly winks at me, shrugs.

"You live together?" She looks at me, then back at Roger. Then at me again. "Tell me something, Herschel ..."

"Yes?"

"You live together?"

"Yes, we do."

"Okay, so who does the cooking?"

Oh. "Uh, me mostly."

"Okay." That seems fine to Bubbe. "And the shopping?"

"Uh, me," I say.

She stares at Roger. "So what do you do?"

"He does the cleaning, Bubbe." I rescue him. And pays most of the bills and the rent. But I don't say this out loud. This I don't think she would understand.

"Very nice," Bubbe decides. "Better than living alone. So you shouldn't be lonely."

"We're not lonely," I assure her.

"But Henry ..." she continues.

"Yes?"

"When will I dance at your wedding?"

"When?" I stall for time. This is crazy. Maybe her mind's going. Maybe it's Alzheimer's. I thought we'd already been through this a few times. I thought she knew about me and Nomi. "Well, tell you what," I say. "When I'm getting married, you'll be the first to know. Okay?"

This seems to satisfy her. She nods, then snaps open the black patent leather purse that rests on her lap. "Here, have a donut." She hands me a stale donut wrapped in an old napkin.

"That's okay, Bubbe. I'm not hungry."

"How about your boyfriend?" She tries to hand it to Roger.

He accepts it, smiles, takes a bite.

"It's good?" Bubbe asks.

"Delicious." Roger, bless his heart, takes another bite.

"Oh, I see we have company, Mrs. Rabinovitch." Dov, the orderly, flits over to our little party.

I smile at him stiffly. Silently beg him to be discreet. "Dov," I say, "this is Roger."

Dov offers a hand, and mercifully he understands. He gives no indication of our former illicit indiscretion in my grandmother's bathroom, up against her stainless steel handrail for the disabled.

"And my father."

"Nice to see you, Mr. Rabinovitch," Dov smiles.

"You're from the Holy Land?" my father asks. Dov's accent is thick.

"Tel Aviv."

"What are you doing here?"

"Getting an education. I'm in nursing school."

"Oh?" This piques Roger's interest. Or is it Dov's boyish smile? Actually I hadn't known about nursing school. Dov has never mentioned this to me before.

"Ryerson?" Roger asks.

"Yes, do you know the program?"

"I graduated from it. What's your specialty?" Roger asks.

Quick blow jobs in the tearoom, I'd like to say, but I remain silent.

"I'm only in my first year," Dov admits. "Part-time, because you know, I have to work."

"Maybe you should think about geriatrics," Roger suggests. "After all your experience here. Plus the boomers are aging. There's going to be lots of openings."

"Seems like there are openings in any part of the field," Dov says.

"Absolutely. Especially for male nurses. You'll be snatched up in no time."

"You think?" Dov actually bats his eyes at Roger. Is he flirting? Or is it just professional schmoozing?

I keep a close eye on both of them.

"So M-A," Solly shouts, "how ya feeling?"

"What's that?"

"How ya feeling!" he shouts louder.

Out of the corner of my eye I spot shawl-woman, Mrs. Rosenfeld, and hope like hell she hasn't seen me. I just don't feel like dancing today. Dov keeps asking Roger nursing questions. They sit side by side on one of the plastic-covered sofas, discussing the latest trends in X-ray equipment. I don't know whether to be jealous or relieved that my lover is getting along so well with one of my tricks.

"You must come to our New Year's Eve dinner, then," I hear Roger tell Dov.

"Well, I wouldn't want to intrude."

"Nonsense," declares Roger. "We'd love to have you. Wouldn't we, Henry?" he calls over to me.

"Hmmm?"

"I've just invited Dov to our New Year's bash."

I smile. Why not?

"I wonder if they celebrate here," my father says sadly.

"Oh yes," says Dov, "but most of the residents don't really know what's going on."

"What's that?" Bubbe asks.

"New Year's Eve is coming up," I tell her, loudly.

"What's that, Tatela?"

"New Year's!"

"New York?"

"New Year's."

"Feh. Who can celebrate with your Zayde gone? I don't have the heart for it anymore. Sixty-five years we were married." Tears form in Bubbe's eyes. "I can't forget him. Should I forget?"

"No, Ma, you shouldn't," Solly tells her. "Should we bring her over?" he asks me.

"For New Year's?"

"Yeah."

"We can. Roger?"

"Course."

"We'll come and get her in the afternoon," Solly says.

"You'll have to do it, Pop. Roger and I have a lot to do that day to get ready."

"All right. Lou will help me. Okay, Ma? You'll come by us."

"What are you saying, Solly? I can't hear you."

"She'll come. She'll come. I'll pick her up, she'll come," Solly says.

Our small dinner party is shaping up into quite the millennium bash.

NOMI'S RIDE TO
THE AIRPORT

"Hurry up, Nom. You'll be late," Betty calls to me from the front door.

I've dashed back into the bathroom to fetch my toothbrush. Betty's driving me to the airport in her Super Shuttle van. She's officially at work today but she's using the burnt-out spark plug trick again. She's supposedly at the mechanic's getting it fixed. If she gets caught, her boss will have her ass. But Betty doesn't care. She's mad at Mona for snubbing her attentions. I think Betty wants to be reprimanded.

"Nomi," she yells again.

"Okay, okay." I rush into the living room, grab my overnight bag, shove my toothbrush haphazardly into my pocket, take a quick look around and follow her outside. In spite of my own protests, I have a feeling it's going to be a long time before I am back here. I am stubbornly bringing only a small overnight bag, leaving most of my stuff at Betty's. I've sworn to everyone I'll be back in four weeks as planned. Somewhere deep inside, though, I wonder if it is true.

I follow Betty to her van, which she has double-parked in the middle of the street. It's only when I'm about to open the door that I notice the others inside waiting. The whole gang has come to see me off. I step up into the van and sit in the front seat beside Guido. Behind in the next seat sit Chester and AJ. Even Patty and Lulu are aboard. Robert must be covering the bar.

"Hey, buddy." Guido punches my arm.

Chester reaches forward and ruffles my hair.

"Is that all you're bringing?" Patty yells from the back seat.

"That's it," I answer.

"For four weeks?" Patty shoots back. Lulu adds her two cents to the discussion with a loud bark.

"I like to travel light."

Betty snaps her seatbelt together, puts the van in gear and tears off up the street.

I am hyper aware of the city's beauty as we drive. The restored Victorian houses, each painted elaborately in several different shades. Palm trees. Deep purple bougainvillea climbing up the sides of houses. Bright red bottle-brush trees. Huge mutant Californian plants and bushes I've never learned the names of. As we pass through the Castro district I notice all the visible dykes and fags wandering the streets. I wonder how the community will feel in Toronto after three years in San Francisco.

"Let's stop at the Clit Club," AJ suggests as we roar down Duboce Street.

"No time," Betty warns gruffly.

AJ went to the club with Betty last Saturday night. She didn't actually participate in any public sex, just watched, but since then it's all she's talked about. She swears she's going back this Saturday and she's going to jump into a scene. We're all holding our breaths. I kind of wish I was going to be here to see that. It's her post-Martha frenzy: AJ's adventures at the Clit Club. It's kind of like lesbian-Gidget goes to Rome.

The whole ride is surreal and melodramatic, as if my friends are escorting me to the ends of the earth. To them Canada *is* the ends of the earth. I keep telling them Toronto is a big city, larger, in fact, than San Francisco. They don't believe me. They can't believe anywhere in Canada is large. They have images of small towns covered in snow, people living in igloos, drinking strong beer out of bottles, wearing red plaid lumberjackets and woolen toques. I've tried. I've really tried in my three years living as an illegal alien in San Francisco to teach my American friends the truth, but in the end it is no use. Even Patty, who was born and raised in Sudbury, has forgotten. Her memories of her native land are of the small town in northern Ontario.

"I grew up in an igloo," she says just to irritate me.

"See?" AJ says.

"You did not," I tell Patty.

"What do you know about Sudbury, Rabinovitch?"

"Well I grew up in Toronto," I insist. "A very large city. In a brick house, with paved sidewalks. No trees. No beavers. No beer, even."

"In your dreams, Rabinovitch."

Why do I even bother? I feel my eyes well up as Betty turns off the highway onto the ramp heading for the airport. I'm really going to miss these guys. If I stay in Toronto, will I make new friends? Will any of my old friends resurface? I'm not much of a letter writer. Probably all my old friends in Toronto hate me now and think I'm a snob for moving to San Francisco and not writing them. What will Julie think of me when she finds out I have no friends?

Betty stops outside the United Airlines departures sign. "This is it, Nom," she says with dread. As if she's just escorted me to the gangplank and I'm about to step into a cold, angry, shark-filled ocean.

I grab my overnight bag. The whole gang de-vans. They all gather around for the final goodbye.

Patty offers a hand to shake. "Well, Rabinovitch, it's been great. Oh, here." She pulls a white envelope from her breast pocket.

"What's this?" I open it. There are two crisp fifty-dollar bills inside.

"Bonus. Kind of like unofficial vacation pay."

"You didn't have to do that."

"Put it away before I change my mind, Rabinovitch."

I stuff the envelope into my jeans pocket.

"Have a good trip," good old Chester says, as if I *am* coming back. "Hey, bring us back some of that Canadian beer, will you?"

"Sure, Chester."

"She's not coming back." Betty punches Chester on the arm.

"She's not?"

"I'm coming back," I insist.

"Sure, Nom."

"Can we visit you there?" AJ asks. "I've always wanted to go to Canada."

"You've been," I remind her. "Victoria is in Canada."

"I mean the other part."

"Course you can visit. But I'm coming back."

"When we see it, Nom."

"What?"

"We'll believe it." Betty is in a foul mood.

"Fine," I say back.

"Aw crap," she says, wiping a tear from her eye. "Just gonna miss you's all," she admits.

I lean over, hug my best friend.

"Awright. Enough with the tears, Rabinovitch. Get going. You'll miss your damn plane and then Julie'll have all of our asses. Go on now." Patty pushes me.

I pick up my bag, wave goodbye one last time, turn and pull open the heavy glass doors.

During the five-hour flight, I think about my life, about San Francisco, about my relationship with Julie. I'm a mixture of sad and happy, but mostly happy. The in-flight movie is a disaster film. I'm only half-watching. Something about a group of young men out in the open ocean on a boat. There's a heavy storm. They're pounded by huge waves. The rain is pouring down in sheets. They'll never make it out of there alive. Why do they show disaster movies on airplanes? I can't bear to watch. I remove my headphones and flip through the *People* magazine I bought at the airport.

When the plane touches down at Pearson International Airport, I notice snow on the ground. I haven't had to live with snow for three years. I glance at my Doc Martens. They're not going to be warm enough, and they're slippery. If I stay longer than a month, I'll have to buy winter boots.

Just through the gates I see Julie waiting for me, her long black hair loose and down her back. The first thing I notice about Julie are her lips. She doesn't see me yet, behind the glass, so I stop for a moment and stare. I've always loved her lips, full and feminine, just like Betty Boop's lips.

I have to wait in the Canada Customs line. It's a long wait. When I finally get to the front, I hold my breath as the agent inspects my ticket and passport. It's always a tense moment. I worry that somehow they will know by looking at me that I have been living in the States without a green card. But the Canadian agent doesn't care about that. He only wants to know what I'm bringing in, which is nothing. He waves me through.

I push open the glass doors. Julie spots me. She rushes over. She is in my arms. My lips are on hers. I don't care that we are in the middle of an airport. She's kissing me on the lips, face, forehead, nose, my neck. I open my eyes. She pulls back to look at me. Her bright red lipstick is smeared all over her mouth. She's crying. Her tears mix in with the lipstick. I brush away the red with my hand.

"Oh baby," Julie says, "I missed you so much."

You'll never have to miss me again, I want to say, but I'm scared to. "I missed you too," I say instead, kissing her again. She pushes her body against mine. We weave, almost topple to the floor in our excitement. I hold her.

"Nomi." She's laughing. "There's lipstick all over your face." She tries to clear it away with her thumb.

"You too."

"And eyeliner. You're a mess."

I smile, throw one arm around her waist, steer her toward the door. "Let's go home." Every reunion with Julie is filled with just a little more pain and joy. She feels so right in my arms. How can I ever leave her again?

It's snowing outside — a light snow, but it's staying on the ground and the cars are covered in an inch of snow. Welcome to

Ontario. I'm such a wimp about winter. How will I cope?

We get inside Julie's car. She takes the wheel. I take her free hand. She backs out of the parking space and onto the ramp, heading for the highway. We have so much to say I don't know where to start, so I simply watch her as she drives. We pass through the flat grey suburbs: strip malls, factories, warehouses, houses built by the side of the highway on what used to be farmland. Every second house looks the same. There are seven-foot high fences at the ends of their backyards to reduce the highway noise. The road is full of other cars. We are at the tail end of rush hour. Julie drives expertly through the traffic.

Inside Julie's apartment, I drop my bag, take her in my arms.

"Babe," she says, leading me to the bedroom, "I can't believe you're here."

"I can hardly believe it myself."

"Take off your clothes," she orders.

"Now?"

"Now."

And I do.

HENRY'S BROKEN HOME

M y mother shows up at my apartment unexpectedly just as I'm preparing dinner. Roger's on day shift, expected home by eight. We're having a late dinner. I'm pan-frying two red snapper filets in garlic and soy sauce, with basmati rice, broccoli and a Caesar salad. The apartment smells heavenly from all the spices.

"Ma, what's the matter?"

She pushes past me, into the apartment, waving a lit cigarette in the air as she speaks. "Where's your father? Is he gone?" She takes a deep draw and blows smoke angrily in a steady stream from her nose. "I know he's leaving."

"Ma." I cough, wave at the smoke. "Please put that out." I throw open a bureau drawer and search for an ashtray.

She ignores me, smokes with a vengeance. "Where is he?"

I lunge for the cigarette, snatch it out of her hand, hold it out in front of me, calmly walk down the hall to the bathroom and toss it into the toilet.

"Henry?" She follows me.

"Ma." I try to remain calm. "I just got over pneumonia. Remember?"

"Oh my God." Her hands fly to the sides of her cheeks. "I'm sorry, sweetie. I forgot. Can you forgive me? I was so wrapped up. I'm furious at your father. I just forgot. Let me look at you." She stands back and surveys my body. "You're thin."

"I know."

"You should eat more."

"I'm trying to cook dinner ..." I gesture to the kitchen.

"How are you feeling?" She reaches up, puts a hand on my forehead.

"Ma, I'm fine. Just don't smoke around me, okay?" I wave at the invisible smoke in the air, cough again for effect.

"Who can remember? These days you can't smoke anywhere. In the old days you could smoke everywhere. Even judges on the bench smoked. Doctors. Nurses. Bus drivers. Everyone smoked when I was your age. There wasn't such a stigma. Now I feel like a criminal." She reaches in her purse, pulls out a fresh cigarette.

"Ma," I warn.

"Don't worry. I won't light it. It calms me to hold one. Where's your father?" She stomps toward the den, throws open the door. "I have something I want to say to him."

He's not in his room. It's empty. The bed is unmade as usual, the covers and sheets tangled at the end, clothes tossed on chairs and the floor, anywhere but the closet. There is a stale odour — old cigar smoke embedded in the walls and fabrics. My father has the housekeeping skills of Oscar in *The Odd Couple*. In an ashtray by his bed an unlit cigar stub rests on top of a pile of ashes. On his dresser sits a family-sized can of Lysol. Against my wishes, he's been smoking in his room again. He thinks the Lysol covers the stench.

"He's out," I tell my mother.

"Where? What a mess." She picks up a dirty sock from the floor, flings it on the bed.

"I don't know. With Lou, maybe."

"Where's he going, Henry? I know he's leaving town again. Where's he going? You can tell me."

"I don't know."

"Oh God." She sinks onto his bed, head in hands.

"Ma ..."

"What?"

"Do you still love him?"

She looks up at me. "What kind of a question is that?"

I shrug.

"I never stopped. He's my husband."

"Ex-husband."

"Husband, Henry."

"What?"

"We're not divorced."

"What? What are you saying?"

"We never got divorced."

"What?" I can't believe my ears.

"We never actually got a divorce."

"But I remember ..." I struggle for the words.

"No, sweetheart."

"I remember you said ... you said you were divorced. I remember."

"Just separated. We never actually went through with it."

"Oh my God." It's my turn to sink onto the bed.

"I'm sorry." She ruffles my hair.

"I can't believe it."

"We thought you knew."

"You told me you were divorced," I accuse her. "When I was little. You said it all the time. You called yourself the gay divorcee. After that Fred Astaire movie."

She shrugs. "It was a figure of speech."

"A figure of speech?"

"That's right."

"All this time ..."

"I'm sorry, Henry."

"You're sorry?"

"Tell me where he's going," she tries again.

I groan. I fall back on the bed and just groan.

Belle is putting on her coat to leave when we hear a key in the lock.

"There he is," she says, a little on the vindictive side.

But it's not Solly. It's Roger.

"Oh, hi, Belle," he says.

"Hello, sweetheart." She peers over his shoulder, looking for my father. Roger doesn't understand, looks behind himself, then back at her.

"Phone me when he gets home, Henry, please. On my cell. Here's the number." She jots the number down on a scrap of paper, presses it into my hand.

"Ma, I can't do that."

"Please, Henry. Just do me this one little favour."

I sigh deeply.

"Thanks, love." She kisses my cheek. "Take care of Henry, Roger. He's too skinny." She pats Roger's arm, leaves the apartment.

Roger hangs his coat in the hall closet. "What's going on?"

"I don't think I know," I admit. "And I don't want to think about it right now."

"Henry?"

"My parents. They're as crazy as usual. And I don't think it really concerns me. I'm not going to let it bother me. Whatever it is. Hungry?" I kiss him.

"Starved. Something smells great."

"It's almost ready."

"I'm going to wash up." He heads for the bedroom. "Your father's out?"

"He's been out all day."

"Good."

The phone rings just as I'm taking the plate of marinated fish from the fridge. I grab the receiver from the kitchen wall. It's Queen David.

"You'll never guess."

"What?"

"Come on, guess."

"You broke a nail?"

"No darling. Not as drastic as that. Did you watch the news?"

"No."

"Our American friend was all over the news."

"Albert?"

"The very same."

"Go on."

"They're suing the U.S. government. The lawyers filed the papers today. He's got the support of practically every AIDS organization in the States ..."

"No mention of us, I guess."

"Actually there was."

I practically drop the fish. "You're kidding?"

"That's why you should watch, dear."

"What did they say?" I have to sit down for this.

"Albert himself was interviewed. He said none of this would have been possible without the help of his Canadian allies at ACTOUT Toronto."

"He said that?"

"In living colour."

"About time."

"Henry, don't be sore."

"Why not? He takes us for granted."

"Sometimes, hon, that's a good thing."

"Why?"

"It means you're family."

"If you want to see it that way."

"Ask me what I'm wearing on New Year's?" Queen David tries to change the subject.

"It won't work, sweetie. I'm still mad at him."

"I know, love. Give him time."

"You're still coming early on Friday to help?"

"Wouldn't miss it for the world, darling. I have a new outfit."

"Can't wait to see it."

NOMI'S MISSING PIECE

"Nomi?"

I'm struggling up from inside a lovely dream, where I'm in bed with Julie. She's touching me all over. I don't want to wake up.

"Nomi?"

"What?" My eyes snap open. Julie stares down at me. I am in bed with her. It's not just a dream. "Hi."

She touches my face. "Tea?"

"You." I reach for her, pull her down on top of me. My lips are on hers. She kisses me back. My arms around the small of her back, her centre. She moans, pushes against me.

"No," she says.

"Babe?"

She pulls away. "I'll be late."

"Who cares?" I kiss her again. She kisses back. I run my fingers through her long hair. Nestle my face against her neck.

"Nomi." She giggles, pulls away, forces herself to stand. "I'm making tea."

I reach for her. She steps out of my grasp. Shakes her head, leaves the bedroom.

I lay back against the pillows. I'm jet-lagged, three hours behind Toronto time. Last night, after we got in from the airport, we made love until three. I don't know how Julie's going to make it through work today on four hours' sleep. I glance out the window. Even the sight of a barren maple tree can't bring me down. I'm so high just being here. It feels so right to have this time with Julie. She's a missing piece of my heart, brought back into place. The kettle whistles. I slip out of bed, step into my jeans and a sweatshirt, go out to the kitchen to join her. It doesn't seem fair that she has to be up and I can linger in bed.

"Nomi, you should go back to sleep." Julie pours boiling water into a teapot.

"Not if you're in here." I sidle up behind her, wrap my arms around her waist.

"Careful. It's hot."

"So are you."

She pours boiling water shakily into the teapot, drops in two tea bags. She likes her tea strong. I'm a coffee drinker, but Julie doesn't own a coffee pot.

I kiss the back of her neck.

"Nomi ..." she warns.

"Hmmm?"

"I can't. I have to get dressed."

"You do?" I undo the belt of her dressing gown.

She moans. "Nomi ... stop."

"Can't help it." I slip my hand inside her robe, fondle her breast.

She leans back into me.

"Do you really have to go to work?"

"No," she moans. "I mean yes." She swats my hand away, pushes me lightly and reties her bathrobe belt.

"Okay, okay." I relent. "I'll stand over here." I go to the farthest corner of the living room, stand ramrod straight.

Julie pours our tea.

"It's the only way," I tell her. "If I'm near you, I can't help it. I have to touch you. I can't be held responsible for my actions. It's all your fault."

"My fault?" She opens the fridge for cream.

"You're too sexy."

She walks toward me with two mugs of tea.

I stretch out my arm, take a cup.

"Come sit with me." She takes my free hand, leads me to the sofa. "What will you do today?"

"I promised Henry I'd help decorate for his party. And I want to check in with him. How has he been?"

"Better, but a little thin. And I think his energy is low."

"Are you sure you have to work today?"

"Yes, Nomi. Tomorrow I only work half a day."

"Which half?" I undo the belt of Julie's robe again, slip my hand back inside before she can stop me.

"Nomi ..." she warns halfheartedly.

I glance at the clock on the stove. "We have thirteen whole minutes before you have to leave." I cup her breast.

"I have to get dressed," she reminds me.

"Then we have ten minutes." I lunge forward and kiss her. She doesn't resist. We fall back on the couch and into heaven.

"Just a minute," Henry calls from inside the apartment. I'm waiting outside his door, in the hall, my arms loaded down with grocery bags. He phoned before I left with a list of things he needed. I stopped at a Loblaws grocery store on the way. The door is flung open. Henry is wearing a frilly pink apron and holding a colourful feather duster in one hand.

"Who are you supposed to be? Julia Child?"

He looks down at himself. "I thought I looked more like Doris Day. Did you get the Pledge?" He peers into my grocery bag.

"I got everything. You look good, Henry." He does look better than I had imagined. Maybe a little thinner.

He slips one arm through mine, steers me inside the apartment. "Coffee?"

"Love some. Julie only drinks tea."

"And she calls herself a Torontonian? Did you eat?"

"I had breakfast. I'm sorry I couldn't come and visit when you were in the hospital."

"I was only in three days. Roger says I'm lucky."

"You always have been."

Uncle Solly wanders into the living room from the kitchen. "Hey! Is that Nomi? Come 'ere." He wraps his arms around me in a big bear hug, lifts me right off the ground, then puts me down. "You look good."

"You too, Uncle Solly."

"How's your mother?"

I shrug. "Getting used to married life." Then I regret my words. Maybe he doesn't want to hear about my mother's new husband — the man who replaced his brother and my father.

He surprises me with his sensitivity. "It's an adjustment."

"Yeah, I guess."

"So you're coming to our big bash?"

"Wouldn't miss it."

"It's the millennium," Solly says, as if I didn't know.

"She knows, Pop."

"Course she knows."

"Come on," Henry says. "Let's get you some coffee."

With a steaming mug of fresh brewed coffee in hand, I'm hard at work on my first task. Henry's asked me to polish the coffee and end tables with the Pledge I bought. I've never polished a piece of furniture in my life. I've always had second-hand furniture that wouldn't really benefit from a polishing. He has to show me how to do it. I find the task actually kind of soothing. Making something go from dull to shiny. There's a beginning and an end. You can see the results of your work instantly.

Henry flits about the room with his feather duster, swiping at the bookshelves, the stereo and anything else in his path.

"So?" he says.

"What?"

"How does it feel?"

"What?"

"To be living here."

"I'm not exactly living here."

"Oh?"

"Well ... I mean I'm here for a month and ..."

"And?"

"Then we'll see."

"Okay, so how does it feel so far?"

I smile. "Great. It feels great to be with Julie. To be relaxed about it. Before we had to say it all and do everything in a couple of days. It's nice to stay put ..."

"But?"

"I still hate Toronto."

"So does everybody."

"They do?"

"Sure."

"So how do you stay here?"

He shrugs. "People. Jobs. The weather."

"The weather?"

"Just kidding. It's people mostly. And ..."

"What?"

"Don't laugh."

"What?"

"I like all the stuff that you hate."

"Like what?"

"The crowds, the sidewalks, the city, the rush. I like the buzz here. I don't think I could live on the coast. Too many trees. Too much fresh air. That can't be good for you."

"You sound like Woody Allen."

"Oh no you don't." He fluffs the duster in my face. "Don't compare me to him. Not after what he did to Mia."

"Well, you do."

"Give it some time, Nomi. You'll get used to it."

We work in silence for a moment.

"So it's still going on?" I ask him.

"What?"

"The AIDS conspiracy stuff."

"ACTOUT New York is suing the U.S. government. Isn't that a trip?"

I shrug. "Sounds dangerous."

"Not any more than living is." He stares at me hard.

"Right."

"It's official now. I have AIDS. My T cells are under two hundred. Before I was just positive. Now I'm positively dying," he says dryly.

"You're not on those protease thingies?"

He groans. "Oh, Nomi. Not you too."

"What?"

"Everyone's been nagging me to go on the drugs. Roger, my doctor, Julie. Now you."

"Why not ... I mean aren't they the best treatment there is?"

"Who knows? That's what they said about AZT, and it killed Steven."

"Steven?"

"A friend. You'll meet his lover Simon on New Year's. Steve went on AZT. He did really well for a year and a half. Then the drug turned on him. He had to quit taking it. After that he got sick real fast. Everything all at once. He was blind. Constant diarrhea, dementia, a tumour in his brain."

"I'm sorry, Henry. That must have been awful."

"Listen, Nomi, I'm doing pretty good without the drugs."

"Yeah."

He puts down the duster, pulls a few CDs from a shelf and flips through them. "Can we talk about something else?"

"Sure, Cuz."

"Tell me about the Drag King Contest again."

"Oh yeah. It was awesome."

"How come you didn't enter it?" He puts the CDs down on the coffee table, pulls out another handful.

"Stage fright."

"I hear you. Tell me about your friend Betty. She sounds great."

"She is."

HENRY'S MIRACULOUS ARRIVAL
AT THE MILLENNIUM

"L'chaim." Michael stands at my apartment door with a full glass of champagne in one hand and the bottle and an empty glass in the other, at eleven in the morning.

"Isn't it a little early?" I open the door wider to let him in.

"We made it, darling. We're having a private little toast. Where's Roger?" Michael follows me into the kitchen.

"The store."

"Here." He hands me an empty glass, fills it.

"I don't want this."

"But you must. Just one little sip. Please."

"What are we drinking to?"

"The fact that we made it."

"To the millennium?"

"Come on, Henry. Haven't there been times when you thought we wouldn't?"

I sigh.

"You see?" He holds his glass up high. "To whatever goddess is looking down on my good friend Henry and me, may we be blessed with another year."

"Just one more?"

"Okay, two."

"Not very demanding, are we?"

"More like realistic."

I look at him with a little more concern. "Is there news from the front?"

He grimaces, knocks back his champagne. "I have to have a mastectomy."

"What?"

"They're removing my breast."

"What breast?"

"All right, just a little tissue above my nipple, but it feels like a mastectomy. I'm going to join one of those self-help groups for women with breast cancer. Do you think they'll let me?"

"Isn't that drastic?"

"The group?"

"The mastectomy."

"I can always buy one of those bras."

Gallows humour. It's become second nature to us. "What bra?"

"You know ... for ladies who've had a touch of surgery." He pats his hair. "Maybe I'll get breast implants. Dolly Parton, look out."

"Is there more?" Bad news, I mean.

"Jeff wants me to go to the ovens."

"Oh." Our code word for radiation treatments.

"The microwave ovens."

I ruffle his hair. "Poor Michael. I'll go with you."

"Would you?" He looks very small when he says this.

"I'll stay with you the whole time." I wrap my arms around my friend, hug him.

He sniffs, refills his glass. "Well, enough about me. What about you, Henry?"

I shrug. "A lot better but ..."

"But?"

"Fatigue. Have to conserve my energy these days. Nap time is a big event around here. Like my kindergarten days."

"Could be worse."

"I know."

He refills my glass. Somehow my one little sip has turned into a full glass. I'm feeling the bubbly effects. Warm and calming. Maybe it's not such a bad idea.

Michael raises his glass again. "To the millennium."

"To friends." I slip my arm through his and we drink our champagne, arms linked.

"What the hell's this?" My father wanders into the kitchen in his Frank Sinatra-style smoking jacket.

Michael and I unlink.

"Champagne?" I ask Solly.

He glances at his wristwatch. "Already?"

"We're celebrating." Michael pours him a glass.

"It's eleven in the morning."

"We wanted to get a head start," Michael says. "Join us?" He hands a glass to Solly.

"What the hell? It *is* the millennium." Solly obliges, silently toasts us, then sips on his champagne.

In our slightly inebriated state, Michael and I commence preparing the petits fours. We put Solly to work cutting broccoli, carrots, cauliflower and peppers for the vegetable platter.

I answer the phone on the first ring, figuring it's Roger calling from the store.

"Did you forget the list?"

"Henry?"

I recognize the voice immediately.

"Hello Albert," I say rather coldly. "What can I do for you?"

"You're mad."

"Hurt is more like it."

"I called to say Happy New Year."

"Happy New Year," I say with no enthusiasm.

"And to thank you, for everything."

"Sure."

"I'm sorry, Henry. I should have called sooner. But you know what it's like in the thick of things. I've barely slept."

"It's okay, Al. We're used to it."

"We?"

"Why wouldn't you drop our little Canadian group ..."

"Stop it, Henry. Who said anything about dropping you?"

"Well, you sure don't need us now."

"Not for the legal challenge. That has to be done here, against the American government. Who said we still didn't need your support?"

"Haven't heard from you and all ..."

"I'm sorry, Henry. Without you, we wouldn't have come this far. Didn't you see that on the news? I said it at every interview."

"I guess."

"Don't be sore."

I take a deep breath. "Okay."

"I mean it, Henry. I couldn't have done it without you."

"You got that right."

"Thank you."

"Don't mention it," I say.

"Look, we'll talk soon. There are things you can help with," Albert says.

"Okay, Al." I can't stay mad at him. "Thanks for calling."

"Happy New Year, Henry."

"Happy New Year." I say it with feeling this time.

Roger returns from the store.

"Did you find irises?" I ask him.

"Yeah. It was hard, though, at this time of year." Roger produces a small bunch, wrapped in paper.

"Irises?" Michael asks.

"For spring," I say.

"Spring?"

"I'm thinking ahead."

"Uh huh." Michael understands.

"Just in case." In case I'm not here in the spring.

I put Roger and Solly to work in the den rearranging the furniture. In order to fit everyone in, we're moving the dining room table against the wall. We'll eat buffet style. Solly's room is being turned back into a den so people can eat in there.

Michael refills my glass.

"So?" I ask him.

"What?" He takes a sip.

"You know very well what I'm talking about."

"Oh. Him?"

"How did it go? What did you do? Can I be a bridesmaid at your wedding?"

"Henry, you can be my maid of honour."

"Thank you for not saying matron."

"He's heavenly."

"I know that. But how did it go?"

"Put it this way, Henry. I can see why you call him David-to-Die-For."

"Are you going to see him again?"

"He's going to be my date," Michael beams.

"For New Year's?"

He grins.

"So that's why we're getting looped first thing in the morning."

"Just one of the many reasons to celebrate."

"Well aren't you little Miss Marvel this morning?"

"David-to-Die-For." Michael holds up his glass.

"Here's to him." I clink my glass against his. We swill the rest of our drinks.

Queen David makes his royal entrance.

"I'll need two of the strongest brutes you can spare, Henry. I've got two cabs filled with extra chairs waiting curbside," he announces, peers at me and Michael, notices the champagne. "What are we celebrating?"

Michael pours Queen David a glass. "Love," he says.

"I think it has more to do with lust at this point," I clarify.

"To love and lust," Queen David holds up his glass, tips it back. "And later I want all the details. Every last one. Meanwhile, the meter's running."

"Right. Roger ..." I call to the den.

He grabs my father and they follow Queen David downstairs. The phone rings. I grab it.

"I know he's there, Henry," my mother says. She sounds agitated. I hear her take a long drag of her cigarette, then blow the smoke out through her mouth.

"Who?" I play innocent.

"Your father. Who else?"

"He's not here, Ma."

"Where is he?" she demands.

"He'll be back in a few minutes. I'll tell him to call you."

"No way, Jose. I'm waiting. So? What's new?"

"Nothing, Ma. We talked yesterday."

"Well, how are you feeling, Henry?"

"Better. Good." I clear my throat.

"What was that?" She sounds slightly hysterical.

"What?"

"You coughed just then."

"I cleared my throat. It was hardly a cough."

"Are you hiding something from me, Henry?"

"No. And I didn't cough."

"So you feel okay?"

"Terrific."

"Listen, I'm worried. Is that so terrible?"

"No."

"So. What about New Year's? What are your plans for tonight?"

Oh boy. What can I do? If I tell her we're having a party she might be hurt we didn't invite her. "Just having a couple of friends over."

"Friends?"

"Yeah, what are you doing, Ma? Are you seeing Bernie?"

"Bernie? Don't be ridiculous."

"I thought you always spent New Year's with him."

"Henry, whatever you may think of me, I'm not that kind of a woman."

"What kind?"

"I ended my relationship with Bernie when I started seeing your father again."

"You did?"

"Isn't he back yet?"

The door flings open. Roger and Solly stagger into the room, weighed down by chairs, followed by Queen David, who directs them. "No. Over there, Roger. That's better."

"I hear him! Put him on the phone," my mother shouts in my ear.

"That's Queen David," I tell her.

"Who?"

"My friend."

"Did you say 'Queen David'? What kind of a name is that?"

"Come on already, Dave!" my father shouts. "These are heavy."

"*That* was your father," my mother declares. "I know that voice anywhere. Now stop playing games with me, Henry. And put him on the phone."

"Okay, okay." I walk across the room, holding the receiver out. "Pop."

"Yeah, what?"

"It's for you."

He drops the chairs where he stands, grabs the phone. "Hello? Oh, hi. No. No. Nothing important. Hang on a second." He cups his hand over the mouthpiece. "I'll take it in the other room," he tells me, as he wanders to his room to take the call in private.

I'm dying of curiosity. On the other hand, I don't think I really want to know what's going on between them. I have enough drama of my own.

"Let's try that one over here," Queen David instructs Roger, who follows orders like a pro and moves the chair. "Lovely." Queen David clasps his hands together. "Now, let me see." He surveys the room. I wink at Roger, leave them to their task and join Michael in the kitchen. He's busy assembling tiny sandwiches on a tray garnished with red peppers and cilantro.

I sink into a kitchen chair and watch him at work. When Michael is lost in cooking he's in another world. A state of beauty. In another life, he could have hosted one of those cooking shows. I think about the millennium. It's almost here and now it feels anticlimactic. Such a fuss has been made over the two years leading up to this day. So far there have been no reports of haywire computers, plane crashes, electricity break-downs. What if it is true, though? What if something happens tonight? At least the people I love most will all be here if the Russians accidentally release a bomb over North America and we're blown to smithereens. Or if the power goes off. Or if the aliens land. I got what I wanted most, anyway. I'm not in the hospital. I'm home, with Roger and my best friends. What more could I ask? I watch Michael work and wonder if either one of us will be here next year.

"If anything happens to me," I say suddenly, "I want you to take care of Roger."

He glances over his shoulder at me. "Oh, you mean like you want me to marry him in your place. Kind of like biblical sisters?"

"No, I don't mean marry him. I mean take care of him."

"But do you mean take care of him in the biblical sense?" Michael pushes.

"You would think that." I throw a tea towel at him.

"Well?"

"I'll break every bone in your body if you do."

"You'll be dead."

"I'll come back and haunt you."

"I really wish you would." He throws the tea towel back. It lands on my head. I leave it there.

"What next, Henry?" Roger asks from the doorway. "What's on your head?"

I remove the tea towel. Smile at my lover. "Is the furniture all set?"

"You'll have to ask the Queen, but I think so."

I stand, snuggle into Roger's arms, kiss his neck.

"Hey ..." he says. "Henry ... ?"

"I love you," I tell him.

He kisses me. "Me too."

I feel a little blue, but I stuff the feelings back into my belly. No point in breaking down here and now. Julie and Nomi are expected any second. We have lots to do. "How about getting glasses and plates ready?" I tell Roger.

"Sure." He kisses me again, slips out of my arms, rejoins Queen David in the living room.

My father bursts into the kitchen, picks up a piece of chopped red pepper, pops it in his mouth.

"Your mother's joining us for New Year's Eve," he tells me.

"What happened to what's her name? Emma?"

"Emma, right. Listen, can you do me a favour?" He grabs the phone receiver.

"No way, Pop."

"Just call her for me and tell her I had to whatchacallit? Unexpectedly leave town."

He thrusts the phone toward me. I hold up my hands. "No way."

"Aw, come on, Henry. Just one little favour."

"No."

"For your old Pop."

"Get yourself out of your own mess."

"Okay, fine." He walks with the phone to the living room. "Roger ... can you do me a favour, buddy?"

"Sure, Solly," Roger responds.

"What's all that about?" Michael asks.

"Don't ask."

By the time Nomi and Julie turn up with the soft drinks and mixers — their contribution — I'm exhausted.

"Henry." Nomi stands on tiptoes to kiss my cheek. "You look tired."

"God," I groan.

"We can stay to help as long as you want," Julie adds.

"Come on in." I take both of them by the arm, steer them inside. They each carry two large grocery bags filled with two-litre pop bottles.

In the kitchen I introduce Nomi to Michael. He puts Julie to work arranging the veggie tray and Nomi chopping onions for his dip.

"I have to lie down," I tell everyone. "Or I won't make it

through tonight."

"Go," Michael orders.

I head for the bedroom.

When I wake up two hours later, I feel groggy but refreshed. I stumble into the living room. The furniture is all in place. Millennium helium balloons have been strung together. There is glitter everywhere. Queen David's huge Liberace-style candelabra sits in the centre of the dining room table, surrounded by empty plates and cups, with room for all the food. There are various candles all over the living room, waiting to be lit. It looks fabulous. I see that Julie and Nomi have left. My father is nowhere to be seen. Queen David is gone. Roger is snoozing on the living room sofa. Michael is adding the finishing touches to his oyster pâté plate.

He smiles at me. "Feeling better?"

"Much. You should go home and get dressed."

He glances at the kitchen clock, screeches. "Oh my God. You're right. I have to do my hair and nails."

"Go. I'll finish here."

"Well ..."

"Just tell me what to do. I can handle it."

"Okay. See how I'm garnishing it?"

He's using parsley around the border with twists of lemon in between. "Got it."

"Okay. Now keep this in the fridge until the absolute moment you're going to serve it."

"You can do that when you come back."

"Right."

I see him to the door. "Michael?"

"Hmmm?"

"Thanks."

He opens the door, turns back toward me. "We'll be here, Henry."

"What?"

"Next year. We'll be here."

"I hope so, Michael."

He gives me a little wave and he's off.

I go into the living room, squeeze onto the couch beside Roger and wrap my arms around him. He opens his eyes lazily. "Just a little nap."

"I'm glad."

"Everyone's gone?" He looks around.

"Just the two of us."

"Your father?"

"I have no idea."

Roger nudges me gently, takes my hand. "Come on."

"Where we going?"

"The bedroom."

"We have to get dressed," I remind him.

"Not if we're getting undressed," he grins.

I follow him into our bedroom.

NOMI'S MILLENNIUM

I'm struggling with a rhinestone bolo tie, the perfect touch to my butch Liberace look, not sure whether to leave it loose with my top button undone or close it right up to my neck, when the phone rings. I hear Julie answer it in the kitchen.

"Nomi." She enters the bedroom. "It's for you." She hands me the portable receiver.

"For me?"

"Your mother." She mouths the words.

"Oh." I lean forward, kiss Julie. "Hi, Ma. What's up?"

"What's up? I called to say Happy New Year. What else?"

"Happy New Year. I thought you and Murray were going out."

Julie leans forward, loosens my bolo, then undoes the top button of my turquoise shirt, straightens the lapels on my matching turquoise sequined jacket and stands back to look. The sequins are a lot flashier than my usual look. We found the jacket yesterday at a second-hand store on Queen Street.

"We are," my mother says, "but first I wanted to call. What will you do?"

I don't want to tell my mother the truth. She might be hurt that Henry didn't invite her, especially since he invited his father and grandmother. "Oh, we're going to some friends' for dinner."

"What friends? Old friends?"

"Friends of Julie's." It's not a total lie. I smile at Julie, shrug helplessly.

"That's nice. Will we see you during the week?"

"Sure, Ma. We'll drop by."

"Come for supper on Friday night. I'll invite the boys."

"Okay, Ma. I'll check with Julie first."

"What's to check? You'll come for supper. Listen, it's important tonight of all nights to make plans for the future."

"Why?"

"To ward off the evil eye." My mother says this as if it's obvious.

"The evil eye?"

"Y2K, Nomi. Where've you been?"

"I know about Y2K, Ma, but what's that got to do with the evil eye?"

She sighs. "It's simple, Nomi. If you make plans like there's going to be a future, it confuses the evil eye, and then all that crazy computer Y2K nonsense won't happen."

"Okay, Ma."

"You don't believe me?"

"I believe you, Ma."

"Murray can tell you. Murray!?" she shouts.

"It's okay. I believe you," I say.

"Just a minute. Murray!" she shouts again.

"Ma, I don't have to talk to Murray. I believe you. Really I do."

"Hello?" Murray has picked up the extension.

"There you are," my mother says. "Tell Nomi about Y2K and the evil eye."

"Uh," I interrupt, "it's okay, Murray. I get it."

"Well, you see," he says, ignoring me, "if we make plans for the future ..."

"I get it, Murray," I say again, firmly.

"What's that?"

"It's okay, I get it."

"Oh. Okay." He seems deflated. Maybe I should have let him explain.

"Anyway, Happy New Year to both of you," I say. "Julie says Happy New Year too." I look at Julie, who looks terrified that maybe I'm going to hand her the phone. She waves the receiver away with her hands.

"Tell her the same," my mother says.

"I will."

"So you'll come?"

"Yeah, Ma. We'll come."

I hang up. "We're going up there for dinner on Friday. Okay?"

Julie snuggles into my arms. "Guess we're a couple now, huh, Nomi?"

"Guess we are."

She licks my earlobe. It drives me crazy.

"Careful ..." I tell her.

"Hmmm?"

"We'll never get out of here if you start that."

"Oh ..." She pulls away. "Okay, then zip my dress." She turns and presents her back. She's wearing a sexy, slinky, purple rhinestone-studded dress that ends at thigh level. The front of the dress is made of thin purple panels that stretch over her belly and breasts, leaving patches of bare skin. Over top she's wearing a glittery cape with a fake fur collar. It's kind of ultra-femme Liberace. He would have loved it.

"Unless you'd rather me unzip it." I lean forward, kiss the back of her neck.

"Later, babe. Later."

We arrive at Henry's precisely at seven. He made us promise we would arrive early.

"You know what happens," he said. "It's always someone you barely know who shows up first. Then you have to sit with them and make small talk. It's excruciating."

He was right. When Roger ushers us into the living room, we find Henry sitting on the sofa chatting with Greta from his ACTOUT group. He looks relieved to see us. Henry is wearing a black and gold satin smoking jacket over pleated black pants with stripes of rhinestones down each leg. His matching gold shirt is open at the collar, loosely fastened with a gold satin cravat.

"You both look divine," Henry gushes, kissing us each on the cheek. "Come with me to the kitchen. I'll pour you drinks. Excuse us, Greta."

"Don't mind me." She tugs at her plain black tuxedo jacket, which is not very Liberace-like.

"Right back," Henry promises her.

"Sorry we're late," I say.

"She's actually different at a party," he whispers to Julie.

"Different?"

"More relaxed."

"She came alone?" Julie asks.

"Yeah. Who can we fix her up with?"

"How about my mother?" I joke. "Maybe she can leave Murray somewhere and scoot over."

"Stop," Henry laughs. He fixes us drinks. We follow him back to the living room, just as Queen David flows into the apartment with his own entourage of three young, beautiful, partially clad men.

"This way, boys. Follow your queen," he orders. "Oh." Queen David stops and admires the decorations. "It looks fabulous in here. Simply divine." Queen David is absolute Liberace. He's wearing a pink, glittery one-piece jumpsuit, covered in more rhinestones than I have ever seen in one place before. His pink shirt has wide lapels and ruffles and he wears a wide pink bow tie. His shirt cuffs are a study in ruffles that end delicately over his hands, which are covered in huge silver and turquoise rings, one on each finger, including his thumbs. Around his neck sits a large jewelled necklace. A stripe of purple rhinestones runs down each pant leg. His peach slip-on shoes have decorative designs done with pink beads and red rhinestones. Resting lightly on his shoulders is a matching pink and purple cape with silver sequins. The collar rises above his head like a huge flower petal. He is wearing a Liberace wig, brown wavy hair, backcombed, blow-dried and sprayed. His young companions wear identical turquoise sequined tuxedo jackets with tails, large white bow ties on bare chests. Their turquoise pants have pink sequined stripes

down each side. They complement Queen David like chorus
boys surrounding the star.

Michael arrives next with David-to-Die-For on his arm.
They both look fabulous. Michael just about outdoes Queen
David, but not quite. His white jacket is covered in sequins. His
pants have a sequined stripe down each leg. His white shirt is
ruffled everywhere and his white bow tie is made of lace. He has
a rhinestone ring on every finger and both thumbs, and is
wearing several dangling earrings. He's holding a portable candelabra in one hand and a long rhinestone-studded cigarette
holder in the other.

David-to-Die-For is in a simple white tuxedo with a
turquoise sequined bow tie and matching cummerbund. Just a
hint of eyeliner highlights his piercing blue eyes. They make
quite the couple.

There is a bit of a commotion at the door as Solly and his
friend Lou enter, holding my grandmother up between them. In
a classic black tuxedo, Solly looks more like Frank Sinatra than
Liberace. Lou is casually dressed in a windbreaker and white
shirt, no tie. But he is working tonight. For a cabbie, New Year's
Eve is too good a night for fares to book off work. Dov, the
orderly from Bubbe's home, trails behind. I don't think he knows
who Liberace was. He's wearing black leather pants with a tight
white T-shirt and a black leather vest. Even Bubbe is a little
dressed up, in a simple blue dress and matching blue earrings.

"Tell me, dear." She turns her back to Queen David. "Can
you zip up my dress?"

"Of course, sweetie." Queen David billows around and
obliges. "You look smashing," he tells her.

"What did she say?" Bubbe asks Solly.

"Come inside, Ma." He steers her farther inside the apartment.

"So tall for a woman," Bubbe remarks.

"Well, I should be going," Lou says.

"What are you talking?" Solly shouts. "Come in and have a
drink."

"Can't. I gotta drive."

"So you'll have some coffee."

Roger glides into the living room from the back. "Hi, everyone." His smoking jacket matches Henry's.

"Nomi, this is my friend Simon," Henry says, introducing me to a handsome, slim Asian man.

"Hi, Simon." I offer my hand.

"So you're the cousin?" Simon's version of Liberace is a bright red sequined tuxedo with a blue feather boa draped around his neck.

"That's me."

"I love San Francisco. Steven and I loved to go to the Freedom Day Parade."

"Yeah, it's great."

"Nomi." Roger holds out a portable phone. "It's for you."

"Oh." I take the phone. "Sorry," I tell Simon. He shrugs. "Hello?"

"Give me a Guinness, Nom. No head."

"Betty!"

"Hi, pal. Just called to say Happy New Year."

"Are you at Patty's?"

"It's too early, you nut. I'm getting dressed."

"Oh yeah. I forgot. How many girls have you kissed so far?"

"Uh hang on ..." I hear the crinkling of paper. "Uh ... four hundred and thirty-three."

"You did not."

"I got up early."

"You started kissing girls this morning?"

"That's right."

"Where? On the street?" I tease.

"Yes, as a matter of fact. I set up a booth."

"Where?"

"Where else? Corner of 18th and Castro."

"You set up a booth?"

"I kissed the first hundred by eight."

"In the morning?"

"On their way to work."

"Betty, you're amazing."

"Only one thousand, five hundred and sixty-seven to go."

"Do you think you'll make it?"

"Do you even have to ask? Hey AJ ..." she hollers. "Nomi wants to know if I'll make my quota."

"Do you have to ask?" AJ yells into the receiver.

"See?" says Betty, triumphant.

"Okay, okay, call me back when you hit one thousand."

"I may be busy."

"Call me anyway."

I hang up the phone.

Henry and Michael announce that dinner is served. The dining room table is loaded with food. It surrounds the huge candelabra Queen David set up earlier. We line up and start filling our plates.

Solly settles Bubbe on the sofa with a plate of food, then rejoins the line to get a plate for himself. Henry opens the door to a late guest. His mother Belle swishes in. She's just about outdone even Michael in the sequin department, in a long silver evening gown.

"Hi, Ma," Henry says. "Come on in. You look great."

"There you are, Belle. Look at you. Don't she look great?" Uncle Solly asks Henry.

"Fabulous."

"And who is this?" Queen David descends on Belle, followed by his entourage.

"David, this is my mother, Belle. Ma, this is Queen David."

Queen David curtsies. "Honey, that dress is fabulous. And your makeup is a dream. Is that Crescent Peach on your lips?"

Belle nods. "Very good."

"You do your own makeup?"

"Every morning. I work in the cosmetic department at Eatons."

"Then we have so much to talk about." Queen David takes Belle by the arm and steers her inside.

Henry approaches me with the phone. "For you again."

I glance at my watch. Eleven-thirty. Eight-thirty San Francisco time.

"Hello?"

"One thousand and thirteen."

"No way."

"It's true. AJ's been keeping track."

"Betty, there couldn't be more than a hundred women stuffed into Patty's Place. What are you doing? Going out into the street and kissing every woman who walks by?"

"As a matter of fact, yes."

"Does that count?"

"Why not?"

Just before midnight Solly starts the countdown.

"Ten ... nine ... eight ..."

We all join in.

"... seven ... six ..." Julie turns to me. "I'm glad you're here, Nomi."

"Five ... four ..."

"Me too."

"Three ... two ... one. Happy New Year!" Everyone's shouting and singing at once, making noise, kissing and hugging. From outside we can hear fireworks, people in other apartments and on the street yelling and whistling. It's the millennium. It's finally here. And I am standing beside the most beautiful woman, surrounded by people I love. We're all dressed like Liberace. It's fabulous. It truly is. Beside me, Henry and Roger stand arm in arm. Henry winks at me. I turn to Julie.

"Aren't you going to kiss me?" she asks.

And I do.

ACKNOWLEDGEMENTS

Material on the origin of AIDS was paraphrased from the following sources: *AIDS and the Doctors of Death: An Inquiry into the Origins of the AIDS Epidemic* by Alan Cantwell, Jr., MD (Los Angeles: Aries Rising Press, 1993); *Queer Blood: The Secret AIDS Genocide Plot* by Alan Cantwell, Jr., MD (Los Angeles: Aries Rising Press, 1993); and *Emerging Viruses: AIDS and Ebola, Nature, Accident or Genocide?* By Leonard G. Horowitz, DMD, MA, MPH (Rockport, Mass.: Tetrahedron, Inc., 1996).

I'd like to thank my editor at Raincoast, Lynn Henry, for insightful editing of the manuscript, and my publisher Michelle Benjamin for her vision and belief in my projects. Thanks also to Tessa Vanderkop, my publicist, and the rest of the Raincoast staff, who continue to promote great books. Thanks to Sheila Norgate for the beautiful cover art, Ingrid Paulson for cover design and Daniel Collins for my fabulous author photo.

Thanks to Dr. Alan Cantwell for answering questions about AIDS and explaining his theory on the origin of AIDS, as outlined in his books. Thanks as well to Dr. Leonard Horowitz, whose book was also valuable to my background research. *And the Band Played On*, by Randy Shilts, gave me additional insight into the politics of the AIDS crisis. Thanks to the Pacific Resource Centre Library, a program of AIDS Vancouver, for information on current AIDS treatments, and Dr. Joan Robillard for assistance with medical research.

Thanks to Terrie Akemi Hamazaki, who read an early draft of *Love and Other Ruins* and offered editorial suggestions. Big thanks to Richard Banner, who continues to bail me out of computer problems as they arise. Thanks to James C. Johnstone, Dianne Whelan, Lisa McArthur, Brian Lam, Michele Karlsberg, Lois Fine, Dix, Eunice Lee, Peter Demas, Nancy Richler, Ann Decter and Jess Wells for encouragement, support, friendship and other amazing feats. Thanks to my parents, Jack and Marion, for supplying Yiddish phrases, and to the rest of my family of origin for inspiration. Special thanks to the Writer's Union of Canada for ongoing work in support of all writers.

Arigato to my fiancée, Terrie Akemi Hamazaki, for standing by me through everything, for love, encouragement and support, and for all of her other amazing talents. And thanks to Mr. Charlie Tulchinsky-Hamazaki for unconditional cat-love.

ABOUT THE AUTHOR

Karen X. Tulchinsky is the award-winning author of *Love Ruins Everything* and *In Her Nature*, which won the 1996 VanCity Book Prize. She is the editor of nine anthologies of contemporary fiction, including the bestselling *Hot & Bothered* series. She has written for numerous magazines and newspapers, including the *Vancouver Sun*, *DIVA* and *Writer's Digest*. She has written several feature-length screenplays and is a graduate of the writers' lab at the prestigious Canadian Film Centre

in Toronto, founded by the legendary director Norman Jewison. Her screenplays have been shortlisted in the Praxis Screenwriting Competition and the Chesterfield Film Project. She also wrote a short film that was produced in the Universal Studios Short Film Programme. Tulchinsky travels back and forth between Vancouver and Toronto but makes her home in Vancouver.

Love Ruins Everything
Karen X. Tulchinsky

Here's the award-winning, much-loved first novel about Nomi Rabinovitch, her cousin Henry, and her ever-entertaining family. Jewish lesbian Nomi is living in San Francisco when her lover unceremoniously dumps her for a burly, buzz-cut man. While Nomi is recovering from her broken heart, her widowed mother calls and summons Nomi to Toronto to attend her surprise second wedding. There, Nomi is reunited with her beloved gay cousin Henry and a long-lost crush, Julie Sakamoto, both of whom are involved in a plot to uncover the shocking truth behind the AIDS epidemic.

"Nomi is a charming and original heroine, and Tulchinsky is at her comic best when describing Nomi's relationships with friends and family, including her earthy grandmother and Uncle Solly, a loveable wiseguy on the lam." — *Publishers Weekly*

"Earnest and gutsy, this first novel by Karen X. Tulchinsky hovers bravely between two worlds, Jewish and gay. As if this were not a tall enough order, Tulchinsky splits her story between two protagonists — cousins Nomi and Henry Rabinovitch. Tulchinsky peppers her fiction wildly with gay vernacular as well as Yiddish. She's very funny, but also dead serious, communicating about AIDS with intense black humour … Tulchinsky not only writes well, she has something important to say." — *The Globe and Mail*

Press Gang • 0-88974-082-8 • $18.95 CDN / $14.95 USA